THE FUGITIVE OF ELDON
World of Samar: Book Eleven

M L Hamilton

authormlhamilton.net

Wayne –
Thank you!
ML Hamilton

After eleven books in a series, if you're still with me, you are my heroes. I cannot thank you enough for your support and loyalty. And to my family, you know how much I love you.
As always,
may Eldon's light shine brightly in your lives.

I have seen many storms in my life. Most storms have caught me by surprise, so I had to learn very quickly to look further and understand that I am not capable of controlling the weather, to exercise the art of patience and to respect the fury of nature.

~ *Paulo Coelho*

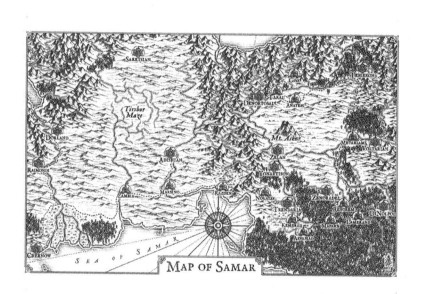

MAP OF SAMAR

PROLOGUE

Karnack Pretorian wasn't an overly imposing man. He wasn't ambitious. He wasn't clever. And he wasn't powerful. Well, in Stravad power, that is. Still, he commanded the Nazarien with an iron fist.

Tarish Enro knew this. He'd been waiting for his moment to challenge the Nazar for nearly two decades, but Tarish was clever and he knew the time wasn't right. Not yet. However, that time, that moment might be fast approaching.

The numbers of Nazarien followers had been dwindling over the years, young people fleeing the order as fast as they were indoctrinated into it. Many felt that the Nazarien had lost their way, that their isolation had made them weak.

In Nevaisser, Stravad were being gathered up and forced to live on reserves, guarded by Human soldiers. The Humans said it was to protect the Stravad, but Tarish knew different. It was to contain them. Land previously owned by Stravad was being stolen and given to Humans. Stravad were retaliating and attacking Human settlements.

Rather than intervene, Karnack had forced the Nazarien into two locations, fiercely guarded day and night. A large contingent of Nazarien worked and worshipped in Chernow and a dwindling force haunted the maze of Tirsbor.

Stravad petitioned Karnack for intervention, but those petitions fell on deaf ears. At first, they turned to Terra Antiguo after being rebuffed by the Nazarien, but Terra Antiguo was stretched thin and the refugees had to leave in order to survive. Terra Antiguo, itself, was being harassed by the Human governments who wanted the fertile valley to enable more homesteads.

Tarish knew the next step would be to petition Temeron itself where Zeran Eldralin held court. Zeran had attempted to corral the Nazarien before and every few years he made a new effort, but Nevaisser was a long way away and it was easy to forget the suffering that happened here.

If Stravad went directly to Temeron, Zeran may have no choice but to respond. Karnack feared that Zeran would command the Nazarien at some point. He was certainly more powerful than his father had been and he was more determined. Karnack's fear of Zeran fueled his isolationism. And age further strengthened it. Karnack knew he was vulnerable and therefore, he had no intention of answering a summons from Zeran, but Tarish would.

Tarish shifted in his seat on the council and watched the aging, stooped form of Karnack. His eyes were clouded and his back rounded with arthritis.

Tarish rubbed a hand over his smooth jaw.

If Zeran Eldralin summoned Karnack and the Nazarien to Temeron, Tarish knew it would give him the opportunity to challenge Karnack's rule. While Karnack was holed up in Chernow with his council around him, he was unassailable, but if he left the caves, it would be so much easier for a stray arrow or a sword strike to find its mark.

Then the Nazarien would be his and he would take the order in a new direction. For too long, they'd been bound by their duty to the Eldralin line. Tarish understood loyalty to the man who had founded the order. He understood loyalty to Eldon, but for too long, the Nazarien had been secondary to the demands of Temeron.

Generations of Eldralins had abandoned and even outright scorned their ancestor's religion. If Tarish had control over the Nazarien, that would stop. If he could succeed in eliminating Karnack and subsuming the order, he might also succeed in ending the Eldralins' stranglehold.

He rose to his feet and stretched. He was sick of listening to the council rehash the same things over and over again. It was time for action. If the Nazarien weren't careful, there wouldn't be any order for him to rule.

To date, Zeran Eldralin had produced three daughters. Daughters mattered not at all to the order. Even Tyla Eldralin had been denied the protection of the Nazarien. That made Zeran Eldralin the last of the Eldralin line.

Tarish walked off the council dais, headed for the door. Now there was a thought.

Zeran Eldralin was the last of the Eldralins.

If he was going to be unseated, if the chains imposed on the Nazarien by the Eldralins were to be ended, now was the time. And yet, Karnack had sat here for the last twenty years doing nothing, biding his time, refusing to take action.

Well, Tarish Enro was a man of action and his time was nearly here.

"Tarish!" snapped Karnack at his back. "We aren't finished."

Tarish slowly turned and faced the aging Nazar. "I am," he said.

"Don't be a fool! I say when you're dismissed."

Tarish felt something go cold inside of him. The Nazarien were a fractured order, the members bleeding away daily, the Stravad forced onto reserves, guarded by inferior Humans. All because men like Karnack Pretorian and Zeran Eldralin didn't take action.

Tarish tilted his head to the side to survey the scene. Maybe now was the time. Maybe now was when he needed to prove he was a man of action. Maybe now was the day when everything would change.

His hand lifted and curled around the dagger on his belt.

Karnack's eyes widened and he struggled to rise. He recognized the situation for what it was. That was the first clever thing he'd done in years. Around him, the council tensed. They also knew what was about to happen, but they weren't going to interfere. Tarish knew this as he knew Karnack was finished.

He drew the knife as Karnack lifted his hand, shouting, "Guards!"

Before the word had died on his lips, Tarish threw the dagger. It caught Karnack in the throat, slamming him back into the chair. He made a gurgling sound and his fingers flexed around the hilt, but he didn't pull it away.

Tarish strode back toward the dais, sweeping the horrified, silent council with his gaze as he came to a halt before Karnack. Karnack looked at him with terrified, cloudy eyes and he opened his lips to speak, but blood gushed from his mouth and ran in a gory clot down the front of his uniform.

Tarish gave him a cold smile as the light in Karnack's eyes died and he slumped in his seat, his hands falling away. Sweeping the council with another glare, Tarish held out his arms. "Genuflect for the next Nazar!" he ordered.

The old men on the council struggled to drop to their knees, prostrating themselves before him. Tarish turned and his cold gaze swept over the guards streaming into the room.

"Bow before me!" he shouted and they also dropped, their weapons clattering on the stones. "Behold Tarish Enro, Nazar of Chernow! Bow!" he commanded.

And they did.

CHAPTER 1

They strode through the avenues, their forest green uniforms blending with the verdant foliage of the Temerian streets, their steps purposeful. Their leather boots made little sound on the rounded cobblestones and the people paused to look at them.

They made an impressive spectacle and it was rare to see them turn out in force. Crime didn't often happen in Temeron, and when it did, it was usually of so slight a nature that the involved parties took their grievance to the Stravad Leader on their own, never needing the assistance of the Temerian guard.

They soon drew a crowd after them. Temeron was a fine place to live, but relatively low in excitement. The appearance of the guard warranted attention and the situation turned into an unorthodox party.

The guard and their tail of concerned citizens stopped before the furniture maker's store. The large, burly woodworker moved to the door of his shop and leaned against the jam, gazing with curiosity at the green garbed warriors and their crowd of spectators. He wiped calloused, stained hands on the leather apron that hung from his thickening waist and stepped onto the shaded walk to greet his visitors.

"What can I do for you, gentlemen?" he said.

The captain of the guard, a middle-aged man, stepped forward and surveyed the store. "You have an apprentice, do you not?"

The woodworker cast a glance over his shoulder into his shop and motioned with a thumb. "I do." He wasn't a man of many words, finding that people, his own people in particular, expended a great deal more energy than necessary at conversation.

The captain held himself straight and lifted his chin a little at the woodworker's confirmation. "This apprentice goes by the name of Trey Almsden?"

"Yes, he does."

The captain nodded, although his expression didn't indicate any pleasure in the answer. The crowd, however, murmured in interest. Trey Almsden was, of course, one of the unfortunates in a city housing the most fortunate on the planet.

His birth was ignoble, his family of questionable reputation, and his own character uncertain at best. Most of the citizens regarded him with moral charity – it was difficult to expect much out of the upbringing he'd had. Still, beyond petty theft as a boy and street brawls as an adolescent, Trey Almsden had led a clean life. Until now.

"Ask your apprentice to show himself," stated the captain.

The woodworker regarded the gathered assembly grimly, heaved a sigh, and ducked back under the narrow door of his shop. He appeared a moment later with his apprentice in tow.

The man who stepped onto the walkway was young with dark hair, nearly black, tied at the neck with a piece of leather. He was dressed in an apron, much like his benefactor, but the shirt and trousers beneath it were worn thin. The sleeves of the shirt had been rolled up exposing a long expanse of muscled forearms. He was tall and slender with a body hardened by manual labor. The face would have been handsome, except for the severe lines of thin lips and sunken cheeks beneath rigid, high cheekbones and penetrating green eyes.

The cold emerald green of the eyes surveyed the crowd and warriors. The eyes were shaped like all Stravad, large and slanted, but the narrowing of them, coupled with the green, made them glitter like cut gems.

The captain took in the large, stoic figure before him and rocked back on his heels, clasping his hands behind him. "Trey Almsden, you are under arrest and ordered to appear before the Stravad Leader Zeran Eldralin."

No expression marred the young face, except a further narrowing of the eyes. He moved forward with grace, like a large cat on the prowl. "Exactly why am I under arrest?" His voice was resonant and deep, rumbling out of a broad expanse of sculpted chest.

The crowd pressed forward, eager to hear the pronouncement.

"For the murder of Trista Lamer."

The crowd gasped and moved backward. Glittering green eyes narrowed even further. The woodworker fixed his hands on hips and frowned.

"Now just a moment, Captain. I'll admit this boy's seen his share of trouble, but to suggest such a thing – well, I can't believe you'd even say it out loud."

"What are you talking about? I saw her just yesterday and she was very much alive," said Almsden.

The captain exhaled on a long sigh. He clearly didn't like this part of his commission. "She was found strangled in her bed."

Another gasp rippled through the crowd. The young man stared hard at the captain with his piercing, gem-like eyes, but he didn't answer or make any attempt to defend himself.

"I request that you accompany us, Trey Almsden, of your own free will. Otherwise, we will be forced to detain you."

The young man was still for another moment. The woodworker watched him, obviously uncertain how to proceed or whether to intervene again. Slowly the young man reached around him and untied the apron, pulling it off his arms and passing it to his master without looking at him.

"Sorry," he said quietly and then lowered his hands to his side.

At a curt motion from the captain, two warriors came forward and bound the young man's hands behind him with shackles. The sight of this broke the woodworker's lethargy and he stepped forward.

"Now just a minute here. You can't just walk up and take away my apprentice. I demand you listen to me."

The captain turned his cool gaze on the woodworker. "And I insist you take your complaint to the Stravad Leader. I am not obligated to do any more than I've already done." He motioned to his men and they led the young man down into the street and back the way they'd come.

The woodworker stared after them, but he recovered again and locked his door, striding off after the detachment with the young man's apron still in hand.

*   *   *

Trey looked at the cobblestones passing by beneath the rapid fall of his feet and those of his captors. He was seething inside, but he'd rather have his heart explode than to let these clowns in costume know it.

Trista was dead? Strangled? How? The thought shocked him. They'd been together the previous night. He'd left her around midnight to go home and sleep. What could have happened to her?

His mother had warned him about Trista. He should have listened. She was good at spotting people just like herself. Still, he couldn't resist all of Trista's flaming red hair (redheads had always been his weakness) or the skill of her fingers. For a few glorious weeks, she'd made him forget everything that he'd never been able to forget in his life. She'd made him feel special. What could have happened to her?

He glanced at the warriors on either side of him. He could see their contempt, their disgust. They'd already tried and convicted him in their minds. It wasn't like anyone, but Master Elefson, would believe him.

Trista was the daughter of a council member. She had money and influence at her fingertips. Trey had nothing. Even the clothes he wore had belonged to someone else.

His hands clenched into fists. Why did this have to happen when he'd finally found his place in this city? He liked working for Master Elefson, he especially liked working with the wood, but most of all, he was good at it. No, he was exceptional at it. Even Master Elefson had told him that and Master Elefson didn't say much in the first place.

For the first time in his nearly thirty years, Trey had seen a future for himself, a way to earn a living that was respected and honest. He'd had so many plans. He would become the best furniture maker in Temeron and those who had scorned him would come to him, begging for a piece of his art.

He lowered his head again and drew a calming breath. The hardest part was the fact that he'd liked it so much. He could get lost working with the wood, molding it, shaping it, polishing it. It took some of his restlessness and channeled it in a positive direction for once. And it was steady.

For most of his life, he'd done odd jobs, practically begging for what little people were willing to spare him. Then Master Elefson had agreed to take him on, give him a chance, even though Trey was considerably older than most apprentices. Now it was all gone. If, by some miracle, he escaped this false attack on him, he'd never be able to return to his job, or in reality, stay in the city. He was guilty by association. There were people in this town who would never believe him, who would always think he'd escaped a just punishment.

The greatest irony of all was the fact that his own mother would shun him, a woman who made what little she did by spreading her legs for strangers, strangers like the man with green eyes who'd given her an unwanted son.

As they neared the Stravad Leader's house, Trey felt his heart pound with the first effects of real fear. No matter how bad life had been for him, he'd never gotten himself in any real trouble and he had absolutely no idea what to expect.

The Stravad Leader had always been kind when Trey was younger, but he shuddered to think what the man would believe now. Would Trey even be given a chance to speak on his own behalf?

He was anything but stupid. He knew the law didn't work the same way for the poor as it did for the rich. He also knew that Trista's father held a lot of influence over the Stravad Leader in council. What hope could he possibly have?

He stumbled when they pushed him at the stairs of the grand house. He glared at them, his eyes glittering with barely suppressed fury. His thoughts focused on Trista. She was dead. Dead. How could that be?

They led him across the wide porch and around to the rear of the house. Covertly he scanned the area, taking in the close press of the Temer forest at the backside of the Stravad Leader's mansion, the bank of windows that fronted his study and private rooms. They paused in the shadows. The captain muttered a command to his men and one of the warriors broke away, hurrying to the study doors and slipping inside.

Trey refused to look at them, refused to meet their eyes. He wouldn't accept the righteousness he knew would be there. They had no way of knowing anything about him. They made their impressions based on the tattered clothing he wore and the reputation of his mother. How could he fight that? How could he prove to them that beneath these worn clothes was a heart that knew real fear and a stiff pride that wouldn't let him bend before them?

The warrior reappeared and whispered to the captain. Trey heard the muffled sounds of a crowd toward the front of the house and knew they'd gathered because of him. Ironic how quickly bad news spread even in a city where there was so much to be grateful for.

The captain motioned to the two warriors on either side of him, and then turned his back and walked toward the study doors. Trey glanced up before he was pushed and commanded to follow. He walked between the two warriors, his hands bound behind him.

They entered the cool study and Trey blinked at the change in light from the bright sun outside. He squinted. The study was filled with rich leather chairs and a couch, accented by heavy oak tables and a desk. A jewel hilted dagger hung by its sheathe on the wall behind the desk.

The desk itself was littered with neat piles of paper and writing utensils. Trey's quick eyes surveyed the area, cataloging everything. He had the ability to walk into a room and remember the exact placement of most items. He wasn't sure if he'd learned the trick when he was forced to steal food as a boy or whether he'd always possessed it, but it really mattered little when his entire life was dangling before him.

His head jerked toward the door when he heard the Stravad Leader's voice. Trey was suddenly ashamed to be brought here bound, even if he was innocent. What would the Stravad Leader think? Would he believe him capable of murder?

The Stravad Leader paused in the doorway, his voice stopping in mid-sentence. He surveyed the gathering with calm, cobalt eyes that shifted and rested finally on Trey. Trey met the look. Something inside Trey wouldn't let him break it. He pleaded with the Stravad Leader in that look to believe him, to see more than anyone else had ever seen in his entire life.

Without taking his eyes from Trey, the Stravad Leader moved into the room. Trey was only vaguely aware of the small figure that followed him, his attention riveted on the man who held his life in his hands.

Stravad Leader Zeran Eldralin was a tall man, as tall as Trey himself. He had broad shoulders with a hardness of years about him. Still he was handsome and dignified, his long black hair lying loose on his shoulders.

Yet it was the kindness Trey saw; the gentleness in his cobalt eyes that had drawn Trey as a frightened boy to confess the truth when he'd been caught stealing. It was that same kindness that had made the adolescent Trey hang his head in shame when he'd been cornered fighting to protect his mother's tarnished reputation. And it was that same kindness that caused an adult Trey's heart to beat with hope and urgency, and made him strong enough to meet Zeran eye to eye.

Zeran moved to his desk and only then broke the stare. He placed his hands, palms down, on the shiny surface and drew a weary breath.

Emerald eyes shifted and focused on the small figure following him. The eyes that looked back were the same cobalt blue as the Stravad Leader's, large and expressive in a face that sported mercurial features – a turned-up, pert nose, high cheekbones, and long lashes. Trey's eyes passed over a lean figure in a baggy shirt and tight trousers that gave evidence to a slight, feminine shape. Long, glistening black hair fell to the small waist of the fey little creature and full, red lips lent an almost absurdly provocative air to the entire effect.

Trey's appraisal lasted no more than a moment before he dismissed the creature and returned his attention to the Stravad leader.

Zeran took a seat and placed his head in his hands. He seemed weary and not pleased by the assembly inside his study nor outside his house. After a tense moment of silence, he lifted his head again and motioned the warriors away. They filed out through the study doors as silently as they had entered. Only the captain stood beside Trey.

Zeran fixed his eyes on the younger man. "Trey Almsden," he said and picked up the piece of paper that had been sitting in the middle of his desk. "I had hoped never to see you standing before me under any such circumstances."

Trey didn't answer. Hell, he'd hoped the same thing, but what good did it do him now?

"Do you realize how serious the charges are against you?"

He knew the charges, but they were false. Is that what Zeran wanted to hear?

Zeran leaned back in his chair, his eyes trained on the younger man. The pixie beside him shifted, but he didn't seem to notice. Trey ignored her as well. He knew everything lay with the man in front of him, no one else in all of Temeron meant a damn thing.

Suddenly Zeran rose to his feet and made a sharp motion toward the door that led into his house. "Do you know there's a crowd gathered on my front lawn demanding to know what's going on? And some of them want blood. They don't care about anything else. They want you strung up now."

Trey blinked, no more. None of these questions had really been directed at him, at the heart of the issue. He knew Zeran was trying to unsettle him, trying to root deeply into the situation and glimpse a shred of the truth lying there.

Zeran's hand came to rest on the desk again. He looked at the pixie and seemed to remember her. "Alana, this isn't for your ears, child. Go find your mother and sisters."

The pixie looked insulted. That look alone captured Trey's interest. She moved to the Stravad Leader's elbow and leaned close.

"You told me I needed to see all sides of your job, Daddy," she said in a level voice that surprised Trey. It wasn't what he'd expected from the pampered daughter of the most elite Stravad in Temeron.

For a moment curiosity overrode Trey's fear. He knew Zeran Eldralin had three daughters. He was familiar with the first two. They were beauties with chestnut brown hair and voluptuous figures. Every young man in Temeron knew them on sight and panted with undisguised lust when they paraded past. They were much like their elegant mother – lovely, feminine, and intelligent. From their father, they'd inherited his cobalt eyes – eyes so piercing they could emasculate an ardent young man with one glance. Still young men lined up for such treatment. Trey numbered himself among their many admirers and he considered he had about as much chance as the rest of the poor saps in the city.

Alana Eldralin was another matter entirely. If the older girls had taken after their mother, Alana took after neither parent. She was said to be opinionated, head strong, and unruly. Many uncharitable young men claimed she was the son her father never had. She was never far from his side, except when she was engaged in a fist fight with a member of the opposite sex (although her father had curbed this tendency in recent years).

Looking at her for the first time, Trey didn't really think much about her. She was a woman-child, obviously spoiled, and obviously naive. Her fey appearance and personality only added to his contempt. She was a flighty little creature who had somehow wormed her way into her father's heart.

But Zeran didn't seem to feel the same way. He looked at her for a moment, then sighed, running the fingers of one hand through his black mane.

"Do you understand the complexities of this case, Alana? Do you understand what this young man is being charged with?"

The pixie looked at Trey, turning back to her father. "I understand, and I want to stay. You said yourself that one of us would take over for you someday. Since Mairin and Selia show no interest in it, I'm all that's left. And since I'm the strongest..."

Trey lifted one brow at that, but kept his mouth shut. The pixie went on and on, chattering and Trey ceased listening. This was another reason why most men steered clear of Alana Eldralin.

The captain let out an exasperated breath and rocked on his heels. Trey shot him a sympathetic look, which he returned. It was the first time they'd had anything to agree on, but it didn't lessen Trey's anger or fear any.

Although her father had a great deal more patience for her prattle than most men, even he grew weary and motioned at her impatiently. "Peace, child, you may stay until your mother discovers that you're missing."

Trey was grateful for one thing. Alana's chatter had allied the men together on at least this point. Zeran gave the other two men an apologetic look and braced his palms flat on his desk again.

"I have only one question before I proceed, Trey Almsden. Did you murder Trista Lamer?"

Without hesitation Trey said, "No."

Zeran studied him a moment. The pixie studied him also, but Trey kept his eyes on the only person who mattered, the Stravad Leader. Finally Zeran gave a short, nearly imperceptible nod.

"You'll be detained in the cellar rather than the prison for your own safety until we can investigate this case."

"I didn't hurt Trista!" Trey said. "I swear to you. I didn't hurt her."

"Were you with her last night?"

Trey glanced at the captain. The captain raised his brows. "Yes," he said. "But I left at midnight. I had work today."

"We know when you left. There are witnesses to your leaving. The doctor who examined her body said she was killed around that time."

Trey shook his head, fear making his throat tighten. "I didn't kill her," he forced out. "I'm telling you, Stravad Leader..."

"Enough," said Zeran, holding up a hand. "You stand accused. You admit you were with her." He looked away. "I can't impress upon you enough how bad this is, Trey. A young woman is dead and you admit you were the last to see her alive."

"None of that makes me a murderer. Why would I hurt her? We've been seeing each other for months."

Zeran shook his head. "I can't explain that. All I know is I have a death and people wanting blood. If there's anything you can do to help yourself, I suggest you think hard about it. Otherwise..." He let the words trail away. Then he focused his attention on the captain. "Take the prisoner away. Make sure he has enough of everything – blankets, food, water. Post a guard outside the door. Then come back. I need you to begin an investigation."

The captain nodded and acknowledged Alana with a short bow. Gripping Trey's elbow, he led him from the room.

Trey was taken to the cellar. He was ushered into a small room and the door was locked. It was dark in the room and he paced the width and length of it until the captain returned with another guard. They carried blankets, a lantern, and a water skin with them. Trey waited anxiously, looking out at the hallway beyond.

The captain came to him and unlocked his shackles. Trey searched his face. He didn't want to be left alone in this room in the dark, but pride wouldn't let him say that.

"I want your word that you'll sit on those blankets and make no move." He pointed to the pile on the floor behind them. "In exchange I'll leave the door open with a guard just outside it. He'll be armed. Do we understand one another?"

Trey nodded, but the captain didn't seem satisfied. "If not, I'll lock this door again and leave you in the dark. Which is it, Almsden?"

"Leave the door open. I won't move."

The captain eyed him sternly a moment more, then nodded and waited until Trey had taken his assigned seat. He led the guard to the entrance and spoke to him. A chair was brought and placed outside the door, and the guard took a seat, bracing his feet against the opposite wall.

Trey pulled his knees in against his chest and wrapped his arms around them. He placed his chin on his knees and sighed. The panic had ebbed a little and so had the anger. What remained was anxiety and confusion.

He'd been with Trista last night. He wouldn't deny that, but it was one of many nights they'd spent together. He'd left at midnight. She'd been fine. She'd even asked him to stay. What had happened between then and now?

Time slipped away as he sat and went over the entire night in his mind. He examined everything that had happened, every word that had been said. He couldn't get his head around the fact that she was dead. Not Trista. She'd been so alive, so vital. How could this be happening?

Footsteps on the stairs brought him out of his thoughts and he looked up. The captain appeared. "You have a visitor."

He moved back and Master Elefson stepped up to the doorway. Trey wanted to stand, but a warning glare from the captain kept him in his place. Master Elefson pushed his bulk into the little room and squatted in front of Trey. Meaty hands rested on his knees and Trey found he couldn't look up from them because of the shame he felt.

"So, this is where they're keeping you," said the woodworker. Trey nodded.

"Ain't much of a cell." Trey glanced at the man, but he was looking over his shoulder at the captain and guard. Master Elefson turned back and caught Trey's eye. "Don't worry, boy. This'll all be cleared up tomorrow, I've no doubt. I'll keep your position just the same 'til it is."

Trey drew a deep breath, trying to fill his constricted lungs. It wasn't easy. No one had shown such faith in him before. He wanted to say something, anything to tell this man how much his trust and belief meant to him.

"I didn't do it, Master Elefson," he said, swallowing against the lump of raw emotion in his throat. "I would never have hurt Trista."

The huge man studied him, then reached out and patted his knee exactly twice. "I believe you." He pushed to his feet with a grunt and headed for the door. "Ain't much of a cell," he said to the captain and then was gone.

Trey watched after him until his heavy steps died away. His eyes lowered to the guard. They were nearly the same age. The guard was watching him without blinking.

"This is for your own safety. The citizens won't bother you if you're in the Stravad Leader's house. He just doesn't know how people will react if you're moved to the jail. We don't have murderers in Temeron."

Trey nodded and turned his head to look at the opposite side of the little room. There was nothing much to see, except some boxes and other stored items. He rested his head against the wall and sighed. What would happen to him if the situation wasn't worked out tomorrow? He couldn't remember in his entire life that a murderer was prosecuted in Temeron. What did they do with murderers?

A cold finger of dread went down his spine. It was strange how he instinctively knew what they did. Death. If you executed someone who was convicted of perpetrating violence against others, you never had to worry about that person again.

He closed his eyes and tried to convince himself he didn't care. It had always worked for him as a child.

When things had seemed the worst, Trey had convinced himself it could always be worse. When other children made comments about his mother being a whore, he persuaded himself that any work which put food on the table was honorable. When his mother drank too much and he had to help her to bed, he made himself believe it was his duty to take care of her since she had no husband to do it for her. When there was no food, he convinced himself he wasn't hungry. When there was no heat, he simply wasn't cold. And when he wanted a father, he knew beyond a doubt that he was lucky not to have one – it was so much easier not to love than to risk getting hurt.

He was surprised when the captain returned, bringing him a tray of food. It wasn't what he'd expected. He figured prisoners got practically nothing to eat, and what they got was what most other people didn't want. Yet that wasn't the case here.

He was served a thick piece of steak with plank potatoes and a generous helping of peas covered in butter. There was also a large slice of chocolate cake and a tumbler full of cold milk. He balanced the tray on his lap and looked toward the door. The guard was watching him with longing.

"Don't you get to eat?" Trey asked, feeling guilty. He hadn't seen this much food in one place his entire life. It certainly seemed like enough to feed two people, but eyeing the single serving of silverware, he figured it was all meant for him.

"Later, when I'm off duty."

Trey looked back at the food and suddenly he didn't have much of an appetite. That bothered him. He couldn't let this much food go to waste. In fact, he figured it would be sacrilegious to leave a single scrap. Even so, he couldn't make himself lift the fork and take a bite. Not here, not now. Not with so much pressing down on him.

He caught the guard shaking his head from the corners of his eyes. "You ought to eat it before it gets cold. Mairin Eldralin's a damn fine cook. If you don't eat it, you'll probably get her mother's cooking for breakfast. Even a starving bear in winter couldn't eat that stuff.

Trey stared at the man in astonishment. He'd never heard anyone remotely suggest Alix Eldralin was anything less than a paragon.

"Oh, don't get me wrong," said the guard. "I have nothing but the deepest respect for Alix Eldralin, but not even her own husband will eat her slop and he's crazy in love with her."

Trey found a smile tugging at the corners of his lips. "How do you know Mairin cooked this?"

The guard's pale blond brows lifted. "Absence of smoke and charcoal."

Trey nodded. That seemed a reasonable answer. He lifted his fork and knife, and cut into the steak. The meat almost melted against his tongue and the hunger that was always just beneath the surface sprang to a demanding, pulsing urge.

He was surprised by how quickly he consumed the entire meal down to the very last crumbs. His stomach was painfully full, a strange feeling for someone who never seemed to get enough. He set the tray beside him and stretched out his long legs, resting his hands on his bulging belly. He saw the guard still watching him from the corners of his eyes.

"Good, huh?"

"Yeah," said Trey. "Mairin Eldralin's a damn fine cook."

The guard nodded. "The man who finally wins her hand will be one lucky bastard."

Trey didn't answer that, but he agreed. He had to admit he'd always been fascinated by both Mairin and Selia Eldralin. Both sisters were gorgeous, that was true, but it was the confidence that most impressed him.

He'd never forgotten the celebration of Valhall five years ago when he'd worked up enough courage to ask Selia to dance. She'd so surprised him when she'd agreed that he'd just stood in front of her like an idiot, until she'd taken his hand and led him into the crush of people.

Even now, he could close his eyes and remember the way her long, chestnut brown hair had brushed against his hand where it rested on her back. He could still feel the curve of her spine, see the spark of mischief in her cobalt eyes. He knew the exact shade of her coppery skin and the pink of her tongue when she'd extended only the tip to lick her lips.

Only the knowledge that she'd left the main square following their dance had allowed Trey to give her up. He'd been so proud to have claimed her last moments during the celebration, so damn proud to have been seen with her in his arms.

Since then, he'd seen Selia and Mairin both on the streets or in the market, but he'd never spoken with either of them. He wondered how they'd act toward him if they knew he was sitting in their cellar, accused of such a crime.

They wouldn't care. They wouldn't even know who he was. Even their pixie of a sister, Alana, had looked at him like he was a curiosity. No, they were so far above him, they probably didn't even realize anything remotely unusual was happening in their home tonight.

He'd almost lost himself in his bitter thoughts when he heard more footsteps coming down the stairs. He figured it was just the captain come to take his tray away and didn't bother to acknowledge him. He was more than a little shocked when the captain announced he had another visitor.

He looked up into his mother's heavily painted face. She stood just inside the door of the small room, her hands braced on her rounded hips. He hadn't seen her in almost a month.

Her appearance surprised him, and his surprise shocked him even more. She seemed suddenly older than he remembered. Her makeup couldn't hide the fine lines that etched her eyes and her pursed lips. She seemed bloated and heavy, and tired.

She was dressed in a low-cut blouse and a short skirt that was supposed to be provocative, but only looked worn and wrinkled on her plump figure. She was glaring at him, her eyes bloodshot and blurry. He could smell the booze on her, and something else he knew he didn't want to identify. The sight of her made him sad.

"Well, I didn't believe it when they told me, but I should'a guessed, huh?"

Trey drew a breath and pressed the tips of his fingers against his temples. He was getting a headache. "Just go, Perrine."

She glanced over her shoulder at the waiting captain and guard. Turning on her simpering whore's smile, she tilted her head coyly. "Might I have a few moments alone with my son, Captain?"

The captain glanced between her and Trey. Trey hoped he wouldn't listen to her. He didn't want to be alone with his mother, not now of all times. She would feel the ridiculous need to chastise him. It almost made him laugh. And he would have if he wasn't afraid they'd think he was insane. It wouldn't be far from the truth. Hysteria lurked just beneath his outwardly calm exterior.

The captain motioned the guard to retrieve the food tray, which he did, and then he disappeared down the corridor and climbed the stairs. The captain moved to the doorway and peered inside at his captive.

"Behave yourself, Almsden, understand?"

Trey nodded half-heartedly. He wouldn't strangle his own mother no matter how much he might want to at that moment. The captain gave him another glare and then turned on his heel and followed his younger guard.

Trey's mother just stood there and looked him over, her lips still pursed. He stared at the opposite wall, wishing she would leave.

"What do you want, Perrine?"

She lifted her right hand and let it fall against a plump hip. "What do I want? Where do I start?" She glared at the opposite wall balefully. "How did you get yourself into this mess? Do you realize what this will do to me? No matter if they let you off, half of Temeron will believe you're guilty. It's certainly going to cut down on customers and what's more, it'll make some of them figure they don't have to pay for it anymore."

Trey stared at her in astonishment. "I'm sitting here in this cracker box and you're worried about yourself? You're some piece of work, *Mom*." The endearment dripped with sarcasm.

She didn't seem to care or notice. "You idiot, what if they find you guilty? They'll kill you."

Trey looked up, his eyes veiled against showing any emotion, but his heart started pounding. Maybe she did care for him, just a little.

"I didn't think that would matter to you either way."

She studied him and he regarded her in return. Finally, she lifted a hand and pushed it through her ash brown hair. "Do you really think I'm that heartless? Do you really think I want my son dead?"

"I'm not sure what to think about you, Perrine."

She sighed. "Did you do it?"

"Would you believe me either way?"

She shrugged. "Guess not."

"So what's the point?"

"They'll bloody well kill you, you stupid fool. You've got to think of something to make them believe you're innocent."

"I am innocent."

She gave him a characteristic Perrine look from her cocked head. It meant she thought anything more plausible than his innocence.

He turned away from her. "Just go, Perrine."

She hunched her shoulders and snorted. "Don't think I'm gonna be there when they string you up. I'll be bloody well damned if I'll watch that. Damn fool! Always knew they'd get you for something serious one day. You're just like your shiftless father."

He opened his mouth to ask about his father, but snapped it shut again. No damn use giving her fuel so she could use it against him. He'd learned to accept whatever she said or gave to him without question. When he got to asking too much, to wanting too much, he always got disappointed. If he didn't demand anything from anyone, ask for anything at all, he didn't get hurt.

Trey had made a profession out of not getting hurt.

"Just go, Perrine. I'm tired and I want to sleep."

"Ungrateful bastard," she muttered.

He looked up at her and he knew, strangely, that it was the last time he'd ever see her. "I'm what you made me, *Mom*."

She had the decency to look affronted and that nearly made him smile, but the sadness of the moment was overwhelming. She turned, her short skirt swinging around behind her, and flounced down the hallway. She paused at the stairs and looked over her shoulder, but she didn't say anything. Trey thought to call her back, but she was already gone, the clomp of her heels a sharp report as she climbed out of the cellar.

Trey sighed and pulled his knees in against his chest, wrapping his arms around them. He laid his forehead on his knees and closed his eyes. Despair and fear filled him. No matter how hopeless his life seemed, no matter how worthless everyone thought him, he didn't want to die.

CHAPTER 2

Merith Daeglor entered the Nazar's cave with trepidation. He'd warned Karnack that his second in command was hungry. He'd seen the want in Tarish Enro's eyes. He knew that want. Coupled with a lack of self-preservation, a young Nazarien could be dangerous. Karnack hadn't heeded his warning. He never heeded Merith's warnings.

And now he was dead.

Merith had been witness to his violent end. Although he'd advised Karnack and he'd sat on the Nazarien Council for decades, he had no love for the past Nazar. Karnack was weak and his weakness had weakened the order. Isolation served only one purpose – survival, but what did survival mean if it was the only goal in life?

Still, Merith wasn't sure the Nazarien's fortunes had changed much. The order was becoming anemic. Too much inbreeding had created unstable leadership. Even the powers that had marked them as superior to their Human counterparts were diminishing. They needed a new infusion of blood, a new life spring to send energy pumping back into a dying people.

"Stop loitering in doorways, man!" snapped Tarish.

Merith inched forward. Once he'd topped six feet, his shoulders had been powerful, his back straight. Years of physical trials had bent his spine, stooped his shoulders, sent threads of silver through his black hair. Even his eyes were not as bright as they'd once been and he had difficulty reading unless the lanterns were at full strength.

Tarish stood with his back to the entrance, a foolish move. Merith fought the urge to scold him for his negligence. Did he think other young Nazarien wouldn't be looking to stick a knife in his back and take over themselves?

He stared up at the tapestry hanging behind his desk. A falcon, the symbol of Talar Eldralin, winged its way across the midnight blue background, the spotted tips of its wings touching the outer edges.

Tarish Enro wore his hair close cropped, scalp showing through. His features were handsome, his eyes brilliant blue. He stood a few inches taller than Merith, lean build, skilled with knives and sword, no powers as far as Merith knew. At least Karnack had never mentioned any.

"You summoned me, Nazar," he said, ducking his head and clasping his hands before him.

Tarish turned slowly and eyed the old councilman, his gaze sweeping from the tips of Merith's boots to the top of his head. His upper lip twitched as if he'd smelt something bad. "You've aged poorly, Merith."

"I'm sorry to displease you, Nazar," Merith answered, biting down on his irritation. Arrogant pup. He deserved to have someone plant a dagger between his shoulder blades.

Tarish crossed the room, his stride silent, his moves graceful. He stopped before Merith and crossed his arms over his chest. "Are you afraid of me?"

Merith chanced a glance up at him, then back down to the floor. "Shouldn't every Nazarien fear his leader?"

Tarish nodded, contemplating. "This is true."

"Why did you have me summoned, my lord Nazar? How can I be of service to you?"

Tarish leaned closer, the scent of his soap wafting over Merith. "Do you know why I killed Karnack?" he said softly.

"To become Nazar," answered Merith. No point in pretending otherwise.

Tarish gave a snort that sounded suspiciously like a laugh, but Nazarien did not laugh. "True, true." A heavy hand landed on Merith's shoulder, making him jump. "This is why I selected you. You aren't afraid to speak truth."

Merith's gaze fluttered up to his face. "Selected me?"

Tarish held out his empty hands. "It seems I might have been a bit hasty in eliminating Karnack. As his second in command, I was privy to most of his dealings, but even I find that there are things I'm not as schooled on as I would like."

"And you want me to advise you?" Merith felt both fear and hope. Perhaps Tarish would be guided. Perhaps he would listen to reason after all.

"I do." He strolled away, walking back toward the tapestry, gazing up at it. "I find that I am displeased with many tenants of our faith."

"Displeased? The order has been much the same as it was on Eldon's founding."

"Exactly." Tarish glanced over his shoulder at him. "I find that unpleasant."

Merith shifted weight uncomfortably. "Others have tried to change us and failed."

Tarish turned and laid his hands on the back of his chair. "True, but they were weak, distracted."

Merith wasn't sure he agreed with that. The Nazarien were anything if intractable. "Jarrett Murata was not a weak man."

Tarish's expression hardened. "Wasn't he? He left the Nazarien to be with a woman."

"She wasn't any woman, Nazar. She was Talar Eldralin's daughter. She was a powerful leader in her own right."

"She was an Eldralin," spat Tarish.

Merith tilted his head. No one in the order took the name of Eldralin in vain. "I fail to understand," he said.

"Our subservience to the Eldralin line ends with me. It has made us weak. It has stripped us of our dignity."

"It is the purpose of our order!" said Merith in disbelief.

Tarish moved so fast, Merith barely registered it. He was suddenly in the elder's face, his eyes glowing, his face tinged with red. "Not anymore! We will no longer dance attendance on Talar Eldralin's bastard spawn. I will rebuild the Nazarien and we will face down anyone who tries to contain us. We will be a force to be reckoned with, Merith, and you're either with me or you're against me." He brought his face so close to the elder's that Merith felt his breath on his cheeks. "So what is it, Merith Daeglor? Are you with me?"

*   *   *

Alana crept to the top of the stairs and looked over into the large tiled entry of the house. Her father was standing beneath the light from the chandelier, speaking in a hushed voice with his captain of the guard. Her father placed his hand on the captain's shoulder and walked him to the door, holding it open until he disappeared from sight. Then he shut and bolted the door.

Alana moved toward the stairs. She wanted to talk with her father, ask him the questions that had been bothering her all day. She knew he'd answer her, he never denied her any information she sought. The appearance of her mother halted her however, and she slipped back to the top of the stairs, peering over at them.

Her father forced a smile for her mother, but Alana knew he was exhausted and troubled by the way he raked his hand through his black hair and dropped it against his thigh. Her mother moved close to him, running her palms up his chest.

Alana adored her father. She thought him the most intelligent, handsome man in all of Temeron. He might not be young anymore, but he'd retained his good looks, his muscular build. He was tall and proud and regal. He was everything a daughter could and did admire in a father.

"You look exhausted," said her mother.

Her father ran his hands up her mother's back and into her hair. Pulling her closer, he rested his chin on the top of her head. Like her mother, Alana was small and petite, but she longed for the tallness of her father and sisters, the strength of their fine Stravad features. She hadn't even inherited her mother's beauty. Both of her older sisters seemed to have taken the best of both sides, while Alana was left with…well, she wasn't even sure herself sometimes.

"I am." He shook his head and sighed again, wearily. Alana felt a pang of worry for him. He worked so hard at being Stravad Leader, trying to balance his duties to his people with the duties of a father and husband. Sometimes Alana thought her mother demanded too much of his time. For a man as powerful as Zeran Eldralin, he was weak when it came to his wife. Alana didn't understand the hold her mother had over her father, or why he seemed so infernally intent on catering to her whims.

Her mother looked up at him. "This whole thing's bothering you, isn't it?"

He nodded. "A girl's dead, Alix. Dead," he said.

"I know."

"I didn't think Trey Almsden capable of such a thing, but I guess part of me isn't all that surprised." Again he raked his fingers through his hair. "With his mother and his background, it was only a matter of time before he did something wrong. Yet…"

"Yet what?"

"When he stood in the study today and told me he was innocent, I believed him." He stared down into his wife's eyes. "I believed him, Alix, and no matter how I look at it, I can't shake the feeling that he was telling me the truth."

"Who else could have killed the girl?"

He shook his head. "He admits he was with her last night. Canto said they had a relationship. He didn't approve of it and I can't blame him. I wouldn't want any of our daughters to see a man like Almsden, but something just doesn't feel right about this, Alix." He eased out of his wife's arms and raked back his hair. "That's crazy, isn't it? Canto's one of my council members. He's an honorable man. I have to believe Trista's father over a man of questionable character."

His wife reached out and touched him in the center of his chest. "What do you feel here, Zeran? That's what matters. That's where the truth is. Which man do you believe more?"

His eyes narrowed. "Trey Almsden."

Her mother didn't say anything, but Alana felt a shiver run up her spine. She hadn't really thought much about Trey Almsden. He'd been a tool to learn more about her father's job as Stravad Leader. She hadn't given a consideration to the fact that he might be innocent and the thought that he might be innocent warred with Alana's innate sense of justice.

If he was innocent, then it was wrong to hold him in the cellar for even one night.

She watched as her mother moved close to her father again. His hands lifted to capture her hips and her mother lifted herself on her tiptoes, bringing her mouth to her father's ear. Alana couldn't hear what she whispered to him and she didn't really care. She'd grown up with her parents' public displays of affection. They had never been shy about embracing or even kissing in front of their daughters. It had ceased to interest Alana years ago. Now she just found it annoying.

She wanted to talk with her father, but it seemed that whenever he had a spare moment, her mother always occupied that time. She rarely found her father alone. She almost never had his undivided attention and looking down at her parents now, she knew that tonight was a wasted opportunity. As always, her mother had managed to capture him first.

She eased back down the hall, then rose to her feet. Mairin's door was open and she could hear both of her sisters inside. Alana rarely found the urge to visit with her sisters. Mairin and Selia were much alike, and Alana was as different from them as they were similar. Both of her sisters were considered beauties. Alana understood why. They had full, generous figures and breath-takingly lovely faces. They were also intelligent and well schooled, but they were too concerned with the opposite sex for Alana's comfort.

Whenever she was in her sisters' company, Alana was reminded of her own inadequacies. They held their father's heart and commanded their mother's undivided attention. Even more so, they had each other and that was a relationship to the exclusion of everyone else, except a current boy of their choice. They never lacked for male attention, a commodity Alana knew little about and cared about even less.

Despite their differences, Alana loved her sisters and admired them. She wished she had just a little more of their flirtatiousness and their beauty, and she wished they had a little more of her intellectual curiosity. For intelligent young women, they were entirely too wrapped up in superficial matters. Yet tonight, Alana found herself hungering for their company. She paused at Mai's door and knocked softly. Mai's lyrical voice called out to her, beckoning her inside.

Alana crossed the threshold with some trepidation. Both of her sisters looked up at her in surprise, then flashed perfect, genuine smiles.

"Hey, Allie, come in and talk with us."

Alana moved to her sister's bed and eased onto the foot of it beside Selia. Selia bumped her shoulder gently against Alana's. "How come you're lurking around up here tonight?"

Alana shrugged, aware as always of her sisters' full, feminine figures and long, shapely legs. "Daddy's downstairs with Mama. He looks exhausted. I didn't want to bother him."

Mai and Selia exchanged knowing glances. "Let Mama take care of Daddy," said Selia with a laugh.

Alana ignored her, looking at her oldest sister. "What do you know about Trey Almsden, Mai?"

"Why ask me? Selia's the one who talks with him every chance she gets."

Selia lifted her dark brows expressively. Alana turned to her. "Selia?"

Selia regarded her youngest sister. "What do you want to know, Allie?"

"Is he capable of doing what they say?"

Selia and Mai exchanged a funny look. Selia started pulling at a loose thread on the bedspread. "I just don't think so," she said softly.

"Why not?"

It was Mai who spoke. Mai had the ability to look into a person's eyes and make a judgment about their personality. Alana always thought it was Mai's Stravad gift, and she trusted her eldest sister's instincts regarding people and situations.

"It just doesn't seem likely. Trey Almsden isn't the sort of man who'd hurt a woman."

"He's been convicted of theft and brought in for fighting in the streets," said Alana with a shrug of her shoulders.

Selia gave her a steely look. It was a look Alana didn't often see on her sister's usually bright and happy face. "That meal Mai and I cooked for him tonight was probably the most food Trey Almsden's seen his entire life. You can't fault a person for stealing when he's hungry. Or fighting when he's defending his mother from the cruelty of other children. Wouldn't you fight back if someone said something bad about Daddy or Mama?"

Alana nodded, still confused.

Mai watched her. "But more than all that is the fact that Trey Almsden could get any woman he wanted. He would have no reason to hurt Trista."

Selia nodded in agreement.

Alana frowned. She knew she was inexperienced in such matters, but she didn't know what that had to do with anything. Trista Lamer was far above Trey Almsden's station in life. If he wanted to strike back at a society he thought had wronged him, that seemed like a plausible, if not horrific, way to do so.

"He said he was with her. Who else could have done it?"

Again Mai and Selia exchanged their enigmatic looks. Alana felt slighted. "What is it? Why do you keep looking at each other that way?"

Mai gave her a grim little smile. "Trista Lamer wasn't exactly the most innocent woman in Temeron, Allie. I'm not trying to speak ill of the dead or anything, but her reputation's well known."

Alana's frown deepened. "What do you mean?"

Selia exhaled in disgust. "Trista Lamer has been with quite a few men. Trey Almsden certainly hasn't been her only lover, maybe only her most notorious." She placed her hand on Alana's knee. "Trey Almsden's a bit of a novelty, Allie. A lot of young women want to bed him, just because he seems like an outcast, like a danger. They hunger for the excitement. He's handsome and intriguing and quiet, and tragic. Trey Almsden has never wanted for female attention."

"For all the good it's done him," added Mai wryly and Selia nodded in agreement. Mai's gaze focused on Alana. "Trista's been sleeping with Trey for weeks. Most people our age know that, and Trista doesn't try to hide it very well, but Trey hasn't been the only one she's entertained."

"Does Daddy know this?"

"Why do you think Trey isn't at the jail? Why do you think Daddy brought him here? Do you really believe our father would bring a suspected murderer into the house with his wife and daughters?"

"But don't you think it's wrong to lock Trey up for even one day if he's innocent?"

"It would be worse to set him free and then find out he's guilty," said Mai frankly. "Or to set him free and let the public decide what to do with him."

Selia nodded again, but Alana wasn't sure she agreed. It seemed horrible to be locked up if you were Trey Almsden. Alana was clever enough to know that even should he be found innocent, he'd never have a life in Temeron again. There were too many people who'd automatically assume his guilt, no matter what the Stravad Council said.

"Well," said Selia, stretching. "It's getting late and tomorrow will be a long day. I'm going to bed."

Alana nodded and climbed to her feet beside her sister. "Good night, Mai. Thanks for answering my questions."

Mai smiled at her and nodded.

Alana and Selia left the room and started down the hall together. At Selia's door, Alana paused. "Why does Mai say you talk to Trey Almsden every chance you get?"

Selia smiled. "Because he's interesting, Allie." She put her hand on her sister's shoulder and touched their foreheads together. "You should get out more and listen to people. You spend too much time hovering around here, trying to listen in on the council meetings. Out there..." She made a move with her hand over her shoulder. "...you learn so much about people. You should spend time with people our age."

Alana considered her words for a moment. "Do you really think he's handsome, Selia?"

Selia laughed. "You don't?"

Alana shrugged. "I'm not sure. I didn't really look at him."

Selia shook her head good naturedly. "You amaze me, Allie. You really have no interest in men."

"They don't seem to have much interest in me, Selia. I'm not beautiful like you and Mai."

Selia fanned her sister's thick black hair over her shoulders and looked at her closely. "You are beautiful, Allie. Maybe in a different way, but have you really looked in the mirror lately? Besides all of that, you're interesting, when you aren't trying to make someone look ignorant. There are a lot of young men who'd love to show you attention if you'd let them."

Alana scrunched up her nose in disgust. "Please, Selia. I couldn't stand to have them drooling over me the way they do you and Mai." She shuddered. "It's disgusting."

Selia laughed, squeezing her sister's shoulders with her hands. "Someday you won't think that. When you meet the right man and he kisses you..."

Alana made a face. "Don't! I can't even imagine what you and Mai find so interesting about that disgusting gesture."

Selia laughed again. "Just wait, Allie." She tapped her sister's nose playfully. "Let's make a bet. You'll be the first of us to fall in love and get married. Huh?"

Alana rolled her eyes. "Not bloody well likely."

"Allie!" scolded Selia playfully. "You'd better not let Mama hear you talk like that."

Alana smiled at her sister. "Good night, Selia."

"Good night, Allie." Selia released her and opened her door, disappearing inside.

Alana headed to her own room, stifling a yawn as she opened the door. She was tired and threw off her clothes, pulling a nightgown over her head and slipping beneath the covers. It wasn't long before she was asleep.

*   *   *

Alana hurried into the kitchen early the next morning. She'd bathed and dressed in her usual trousers and loose shirt, but she'd taken a little time to fix her hair.

Selia and Mai were good at choosing flattering outfits and applying the scantest bit of makeup to enhance their already lovely faces. They both had nice heads of shimmering chestnut brown hair, but Alana's hair was by far the best.

What she didn't have in a figure and facial features, she made up for in her shining, thick mass of black hair, she thought. And she had the ability to style it, something that neither Mai nor Selia were very good at themselves. In fact, they often pleaded with their youngest sister to arrange their hair for them in flattering designs.

This day Alana had taken the heavy sides of her hair and wound it into an intricate ponytail. The end of the ponytail and the rest of her hair hung down to her waist, the sides curving over in a smooth roll. It made her small, pert features more prominent and gave emphasis to her heavily lashed cobalt eyes.

She pranced into the kitchen and both of her sisters immediately pounced on her as she knew they would. The hairstyle was attractive, but best of all, no other young woman would be wearing it since she'd invented it herself that morning. She was hoping it was intriguing enough to earn her their cooperation.

"Look at that," said Selia, turning Alana around to examine the back. "When did you think this up?"

"This morning," said Alana over her shoulder. "Do you like it? I wasn't sure, but I've been wanting to try it."

Mai and Selia praised her and Alana pretended a false modesty. They both begged her to try it out on them, after breakfast was finished, but Alana shook her head and told them she would be too busy to assist them. In truth, she had the entire day free to do with what she willed.

She wandered over to the stove and looked down at the meal they were preparing. "What are we having, Mai?"

Her sisters returned to their chores reluctantly. Mai picked up the bowl and spoon, and began stirring batter with quick, efficient strokes. "I thought I'd make my strawberry pancakes. Are you hungry, Allie?" She asked so pointedly that Alana knew what she was hinting at. She left the bait dangling.

"Not really." She leaned on the counter and braced her chin on a hand. Selia and Mai exchanged a look. Alana didn't consume much food. In fact, both her sisters remarked often that she seemed to exist on air.

Alana had a very good appetite, but she only ate when she was hungry and only enough to satisfy that hunger. Both Mai and Selia, with their more voluptuous figures, had to be careful of what they ate.

She watched Mai cook a large pancake to a golden brown. She placed it on a plate and then handed it to Selia. Selia carefully spread butter over the pancake and then lifted a bowel, spooning a generous helping of syrupy strawberries over the entire thing. She added a few large sausages that were browning in a pan beside the pancakes and set the plate in the middle of a tray, placing a napkin over it. She filled a glass with fresh orange juice and added a cup of cut fruit.

She looked up at Alana finally. "Go call the guard. Tell him Trey's breakfast is ready."

It was the opportunity Alana had been waiting for. She grasped the tray in her hands and started to lift it, but Selia stopped her. "What are you doing?"

"Why make the guard come all the way upstairs for it when I can take it down just as easily? He'll have to lock the door and then be worried about opening it again once he gets to the bottom of the stairs. I don't mind taking it down."

Mai looked over her shoulder and frowned. "What? What's this nonsense about all of a sudden?"

Selia stepped back and crossed her arms over her chest. "You want to see Trey, don't you?"

Alana took a deep breath, cursing her own innate honesty. Sometimes she wished she could be just a little more deceitful. She always caved whenever anyone got suspicious.

"You told me last night that I needed to get out more and talk with people my age."

Selia's dark brows lifted. "Yes, but I meant people who aren't being held for murder."

"You and Mai both said you think he's innocent. I want to judge for myself, but I can't do that if I can't talk with him."

Mai turned from the stove. "No offense, Allie, but what good would it do him if you did think he was innocent?"

"None, but it would do me good to make that judgment for myself."

Mai and Selia exchanged a curious glance. "That's ridiculous. Daddy would tan our hides if he knew you went down there."

"He doesn't have to know if you don't tell him." She moved forward and laid her palms flat on the counter beside the tray. "Selia, you said I needed to talk to people our age."

"Your age! Trey Almsden's closer to Mai's age than yours."

Alana waved that argument away. "Mai's close to my age and I only want to talk to him, not marry the man."

"Have you considered he might not want you asking him questions, Allie?" said Mai.

Alana wrinkled her nose. "I hadn't planned on asking him for an outright confession if that's what you're worried about. I'm not a complete social imbecile, Mai."

Mai exhaled, then made a motion at Alana's hair with her spoon. "You mean to tell me you spent all that time designing a hairstyle just so you could assuage your curiosity? I didn't think you were so devious."

Alana took her words as praise and beamed at her. "I'll fix your hair this way if you'll just keep your mouths shut about me taking the tray of food down." She fixed a hand on her hip. "Really, it isn't like I'm doing anything remotely dangerous. I'm taking the man breakfast with an armed guard standing by me."

Selia gave her the same expression. "And what will you say when that same armed guard tells Daddy you've been down there?"

Alana's face fell, but she recovered. "He won't, but if he does, I'll handle Daddy."

"She always does," said Mai, turning back to the stove.

Selia glared at Alana for a moment. "All right, Allie, but if Daddy finds out, we're gonna tell him we knew nothing about it."

"Fine."

"And you'd better come right back," she scolded, waggling a finger at her.

"I will, as soon as breakfast's served."

Before either of them could protest further, Alana caught up the tray and headed for the cellar stairs just outside the door to the kitchen and off the pantry. She descended quickly and was surprised to see the clean shaven young guard waiting at the bottom for her. He also looked surprised.

"What are you doing here?"

Alana flashed her best smile. She knew it wasn't anything like the flirtatious smiles of her sisters, but she hoped it might have a little effect on the guard.

"I'm bringing the prisoner breakfast."

"Give me the tray and go back up stairs, Alana. Your father would kill us both if he knew you were down here."

Alana frowned at him, then remembered she was supposed to flirt. "Oh please," she simpered, balancing the tray with one hand and waving him away with the other. She wasn't good at this and she hoped she didn't look utterly ridiculous. "If I give you the tray, you'll have to take your hands off your weapon. Then we'll both be vulnerable, won't we? It's just better if I deliver it to him. Besides..." She had to look down so he wouldn't detect the lie in her eyes. "...my father already knows. He told me to make myself useful and take the prisoner his meal." She glanced at the guard through her lashes and saw the uncertainty on his face. "You don't want to disobey his orders, do you?" She delivered the final barb home with a rapid flutter of her eyelashes.

He opened his mouth to speak, but nothing came out. Finally he stepped back and gave her a curt motion into the little cellar room.

It took a moment for Alana's eyes to adjust to the dimness. She stood just inside the room and blinked until it all came into focus. Trey was sitting on a pile of blankets, his long, dark hair neatly combed back and tied with a piece of leather, his jaw and chin shadowed by a day's growth of beard.

Even in the dim light, Alana could see the cold, gem-like glitter of his strange green eyes. She shuddered and looked away, advancing with the tray before her. She set it at his feet and then backed up, but she made no move to leave the room. The guard behind her sighed in annoyance, but she ignored him.

"Did you sleep all right?" She clasped her hands at her back and clenched them tightly. Damn, she wasn't any good at this either. She'd never been one to make small talk.

His glittering green eyes lifted from the food and fixed with absent curiosity on her face. "Not particularly," he said. "Something about unlawful incarceration spoils a truly good night."

Alana had told herself she wasn't going to discuss his situation. She rocked on her heels and clenched her hands tighter. "My sister, Mai, made it. I'm sure it's delicious. She's one of the finest cooks I know and this is her specialty. She's been doing the cooking for years. I think she enjoys it."

She stopped abruptly when she caught the stunned look on his face. She tended to ramble when she was nervous and this was certainly a time for a young woman to be nervous. He was staring at her from behind his veiled expression and she truly didn't know what he was thinking. His eyes searched her face for another long moment.

"Either go back upstairs or stop doing that. You're making me nervous as hell."

Alana stopped moving when he motioned at her rocking hips. "Sorry," she said, "it's a habit I revert to when I'm nervous." Honesty seemed like the best policy. "And I am nervous. I've never…I mean I've…but…not…oh, this is so difficult. I don't usually speak to people my age, let alone…let alone…"

"Criminals?"

She nodded vigorously. "When I was younger and got nervous, I tended to wring my hands, but that bothered my mother, so I learned to tap against something to relieve tension. But that quickly became annoying to everyone, including myself. So I…" She shrugged.

"So you chatter."

Alana let out a nervous little laugh. "Guess so."

"It's annoying too," he said, lifting the plate from the tray and balancing it on his knees.

Behind them the guard snorted in what sounded like smothered laughter. Alana shot him a dirty look, but he was too busy sitting down to notice. She looked back at Trey.

He'd cut a piece of the pancake and was looking at it with an uncertain expression.

"Strawberries," she said brightly.

His glittering green eyes shifted to her. "Strawberries?"

She nodded. "On the pancake?"

He was still looking at her, but he nodded indulgently. "I'd sort of figured that out myself." He leaned toward her and dropped his voice conspiratorially. "See, I might be a criminal, but I'm not altogether an idiot."

She blinked at him. "No, but you're certainly rude."

He looked just the slightest bit surprised by her honesty, then to her amazement, threw back his head and laughed. Alana had never heard such a rich, vibrant sound in her life. Her father's laugh was infectious, but not nearly so much as this man's. She couldn't stop the curve of a smile on her lips.

Trey finally quit laughing and looked up at her with amused green eyes. "So, since we're being blunt with one another, why are you really here?"

She wrinkled her nose. "I guess I wanted to hear your side of the story."

"My side, huh?"

"Yes. Did you do it?"

He studied her a moment silently. What he saw in her face she wasn't sure, but he finally drew a deep breath and exhaled. "No."

She cocked her head and then squatted just outside the door of the cellar. "You must be furious at being locked up, then."

"You might say that. You believe me?"

"Do I have reason not to?"

The green eyes narrowed. "You have no reason to believe either way. Why do you care?"

"I'm not sure, but I don't think I'd like being locked up…" Her eyes made the circuit of the cramped, dark little room. "…anywhere if I were innocent. If you're furious, you don't act it."

"How should I act?"

She considered that. "When my mother gets furious, she voices it, loudly. My sisters make everyone miserable with their complaining, and Daddy, well, Daddy retreats. You can't get him to talk with you for nothing."

"And you?"

Again she wrinkled her nose. "The only time I got really furious, I fought. Daddy about turned me black and blue, but I didn't care. That bully deserved to be knocked in the head many more times than I actually did."

"Somehow I don't think your father's ever lifted a hand to you or your sisters."

"Well, I was speaking figuratively of course." She pinned him with her curious gaze. "Did you ever get beaten?"

He gave a little bark of laughter. He was handsome, when he wasn't scowling at her. "No, I didn't get beaten."

"That's good."

"I guess."

"Alana," snapped the guard behind her. She jumped a little, but quickly recovered and glared at him over her shoulder. "You better go. Your daddy's gonna beat *me* if he finds you down here, no matter what you say."

"I'm going, but that doesn't give you excuse to be rude to me."

Alana was annoyed when Trey and the guard exchanged an enigmatic look between them. She pushed herself to her feet and pointed at his breakfast.

"You really ought to eat. It'll get cold and then won't be as good. Mai's cooking is a terrible thing to waste."

He looked down at his plate. "Wouldn't think of doing that," he said stiffly, then shot her a curious look. "You'd better go."

"I am." She turned her back and walked to the stairs. "Enjoy it."

"I will," he said as she started ascending.

She paused.

That wasn't what he was supposed to say, the ill-mannered barbarian. Hadn't he ever heard the words *thank you* before?

CHAPTER 3

Trey was led to the doors of the Council Chamber, his hands shackled. It was difficult to keep your dignity when you were being led like a market animal, and nothing could make him believe he wasn't going to his own slaughter.

The doors were thrust open and he was pushed inside. He glanced at the young guard, Roe something-or-other. He'd been Trey's guard almost since the beginning, except during the night when Trey had been left alone in the darkness of the little cellar. In a day, Trey felt as if he hated that room. The guard met his look sympathetically.

They were nearly the same age and although their status in life was vastly different, they understood one another. Roe knew Trey was scared and Trey knew Roe was grateful he was on the other end of this situation.

He led Trey into the center of the large room. Trey's shrewd eyes took in the entire scene, cataloging everything in detail.

The room was white and stark and intimidating. The only splash of color, a long red carpet, rent the room precisely down the middle. Before Trey was a single stair, rising to a low dais and an ornate, high backed chair. Along both sides were risers and benches, partitioned off by a solid, half-wall, where the council members sat, hands folded in their laps, their eyes trained on the empty chair.

Trey's eyes passed over each of them – he saw a multitude of blue eyes in varying shades; bronze skin, some wrinkled, some smooth; long hair – black, blond, brown, grey, even a startling red that stood out like a beacon. There were old and young, women and men on the council, a fairly good assembly of the Stravad in Temeron; but it was the single empty place on the lowest bench, the closest spot to the dais that occupied his attention.

The Lamers, Canto and his wife, stood just to the left of the dais. The older man turned and spoke something into his wife's ear. She nodded and continued studying the ground.

Trey absorbed Canto's short, stocky form, his grey flecked brown hair, his rounded cheeks, and his short fingered hands. He digested the man's well tailored suit of pin stripes and dark colors, the collar of the shirt seeming just a little tight, forcing his heavily laden chin to hang over.

Trista's mother was tall and thin, almost the exact opposite of her husband. Trista herself had leaned toward her mother's side of the family. Her mother was a handsome woman. There was a hardness about her mouth that drew Trey's interest. She'd aged well, better than her husband, so the lines about her mouth had to be for an entirely different reason. The downward cast of her eyes and the line of that rigid mouth engrossed Trey. A strange restlessness set up in his limbs, making him shift uncomfortably.

"What is it?" whispered the guard at his side.

Trey shook his head, his brow furrowing.

"All rise," came the shouted command and the entire council surged to their feet. The quickness of their reaction didn't bode well.

Trey's eyes shifted back to Trista's parents. The idea of Trista being murdered ambushed him over and over again, but nothing had sent it home quite as forcefully as looking at her grieving parents. He glanced toward the dais when Zeran stepped up on it and strode to the chair. His was a regal presence that demanded attention.

"Be seated," came Zeran's calm, authoritative voice. The council sat noisily.

Zeran regarded the younger man with a veiled expression. It was an expression Trey had always admired and as a young boy had tried to imitate. No one knew exactly what was going on inside Zeran Eldralin's head, but most bet it was a good deal more than they wanted to know.

"Step forward, Trey Almsden."

The guard put just a little pressure on Trey's elbow and Trey moved closer. He didn't like any of this. He knew that somehow everything was about to be twisted around, until Trey would wish to confess just to feel he understood some small part of it. The sense of doom was overpowering. Trey had known since the start that nothing good would come of this; he knew he was finished, ruined (as if he'd ever had any real prospects before).

He trained his eyes on the single stair. Why look up at Zeran and give him the psychological advantage over his prisoner? He had the physical advantage already.

"Trey Almsden, you are being tried for the brutal murder of Trista Lamer. You have the right to select a council member to represent your interest in this case. Have you given it any thought?"

Trey looked up. "I'll represent myself."

"I wouldn't advise it," said Zeran, but there was no surprise or even interest in his voice.

"Can I though?"

"Of course, but you don't have the knowledge or the time to prepare a sufficient counterargument."

Trey raised his brows. "Seems to me it doesn't matter much either way. I don't think I'll have an opportunity to tell my side, and if I do, the council is predisposed to hear only the opposing view."

"This is a fair and just council..."

Trey nodded. "For those whose mothers are paragons of the community. Can't exactly say the same for myself, can we?"

"Your mother isn't the one on trial here, Trey Almsden."

Trey sighed, narrowing his green eyes on the man he'd admired so much his entire life. "I know I don't stand a chance in hell, Zeran Eldralin, so don't start lying to me now."

A murmur of surprise rippled through the council. Trey felt the guard's hand tighten on his elbow. Still he met Zeran's cobalt gaze and refused to back down.

"What exactly do you think I'm lying about?"

Trey couldn't help but be impressed. Zeran looked him straight in the eye, giving him his most contained expression. "Everything about my life is on trial here today – my past, my present, my future, and especially my family." He didn't bother to look at the council, he could feel their affront from where he stood. In truth, Zeran Eldralin was the only one that mattered in this room and practically speaking, he didn't matter a damned bit either. Trey was a dead man in their eyes. "Get on with it. Play the game and then let them convict me. Pass your sentence and send me back to your little cellar room while I wait for you to carry it out."

Zeran stood for a long, tense moment regarding the younger man before him. Finally he stirred and moved back to take a seat, folding his hands over the arms of his chair with slow precision. Trey followed each movement, etching it in his mind even though he'd have liked not to remember.

*   *   *

Alana balanced the tray on her hip and opened the door leading down to the cellar. She heard the immediate scrapping of the guard's chair as he rose to meet her. She headed down the stairs, careful to protect the contents of the tray and keep her dignity intact.

No one knew she'd come down here again the same day. Mai had prepared the meal, then commanded Alana to call the guard. Alana had assured her sister she'd take care of things and then had waited for Mai to leave the house. It hadn't taken long.

The entire city was in an uproar. Her father had returned from the Council Chambers an hour ago and locked himself in his study, refusing to speak with anyone. The captain of the guard had dispatched his company, surrounding the Stravad Leader's house and keeping everyone at bay. The council, as far as she knew, was still in session, but they'd returned Trey Almsden to his cellar room.

Alana itched to know what had happened. Mai had been silent and Selia was absent. As soon as she could, Mai had taken off, claiming a need to be with her friends. Alana was just as grateful, but she wanted information. Since her father was sequestered and her mother wouldn't divulge anything no matter what, that left Alana with only one choice. Trey Almsden himself.

The guard gave her a severe look. Alana smiled brightly. She could charm her way past him, she told herself, and if not, she had an ace in the hole. The poor guard, Roe Manes, was hopelessly in love with Mai. The fact that Mai gave him only a passing glance didn't seem to lessen that ardor. Alana knew she'd use Mai as a tool to get to Trey Almsden, but she hoped she wouldn't have to – it seemed underhanded and dishonest.

"I brought the prisoner his lunch," she said with another false smile.

Roe rolled his eyes. "Your daddy know you're down here, Alana? 'Cause if he doesn't, I surely don't want to cause him any more grief today."

Alana fought to keep the excitement from her face as she gave the guard a haughty look. "Do you think I'd want to upset Daddy on a day like today, Roe Manes?"

The guard studied her, then heaved a reluctant sigh. "Hurry up. Give him the tray and get out of here."

41

She wrinkled her nose at him. "Don't you think even a prisoner deserves some intelligent conversation," she remarked, shoving past him. If he picked up on her jibe, she didn't wait to find out.

She moved into the little room, pausing only momentarily to let her eyes adjust. She perceived the prisoner sitting on his blankets and walked forward, bending to place the tray at his feet.

"What's this?" he snarled in a hostile voice.

"Lunch, you ignorant baboon." She caught the glittering amusement in his eyes as she set about organizing his food. It gave her something to do, anything to avoid feeling disconcerted by his frank appraisal.

"I just ate."

She glanced at him. He seemed genuinely surprised and something else. What? Appalled? "You ate breakfast nearly four hours ago. This is lunch, the typical midday meal for most people. Don't tell me you haven't at least heard of it."

"Eldon's star, Alana, your tongue's as sharp as a razor," said Roe.

Alana glared at the nosy guard and then returned her attention to the prisoner. His quick green eyes passed between the two of them and fixed on her. "She speaks her mind. It's something at least," said Trey.

The guard grunted in disagreement, but settled back in his chair, bracing his feet against the opposite wall. Alana noted his lack of attention and turned hers on the prisoner.

"I know you haven't led the most privileged lifestyle…"

"Clever pixie," he said with a nasty, cold smile.

She started to protest his words, but thought better of it. She didn't have much time and needed to get to the bottom of things. "Anyway, I didn't mean to offend you…"

"Yes, you did. Admit it, pixie. You impressed me earlier. Don't disappoint me now."

She met his frank gaze. "All right, I did mean it. You can't hide behind your poverty forever."

He gave a short laugh. "Can't hide from anything, it seems, but then you wouldn't know because Daddy shields you from anything bad."

"You don't know that."

His eyes made the circuit of her small, delicate frame, but he didn't answer. He lifted the plate off the tray and studied the sandwich on it. He looked at Alana over the top of it.

"You're not afraid of me, are you, pixie?"

She didn't know what the name meant that he kept calling her, but she hated it. From the sound of it, it couldn't be anything good. She met his stare coldly. "Why should I be afraid of you?"

"You shouldn't, so stop crouching there in the doorway and sit down or leave."

Alana caught the challenge in his voice and sat down, tucking her legs beneath her and folding her hands primly in her lap. He watched her with those damn glittering green eyes and then smiled.

"What's so funny?"

"You Eldralins," he said, lifting one half of the sandwich. He reached over her and Alana forced herself not to flinch away. "Here, Roe, take this. I know you're hungry."

Alana fixed a hand on her hip. "That sandwich is for you, not the guards." She glared over her shoulder at Roe.

"The man's hungry, sprite. You and your kin haven't been considerate of his situation. You think he wants to be stuck down here underground all day, watching me." He looked at the guard and gestured with the sandwich. "Take it."

"Thanks, Almsden," said the guard, grabbing the half and glaring back at Alana. "You might learn something down here after all, Alana."

"What?"

"Manners," said the young man, placing the sandwich at his mouth.

Trey chuckled and Alana's head swung back around to glare at him now. He lifted the remaining half and broke that in two. "The pixie's got manners, she just doesn't have to use them. She's an Eldralin."

"Humph," said Roe around a mouthful of sandwich.

"I don't need you to defend me," spat Alana, then frowned, not sure that's exactly what he was doing. It was hard to tell with a man like Trey Almsden. Eldon's star, she hated that name he'd made up for her, but pride wouldn't let her tell him that.

He held out a part of the sandwich to her. She looked at it, then into his amused eyes. What did he find so damned amusing?

From the rumors she'd heard, he was as good as dead. Only her father stood in the way and if he thought her father could veto a unanimous vote of the council, well...

"What? That's your lunch."

"I'm not that hungry after the enormous breakfast your sister made me. Besides," he said, looking over her figure again. "You need it more than I do."

Alana's jaw clenched tight with anger and she started to scramble to her feet. His hand came out and wrapped around her wrist, pinning her. Alana stopped moving immediately and stared at his large, strong hand. Her wrist looked like twigs caught in his grasp. She felt Roe come alert at her back and she lifted her eyes to Trey's face.

He was staring at her with unnerving green eyes. Alana felt a strange heat pass between them. For some unknown reason, her gaze slid down to his tightly pressed lips and hers felt suddenly, unbearably dry. Slowly she licked them and saw his strange green eyes follow every second of the nervous gesture.

"Alana," said the guard, rising to his feet.

Alana parted her lips, her breath coming in a quick pant. She let the pressure Trey exerted on her arm push her back to the floor and then his fingers were sliding away from her, sliding away in a motion that was slow and deliberate. Alana felt an odd tightening in her stomach. She broke his stare and looked over her shoulder at the guard.

"I'm fine," she said, surprised by the tightness in her own voice. She looked back at Trey and found him watching her. "I'm fine."

Roe exhaled audibly and sank to his chair. "What happened?"

"I got up too fast and got dizzy. Trey steadied me or I would have fallen into his lap."

The green eyes narrowed. "More's the pity," he said and Alana's brow furrowed. Now what did that mean?

He held out the sandwich to her again. "Take it so you don't get dizzy anymore."

Their fingers brushed as she took the sandwich and again Alana felt the weird response. An errant lock of dark hair had fallen over Trey's eye and she longed to brush it back with the tips of her fingers. Instead she looked at the sandwich.

"It didn't go well in the Council Chambers, did it?" she asked quietly.

His hands paused just before his mouth. He brought them down into his lap again. Alana looked at him through her lashes. "No, it didn't go well."

"What happened?"

"Alana," scolded Roe. "I'm sure that's the last thing he wants to talk about now. You'd better go."

Alana ignored him. "What happened?" she said again.

Trey glanced between the two of them. "They brought Trista's parents to testify against me. After that there wasn't much left to say. I was surprised when your father demanded they hold their verdict until he had time to investigate. Didn't seem to be much to investigate after that."

Alana wrinkled her nose. "Maybe he believes you when you say you didn't do it."

Trey glanced at her, then stared at the opposite wall, his eyes growing distant. "Maybe." His voice trailed off. "Here's the thing. I didn't do it. I didn't kill Trista."

"Okay," said Alana.

"But that means there's a murderer still running around Temeron."

"Attacking women," remarked Roe around a mouthful of food.

Trey looked at the guard and then nodded. His eyes lowered to Alana. "When I left her that night, she was fine. Who came in after I left?" He stopped and seemed surprised he'd been saying so much. "It doesn't matter either way. Your father's stalling the inevitable. I wish he wouldn't prolong it, 'cause there's not a damn thing he can do to save me."

"If my father believes you, he'll work nonstop to see you freed."

Trey leaned closer to her. "There's nothing your father can do, pixie. He'll have to agree to the execution just to keep his position as Stravad Leader."

"My father's a good man."

"I didn't say he wasn't, but he also has to protect his political career and his Eldralin name. One less Almsden would actually be a boon."

"How dare you…" she snapped, but caught herself. She'd heard her father say many times that he was a servant of the people and he had to follow their wishes even when he knew they were wrong. He could only try to convince them otherwise, but in the end, he had little choice. Was this one of those times? She stared at the man before her and felt an overwhelming sense of confusion and divided loyalties. She adored her father and her people. Her fondest wish had been to lead them herself one day, but if it meant hurting innocent people in the name of justice or letting a true murderer go free.

Without thinking, she reached out and placed her hand on his arm. He looked down at it, startled by her touch, but she didn't pull away. "You've got to remember something about that night, something that will help my father prove your innocence."

"It won't work, sprite."

"It will, if you just try. You can't give up."

He lifted his eyes and pinned her with his wide, green stare. The lines around his mouth softened. For a moment, Alana saw how handsome he was. "I haven't given up, sprite," he said, and his eyes narrowed on her again. "In fact, I've just figured out what to do."

He lifted his free hand and reached toward her, but Roe came to his feet. "Come on, Alana. That's enough." He grasped her arm and hauled her to her feet. "You've got to go. Don't come down here again." He pushed her toward the stairs and Alana stumbled on the bottom one before she caught herself.

"I'm going," she said, yanking away from him. "Don't you manhandle me, Roe Manes. You're acting just like an animal and I won't stand for it."

She marched up the stairs before him, her back straight, her long black hair swinging against her waist.

*   *   *

Trey chuckled to himself. *Don't you manhandle me, Roe Manes.*

Eldon's star, that one was a spitfire. He'd never given her a second glance her entire life, but he was watching her now. Her older sisters might have the more voluptuous figures, but Alana had gotten more than her share of passion.

He thought of all that shining black hair and those enormous cobalt eyes. Damn but he'd wanted to sink his hands in that hair and lose himself in those eyes. Her wrist had felt so small and fragile in his hand and he knew that he'd probably be able to span that waist with no problem. She had to weigh nothing, which was good, because for his plan to work, he'd need to be physically stronger than her. He had no doubt Alana Eldralin would put up a fight. A smile curved his lips. He was actually looking forward to a battle with the little thing.

Roe trooped back down the stairs and collapsed in his chair again. He looked over at his prisoner with a weary sigh. "Someone ought to turn that girl over his knee and paddle some sense into her."

Trey smiled, but looked away. He could think of a better way to tame pretty Alana Eldralin.

He leaned his head against the wall and closed his eyes. He had a lot to plan before the evening meal. He calculated that to be about four hours away, the way these people ate continually. He hoped Alana wouldn't listen to the guard's admonishment because he needed her down here for his plan to work.

Not that he thought for a moment she'd listen to anyone. Again a chuckle rumbled in his chest. She'd looked so concerned that he might give up. If she knew what he'd been thinking at the time, she would have either kicked him or fled like a frightened rabbit.

Fleeing, though, didn't seem like Alana Eldralin's style. No, the ridiculous little sprite would have flown into him, trying to punish him for assuming too high.

* * *

Alana heard Selia return home a few hours later. She left her room, where she'd been hiding, and hurried to her sister's door. She tapped and looked down the hall, hoping her mother wouldn't hear her and come to investigate. She wanted to talk with her sister alone.

"Come in," came Selia's voice.

Alana slipped into the room and found her sister playing with her hair before the dressing table mirror. She walked up behind her and looked at her sister's reflection.

"Do my hair in your new style, Allie," said Selia, dropping the chestnut mass with a sigh.

Alana picked up the brush and set to work. "Where have you been all day?"

"Out. The whole city's in an uproar over this Trey Almsden thing. How's Daddy?"

"Worried," said Alana, brushing her sister's hair until it snapped and glistened. "He ended the council and demanded some time to research it." She placed her hands on Selia's shoulders and looked into the mirror. "You really believe he's innocent, Selia?"

"Yes, I do."

"But unless Daddy finds something soon, they'll execute him, won't they?"

"I'm afraid so, Allie," Selia said sadly. "And Daddy will have no choice. He has to do what the council demands."

Alana looked down. "It'll hurt Daddy, Selia."

"It'll hurt all of Temeron, but people don't see that. Everyone pays when an innocent man is harmed. Not to mention someone else has gotten away with murder."

Alana began working with her sister's hair. She wanted to change the subject. "Trey Almsden ever kiss you, Selia?"

She felt Selia go still beneath her hands. She glanced at her in the mirror. "Why do you ask that?"

Alana shrugged, but she was dismayed to see the spark of color in her cheeks. "Curious."

"Yeah, but he probably doesn't remember it. He was a little tipsy at the time."

"He was?"

Selia smiled and nodded. "And I kissed him."

"Selia!"

"Oh, please, Allie. It was fun."

Alana lowered her eyes, embarrassed by the rush of heat in her face. She remembered her reaction to Trey in the cellar when he'd touched her arm. If he'd kissed her…

She'd been too sheltered, she decided at once. "What was it like?"

"The kiss?"

Alana glared at Selia in the mirror.

Selia laughed. "It was nice."

"Nice?" Alana was appalled. She'd thought many things about a kiss, but nice hadn't been one of them.

"All right, Allie, what did you want me to say?"

"The truth."

Selia's eyes went dreaming. "Okay, it was hot and spicy and dangerous, and I didn't want it to stop."

Alana flushed again and snagged the brush in Selia's hair. "Sorry," she muttered and set about trying to free it. "You liked it then?"

"Liked it?" Selia sighed. "I'll bet Trey Almsden knows tricks with a woman that would make her melt."

"Selia!"

"You asked." Selia shrugged matter-of-factly. She placed her hand under her sister's chin and lifted Alana's face. "Why are you asking all this?"

Alana shook her head. "No reason."

"Don't lie to me, Alana Eldralin."

Alana played with the brush. "I brought Trey his lunch."

Selia's eyes widened. "If Daddy finds out..."

"Don't scold me, Selia, please not now."

"All right, Allie," said her sister with concern. "Go on."

"I don't know what it is, but I'm just so curious about him. I had to go back down there and talk with him, make sure he was all right."

"And was he?"

Alana nodded. "Surprisingly so. He didn't even seem down at all. He did make me mad though and when I stood to leave, he grabbed my wrist."

Again Selia's eyes went wide.

"Oh, don't be worried. Roe Manes was right there, hovering like a fly." Alana looked up into her sister's eyes. "It was so strange, Selia. We just looked at one another and I got the funniest feeling."

Selia smiled. "In the pit of your stomach?"

Alana looked down. "Yes."

Selia gave a laugh. "I'm familiar with it." She lifted Alana's head. "So you find him attractive. You're not the first person."

"But this hasn't ever happened to me." She stared at her sister a moment in silence, then sighed. "I like to be near him, but what if they execute him, Selia?"

"I don't know, Allie."

Alana turned the brush over and over in her hands. "That's why I have to see him as much as I can. Help me, Selia."

"I don't know, Allie, if Daddy…"

"I'd help you. Please Selia, please!"

Selia sighed. "All right, Allie, but only if Roe's there with you. Agreed?"

Alana smiled. "Agreed," she said.

CHAPTER 4

Merith rapped on the Nazar's wooden door, glancing down at the missive he held in his hands. He'd been to the trill cote, the avian messenger system Shadar Haldane had created so many generations ago. The message they'd received alarmed Merith. News had traveled fast, faster than he'd expected and Loden knew the Nazar had changed yet again.

"Come!" shouted Tarish Enro.

Merith pushed open the door, tamping down on the annoyance he felt whenever he danced attendance on the arrogant pup. He had to give Tarish credit. He'd been forcing the Nazarien to get into shape again with physical trials, weapons training, and hand to hand combat, but the reason for so much training worried Merith.

Tarish turned from the tapestry that he studied endlessly. Merith had once suggested he have it removed if it bothered him so much, but he'd said it was good to have a reminder that they were tools to be wielded by another. Someday, he swore, they would burn the tapestry and everything that had ever linked the Nazarien to the Eldralin line.

The other council members spoke of this as blasphemy, but Merith kept his peace. If Tarish Enro thought he could pit himself against the Eldralins, so be it. Lesser men had learned the lesson of that folly.

"You received a missive."

Tarish turned and regarded him, his eyes sweeping over Merith. "A missive? From who?"

"The Lord of Loden."

"Falco Leonhart? Are you serious?"

Merith ducked his head in agreement.

"Give it here."

Merith held it out and Tarish snatched it from his hand, breaking the lion seal on the back. His eyes swept over the paper, then he threw back his head and laughed. Merith jumped. It had been many years since he'd heard laughter. The last time was when they'd gone into Dorland after supplies and they'd passed a Human tavern.

"May I caution you about dismissing such things?" he pleaded, keeping his eyes downcast.

"Caution me? About Falco Leonhart? The spineless ass!" He shook the missive in Merith's face. "Do you know what he dares?"

"I can only speculate."

"Well, don't. He orders me to present myself before him in Zelan at the start of Autumn. Orders me? The Nazar?"

"I would caution you against ignoring such a summons."

Tarish went still and Merith glanced up, feeling his stomach clench in dread. Slowly, Tarish crumpled the missive and dropped it onto his desk. "This is what I think of Falco Leonhart's summons. He does not order me. He does not command the Nazarien."

Merith swallowed hard. If Tarish wanted his advice, why wouldn't he listen? What was the point of having an advisor if you ignored what he said? "And if the summons comes from Temeron?"

A hellish light blazed in Tarish's eyes. "Oh, let it come," he breathed. "Let it come!"

*   *   *

Alana stood in the hallway outside the dining room, listening to her family take their usual places. It was quieter than usual and Alana wondered when her absence would be noticed. She bit the side of her forefinger nervously, more to keep herself from drumming against the wall.

"Where's Alana?" came her mother's voice.

Alana went still, holding her breath.

"Did you tell her dinner was ready, Selia?" asked her father.

There was a long pause. "She said she wasn't hungry," said Selia, then she went silent. After a moment, she spoke again. "She wanted to meet up with some friends in town."

Alana frowned. That wasn't what Selia was supposed to say. Alana didn't go into town to meet friends. That's what Selia and Mairin did.

"What friends in town?" said her mother, concern evident. Alana grimaced as a chair scraped across the dining room floor.

"Some people from her legislative class," said Selia. "I think this whole Trey Almsden thing has her upset. You know how she's always wanted to follow in your footsteps, Daddy. Well, Allie's

52

getting a glimpse as to how hard your job really is and she wanted to discuss it with them."

Well, that was better. Plausible even.

"Why didn't she tell me she was going?" said her mother.

"She told me. She knew you and Daddy were busy with this case."

"Sometimes it's best for a person to work things out by herself. Allie knows she can come to us if she wants to talk," said her father.

"Still, she should have told me she was going."

"She's grown, Alix," said her father. "She doesn't have to tell us everything she does anymore."

Alana breathed a sigh of relief and closed her eyes momentarily.

"She'll be fine, Mama," replied Selia.

Alana heard her mother's sigh. "Let's save something for her, Mai, in case she's hungry when she comes home."

"Sure, Mama," answered Mai.

Alana suppressed the wash of guilt at her mother's concern, but she'd be guiltier if Trey Almsden was sentenced to die and she hadn't spent as much time with him as she could before that end.

She slipped away from the wall and angled around to the kitchen. She crept stealthily and quietly to the pantry and eased open the cellar door. She tried not to make a sound as she hurried down the stairs, but Roe was waiting for her just the same.

"I told you not to come down here, Alana. Trey's already been brought his dinner."

Alana faced him, but that was difficult because she had to look up to do so. "You have no control over me, Roe Manes, so step aside. I've told you before my father knows where I am. If you'd like to take it up with him, be my guest. He just sat down to dinner with my family." She made an expansive motion toward the stairs.

Roe glared down at her and she met his look, hoping that the racing fear inside of her didn't show on the outside. It seemed to take an inordinate amount of time, but finally the guard exhaled and stepped back to make room for her.

* * *

Trey heard the door to the stairs open and he glanced toward Roe. His muscles tensed as the guard rose to his feet with a muttered curse and went to the bottom of the cellar stairs.

Every nerve inside of Trey was screaming. He prayed that the intruder was Alana because if it wasn't he was in deep trouble. His entire plan centered on her appearance here tonight as he'd predicted. She just had to show, she just had to come. His life depended on it.

At the first sharp words from Roe, Trey eased into a standing position. For the last few hours he'd been flexing and relaxing his muscles, trying to work out the tension sitting all day had placed on them. He reached out and curled his fingers around the small crowbar he'd found the previous night. He was sure it had been used to open crates stored in the cellar. It had fallen in the very back, behind some crates holding fine china. It wasn't very heavy, but for now, it was the only weapon he had available.

He eased to the door of the cellar room, careful to keep himself in the shadows. Alana's clipped, irritated return set his heart to beating frantically. She was there. His plan would work. It had to work.

And then she was stepping toward him, blinking in the unfamiliar darkness. He moved swiftly, catching her arm and hauling her against him. She gave a little cry of surprise, but he silenced her with his free hand over her mouth. Strange how the clean, floral scent of her hair distracted him momentarily and he breathed deeply, filling his lungs with it. Recovering, he lowered his head.

"Scream and I'll kill you both!" he hissed in her ear, pulling her further into the cellar. "Nod if you understand me!"

She didn't respond.

He shook her. "I don't want to hurt your family. Promise me!"

She gave a jerky nod. He could feel the flutter of her heart beneath the arm he'd wrapped around her waist.

"Alana!" came Roe's cry as he hurried into the hallway outside the cellar room.

Trey's fingers tightened on the crowbar and Alana at the same time. He had to be very sure where he hit the guard. He didn't want to have to do it a second time.

"Alana!" Roe reached for his sword hilt and stepped through the door.

Trey cast Alana to the ground and struck out, catching the guard at the base of his skull. Roe gave a grunt of pain, his head shot back, and then he dropped.

Trey glanced down at Alana, surprised she hadn't screamed, and stepped over the downed guard, straddling him as he slipped Roe's dagger free.

Alana scrambled toward the guard. "Did you kill him?" Her voice trembled.

Trey placed his fingers against the hollow of Roe's throat. A strong, steady heartbeat met his touch. He sighed in relief. He didn't want to permanently hurt the guard, not even for his freedom.

"No, he'll have a hell of a headache, but he'll be fine."

Alana stared up at him in shock, then reached out a trembling hand and stroked the guard's hair back from his face. The tender gesture made Trey restless. He didn't like seeing her touch another man. Then she jerked her hand back and her entire body stiffened. She scrambled against the nearest wall and pushed herself to her feet.

"Don't scream!" he warned her.

"Why did you do that?"

Trey rose also, tightening his grip on the dagger. "I had no choice."

He could see the rapid lifting of Alana's chest in the darkness. He could also see the terrified whites of her eyes. He stepped toward her and she bolted.

He caught her easily about the waist and brought her back up against the wall, stepping in to pin her there with his body. She stared up at him wildly and he felt the flutter of her heart against his chest. Carefully he held the dagger up in her line of vision.

She went still beneath him. "Don't hurt me, please," she whispered.

Her plea caused a drop in his stomach. He really didn't want her afraid of him, but for now, he had little choice in the matter. "You listen to me, little girl, and you won't get hurt. You understand?"

She nodded.

"Good," he said, and then couldn't resist lifting his free hand and brushing back the strands of black hair that had fallen over her face. Her hair was soft and he threaded his fingers into the dense mass of it at her temple. She shivered beneath him. "Damn it," he muttered, but he didn't release her.

Still, he hated himself for doing this to her. He'd chosen Alana Eldralin because she kept forcing herself into his presence, and because he was fairly sure he could control her.

"You've done really good so far, pixie. I'm impressed. Keep quiet and your family will live out the night."

She nodded, her breath hitching.

"We're leaving here as soon as I tie Roe up. We've got to get out before they shut the gates."

He eased back just enough to grasp the bottom of her shirt and pull it from her trousers. She shuddered and a little whimper escaped her lips. He used the dagger to cut a thick swatch of cloth from her shirt.

She whimpered again as he used the knife.

"Shh," he whispered, close to her ear. "It's all right, little girl. Stay quiet and I won't hurt you."

He pressed the cloth into her hands and then turned her around until her back was flush against his chest. He urged her to sink to her knees beside the downed guard.

"Put that in his mouth and then tie it at the back of his head."

"Please don't make me do this," she whispered.

"Either this or I slit his throat," he said, hoping she believed him.

Her hands shook as she did what he said, but he was satisfied that the knot was secure. He reached behind him for the pieces of rope he'd pulled off the crates and tied together during the previous night. He pressed that into her hands also. "Tie his hands behind him and then we'll do his feet." He moved her to the side of the guard and waited while she secured the man's hands.

Although she was terrified, she managed. He couldn't help but be impressed. He didn't think he'd have maintained such composure in this situation. He took a remaining bit of hemp and pulled both her hands behind her back, tying them together. Sliding his arm across her back and through one of hers, he urged her to her feet. "Let's go," he said, directing her to the stairs.

She balked for the first time. Frantically, she lifted her eyes to his face. "Don't do this, Trey," she said, her voice quivering. "You can still get away. Leave me here and I swear I won't cry out until someone comes looking for me."

For a moment, he almost relented, then he remembered what they intended to do to him, especially now that he'd struck a guard.

"I can't, sprite. You're the only insurance I've got. Get me out of here and I'll let you go. Scream and I'll have no choice." He left the threat hanging. He wanted her to believe he'd kill her family if she fought him.

Her face crumpled momentarily and he braced himself for the flood of tears or screams of terror he knew were coming. Then to his amazement, her chin firmed and she lifted it regally, shaking the hair from her eyes.

He forced her to climb the stairs and then paused in the pantry a moment, listening. She was stiff in his arms, but she didn't cry out. He wasn't sure if it was fear for herself or her family that kept her quiet, but he didn't need to question it. He carefully closed and bolted the cellar door, then eased along the wall until they could peer into the kitchen.

The dull rumble of conversation from the dining room reached them and Alana gave a gasp. Trey showed her the dagger again. "I don't want to hurt them, sprite," he said ominously. "Show me the back door."

"Don't hurt my family," she whispered. "Please, please don't hurt them."

"Show me the door and I won't have to."

She started across the kitchen floor. It was by far the tensest couple of seconds for both of them. They knew that should one of the family enter the kitchen to refill a plate or clear off the table, they were in trouble. But they reached the back door without mishap.

Trey peered out the window. It was after seven, but being summer, it was still light outside. He didn't see any movement or any other signs that someone was guarding the grounds. Remembering the day, he figured the guards must all be posted out front to calm the crowd of angry citizens waiting there.

He reached around her and opened the door and they slipped out onto the porch at the side of the house. He led her in a loping, awkward run toward the back where the Stravad Leader's house gave way to the Temer forest. So far everything had gone much smoother than he'd dared to hope in his dank, cellar prison.

Now, he had to get through the gate before it closed. They came to where the Stravad Leader's property butted up against the house next to it. He hoisted her over the short fence and they ran to the end of the yard. He climbed over the second fence first, catching her when she tried to bolt, then he lifted her over. Thank Eldon's bloody star, he'd picked the sister that weighed next to nothing.

On the side of this house, he found a clothesline. He stripped a cloak off it and draped it around Alana, pulling the hood over her head to hide her features and tugging it down her back to hide the rope on her wrists. There was nothing for him to disguise himself.

He turned her to face him and looked her in the eyes. "Help me get beyond the gate and I'll let you go."

She searched him with those cobalt eyes, looking for sincerity. "And if I don't?"

"I don't want to kill you." He tilted his head, trying to put as much menace in his words as he could. "How much do you love your family, little one, because I've got nothing left to lose."

"You'll never get past the guards at the gate. You think they won't recognize you."

"I have to try. Get me out of the gate and I'll let you go."

She considered for a long time. Trey didn't want to hurt her, but he'd have to do something if she wouldn't help him.

"We're running out of time, sprite."

A tear ran down her cheek. He wiped it away with his thumb.

"I don't have a choice," he said. "You know they're going to hang me. I don't want to hurt you, but I don't have any choice. It's you or me, sprite. Please don't make me choose."

"There's another way," she said so softly he wasn't sure he heard her. A second tear chased its way down her face, dropping off her chin.

"What do you mean? What other way?"

"There's a break in the wall. I found it a long time ago. The stream eroded the land back under the trees along the edge of my family's property and the wall has crumbled. It's just big enough for someone to pass through. You can get out that way."

"Show me," he said.

"Then you'll let me go?" she pleaded.

"Show me!" he growled at her.

And Alana Eldralin, pampered daughter of the Stravad Leader, lowered her head and obeyed.

* * *

Alana sank to the ground beside him. He was still holding her elbow. She jerked her chin at the break in the wall where the stream had eroded the land on either side of it, creating a breech. Her knees felt weak and she fought the tears that streamed down her cheeks, but she'd be free of him in a few moments.

He dragged her to it and braced his hand on the wall, peering into the breach. It was hard to see in the gathering darkness, but she could visualize the green of trees on the other side. He'd have to drop into the stream and wriggle under it, but he'd be able to get his large frame through. Then she'd run. If she could make it back to the edge of the yard, she knew soldiers swarmed all over the grounds, keeping the crowds at bay. She just had to get him to release her.

She damned him, she cursed him. How could he have done this to her when she believed in him?

She was so afraid.

Why hadn't she listened to her sisters and Roe? Why had she insisted on going into that cellar? Everyone had told her it was wrong, but she hadn't listened. And then she'd made up that lie about going into town. It could be hours before her parents or sisters decided to look for her.

She should have known he was clever enough and desperate enough to plan something like this, but still, the ease with which he'd accomplished it was staggering. Here she was at his mercy and there was absolutely nothing she could do about it...

Yet.

Her mind returned to thoughts of Roe. It was her fault that he'd been hurt. If she hadn't kept coming down to the cellar, this would never have happened. Tears burned behind her eyes, but she fought them away. No matter what he did to her, she wouldn't let him see how afraid she was.

He turned to her, his green eyes glittering in the half light. "You go first."

"You said you'd let me go if I brought you here!" She hated the quiver in her voice. "You promised me!"

"I said I'd let you go when I was free." His hand fingered the dagger he'd shoved into his belt. "Go through first."

She eyed the breach, knowing it would be difficult with her hands tied behind her back, but she couldn't deny he looked desperate enough to hurt her if she refused. And then there was her family, not so far away. He'd threatened to kill them if she didn't cooperate.

He grabbed her elbow and forced her into the stream. Her feet scrambled on the shifting stones. She could see the branches of the trees on the other side and she knew if she went through, she was beyond all help.

And yet, there would be a moment when he was trying to force his larger bulk through the tight space that she'd have an advantage. She glared at him, then she ducked her head and scrambled awkwardly through, falling to her knees.

She felt the stones in the streambed cut into her as she crawled forward, but she ignored it, fighting her away to the other side. Then she stumbled to her feet and lurched her way free of the wall. Before he could come after her, she bolted, losing her footing on the bank. She surged to her feet and started running for the forest, away from the stream. It was difficult keeping her balance with her hands tied behind her, but she made the cover of the trees.

Once they closed about her, she stumbled on a tree root and nearly fell, catching herself against the trunk, then she started running again. She didn't dare look over her shoulder, but the terror of not knowing where he was or what he was doing almost overwhelmed her. And then she felt his hand snag the back of her shirt.

She gave a terrified, frustrated cry and felt herself being whirled around. Sudden impact jarred her arms, hands, and reverberated up her spine. His weight descended on her and she gulped for air. She looked into his glittering green eyes. He was sprawled over the top of her, pinning her into the loam of the forest floor. Alana's arms felt as if they were coming from their sockets, but she wouldn't let him see her pain. As if he sensed it, he eased off her a little.

His hand lowered to his belt and Alana couldn't suppress the whimper of fear that escaped her. He pulled free the dagger and flipped her over onto her belly. She tried to kick him with her legs, but he had his thighs clamped against hers.

She felt the pressure of the knife's blade against her bonds. She stiffened, but suddenly the rope snapped and Alana's hands moved apart. He replaced the dagger and then flipped her over again. Hauling her into a sitting position, he straddled her thighs and rubbed both of her wrists with his hands. "Are you all right, little girl?"

She blinked at him in astonishment. Was the man mad? She'd been trying to escape him and he was asking if she was all right. She wasn't all right, damn it. Nothing was all right.

"How dare you..." she snarled at him.

He didn't even look her in the eye, but continued chafing her abused wrists.

"I was trying to get away from you, you animal!" she spat.

He looked up then, meeting her eyes. "I know."

"You promised you'd let me go if I got you past the wall."

"I know," he repeated.

"I hate you!" she sobbed.

He blinked suddenly as if she'd thrown cold water in his face. "I guess you do." He released one of her hands and reached out to brush back an escaped strand of hair. "It would be too much to ask you to understand."

It was her turn to blink in astonishment. "Understand? Understand what?"

He didn't answer. Alana jerked her hands out of his hold, wanting to throw him off, but he had her pinned.

"What am I supposed to understand?" she asked.

"Why I had to take you with me."

"You needed me to escape the house, but we're out. You promised me you'd let me go. Please let me go."

"I can't. Not until we reach a place with more people and I can get lost in the crowd. I promise I'll let you go. I promise you, Alana."

She blinked at him. He'd never used her name before. "Your promises don't mean anything!" she hissed at him. "You already promised me and broke it."

He shrugged. "You'll just have to trust me. My word will have to be enough for now."

"I want to go home," she said softly. "Please just let me go home."

"I will. I promise. Once we get somewhere safe."

"I'll try to run again," she hissed at him. "And if I get the chance, I'll kill you myself."

He sighed. "I know that too. I'd be disappointed if you tried anything less." He curved his hands around her elbows and stood, pulling her up with him. Then before she could react, he bent, found the pieces of severed rope, and knotted them together. He held it up for her to see. "Hold out your hands, sprite."

"Go to hell!"

He sighed once more. "You know I can force you. You know I can gag you. You decide."

Alana glared at him, wishing him dead, praying that he'd be caught. She'd be the first one to line up to watch him hang. He quirked a brow at her and she held out her hands.

*   *   *

After her failed escape, he took them through the little stream that ran through the forest. Alana's feet grew numb in the chilling water and her legs ached with the hours of walking. Most of all it was difficult to walk in the shifting stream bed in the dark. She stumbled and fell more times than she cared to remember. Every time, when she thought she couldn't keep going, he would haul her to her feet, keeping a hand at her elbow until she shook him off.

She marked the progress of the moon and stars in the sky. She was trying to keep track of the direction they travelled. She had every intention of getting away, and couldn't admit to herself that she'd lost her bearings hours ago.

Trey was a difficult task master. He didn't seem to tire and he didn't seem to have the same difficulties as she did, walking in the darkened stream. His long legs ate up the distance and forced Alana to quicken her pace when her body was screaming at her to stop. Worst of all, he didn't talk.

Although Alana hated him, she still wished he'd say something. He'd closed himself off from her completely. If he didn't talk, didn't communicate with her, she'd never be able to convince him to let her go.

"My family will be looking for me," she said, despite the nagging worry that they wouldn't miss her until morning.

No response.

Minutes passed until she tried again. "They might have acquitted you. They'll never do it now. You'll be executed for sure."

This garnered a grunt, which was more noncommittal than his silence.

"My family will be worried sick. Doesn't that matter to you?"

The rocks in the stream twisted under foot and she went down, a spray of wetness cascading over her. This time she didn't even try to rise, but hung her head and fought the tears that threatened.

She felt the heat of his body as he crouched behind her and then the pressure of his hand as he eased it around her elbow. "Come on, sprite. You're getting soaked and we don't have any other clothes."

"I don't care," she whispered, lifting her bound hands to brush away the damp tendrils of hair that clung to her face. "Just end this already."

"While the drama of that statement isn't entirely lost on me, you should know I have no intention of killing you anymore."

She lifted her head and stared at him, blinking around the mass of hair that spilled over her face. Hysterical laughter bubbled out of her. He had the decency to look alarmed before he slipped one arm beneath her legs, the other around her back, and lifted her.

Alana's laughter ended. She was so startled that she threw her arms around his neck and clung to him.

Trey carried her up the bank and into the trees. "Don't do this to me, Alana," he said in a low, steady voice. "I know you're afraid and you miss your family, but this is my life. It may not seem like much to you, but it's all I have and I'm not going to give it up. This isn't some game for pampered little girls. This is real. This is serious. Cooperate and you will go home a little wiser, a little smarter. Fight me anymore and I don't know what I'll do."

He paused before the gaping black hole in the side of a hill and set Alana on her feet again, then he bent to look into the narrow opening. Standing once more, he faced her. "Do you need to relieve yourself?" he said softly.

Alana felt her face flame. She did, but she didn't want to disclose such personal information to this beast.

He narrowed his eyes on her. "Don't give me this maidenly modesty, sprite. Do you need to go or not? It'll be a long night if you don't go."

"Fine," she whispered, dropping her head to hide her embarrassment.

He motioned to a few rocks beside them. "Go over there, just behind the rocks. Don't try to run because I'll be watching for you. You've got just a few minutes before I come after you."

Alana forced down her humiliation and held up her bound hands.

Trey shook his head. "No way. That's my only insurance for being such a gentleman."

Alana gave him an astonished look, but immediately turned her back and went to where he'd indicated. Crouching behind the rocks, Alana realized he had to see her head since the rocks were so low. She hated him with a new fervency that surprised her.

She quickly finished her business and returned to him. Thankfully he didn't say anything regarding her compliance. Still it bothered her that he thought her cowed. However, she'd looked around, judged her chances, and decided that it was too risky. There were other creatures in this forest probably more dangerous than Trey Almsden (she hoped). Escape would have to wait for daylight or a better opportunity, say when her hands were no longer bound or he was asleep. He had to sleep sometime, didn't he?

He motioned to the dark, narrow hole in the hill. Instinctively Alana balked at the silent command. She wasn't going in there.

"It's safe. I just checked it out. It's also dry and hidden. Go on, sprite."

"No!" She said it as firmly as she could.

"Yes," he answered, catching her elbow and directing her to the entrance with a gentle, but insistent shove. The pressure of his large hand forced her to drop to her knees. Then the beast did the unthinkable and placed his hand on her bottom, exerting not a little coercion.

Alana scrambled into the cave, fleeing the intimacy and familiarity of his touch more than anything. The cave immediately widened into a low ceiled room and she spun around on her knees to meet him as he came through.

The moment his head appeared, Alana let loose with her fists, pelting him. His fingers closed on her wrists and she found herself on her back, staring up at the roof, the weight of his body immobilizing her. She tried to pull her bound arms free, but he had them pinned again. She looked into his face and found she could see very little in the oppressive darkness surrounding them.

Shifting, he rolled her from beneath him, slid his arm up between both of hers, twining the bit of loose rope around his wrist. Then he hauled her bodily into him, her back against his chest. With his free hand, he cleared the hair from her face and his breath puffed against her ear again.

"Go to sleep," he said in a tight voice.

Alana blinked frantically in the darkness. He couldn't be serious. How could anyone sleep with such a beast curled around her?

"I hate you."

"Good. It should keep you warm."

Alana was sure she wouldn't sleep. Her heart continued to pound against her ribs and she couldn't stop the trembling. He tugged the cloak he'd stolen over the both of them and settled his head on his arm behind her.

Alana never remembered being so afraid in her life, and the thought of her family, her parents searching for her brought her to tears. She tried to suck in air and stop it, but sobs wracked her body and she gave way to it.

In the midst of her turmoil, she felt his hand in her hair, stroking it gently. "Shh, little one, it'll be all right," he whispered.

The incongruity of it was almost more than Alana could bear.

CHAPTER 5

Alana awoke suddenly. Her eyes fluttered open and she found herself staring at the domed ceiling of a cave. She was momentarily disoriented, allowing her gaze to sweep her surroundings.

Her head was cradled on Trey's shoulder, her bound hands entwined with one of his, their bodies pressed so tightly together she could feel the steady rhythm of his heart against her back. She turned her head just enough to look at him. He still slept, his face at ease, his dark lashes resting against his bronze cheeks.

Beyond him, daylight cast a weak, grey light into the small cave, illuminating that which had been blackness the night before. The cave was shallow and narrow, the roof just a few feet above them while they lay reclined.

Looking to the deepest part, Alana noted the joining of stalactites and stalagmites in haphazard columns of limestone. If she hadn't turned back to the entrance immediately the previous night, she would have knocked herself senseless on one of them.

Her thoughts shifted to the previous night and then to her family. An ache rose within her. They had to know she was missing by now. Were they panicked? Did Selia feel responsible?

She wasn't. It had been Alana's own curiosity that had led her to this pass. It was Alana's fault…well, not entirely. The man lying beside her also bore the brunt of that burden, and yet he slept as soundly as if he'd done nothing wrong.

Alana shifted again and looked at him. He had done something wrong, but not what she'd feared he'd do or even what they accused him of doing. Strange as it seemed, he'd been gentle with her since he'd bludgeoned a guard and kidnapped her.

So, she kicked him.

He reared up in shock and struck his head on the low ceiling, collapsing again with a curse. Alana tried to wrench her hands free, but he had them wound around his own. Still, she scrambled over him and tried to reach the entrance.

He hauled her back, slamming her into the ground, then he was glaring into her face, one eye squinted. She could see a bump already forming on his forehead. When he lifted his free hand, Alana flinched, but he just brushed the tangled hair off her face.

"This is getting old, little one," he said.

She jerked her face away from him. "Then let me go."

He shook his head. "I would. Believe me. I would if it was safe to do so, but you're all the insurance I have."

Alana lay still as Trey moved to her feet, but when he began removing her boots, she kicked him again. "What are you doing?" Panic rose in her as he tossed a boot outside the cave and reached for the other. She kicked harder, pelting him with her bound fists.

He threw his weight on her and tore free her other boot, casting it outside. "I have to get us supplies today, so I can't take the chance of you getting away. If you try to escape, you won't get far without shoes." He motioned to the cave entrance. "After you."

Alana didn't move for a moment, thinking about what he said. He was leaving her here, alone. She would definitely try to escape, but if he took her boots, she'd cut her feet on the brambles and rocks. And sometime in the night, she'd lost track of where they were.

But if he thought there was some place to get supplies, he must think there was civilization nearby. She just had to reach help.

"Let's go, sprite."

Alana didn't need a second invitation. She wanted nothing more than to be free of this cave. She crawled to the opening and clambered out, climbing to her feet and stretching taut muscles. Trey was right behind her.

He motioned to the rocks she had used the previous night. "Go relieve yourself, but come back immediately. I don't want to have to search for you."

Alana blinked at him. "You aren't serious?"

"Very."

Her eyes shifted from her boots to her bare feet and back. "The ground will cut up my feet. Don't make me walk over it."

"Would you rather I carried you?" He moved toward her and she started back, holding up her bound hands.

"All right. I'll walk, but at least untie me."

He shook his head again.

"Bastard!" she spat and limped toward the rocks with her back as straight as possible.

She relieved herself and picked her way carefully over the rocks again, her eyes cast down. This entire situation was so absurd. She had to talk him out of it before any more time passed. Her mother would be frantic, her father enraged. The entire town would be turned out after her and there was no point in her being here to begin with.

She gasped when he swept her into his arms and carried her to the cave entrance. She looked about for her boots, but saw nothing. He set her down at the entrance and motioned toward the opening.

She blinked at him. "No."

Dark brows lifted quizzically. "No?"

She held up her bound hands. "Look, you escaped. I helped you out of the house, I helped you get through the night. Now give me my boots, untie my hands, and leave."

He moved so suddenly, Alana couldn't help but start back. She found herself pressed into the cave face, her hands jammed against his chest to ward him off. He braced his palms flat against the rock wall on either side of her head and leaned in until they were nearly nose to nose.

"Now you look here, Alana Eldralin. I haven't escaped anything yet. I'm still trapped, so until I'm far away from Temeron, you're my insurance policy. Don't become a liability."

She met his look, forcing her expression to be braver than she felt at that moment. She'd been safe with him the previous night and part of her believed he hadn't killed Trista, but the small part of her, that was afraid now, whispered that she just didn't know what he was capable of doing. He lived outside the bounds of any person she'd ever associated with. Hadn't her father told her desperate men did desperate things?

His green eyes hardened to a glittering jewel-like coldness. "Get inside the cave." The authority in his voice broached no argument, but Alana wasn't like most people. She'd been raised as an Eldralin with an Eldralin's indomitable pride.

"No. I hate that cave."

His jaw hardened, a single muscle bulging. His left hand shot out and wound in her hair, and he pulled her up against him. A cry escaped Alana's throat, a cry of surprise more than anything else.

"I warned you, sprite. Don't push me. We'll both be sorry at the outcome."

She met the look in his eyes. Her stomach knotted in fear, but her spine was ramrod straight and her own eyes glittered with a mixture of fury and rebellion.

It was his towering size and the tiny thread of self-preservation that finally backed her down. She stifled a sob and closed her eyes. He released her hair, dragging her to her knees by a firm pressure on her bonds. She felt the cold ground against her fingers and opened her eyes again. He turned her toward the cave entrance and gave her a slight shove against her lower back. She crawled in and sat up on the floor, staring at the opposite wall, her back straight, her chin held high.

He crawled in behind her, looked at her a moment with his hands braced on his thighs, then grasped her elbow and directed her deeper into the cave. Alana did as he commanded only because he was blocking the entrance. She could wait, she had patience. Sometime he would let down his guard and she would escape. Then she would make him pay for every single humiliation he'd heaped upon her during this time. That thought single most in her mind, she didn't even realize what he was doing until it was too late. She felt the tightening of the bonds and looked down. He'd taken the loose part of the rope and hooked it around the width of a connected stalagmite and stalactite.

With a cry of disbelief, she yanked back, but only succeeded in tightening the bonds around her own wrists. Her hands were not only tied together, he'd secured her to the column of limestone. Her eyes flashed to his face in disbelief. He met her look momentarily and she caught a hint of regret or apology in his stare.

"Why are you doing this to me?"

He smoothed the hair from her face with a touch that was gentle. She was so terrified, she couldn't find her voice to speak. What was he going to do?

"I won't be long," he said softly.

Alana stared at him, her lips parted in shock. His words repeated in her mind, but didn't sink in until he turned away and began crawling toward the cave entrance.

"NO!" she cried out, understanding dawning on her. "Don't do this! Please!"

He didn't hesitate as he ducked out of the cave and rose to his feet. His figure blocked the entrance, casting her in darkness. A low sob tore from Alana and she yanked back.

Then the pale light filtered into the cave again and Alana halted, staring at the entrance, hardly breathing, her heart hammering wildly inside of her.

He was leaving her tied inside a cave beneath miles of stone and dirt. Generations of Eldralin pride gave way in the face of this, but if her cries reached the man striding away from her, he gave absolutely no indication of it.

*   *   *

Alana's eyes opened slowly. They were swollen and sore. Her head was resting on her bound arms, making them ache. She rolled her neck, letting her head swivel until it was leaning against the cave wall at her back, and licked her dry lips. Shifting her knees a little, she tried to ease the burning in her bloodied, raw wrists, but only succeeded in momentarily increasing the agony. A whimper escaped her parched lips, a sound so detached and empty, it surprised her.

She shut her eyes again, unable to bear the darkness closing in on her. Alana had never felt this close to madness before in her entire life, but this must be what a caged animal felt. Sometimes the panic welled up inside of her so much, she found herself screaming, tearing at the bonds in a rage, but the ropes didn't fray. They'd been soaked in wax or something that made them pass over the stone without tearing.

Day had passed into night and now she was too exhausted to fight anymore.

An ache in her belly reminded her she was hungry and the dryness in her mouth was a constant notification of her thirst.

Blissful sleep claimed her yet again, pulling her down into a numbness that not even her terrifying predicament could invade. She was faintly aware of a scuffling noise, but she just didn't care anymore.

*   *   *

Trey approached the cave, his heart pounding. He hadn't intended for this errand to take all day, but it had. It had been difficult to find a safe place to get what he needed. A few homesteads dotted the area around Temeron, but they were further away on foot than he'd thought. He'd finally found one, but the people had been around all day. He crawled into the brush and dosed until nightfall, then he'd watched the lights in the house until they'd been extinguished and the residents had gone to bed.

Living so far out, they hadn't bothered to lock their doors, something he'd figured was pure serendipitous fortune. Gathering some food, fire starting materials, and a packet of medicinals, he'd slipped back into the forest and worked his way to the cave, running through the stream, hiding in the trees, avoiding the patrols that swept the area outside of Temeron.

He stood at the entrance of the cave, staring at it. It was quiet inside. Either Alana was asleep or someone had heard her panicked cries for help and set her free. He didn't see any footprints outside the entrance (he'd carefully swept his own away), but that didn't mean anything.

More than fear for himself, he was worried about Alana. She'd been terrified when he'd left, more than he'd thought she'd be. He could only imagine what she'd been thinking in the interim. Propelled by worry for her, he dropped to his knees and crawled into the tight space. He stopped immediately in the overwhelming blackness, his heart catching. He hadn't remembered it being so tight or dark last night.

He fumbled for the pack on his back, pulled it in front of him and clawed it open, searching for the fire starting kit. As he hastily struck flint together and applied it to a small handful of tinder, he was aware of the unnatural quiet. The tinder flared to life, providing him with a makeshift torch. He held it aloft and its flickering light fell on Alana where she was still tied to the limestone column.

Trey almost dropped the tinder at the sight of her. Her head was lolling back against the wall, her eyes were shut but red rimmed and swollen, and her wrists bloody and abraded where she'd been trying to free herself. Guilt and fear assailed Trey, two emotions so powerful he couldn't move. His hands shook as he placed the tinder on the ground beside him. And then he was moving toward her, pulling the knife from his belt and cutting the bonds away.

Her eyes fluttered open at his first touch on her bloodied wrists. She stared at him blankly, then recoiled. Trey released her, every muscle in his body tense. With a low wail, she threw herself at him, striking him with her fists, her hair falling forward to cover her face.

"You bastard!" she sobbed. "You bastard, you left me alone! You left me alone!"

He let her pelt him, feeling he deserved whatever she dealt him, but a few small stones struck him on the top of the head, distracting him. He glanced up, seeing a hairline fracture running through the stone. More dust and debris rained down on him and the crack widened.

Grabbing Alana around the waist, he tossed her toward the exit and snagged the pack, scattering the tinder he'd collected as he hurried after her. The moment she felt the air on her, she scrambled for the opening and he tumbled after her, both of them tripping and landing on their sides.

Behind him, he heard a loud rumble, then a cacophony of falling rocks. Dust and debris shot out of the cave and Trey threw himself over Alana, covering her head. They lay still for a long moment after the rumbling had died away, then Trey eased off Alana and studied her. Her eyes were glowing with a strange light.

What the hell!

The cave had been solid all night and day. Why had it suddenly collapsed?

He rolled to his knees and reached out to touch her shoulder. "Alana?"

She blinked and the light faded from her eyes, but she didn't seem to recognize him.

"Alana, can you hear me?"

She sucked in a breath, then started coughing as the dust from the cave settled around them. He fumbled for the pack and dug out the water bottle he'd stolen from the homestead. Uncorking it, he held it out to her. She snatched it from his hands and drank greedily.

He felt another wash of guilt. She was so thirsty. He hadn't thought to leave her with water. Not that they'd had any. He cautiously reached for the bottle. She still seemed dazed, her eyes fixed on the collapsed cave entrance. He took one of her hands and held it to the side, then he bathed the abrasions. She hissed and tried to pull away, but he tightened his hold. He rummaged inside the pack until he found the medicinal kit and pulled it out.

He found the Stamerian easily. No Stravad would go anywhere without it. He uncorked the little vial and applied the salve to her cuts. She gave a shuddering sigh and shut her eyes, bracing her wrist against her thigh as he worked on the other one.

He kept an eye on her as he took out the loaf of bread and the dried meat he'd stolen. He tore the loaf in half, then in half again, offering her the larger portion. Then he divided the meat in the same way. She didn't eat for a moment, still staring at the cave.

"That could have collapsed on me while you were away."

He took a bite of his food, considering her. The glow in her eyes was gone, making him wonder if he'd really seen it or not.

She met his gaze. "Did you hear me?"

"I don't think it would have," he said.

She narrowed her eyes on him. "What?"

"Has anything like that ever happened to you before?"

The look she gave him said she thought him daft. "Has a cave I've been tied up inside all day by a lunatic collapsed on me?"

He sighed. "When you say it like that…"

"Where are my boots?" she demanded, then held out her hand. "Give me the water again."

He passed it to her, but he didn't bother to pull her boots out of the pack.

"I want my boots."

"You need to eat."

"Go to hell!" she said, struggling to her feet. "I'm going home."

He was a little afraid of her, but he kept his features neutral. "I can't let you do that."

She whirled on him, her hair whipping around her face in a tangled, black mass. "Then you're going to have to kill me." She held the water bottle in one hand and the bread in the other. She looked ridiculous, but he felt a sudden desire to pull her into his arms and kiss the anger away.

"Please sit down," he said in as level a voice as he could muster. There must be something wrong with him, he decided. One minute he was afraid of her and the next he wanted to kiss her. What the hell!

She sank to the ground, her breathing labored. "I just want to go home."

"I know. I know you do."

She drank more of the water, then held it out to him. "I'm tired. I'm dirty. And you left me tied up all day."

"I shouldn't have done that," he said, taking the bottle.

She blinked at him. The light was growing as daylight approached and he could just see her. "What did you mean when you asked me if anything like the cave collapse had happened before?"

"It was solid. There was no reason for it to collapse."

"What are you saying?"

He wasn't sure he should explain it to her. She might use it as a weapon against him, but he felt so damn guilty for leaving her like that. He could see the raw, abraded lines on her wrists even in the moonlight.

"I think you brought it down."

That got a lift of a brow. "I brought it down?"

"Have you ever done anything like that before?"

She thought for a moment. "I cracked a mirror once when I got angry at Selia. I screamed and it shattered."

He took that in, wondering if he shouldn't just give her back her boots and get the hell out of here.

"My father can move things," she said absently. "He's showed me a few times."

"Have you ever tried to do that?"

She glanced over at him. "No. I've never thought about it."

He took a bite of his bread. "You need to eat and we need to get walking."

"I'm going home."

He sighed. "Listen, sprite, what's say we make a deal?"

"Make a deal? You want me to make a deal with you?"

"Yes."

"Why would I do that? Why would I do a damn thing for you?"

"Because I'll die if you don't."

That made her pause. He was glad to see it, until she spoke again, "As if I cared."

He didn't believe she was that heartless. She was furious with him for leaving her all day, that was all. She didn't really want him dead. He had to believe that. He had to believe the curious Alana Eldralin that kept coming to see him even when she was told not to still resided in her.

"Give me a few more days and I'll let you go."

She made a scoffing sound, shoving a bite of bread and meat into her mouth. "You keep saying that, but the letting me go keeps getting further and further away," she said with her mouth full. She swallowed and jutted out her hand for the water again. "My family must be panicked. Besides, you'll make better ground by yourself. You don't need me anymore."

"So you know how to get home?" he asked her, taking a shot in the dark.

Her hand paused midway to her mouth and she lowered the bottle. She glanced around the dense forest. In that moment, he knew she had no idea. He, of course, knew exactly where they were. He couldn't forget if he wanted to.

"The first town we'll reach is Anatem. Come with me that far and I'll make sure someone escorts you home again."

She considered for a moment. "That could be days."

"True, but your father might pick up our trail sooner than that. I might be dead in a few hours."

"One could hope," she said hatefully.

He shrugged. "Or not. I could let you go here and head out. Odds are your father and his men will pick up my trail and follow it. I leave a slightly larger mark than you do. Which means you could wander around out here for days, weeks, with bears and mountain cats and Orahim."

"Orahim?"

"You didn't see the warnings in Temeron posted on the bulletin board? We're near the Madronic Range. Orahim have been sighted here, moving down to find game."

She glanced around again and he knew he'd found something this spitfire was actually afraid of, besides him. Although he suspected she wasn't as afraid of him as he'd planned for her to be. "You're bluffing!" she said, shoving the rest of the bread in her mouth.

"Maybe." He stretched out his legs. "Maybe not. You dog your father's footsteps. What have you heard?"

By the expression on her face, he knew she'd heard plenty.

"Just a few days," he said. "I know plenty of wealthy merchants who would be delighted to do a favor for Zeran Eldralin. To bring his daughter home safe and sound. Think of the trade benefits he might grant."

She looked down at her abraded wrists. "If you tie me up again, I'll kill you."

"I won't tie you if you promise not to run."

"What protection do you think I offer you anyway? If my father finds us, he'll kill you on sight."

"He won't risk it as long as I have you near me. I'm more worried about an arrow in the back before I have a chance to run. He won't authorize anyone to shoot if he thinks you could be hurt."

She chewed on her inner lip. "As soon as we reach a town, I will try to escape."

"I wouldn't doubt it." He held out his hand. "Do we have an accord?"

She studied the hand like she thought it might bite, then she shook it.

"Good. See, you can be reasonable."

"Only until my father strings you up from the nearest tree," she said, smiling wickedly at him.

He shrugged, releasing her. "There are worse ways to go. I hear the Orahim sometimes eat Stravad." His eyes tracked down her slight form. "Especially tender, sweet ones like you, sprite."

She recoiled, a shudder passing through her, and he fought hard not to burst out laughing.

CHAPTER 6

Selia sat on the couch in the parlor, watching her mother working frantically on the canvas she'd set up on her easel. She'd been at it for most of the day, not even stopping to eat a meal. When Selia had awaken that morning, her mother had already been painting. She barely answered whenever she was asked a question.

Mai entered the room, looked at their mother, and then crossed to her sister's side. "We've got to get her to stop."

Selia's gaze shifted between the two of them. Mai looked exhausted, dark circles under her eyes, wisps of chestnut hair escaping the hasty bun she'd made, but she looked stronger than their mother right now.

"I've tried. She hardly answers me."

Mai watched their mother paint for a moment. "I've never seen her act like this before," she said quietly.

Selia shrugged. She'd never seen their mother like this either. Their mother was always so strong. Selia had believed her mother was the backbone of their family, holding them together and keeping their father in equilibrium when his position as Stravad Leader became too demanding. To see their mother falling apart was terrifying for both of them. They needed her calm, her resolve, her fortitude.

They both looked up when their father appeared at the door. He glanced at them, then his entire focus went to his wife. As if sensing him, she turned, paintbrush in hand, and regarded him. Their look held for a long time as if they didn't need words to communicate between them.

Selia watched her mother shrink before her, curling in on herself. She set the brush down and stared at the floor without moving. Both Selia and Mai got to their feet, apprehension filling the room.

Zeran crossed the floor. He reached out a hand as if he'd touch his wife and drew it back again. Alix lifted her head.

"Nothing?" It was more a plea than a question. Selia's heart stopped beating and her mouth went dry. The anguish in her mother's voice was palpable.

Zeran swallowed hard and closed his eyes for a moment. "Nothing yet," he said.

Their mother nodded and turned, reaching for her paintbrush. Their father's hand shot out and closed around hers, stopping it.

"Don't." The single word was wrenched from him. "Please."

Their mother looked up and a sob broke from her parted lips. Her body began to tremble and she melted, right before their eyes, into their father's arms.

He gathered her up, kissing the top of her head. "I need you, Alix," he whispered against her chestnut hair. "I need you."

"I know," she said, her voice muffled against his shirt.

Mai tugged at Selia's sleeve and Selia went with her, following her sister to the door. She paused on the threshold and looked back at her parents, clinging to each other for support. Tears blurred her vision and she blinked furiously, turning into the hallway and moving with blind purpose toward the stairs.

* * *

Alana stopped and threw her head back, letting the cool breeze blow over her heated flesh. The muscles in her legs felt knotted and stiff, and her wrists hurt where the sting of sweat invaded the cuts. She opened her eyes again and studied the rising incline. She knew they were deep in the Temer, almost to the outskirts of her land, walking straight across the low rise of foothills marking the Boline Plain from the Madronic mountain range.

At least it was dark, so the sun was no longer a problem. For hours this afternoon, it had beat down on them, wringing their bodies of any natural moisture they had. Trey had filled the single water bottle before they broke camp. Alana studied it as she tried to catch her breath. Even in the dark she could see it wasn't even half full anymore.

As if prompted by her thoughts, he eased it off his shoulder, uncorked it, and lifted it to his lips. Alana watched the muscles in his throat work as he drank, licking her chapped lips in anticipation. He handed her the bottle and watched her bring it to her own mouth.

She might guess where they were by instinct, but she had no idea where they were headed or if there was fresh water anywhere close. And Trey had been circumspect on all accounts. She wiped a damp strand of hair from her forehead. The braid helped, but her clothes were sticking to her body and her skin felt clammy. She wanted a bath, she wanted a soft bed, and she wanted to go home.

"How much farther?"

He studied her a moment in the darkness. "You've done good, sprite. I'm impressed. You haven't even complained today."

She looked back at him. The hair near his temples was damp and he was panting, but he still stood straight, his shoulders squared. She envied his strength. She felt as if she might drop where she was.

"How much farther?"

He looked away, giving her a view of his strong profile. His right hand clenched and unclenched. "Not too far." He grabbed the water bottle from her and started walking again, his long stride eating up the terrain.

Alana stared after him. *Not too far.* Just that and nothing more. He didn't even bother to look over his shoulder to see if she followed. She had half a mind to turn around and retrace their steps, except she was lost and the bastard knew it. Whatever water and food there was, he had.

She forced her knee to bend, her thigh to straighten, her other leg to follow. The first step was the most painful, she told herself, and soon fell into the rhythm once more. Anger helped fuel her, so she stoked it.

Last night and this morning he'd practically begged her to help him. Now he didn't even seem to care if she was there. He'd hardly spoken to her all day. He said he was *impressed*. Well, wouldn't he be impressed when she kicked his arrogant ass!

Trey Almsden was perplexing. He could be gentle, beguiling, and then so maddening. His dark, good looks attracted her, had from the first time he'd stood in her father's den. His attention enchanted her and nearly made her act like an idiot for him. But then he always tempered it with this confounding indifference.

She stumbled and fell on her hands and knees. Lifting her head, she noticed Trey had actually stopped walking. He was standing on the incline, hands on hips, staring at her. Alana sank back on her heels, resting her palms on her thighs, trying to catch her breath.

He came back to her side, bent and curled a hand beneath her upper arm, hauling her to her feet. He looked down into her face. "You all right?"

"No, I'm tired, thirsty, and hungry. I want to go home."

"I know," he answered as always. He turned and started walking again, keeping his hand on her arm for support. "Just a little further and we'll rest for a while."

Alana didn't answer, but stared at the ground dropping by beneath her feet. She thought again of her mother and father, her sisters. She wondered how they were and what they were doing right now. She missed them. She was worried about them. Strangely, she was most worried about her mother. With that thought plaguing her, she stumbled on beside her captor, wondering how she was ever going to get herself out of this mess and back home.

*   *   *

Trey peered over the hill at the plain below them. Lifting his eyes, he studied the sky, noting the pale pink fingers of dawn tracing her path into the heavens. The fires from the Temeron guard twinkled below them, only a faint glimmer against the failing darkness now.

He sensed Alana as she eased to his side. Every muscle in his body went taut when she caught her breath and her hands closed into fists before her.

He felt her eyes on him, but didn't turn to meet her angry stare. "You planned it this way, didn't you? You knew they'd go out on the plain to catch you, so you dragged me through the forest, into the foothills and beyond them, letting them try to outflank you. You knew you could outflank them."

He glanced at her and returned to his study of the guards. There weren't as many as he'd expected and that made him a little nervous. She was right, he'd figured they'd try to outflank him. He also knew a large force was moving through forest, attempting to trap him between the two, forcing him to surrender his captive.

Trey didn't know where the second group was located right now, but he'd bet they weren't far behind. They might not have been able to follow his convoluted trail, but they'd soon piece it together when he didn't emerge from the forest the next day.

He and Alana had to put many miles between them after darkness fell once more. They couldn't move during the day because their elevated position on the foothills would easily give them away. He needed Alana's full cooperation and he needed it now.

He shifted and stared at her. He only hoped she'd consider his proposal if only long enough to get him to Anatem. After that he'd figure out the rest on his own if necessary, but he hoped it wouldn't be necessary.

He grabbed her arm and pulled her down off the rise. She went with him, but he felt the tautness in her muscles and caught the flashing of her eyes. She knew what he knew, that if she but screamed, the guards would know exactly where they were.

"Now I need you to listen to me, sprite."

She stared at him, her chin cast at a haughty angle. She wasn't going to make this easy and he damn well knew it. "There are Temerian guards all over the plain down there."

He nodded and drew a deep breath. "And you've only to scream. They'd be swarming all over the foothills."

"So I don't see why I need to listen to you."

Trey braced his foot on a rock and leaned his forearm on his thigh, studying her. "You say you hate me, Alana, but do you really want me dead? Because that's what will happen if you scream right now. There's nowhere for me to go and they won't hesitate to fill me with arrows."

Her look softened. "I don't want you dead." She spoke so quietly, Trey had to lean forward to hear her. She lifted her head and stared him straight in the eye. "But I want to go home."

"I know."

"Stop saying that!" she spat in frustration.

He held up his hands in surrender. "All right. Here's the point. I can't go back to Temeron. If I made it alive, they'd execute me just for kidnapping you and hitting Roe."

"Maybe you should have thought of that before you did both of those things."

Trey's eyes narrowed. "You're smarter than that, sprite. They were going to kill me anyway. It was only a matter of time before your father had to accommodate the council."

She looked away and drew a deep breath.

Trey pressed his advantage. "We may have outflanked them, but they're following us, you can be sure. I've confused them a little with our aimless wandering and hiking through the water, but it won't last for long. They'll find our trail and then they'll be after us quicker than we can travel."

"On horseback," she said.

"On horseback." He reached over and placed his fingers under her chin lifting her face. "So here's my proposal. I've changed it a little since we talked last. Help me get away, help me get to Denortosal and I'll drop you off at the castle. The king will send a messenger to your father and you'll be home before you know it, no worse for the wear."

She wrinkled her nose at him. It wasn't a good sign. "I want to go home now. All I have to do is walk off these hills and the guards will take me home. I won't tell them where you are. I'll tell them I escaped."

"And they'll be swarming all over here in an hour. I can't get away that quickly. Without you, Alana, I'm a dead man. You're the only insurance I've got."

"Why are you telling me this? You abducted me without asking."

"Because I want your help now. I want us to work together, a partnership."

"Why?"

"Because…" He looked away and stared at the hills rising around them. "Because I never meant it to go this far, sprite. I never meant to hurt you or scare you." He looked back at her. "I hurt you and I can't stand the thought of what I did. I want you to help me because you choose to do so."

She was silent, staring at him. Finally she blinked and looked away. "What about my family? They must be worried about me. My mother?"

He nodded. "We'll pass through Anatem on our way to Denortosal. We'll stop there and send a message to your father. I promise."

"My father will never believe I'm with you by consent. They'll be sure you forced me."

He shrugged. "It doesn't really matter, does it? The minute they arrested me, I was a dead man. If they catch me, nothing's changed."

She studied his face with those piercing Eldralin eyes. "You didn't kill Trista, did you?"

"No," he said. What more was there to say?

"You might have gotten off."

"Do you really believe that? Really?"

She looked out over the plain. "No. No, I don't believe that. They would have executed you."

His eyes scanned her pretty face, her rope of black hair, wisps of which had escaped to tangle in her long lashes. How had he never noticed how pretty she was before this? How had he dismissed her? She had strength and intelligence and character. She was no bigger than a minute, but he didn't think any other woman would have fared half as well as she had.

"I didn't kill her. I swear to you on all that I hold holy."

She looked back at him. "Do you?"

"Do I what?"

"Do you hold anything holy, Trey Almsden?"

He took her hand, gently stroking his fingers along the lines made by the rope. He hated that she bore these marks. She didn't pull away from him and he looked up. Her breathing had quickened and she stared at him with wide, vulnerable eyes. He pressed his fingers to her pulse and found it jumping. So, she didn't hate him as much as she said.

"I don't hurt women, Alana. That I hold sacred. I spent my life watching my mother be used and discarded by one man after another. I swore that I would never treat a woman the way she was treated. I hated it." He stroked her pulse, his eyes narrowing as she slowly licked her chapped lips. He wanted to follow her. He wanted to place his mouth over hers. "This I promise you, sprite. I will hold to my word, I will hold it as holy from here on out."

She gently drew her hand away, but she didn't break their eye contact. "I believe you," she said. "I don't want you dead. I'll go with you to Denortosal, but you have to keep your word and let me send a message to my father in Anatem. You have to swear it on your life, Trey."

He crossed his heart. "On my life," he repeated.

*　*　*

"There's a little soap in the pack," said Trey, motioning to it with his left hand.

Alana reached around the small cooking fire Trey had built and pulled his pack to her. "How did you get all this stuff without being caught?"

Trey glanced up from spearing potatoes on sticks and hanging them over the open blaze. "To be honest, it was luck, pure dumb luck."

A laugh escaped her. He smiled, the hard lines of his face softening. She couldn't deny he was handsome when he smiled. Distracted, her fingers fumbled with the drawstring on the pack, knotting it. She tugged and pulled, finally pushing it away in frustration. She startled when Trey's arms eased around her sides and began working on the knot, his long fingers gliding deftly over it.

She tensed. He was so close, the heat of his body warming her back. Her eyes fixed on his hands as his breath puffed against her cheek. She shivered despite herself.

"Are you cold?" he purred into her ear, brushing his lips across the stray hair that had escaped her braid.

"N-n-no," she stammered, mortified at the way her voice failed her.

"There," he said, sliding his hands to her upper arms and giving them a light squeeze.

"There what?" she snapped, afraid of her own unruly response to him. No man had ever unsettled her the way Trey Almsden did. In fact, no man or boy had ever interested her in the least.

His mouth curved into a seductive smile. "There, the pack's open."

If her face got any hotter, she'd likely burst into flames. "Oh," she said, curling her fingers in the pack's rough fabric. "Thanks."

He made a noise that sounded suspiciously like a chuckle. Alana glared up at him as he rose and walked back around their small fire to turn the skewered potatoes. Wrenching the mouth of the pack open, she dug inside. She pushed beyond a man's coarse shirt and

84

matching trousers. Her fingers caressed something smooth and soft. She drew a corner out, staring at a pale blue swatch of silk. She looked up at Trey.

"What's this?"

He glanced at the material in her hands. "A dress."

"For who?"

"You."

Alana shoved the dress into the pack. "I don't wear dresses."

For a moment, she caught the vulnerable flash of surprise in his eyes, but they quickly frosted over into icy emeralds again. "Pull the dress out and look at it."

"No."

He drew a deep breath and waited. He had a stillness about him that unsettled Alana. She'd been with him long enough to notice that it usually proceeded some strong arming on his part.

"Why do I need a dress?" she added to forestall him.

His look softened. "When we hit Anatem, you'll need to look like a lady, not a boy on the run."

Alana looked down at herself. She might not have the luxurious hips of her sisters or their lush bust-lines, but what she did have was obviously female. She angled her chin up haughtily.

"I don't think any other man, besides you, would mistake my figure for that of a boy's."

Trey's smile was feral. "No, sprite, I don't think any male would mistake those curves, especially not me."

"You..."

"Bastard," he supplied. "Undeniable. At any rate, I thought a young woman in a dress would attract a lot less attention, than a hoyden in trousers. My idea is to attract less attention of both male and female variety." He reached out to turn the potatoes, deliberately taking his eyes off her. "Pull out the dress and assure yourself I haven't brought you a strumpet's costume."

"No, thank you. I've never worn dresses and I don't intend to start now. Nothing would look more out of place on me. I'll be fine in my trousers and shirt."

"We'll see," muttered Trey under his breath.

Alana started to demand an explanation, then wisely decided it didn't require a verbal battle right now. She'd get her way later. She always had with her father and Trey was reminding her more and more of him the longer they were together.

She forced aside the wash of pain at the thought of her family and reached into the pack again. Her hand met the raised, hard side of a book. Curious she pulled it out and looked at it. It was a book of short stories. Turning it so she could see the cover, she discovered it was a book filled with Ancient legends and myths. Alana opened to the first page and ran her fingers over the worn binding.

"So this is where you get all these fanciful ideas of pixies and sprites?"

Trey glanced at the tome in her hands and then rubbed his palms against his thighs to dust them. "One of the places. My mother had a few books like this. She couldn't read so I'll never know why she had them. As a child, she wouldn't let me touch them; although I stared at them everyday, just wishing I could slip away into the adventure between their pages. I guess she was afraid I'd damage them. They were precious to her."

"Then how did you get to read them?"

Trey's eyes lowered to the small blaze. "I never did. I snuck them out of the house one by one and took them to whoever was available that week, begging them to read to me. Your sister Selia was one of my favorites. She liked to change the voices of the characters, which made it much more exciting."

"Selia?" Alana was surprised by the stab of jealousy that went through her. "Selia?"

"Yes, Selia was always kind to me."

"I guess so. Why, she was a paragon where you're concerned. You should have married her instead of messing with Trista."

Trey shrugged. "You're probably right."

Alana looked down, hiding the hurt on her face. She was the one he'd kidnapped, yet he was thinking of Selia.

"Where did you get this book?" she asked to change the subject.

"It was sitting by the fire in the house where I got everything else."

"You risked a lot just to take a book."

He shrugged.

She found that fascinating. So many things he could have stolen and he'd stolen a book.

"So why didn't you read the stories to yourself if you wanted to hear them so badly? Why ask other people?"

Trey was silent for a long time, his green eyes glittering in the firelight. "I can't read."

Alana stared at him in amazement. She wasn't sure she'd ever met anyone who couldn't read. "I'll teach you," she said before she thought better of it.

His head lifted and his eyes sparkled with something besides anger. "You would?"

"Yes," she said, even though she didn't know how to begin such a process or whether she'd ever have enough time. Looking into his hopeful face, Alana knew she had to try for both of them. Despite his arrogance, she was drawn to him.

His lips curved in a smile. "Thank you. I'd never be able to repay you that kindness. It would be an immeasurable gift."

"Nonsense, I'd enjoy it." She set the book down and began rummaging through the pack until she found the soap. "Finally," she said, holding it up. He gave her another smile, but Alana looked away. If he kept smiling like that, he'd have her captive in every sense of the word.

CHAPTER 7

Mairin was kneading the dough on the counter when she heard the soft tap on the kitchen door. She blew the stray hair off her forehead, dumped the dough into a bowl, and draped a clean cloth over it. Then she set it in the middle of the stove and wiped her hands on her apron, hurrying to the door and parting the curtain to peer out.

Roe Manes stood on the porch, rocking back and forth on his booted heels. Mai unlatched the door and opened it, motioning him inside and looking around the yard at the same time. Since Alana's abduction, any number of people were lurking about the Stravad Leader's house, trying to catch bits of information.

Placing her back to the door, Mai stared up at the handsome guard. Roe met her gaze, lifting a hand and passing it through his golden locks. He looked haggard and tired. Both of his eyes appeared bruised and swollen.

"Hello," she said, a catch in her throat. She couldn't look at Roe without remembering him lying at the bottom of the stairs, blood caked at the back of his head. She couldn't look at Roe without remembering the monster who took her sister away from her family. "Any news?"

His lips thinned and he looked away. "Has your father come home yet?"

"No."

He looked back at her and narrowed his blue eyes. "They must have left the forest at least a day ago. The trackers have been over nearly every inch of it and found hardly any signs. It's very unlikely they're still in the forest now and they're certainly not in the city."

"Then where?" Mai moved away from the door and closer to the guard. Her hands closed into fists at her sides.

Roe watched her and then shrugged. It wasn't meant as a negligent gesture, but something about the hopelessness of it chilled Mai and brought the tears rushing to her eyes. She choked on a sob and her hands flew up to cover her mouth.

Roe looked uncomfortable, but when the tears welled in Mai's eyes and overflowed, he moved forward and pulled her into his arms. Mai clung to him, burying her face in his chest, her hands knotting into fists on the lapels of his uniform jacket.

It took awhile for her sobs to quiet, but she finally regained control, yet she didn't move out of Roe's arms, not yet. It felt safe there and comfortable. She turned her head and pressed her damp cheek over his heart, listening to the pounding of it.

"Do you think he's hurt her?" she whispered.

Roe's hands stroked across her hair. "I don't know, Mai. I wish I did."

Mai gave a hitching sob and closed her eyes. "I keep seeing her, my little sister, afraid and needing us and we're not going to her."

"And I keep reminding myself that this whole thing is my fault."

She lifted her head and stared into his face. She saw hurt and sincerity and guilt warring in his eyes. "Your fault?"

"I should have protected her. That's why I was there."

"And Allie shouldn't have been down there."

"You can't blame her for trusting that bastard, Mai..."

"And you can't blame yourself for not guessing he was that ruthless and desperate."

He moved away from her, walking toward the kitchen door. Again he ran his fingers through his hair. "I still feel responsible. I never thought he was a criminal. I never thought he'd really hurt a woman..." His voice trailed away in an anguished moan.

For the first time, Mai realized that her family wasn't the only one hurting because of this. Roe Manes was probably hurting more than any of them because right or wrong, he carried the most guilt.

She moved up behind him and placed her hand on his shoulder. "Roe, no one blames you for what happened to Allie. And you've been there for us since then. You're practically asleep on your feet. Stop beating yourself up about this, please. It doesn't help anyone, especially not Allie."

He didn't answer, simply bowed his head lower.

Mai felt a touch of fear that had nothing to do with her sister at the moment. "Roe, please?"

He turned suddenly, his eyes so anguished, so filled with pain, and then he was reaching for her, pulling her into his arms. She was momentarily surprised, but went with him, and then his head came down and he claimed her mouth.

His kiss wasn't tender or seeking. It was possessive and hot and demanding, and she surrendered beneath it with a gasp of surprise. Head spinning, Mai clung to the blond-haired guard and returned his kiss with equal fervor.

*   *   *

Alana rolled to her back and stared up at the bright noon sun. Every muscle in her body ached and she was exhausted, but she couldn't sleep. Trey stirred beside her and angled up on an elbow, looking down into her face. She met his eyes and sighed.

"I can't sleep. It's too bloody light out here."

His lips curved in a smile and he rolled to his back, folding his arms beneath his head. "It's almost noon, sprite. What do you expect? Aren't you tired enough? We walked all night."

Alana lifted herself up on one elbow and looked down at him. "How much longer do we have to switch around our days and nights?"

He shrugged. "We've left the soldiers behind, but I don't know how far back they are. We can't take any chances."

"How much longer until we reach Anatem?"

"Another couple of days."

Alana groaned and rolled onto her back again, placing an arm over her eyes to block the sun. She felt Trey leaning over her, his breath warm on her arm.

"Why don't you read to us for a little while until we're sleepy?"

She looked at him from beneath her arm. "Why don't I give you a lesson?"

One dark brow arched and a lock of hair fell over his forehead. He brushed it back. "You really feel up to starting now. I tell you I'm dense."

Alana wrinkled her nose. "Like a bloody steel trap."

Trey laughed and touched her nose with the tip of his finger. "Your mother ever hear you talk like that?"

"You can't be serious," said Alana, sitting up and reaching for the pack.

Trey had managed to steal a change of clothes for each of them (albeit a dress for her), the book, a small sliver of soap, a brush, one blanket, a medicinal pack, and a water bottle. Thankfully they'd found water that morning when they made camp. A stream gurgled even now beside them.

She pulled the book free and set it on her lap, opening to the first page. Trey eased closer to her, scattering her thoughts. He looked over her shoulder, his forearm resting on her thigh as he angled the book for his sight. Alana couldn't get him out of her mind, especially when circumstances forced them together so intimately.

"I'll drag my fingers over each word as I read it the first time. Look for those that appear familiar to you and try to remember them."

It didn't take Alana five minutes to learn Trey had an amazing memory. He learned half the alphabet before the first page was finished and knew at least ten words on sight. He might have had no formal education, but he was intelligent. The reading lesson became a fun distraction for both of them and they lost track of time.

Suddenly Trey placed his hand over Alana's and closed the book. As he drew away, his fingers caressed the back of her hand and Alana twisted to look into his face. He reclined on his side, his hand resting on her inner elbow.

"Thank you, sprite," he said huskily. "I enjoyed reading with you."

Alana couldn't stop herself from licking her suddenly dry lips. His green eyes followed the motion. "We can read more tomorrow." Heat flared in her cheeks at the huskiness in her own voice.

"That we can."

He lifted a hand and curved it over her right cheek, caressing her with his fingertips. "I appreciate the gift, Allie."

A stab of homesickness followed his use of her nickname, but he chased it away with his touch on her face. A strand of hair had fallen over his forehead and impulsively, Alana reached up to push it back.

He caught her hand and turned it over, bringing the inner part of her wrist to his mouth. First he ran it over the stubble on his chin, sending a shiver up Alana's spine. Then he kissed it and Alana's breathing broke.

He looked up and locked eyes with her.

Alana licked her lips again. "Trey?"

"Hmmm?" he purred.

"Did you love Trista?"

He narrowed his eyes on her, those green eyes, so clear, so focused. "No, Allie. I didn't."

"But you slept with her." She didn't know why she cared, why it mattered to her.

He nodded. "I did."

She swallowed. "I don't understand that."

His fingers pressed against the pulse point in her wrist. "It's just biology, sprite. Nothing more."

"Did you know she was sleeping with other men?"

"I suspected."

"That didn't bother you?"

"Why should it?" He sat up, bringing himself closer to her. He reached for the end of her braid, running the hair through his fingers, the back of his hand sliding along her collarbone. "Does it bother you that I was with her?"

She knew she should pull away, but she didn't. He released her hair, then placed his hand under her chin, tilting her face toward his.

"Allie, does it bother you that I've been with Trista?"

Her eyes lowered to his lips. She knew he wouldn't stop her if she just leaned forward and kissed him, but she wasn't ready for whatever else he might expect. "No, why would it bother me?"

He leaned closer still. She could smell the evergreen of the trees around them on his skin. "Because you like me."

That broke the spell and she pushed him away. "You kidnapped me. You stole me away from my home and my family. I hate you."

He caught her hand and held it against his chest. She could feel his warmth and the beat of his heart. "You're lying to both of us and you know it."

She tugged at her hand. She wasn't lying, but he was right. She wasn't exactly sure what she felt. She wanted to go home, but she didn't hate him. He lifted her wrist and pressed his lips to the marks the ropes had left.

"I'm so sorry about this," he said in that same husky voice that sent shivers over her.

"Well, you can't take it away!" she snapped, yanking her hand free. "You can't take any of it away." With that, she turned away from him and rolled onto the blanket, closing her eyes.

He didn't move for a moment, then she felt him lay down next to her without touching her. Homesickness washed over her and she wished she could see her mother just one more time. Picturing her family sitting around the table for a meal, she fought the tears and drew in a deep breath, holding it until the ache in her chest eased. Soon, she found herself drifting toward sleep.

* * *

Trey came up from a dead sleep, hearing his name spoken in Alana's voice. He blinked and opened sleep heavy eyes and found her leaning over him.

"Wake up. It's about an hour before night fall. We've got to get moving."

Trey groaned and dropped his arm over his eyes again. They'd been walking all night for the last three days and sometimes long into the next morning. The effort of running for a week had finally caught up with him.

"Trey, please. Wake up!"

He braced himself on an elbow and watched her rummage through the pack, finally pulling free the sliver of soap. She held it up for him to see.

Last night they'd crossed the rushing waters of the Rovarn River and were less than a day out of Anatem. Trey had been saving their clean clothes for that occasion, but they both needed baths and a decent night's sleep in a bed. Not to mention a multi-course meal.

In the bottom of the pack was a few carefully hoarded bills that he hoped would provide them with what they needed when they arrived in the city. And then, he'd let Alana send a message to her father. He'd promised her he'd let her do that once they reached Anatem. He promised her and he meant to keep that promise.

Sometime over the last week, he'd come to enjoy her company and he didn't want her to try to escape once they were around other people. She still told him she hated him, but he also got a glimpse of her quick wit and her intelligence. In fact, he found her fascinating. She knew a lot about a variety of topics, and best of all, she was teaching him to read. He looked forward to the few minutes she spent instructing him before they bedded down in the morning.

Alana was in good spirits this evening, but Trey didn't like the dark circles under her eyes, or the thinning of her waist and face. For himself, he was exhausted and filthy. He just wished they could stay in this spot for another day and leave tomorrow night. If he could have just a little more time with her, maybe he'd convince her she should go all the way to Denortosal with him. He marked that the number of times she told him she hated him each day had lessened. Sometimes an entire day would pass without her saying it at all.

He looked over at Alana. Although they had an agreement that she'd go to Denortosal with him, where he'd drop her at the castle, he wasn't stupid. He knew the moment they entered Anatem everything changed. If she told someone she was being held against her will, he'd have to run without her, deal or no deal. And while he enjoyed her company, he just didn't trust her to stand by him when that quick mind of hers would instantly see a way out.

"I'm going to the stream to try to wash off a little trail dirt."

Trey shook his head. "I don't know why you bother. We both need to soak for hours in a hot tub with straight lye."

She laughed, shaking back her heavy, limp hair. "I do the best I can," she said, rising to her feet.

Trey smiled and his eyes followed the tempting sway of her hips as she walked beyond him toward the tributary they'd been following for a day now. Dropping one arm over his forehead, he tried to go back to sleep.

"You've only got until I'm finished," Alana called over her shoulder. "I'm ready for civilization."

Trey started to smile and then a sick feeling struck him low in the stomach as his mind's eye conjured up an image of her near the bank. He reared up and twisted at the same moment.

"Alana, no!"

His shout echoed over the creek, but he still heard her cry of pain. He was on his feet and running, his hand closing around the dagger at his waist. He wrenched it free and flung it. It split the snake's head in half and buried it in the sand. He grabbed Alana from behind, his hands curving around her elbows, his heart thundering. He was muttering frantically, fragmented prayers he'd learned as a child, but the moment he looked over her shoulder, he knew they meant nothing.

"It bit me," she said in a small voice.

Trey's hands tightened reflexively and then he bent, sweeping her up into his arms. He pressed his face against her hair and held her tightly, carrying her back to their campsite. He set her down and stared for a moment into her pale, tear-streaked face. The fact that she hadn't screamed or that she wasn't sobbing now surprised him, then he remembered it was Alana. He brushed the hair from her face.

"How many times did it bite you, sprite?"

She shook her head, her eyes so enormous they almost swallowed her face. "I don't know."

"You've got to know, Allie," he demanded. Fear coiled in his stomach and he grabbed her arms, giving her a little shake. "How many times?"

"Once," she sputtered and her eyes drifted to the headless body lying in the sand. "It's a sand snake, isn't it?"

Trey nodded, unable to make himself release her. There was something he must do, but for all of his amazing memory, he couldn't form a coherent thought.

Her eyes found his face again. "It's poisonous, deadly."

Thoughts snapped into place. He released her arms and looked down at her leg, grasping it and turning it into the failing sunlight. She gave a cry and clutched at his hands, but he released her again.

He rose to his feet and retraced his steps to the dead snake. Bending, he pulled free the dagger and hurried back to her. No time to stall anymore. He knew what he had to do. He straddled Alana and lifted her wounded leg over his thigh, bracing it with his hands. She was watching him, her chest rising in a frantic pant as he met her eyes.

"If you know it's poisonous, Allie, you know what I have to do now."

She nodded and dropped her gaze to her leg. "I trust you," she said.

Trey felt his heart pounding. He wished she hadn't said that. *He* didn't trust himself. His hands were trembling and sweat was making a sickly path down his spine, but he had to do it, for her. There was no other way.

He pulled off her boot and placed the dagger against the inseam of her trousers. He cut upward, slicing the pants apart as he went until he came to the wound in her thigh. The flesh was raised and puckered, and a mixture of blood and venom oozed from the twin puncture marks.

There was no time to sterilize the dagger, no time even to run to the creek and wash it. He ran the risk of infecting her, but there wasn't time to consider that problem now. Already poison was pumping through her body and she was so damn small, he didn't know how much it would take to be fatal.

His hands trembled as he positioned the knife. He looked up into her eyes and took a deep breath. "I'm sorry, honey."

She didn't answer, but her expression spoke volumes of her trust. He focused on her thigh again and made two quick incisions, one above and one below the bite marks. Moving quickly, he pressed until blood poured from the wounds. She whimpered, but amazingly, she held herself still as he pressed the poison out.

He continued the process until she was trembling violent, her breath sawing in and out of her lungs. He figured he'd gotten as much as he was likely to get and he couldn't risk any more blood loss. He lifted his eyes to her face and found her pale, her eyes closed, and a sheen of perspiration coating her brow. He snagged the pack and pulled out the shirt he'd stolen for himself, then he ran to the stream and soaked it. He remembered his mother telling him something about Stamerian drawing out poison.

He cleaned off her leg, then packed the Stamerian around the wound and using the knife, cut a strip off his shirt and bound her leg. She was swaying, so he gathered her in his arms, and moved her away from the bloody ground. She clung to him, moaning as he carried her to the blanket, settling her on it.

When he tried to get up again, she clung to him, shuddering. "I'm afraid," she said softly.

"So am I, honey," he answered, sinking down beside her. "But I'm here and I'm not going to leave you. We'll get through this together."

Her breath sawed against his throat and she shivered in his arms. Trey kissed the top of her head and began muttering his incoherent prayers once more. It was all he could do at the moment, but he was terrified it wasn't going to be enough.

* * *

Trey lay on his back cradling Alana in his arms. Her head was resting against his chest and he'd carefully positioned her injured leg atop the pack to cushion it. He ran his hands over her hair and watched the stars, but most of his concentration was on her rapid breathing.

"Allie, you all right, honey?"

She mumbled something against his chest, but her hand clenched and unclenched against his shirt.

"How about some water?"

She didn't answer. Still, he knew he had to keep her hydrated. He eased out from beneath her and grabbed the water bottle. Kneeling beside her, he pushed the tangled mass of hair from her pale, damp face. She blinked and opened her eyes, then narrowed them as if the small light of the fire hurt her.

"Come on, honey. You need to drink something."

He angled an arm beneath her head and helped her into a sitting position. He braced her back against his chest and lifted the bottle to her lips. She drank and then her head lolled against his shoulder. Trey fought his growing panic and reached down to part the tear in her trousers.

Her leg had swollen to twice its normal size. The wound itself was puckered and angry, still oozing a sticky mixture of blood and pus. He didn't like the way it looked, but he was so damn helpless right now.

He cursed. This was his fault. If he hadn't taken her from her home, she'd be safe now, but then he'd never have gotten to know her or gotten to experience her indomitable will and spirit. He picked his way back to the creek and washed out the cloth, then he carried it back to her and laid it over the swelling. Even though he was being as gentle as he could, she drew in her breath and shuddered.

"Sorry, honey," he whispered against her ear, pulling the cut ends of her trousers back into place. Then he sat behind her again, bracing her with his chest and urging her to drink some more. When she finished, she pressed her face against his jaw.

"That feels good," she murmured.

"What, sprite?"

"The cool water."

He pressed his lips to her temple. It was too warm. A fever was starting. He cursed again and looked up at the stars. He'd do anything to see her through this safely, anything – even surrender to her father.

"Hopefully, the Stamerian will draw out the poison."

"This isn't your fault," she whispered, her eyes fluttering closed.

"How do you figure that?" he said, smoothing her hair over her shoulder.

"I should have seen it in the grass. I stepped on it."

"I shouldn't have taken you from Temeron."

Her breathing was shallow. "I was suffocating in Temeron," she said. He was afraid she'd become delirious. "If I die, at least I'll have had an adventure."

Trey's body went still. His arms tightened about her waist. "Don't say that, Allie," he whispered in a strained voice.

She shrugged. "I'm just saying what we're both thinking right now."

"No, you're going to be all right."

She didn't answer.

He settled her more comfortably against him. He was silent for a long while, wanting to say so much to her, but not sure how to start. He'd never been at a loss for words with any woman before. Those he bedded he spoke little to and those he didn't, like Alana's sisters, he didn't really care what they thought of him.

But he cared with Alana. He cared a lot.

"Allie," he began, but his voice faltered.

"Hmmm."

"I'm sorry I dragged you out here. What happened today…"

She shifted suddenly and a cry of pain escaped her.

"Allie?"

"Don't blame yourself. What happened to me happened because it just did. If anyone should take the blame, it's me. My father taught me how to watch for sand snakes on the Boline Plain. I knew better than to go rushing off toward water at sunset. I just forgot and it was an unlucky time to forget."

She leaned more heavily against him again. Her breathing was ragged and Trey felt another wash of fear.

"Allie, I need to apologize. I was wrong when I kidnapped you, then I made the situation worse by begging you to help me get to Denortosal."

Her head rolled against his chest. "Even after being bit today, this has still been an adventure. I never realized what I was missing being the pampered little girl of my parents. I wouldn't trade a moment of this for anything..."

She was definitely delirious now.

"Except..."

"Except what, honey?"

"I wouldn't have my parents worry."

He swallowed at the lump in his throat, but before he could say any more, she shifted again and looked up at him. He could see even in the fire's light that her eyes were fever bright.

"Trey, this is serious, so please listen." She waited for him to answer, but he could only nod. He already guessed what she was about to say and he didn't want to hear it.

"If I die, promise you will send a letter to my parents and explain how it happened and where my body is." She reached through the darkness then and caught his hand, clasping it in both of her own. Her fingers were hot and he almost pulled away in shock. "But swear to me you'll keep heading toward Denortosal. Don't go back and don't let my father catch you. Swear to me, Trey."

He blinked at her in astonishment. He'd expected the first part, but he'd never dreamed the second. He couldn't move, he couldn't speak, he could only stare at her and be amazed. She humbled him. After what he'd done to her, she was trying to protect him. He'd never met a more incredible woman in his life. Why hadn't he met her before everything had gone so wrong?

If he had, if he'd known her in Temeron, she might have saved him.

He kissed her hot forehead. "I will do whatever you ask of me, Alana Eldralin. Just promise me you'll keep fighting no matter what. Promise me that, honey, please."

"I promise," she whispered.

CHAPTER 8

Zeran stood, looking out the windows of his study over the grounds down to the creek. Tyrane, his foster brother, stood beside him, a supportive presence as he'd always been. He and Tyrane were family, but even Tyrane couldn't fix this for him.

Alana had been gone for more than a week now, taken by a man Zeran had trusted. He knew Trey Almsden had a hard life, but he'd never suspected the young man would be a threat to Zeran's family. The realization of what had happened kept ambushing him, crippling him with its intensity. His daughter was missing. How did any father continue knowing his daughter was at the mercy of someone else?

"Have you eaten anything?" asked Tyrane.

Zeran shook his head, fighting the hum of power that raced through his body. He couldn't lose control now. He couldn't let it sweep him up. He lifted his hand and curled it around the emerald at his throat, drawing calm from the weight of it.

Tyrane turned and faced him. "You won't be good to anyone if you don't take care of yourself."

A knock sounded at the study door. Tyrane gave him a final pointed look, then he went and opened it. The Human Reverend, Jarvis Talmar, stepped inside. Talmar had accompanied Alix and Zeran to Temeron from Nevaisser and he'd stayed on to become one of Zeran's closest advisors. He'd aged in the years since, his golden blond hair threaded with grey, lines etched around his mouth, but his mind was still as quick and his loyalty unwavering. He and Tyrane exchanged a muted conversation, drawing Zeran's attention from the window.

"What is it!" he demanded, his patience snapping.

Talmar ducked his head. No matter how many years he advised Zeran, he'd never gotten over his intimidation. "A message from Zelan," said Talmar, moving forward and holding a letter out to Zeran.

Zeran took the envelope and turned it over, seeing the seal of Falco Leonhart, the Lord of Loden, embossed on the back. He turned to toss it onto his desk. He didn't have time for whatever Falco wanted, but Talmar made a noise of protest, holding up a cautionary hand.

Zeran's gaze swung to him and pinned him where he stood. "It's urgent," said Talmar.

Zeran drew in a slow breath and held it, fighting the surge of power that pressed at the edge of his control. Then he broke the seal on the envelope and pulled out a single sheet of paper, scanning it.

"What does it say?" asked Tyrane.

Zeran chewed on his inner lip, trying to absorb the ramification of Falco's letter. He wasn't sure what it meant, but a frisson of anxiety snaked down his spine. "The Nazar, Karnack Pretorian, is dead. He was eliminated by a Nazarien named Tarish Enro."

"Eliminated?" said Talmar in shock. "What do you mean eliminated?"

Zeran's eyes lifted to him. "Killed."

Talmar looked between Tyrane and Zeran. "Killed? Who's Nazar now?"

"Tarish Enro."

Talmar's mouth dropped open. Tyrane rubbed the back of his neck, staring at the ground. He understood they didn't need anymore bad news right now.

"Wait. I don't understand. The man who murdered the Nazar is now Nazar," questioned Talmar.

Zeran nodded, moving to drop the letter on his desk. "That's their way. When the Nazar becomes weak, a rival will eliminate him and take his place."

"That's barbaric!" said Talmar.

Zeran considered that. It was, but the Nazarien were barbaric. "It's problematic."

"In what way?" asked Talmar.

"Zeran is an Eldralin," said Tyrane. "Ultimately, the Nazarien answer to him."

"Then you can order this Tarish Enro to step down. You can change this."

Zeran rubbed his eyes wearily. "My great grandfather, Jarrett Trauner, tried to change the order and failed miserably, but you're right about one thing. I need to establish my authority with this

Tarish Enro. He can't be allowed to think he has full rein to rule as he pleases."

"What do you want to do?" asked Tyrane.

"Falco demanded Tarish present himself in Zelan by the start of Autumn. Send our own command to Chernow and tell Tarish I also demand his presence." He stared out the window at the rolling grass, his thoughts returning obsessively to Alana. "Block out that time and arrange an entourage to accompany me there for the meeting."

Tyrane nodded. "On it," he said and turned for the door. When he opened it, he stepped back.

Zeran's captain, Valmir Petric, stepped into the room, followed by a man in forest green clothing. The second man had wheat gold hair hanging to the middle of his back, Stravad blue eyes, and a skin tone that was surprisingly pale for a Stravad. He was handsome, but there was a hard set to his mouth.

"Stravad Leader," said Petric, ducking his bald head, his fist against his breast.

"Valmir, speak," said Zeran.

Tyrane and Talmar hesitated, waiting to hear what the captain had to say.

"This man is Folen Tesseran. He's the finest tracker in Temeron."

Zeran's chin lifted. "Tracker?"

Tesseran bowed his blond head and pressed his fist to his chest as Petric had done. "At your service, Stravad Leader." When he rose to his full height, Zeran could see him playing with a wooden medallion at his throat.

"Tracker?" Zeran repeated. "Can you track my daughter?"

Tesseran gave a nod. "I believe I can."

"No one else has been able to find signs of her."

Tesseran tilted back his head. "To be honest with you, Stravad Leader, they are not me. I can find her. No matter what happens, I can find her."

Zeran's gaze shifted to Petric. "You've seen this man's skills firsthand?"

"I have, Stravad Leader. He's the finest we have."

Zeran felt a wash of hope sweep over him, but it dissipated. Alana had been missing for more than a week. The thought of his daughter at any man's mercy made his power surge inside of him. He took a step toward Tesseran, staring into his eyes.

"Find my daughter, Tracker, and I promise you, you will never want for anything again."

Tesseran smiled slowly. "As you wish, Stravad Leader," he said.

*   *   *

Bane Greyson stopped in the midst of his hoeing and placed his hand over his eyes. The sun was shining, a shimmer of heat in the distance, but it didn't prevent him from noticing the stranger walking across Greyson land, carrying the body of what appeared to be a child.

The stranger staggered, then went down, clutching the limp form against him. Bane whistled at his brother and dropped the hoe. Then he was running across the land. He came to a panting halt and looked down at the stranger. Emerald green eyes lifted to his face.

"Help me please!" the stranger whispered and then dropped his head again, cradling the limp body closer.

Bane studied the strangers. The first was a man, large and muscled, but thin. At close sight, the second was a woman with a mass of thick black hair and a pale complexion. One leg of her trousers was cut and her thigh was covered with a stained cloth.

Morvan came up behind him. "Who is it, Bane?"

Bane shrugged. "Stravad."

The stranger lifted his head a little. By the fine sheen of perspiration across his brow and the tattered filth of his clothes, Bane guessed he'd been travelling quite a distance trying to find help.

"What do you want?" he said, bracing his feet and studying the man.

Green eyes fixed on Bane with a bone weariness. "My wife is hurt. Please help her."

Bane studied the woman in the stranger's arms. Her head lolled over his arm, her own arms hanging limply. Her breathing was too rapid. His eyes went back to the dirty bandage across her thigh and the obvious tearing of her clothes.

"What happened to her?"

"Sand snake," said the stranger, his Temerian accent noticeable.

Bane and Morvan exchanged glances. Bane hadn't been many places in his life, but he could guess the strangers' race by the color of their skin and the cast of their features, green eyes notwithstanding.

"You're Stravad, right?"

The stranger nodded.

Bane took a deep breath. "How far you been carrying her?"

"I don't know. I left a tributary of the Rovarn just south of here at daybreak. I've been walking ever since. I was afraid to stop. Please help me."

The woman moaned and her head rolled limply. Bane couldn't stand the sound of her pain. It reminded him too much of Noni, his dead wife. He knelt in front of the stranger and held out his arms.

"Give her to me."

For a moment the man's eyes took on a wild, feral light and he clutched the woman tighter. Bane understood the man's reaction, probably better than any of his brothers might have.

"I want to help," he said and the look passed in the stranger's face.

He allowed Bane to take her into his arms, cradling her. When Bane rose to his feet again, the woman whimpered and tried to lift herself, then went limp once more. Bane nodded at his brother and Morvan helped the stranger to his feet, bracing him with his shoulder as they made their way off the hills and toward the main house.

* * *

Trey leaned heavily on the man who walked beside him and kept a wary eye on the man carrying Alana. They seemed like decent men, but Trey had learned little about trust in a lifetime of deceit. Alana was so sick and she needed help, but Trey had to stay alert in order to make sure she got it.

The problem was he was exhausted.

He'd been walking since before the sun had risen, carrying Alana and praying he'd find someone else, even a Temerian Guard to help him. He'd been determined to walk until he dropped, a prediction that had almost come true, before he'd accept defeat.

A white farm house rose before them. A screen door banged in the distance and a woman appeared on the porch. She caught sight of the strange procession coming to her door and hurried off the porch, running across the dusty yard despite the considerable bulk she carried.

She came to a halt before the man carrying Alana. "Eldon's star, Bane, what's happened?"

"Strangers," said the man, nodding at Alana's limp form. "She's hurt bad, Mama."

Trey looked the older woman over. Her hair was grey and tied up neatly in a bun on the top of her head. She stood a good foot shorter than her son, and he nearly a half-foot shorter than Trey himself. Although her clothing was worn and faded, she was clean and had a bright look in her eyes.

She glanced at Trey, but her attention immediately focused on Alana. She stroked the tangled hair off Alana's damp forehead and then parted the tear in her trousers, looking at the haphazard bandage Trey had managed to tie around the wound.

"What happened to her?"

"Her husband says sand snake."

The woman lifted her eyes to Trey's face again. Trey eased away from the second man, shifting the pack carrying everything they owned higher on his shoulder. He met the older woman's gaze and hoped she'd see the desperation in him. If she turned them away, he'd do something crazy.

"Please, ma'am," he said, surprised by the breaking of his voice. Although his Lodenian was perfect, (there were few things he learned that he ever forgot), he was exhausted and his head felt fuzzy. "My wife needs help. I know you probably don't see many travelers out this way, but if we don't get some help, she…" His voice failed him. He just couldn't put words to the fear that had kept him awake all night and walking all day.

Her dark, bright eyes shifted back to Alana. "Poor darling," she whispered. Then her back went ramrod straight. "Take her into the house and lay her on the guest bed, Bane. As soon as you're done, go find Imre and send him after Doc Ingers. Morvan, help the young woman's husband to the house. He looks like he's ready to drop."

Both men obeyed her commands immediately. Trey was ushered along behind Bane and his mother, his eyes scanning the farm and lands. He climbed the porch and ducked beneath the low door frame. Bane was just disappearing into a room off the kitchen, but he reappeared, shoving his way past everyone as he went for the door.

"You stay here, Morvan. Keep an eye on things," Bane said.

Keep an eye on me, thought Trey, but he didn't mind. He was so damn grateful these people had decided to help them. If they wanted Trey to get out, leaving Alana behind, he'd do it. He'd do anything to help her now, but he wanted to be near her, make sure she was all right before he left.

He moved to the door of the room and leaned against the jam. Alana was lying in the center of the double bed, her midnight black hair fanned out around her. Her lips were parted and she was breathing rapidly, her face too damn pale. Trey felt a tightening in his chest and he wanted to go to her, but the room seemed much too small for his bulk.

He eyed Morvan. Like his brother, Morvan was short and stocky, huge arms and legs, and a short torso. He had the same dark brown hair and dark eyes of the older woman and Bane. They were family, Trey decided and then dismissed him.

His attention was drawn back to the older woman. She was unwinding the bandage around Alana's leg. The leg was badly swollen, the wound itself puffy and red, and it was still weeping a sticky yellow pus. Just looking at it from this distance frightened Trey.

The woman's expression was pained, but she didn't pull away or gasp in horror. Trey was impressed. Maybe he'd brought Alana to the right place. She dropped the soiled bandage on the ground and then turned to the door where both Trey and Morvan were watching. She fixed her hands on her ample hips and frowned.

"Go run to your cottage and get Glynis. Stop by Bane's and tell Moya. No use upsetting Zoel though. You know how she is when she's breeding. Tell the others I need their help. Have Moya bring a sleeping gown, she's likely the smallest." She cast a look at Alana on the bed. "Poor little thing, she's no bigger'n a sparrow."

Morvan stood in the doorway, awaiting more orders. The older woman turned back and glared at him. "Well, go on now,

Morvan. Don't stand there like you're deaf. You want to see me strip this little bit down buck naked or what?"

Trey blinked in astonishment and looked at Morvan. The man blushed and shook his head. "No, Mama, I mean, yes, Mama," he stammered and then he was gone.

Trey watched him scramble through the kitchen and disappear into the yard. He looked back at the older woman and found her studying him intently.

"So, you're her husband. Is that right?"

Trey nodded slowly.

"Well, you certainly got her in a fine mess, didn't you?"

Trey flinched. He blamed himself for Alana's predicament, but it sounded brutal coming from a stranger.

"She breeding?"

Trey blinked again.

The woman held up her hands and let them fall against her hips. "Don't tell me you're deaf?"

"No, ma'am," he said, recovering. "My wife, Alana, got bit just before nightfall yesterday. As soon as the sun came up, I started walking, carrying her. I've been walking since then. I didn't dare stop, even to catch my breath. Right now, I'm exhausted, not to mention damn worried about her, ma'am."

"No need to swear at me, boy," she said sharply, but her look softened. "Is she breeding, boy?"

"No, ma'am," he said abruptly.

"You sure about that. I was married near thirty years to the same man, had three boys of my own, and seven grandkids. It seems to me like the papa's usually the last to know these things."

"Allie's not pregnant, ma'am. Of that I'm sure."

The woman nodded. "You can stop the ma'amin'. Folks just call me Miss Leev. You can do the same."

"Thank you, ma'am...Miss Leev."

"Well, guess you better come on in. You can help me undress her."

"Ma'am?" Trey's voice broke again. Damn, but he must be thirstier than he'd first thought.

Miss Leev just shook her head reproachfully. "Ain't a one that doesn't get all bashful over such things, 'cept when the moods on them. I want to get these dirty things off her and make her more comfortable until Doc Ingers gets here, so you come on over here and lend me a hand."

Trey staggered to the bed and stood beside Alana, looking down at her. She moaned in her sleep and her head rolled on the mattress. Trey suppressed an urge to cradle her in his arms again. He looked up into Miss Leev's eyes. She returned the look with one of gentle understanding. For all her bossy ways, she did seem like a good, honest woman.

The softness evaporated at once. "Start with that filthy shirt, while I put on some bathing water and get some towels." She left the room without looking back.

Trey sank onto the bed beside the woman who wasn't his wife, but his captive. His hands trembled as he reached for the buttons on her shirt. He might have thought about undressing Alana frequently in the last few days, but certainly not under these circumstances.

He managed to work free the first button. It seemed like a great feat. A sheen of perspiration covered her skin, her black hair dark against the white bedspread. He reached out and ran his fingers over her cheek, letting them trail down to the pulse point in her throat.

He'd never beheld a woman who moved him the way Alana did. He found himself letting her slip past the barriers inside of him, making him care – not just about himself, but about her, so very much. Laying there, she seemed so lost and alone, he wanted to shelter her, protect her, and he'd never felt that way about anyone or anything in his entire life. Yet Alana's beauty was illusive, like her spirit. He sensed no matter what he did to prove himself to her, he'd never really be able to claim her as his own. Even now he felt her slipping away.

Fear choked up tight in his throat. Unable to resist himself he bent down and curved his arms around her, shutting his eyes and placing his face against the side of her throat, holding her gently. He kissed her feverish cheek and allowed the thought of being her everything sink into him, moving past barriers, making him care and want what he could never have.

"I'm so sorry, Allie. I never meant for this to happen to you." He whispered into her ear and pressed his lips to her cheek again, needing to feel her heart beating against his chest.

Loud, feminine voices sounded outside the room and Trey sat up, releasing her. He looked at the door and found Miss Leev there, watching him. She'd obviously been standing there for a good while. Trey was surprised he didn't feel any embarrassment. Without a word, Miss Leev turned and placed a single finger to her lips to quiet the women who'd just arrived.

"Glynis, you come here and help me undress her," she said in a scolding tone. "Moya, show this young man where to wash up and get him some clean clothes out of Papa's trunk. Something in there is bound to fit."

Two short, plump women appeared in the doorway. They looked a great deal like Miss Leev with their tight buns and faded dresses, but they were much younger, their hair brown, not grey. They surveyed Trey first, their eyes passing over him curiously from head to toe, then their attention went to Alana.

They both gasped and pushed into the room. Trey felt claustrophobic. The three women together took up a good deal of space and there wasn't much to spare in the little ranch house.

"Is she Stravad?" asked the first.

"Isn't she lovely?" said the second.

"So small."

Miss Leev shooed them both away and came to the side of the bed to look down at Trey. "Go with Moya here and get cleaned up." She indicated one of the women. They looked the same to Trey, but he noted Moya was just an inch or so taller than the other one.

"What if she wakes and wants to know where I am?"

"You can come back and stay with her as soon as you're presentable."

It didn't seem like the time to argue. He cast one last glance on Alana, then rose to his feet, hunching his shoulders to avoid the low roof. The moment he moved away from the bed, Glynis and Miss Leev took his place hovering over Alana. He watched them as Moya led him from the room. He sensed they were good women, but he didn't like leaving her.

*   *   *

Alana came awake and tried to open her eyes. They were too heavy as was the rest of her body. She knew then that she was ill. Her head throbbed with fever and there was a burning pain travelling up her right leg. She rolled her head on the pillow. The bed felt hard beneath her. She tried to get comfortable, but the pain only intensified. Her lips were dry, so was her throat, and she tried to ask for water, but couldn't find her voice.

She heard the voices talking over her. Daddy and Mama. Her mama would know she wanted water. Just as she knew that Alana needed comforting now. She must be very sick because the cool hand that pressed to her forehead didn't seem like her mother's.

She remembered the scattered snatches of her fever dreams, but it was all so outlandish, she had to dismiss it. Somehow she'd gotten sick and had forgotten what happened to her. Her mind drifted again, filtering through strange images.

She was tied up in a cave with a low ceiling that got lower and lower until she couldn't breathe anymore. Then she was on a hill, looking over at Temerian guards with a man beside her. At first she assumed the man to be her father, but then she looked up into emerald green eyes. The worst was the hissing of snakes that filled her head and made her tremble.

And then there was a fire in her right leg, which shot through the entire extremity, making her shudder. It ebbed away, tiny explosions that rippled through her body. In the wake of the pain, she heard the voices again.

Her mother and father, discussing her illness.

"It'll have to come off. There's no other way. I've seen it before."

Alana tried to open her eyes, tried to understand what her father was saying. *What was he talking about?*

"Such a shame. Such a beautiful little thing."

Her mother? But it didn't sound like her mother. Was she talking about Alana's illness? Why wasn't there more concern in her voice?

"It is, but it's the only way to be sure."

"It's not safe to wait? It's such a shame to mutilate her. She's such a pretty little thing."

Fear coiled through Alana, making her cold. She tried to open her eyes again. Why was her mother talking about mutilating her? The answer came then. Her leg. Something was wrong with her leg.

"I'm not an expert on Stravad, mind you, but with Humans we'd have done it immediately. I hate mutilating her too, but she'll do fine on one leg and at least she'll be alive."

"Of course, you know best."

NO! Alana longed to scream the word, to beg her father and mother to protect her, but they were talking about taking off her leg as if it was only an unfortunate occurrence. Terror and desperation mounted within her and she fought her way to the surface, but when she broke, it wasn't her mother or father she called for.

"Trey!"

* * *

Trey bolted awake and rose to a half-sitting position, instinctively reaching for Alana and angling his body to protect her. Her arms came around him and clutched tight. Her heart thundered against his ribs and her breathing was marred by hitching sobs. He looked wildly around and found himself back in the small ranch room. Miss Leev and a strange man were standing beside the bed, looking startled. Glynis and Moya appeared in the doorway, a similar expression on their faces.

Trey took a deep breath and folded his arms around Alana, lowering his lips to the back of her head and whispering to her. "It's all right, sprite. I'm here."

"Don't…don't let them…please, don't, Trey."

"Shh, honey, it's all right. It's all right."

He watched the strange man and Miss Leev from the corner of his eyes, praying Alana wouldn't say anything in her hysteria to give him away, but if she was going to condemn him he didn't understand why she was clinging to him so desperately.

She lifted her feverish face and angled closer to him. "Don't let them take off my leg," she moaned, her fingers clenching and unclenching.

Trey's eyes shot to Miss Leev and the strange man as they both gasped. "Oh lord, she must have heard us," whispered the older woman.

The strange man nodded. "I thought she was unconscious. Poor little thing."

Trey's arms tightened instinctively and he could only stare at the two strangers in horror. What had they been planning while *he* lay unconscious beside her? Would they have done it with him right there, unknowing?

The man recovered first and held out his hand. Trey stared down at the hand unblinking, while Alana wept in his arms. The hand was smooth, clean, the nails neatly trimmed. Trey followed the hand to the man's lean, angular face. He was only a few years older than Trey himself, Human, well-dressed and moderately handsome by another man's standards.

"I'm Doctor Ingers. I should have introduced myself, but matters being what they are, I'm not always given that luxury."

"Doc Ingers is the doctor in Anatem," offered Miss Leev.

Trey's eyes shifted to the two women peering at him through the door. They both nodded encouragement.

Doctor Ingers drew back his hand and folded his arms across his chest. Alana was still weeping and Trey bent his head to press a comforting kiss against her tangled hair.

"Don't let them," she moaned softly.

"Shh, honey, I won't let anyone hurt you. I swear it."

The doctor cleared his throat at Trey's words. "Mister…"

"Almsden," Trey offered before he thought better of it. He grimaced and then let it go. What difference did it make if they knew who he was with Alana shivering and weeping in his arms, facing the real prospect of having her leg amputated by strangers?

"Mister Almsden, your wife's wound is unfortunate, but grave. I understand you attempted to draw out the poison yourself, but despite your efforts, it appears to be badly infected."

Trey's face blanched and he choked down a rush of guilt. "I didn't have time to clean the blade."

The doctor held up a hand. "Notwithstanding the infection, Mister Almsden, your wife's chances of surviving a sand snake bite are not very good."

Trey's jaw clenched.

"I know it seems brutal, but I'm being honest. The best chance she has, we've found through experience, is to amputate the affected limb."

Alana's moan of anguish shot straight to Trey's heart. He clutched her tighter as she began shivering again.

"The only chance she has?"

The doctor nodded, followed by Miss Leev's nod.

"I've treated a least fifty cases since starting up practice in the Boline plain. It is an unfortunate reality of my occupation."

"We aren't talking about an occupation, Doctor. We're talking about my...about Alana's leg."

"And her life."

Trey looked down at the young woman in his arms, then trailed his look to the distorted flesh that had once been a healthy limb. Was this the only answer?

"Certainly you'd rather have your wife without a leg, than to have no wife at all," said the doctor gravely.

Trey's eyes flashed to the man's face. Without a doubt Trey figured he'd probably want Alana no matter what, but it wasn't his decision to make. She wasn't his.

"What are the chances she'll survive if you do the operation?"

"No...no," moaned Alana against his shoulder, her hands clenching and unclenching again.

"Better."

"But you can't give me odds, can you?" demanded Trey.

The doctor opened his mouth to speak, but Alana cut him off. Trey turned to her, pressing her back on the pillows. She tried to get up, but pain twisted her flushed, damp face and she lay back, panting.

"Listen to me, Allie. Listen." He gave her shoulders a little shake. Enormous, terrified cobalt eyes opened and fixed on him. Her lips parted as if she would speak, but they were trembling so violently, nothing came out.

Trey's expression softened. "What if he's right, Allie? What if this is the only way to save you?"

She lifted a trembling hand and touched his cheek. He clasped her hand and pressed a kiss to her hot, dry palm. "Don't let him do this to me, Trey," she begged, her voice breaking on a sob. "Please don't let him do this to me."

Tears flooded Trey's eyes for the first time since he could remember. He tried to blink them away, but they overflowed and ran down his cheeks, dampening her fingers where they were clasped to his beard-stubbled jaw.

"I don't want to lose you, sprite. It doesn't matter to me what you look like. It won't change the way I feel about you." He wasn't sure what he was saying, but the words poured forth and they were true. "Please, honey. Think. There's so much life left. If this is a choice between life and death, there isn't a choice."

She blinked rapidly, her lips trembled, and her fingers curled in against her palm. Trey kissed her hand.

"Please, honey. Think."

Her eyes fixed at a spot over his shoulder. Trey held his breath, praying she would see the reasoning behind it, that she would take the decision from his hands. And he knew in that moment he'd make the decision no matter what it meant, if it would save her.

"A poultice," she said in a strangely calm voice. Her eyes shifted back to his face. "We can make one from..." Her brow furrowed and her eyes narrowed.

"Mister Almsden, this is wasting precious time..."

"Shh!" hissed Trey without turning around. "What, Allie? What are you thinking?"

"I saw the healers do it once." She shook her head and took a hitching breath. "A boy cut his hand and it was infected. They made a poultice from Datel weed and willow bark and Stamerian, I think."

"Stamerian?" Trey prompted. He felt the doctor shift impatiently behind him. "Are you sure, Allie?"

She nodded absently, her eyes locked on his. "Stamerian. Of course, what else would a Stravad use." Her voice had lowered until it was nearly a whisper, but Trey didn't mistake the hint of humor in it.

He gave a laugh and brushed the tangled hair from her feverish forehead. She closed her eyes at his touch. "Of course," he whispered, then swiped violently at the ineffective tears on his own face and turned on the doctor. "Well?"

The man looked confused. "Well what? I don't speak Temerian." He held out one perfectly manicured hand.

Trey hadn't realized they were communicating in Temerian. "She says a poultice of Datel weed, willow bark, and Stamerian will draw the poison out. Will it work?"

"That concoction? To take away her pain, maybe, but..."

"No!" Cobalt eyes opened again and fixed on the doctor. She narrowed them, struggling to remember Lodenian. "It's the combination. It draws out the poison, reduces swelling and helps with the pain." Her gaze shifted to Trey again. "But it worked on this boy, I saw it, and they were talking about amputating his hand too." She lifted her hand to his face once more and touched it with a trembling stroke. "Please, Trey. I want to try this. Please."

Trey searched her eyes. She was begging him to stand behind her now, when he'd gotten her into this predicament. He gave her a nod and turned to the doctor.

"Will you put it together?"

The man drew a breath and glared at Trey. "I'm against this course of action…"

"Will you put it together?" Trey ground out through clenched teeth.

The doctor looked like he was going to protest, but Miss Leev placed a hand on his shoulder. "Doctor, the young woman wants to try. Isn't it her decision?"

The doctor broke the stare with Trey. "I hold you responsible."

"Fine!" said Trey. "We don't have time to waste."

The doctor turned to the door. "Moya, Glynis, get some water boiling." He turned to Miss Leev. "I'll need a mixing bowl and…" He ushered the woman to the door and their voices echoed back down the hallway.

Trey watched Alana and offered his fervent, silent prayers that they'd made the right decision.

"Thank you," she mouthed and closed her eyes.

Trey eased forward and kissed her forehead. "You don't have to thank me, sprite. You should be blaming me."

She opened her eyes again and gave him a stern look. "The only thing I'll be blaming you for is treating me like a child."

Trey frowned, but she lifted her hand and cupped the back of his head, urging him down to her lips. She gave him a short, passionate kiss and released him again. Closing her eyes, she exhaled. "There. That's more like it, *husband*."

Trey wanted to laugh at her audacity in the face of what she was going through, but he was still too damn scared to do more than angle his arms around her and hold her close, his face pressed against her neck.

CHAPTER 9

"Merith!"

The councilmember jumped and closed his eyes, drawing a deep breath. Tarish Enro blazed into the library, his clothing in disarray, sweat stains on his leather tunic, his hair slicked back away from his face.

"My lord Nazar," Merith said, keeping his eyes focused on the book before him.

Tarish's gloved hand slammed a missive onto the open book. Merith's mouth fell open when he saw the royal blue falcon emblem embossed on the back of it. The mark of an Eldralin. He raised his eyes to Tarish's.

Tarish gave him a grin. It wasn't a happy grin and it made Merith's spine crawl. "What do you make of that?"

"It came today?" Merith asked.

"It came today. It was brought to me from the trill cote. It's the Eldralin seal."

Merith nodded, his gaze fixated on it.

Tarish swiped his sleeve across his upper lip, wiping away the sweat. "Open it." The smell of sweat permeated the room. Merith knew the Nazar spent hours on the training grounds, honing his body and mind, forcing his followers to do the same.

"Open it! Open it!" he ordered, motioning impatiently.

Merith reached for it, dismayed to see his hands shaking. A missive from Temeron, coming on the heels of one from Zelan could not be good news, yet Tarish acted like they were inviting him to a Valhall Celebration. He carefully broke the seal and opened the letter.

An elegant script danced across the page and Merith felt his mouth go dry as he read it to himself.

"Read it out loud!" said Tarish, an almost gleeful note in his voice.

"Nazar Tarish Enro," Merith began. "Recently I was made aware of your elevation from second-in-command to Nazar upon the death of Karnack Pretorian."

Tarish barked out a laugh and paced away from the table, waving one hand in the air, the other braced on his hip. "Upon the death? Upon the death?" His humor faded and he turned back to face Merith, his features grim. "Try execution."

Merith shot him a shuttered look, then scanned the letter again.

"Go on. Continue," growled Tarish.

"I know you have received greetings from the Lord of Loden, Falco Leonhart. I have also been made aware he has commanded you to present yourself in Zelan at the start of Autumn. I am desirous of the same favor."

"Favor?" scoffed Tarish, rolling his eyes. "Favor! Eldon's bloody star, the way these fools speak."

Merith met Tarish's gaze fully for a moment. He felt a chill race over his body. If Zeran decided to abolish the Nazarien, he'd be in his right to do so, but Merith had never known anything but the order. So had most of the men around him. They couldn't survive in the Human world, not in Nevaisser. They'd be killed for their association with the Nazarien. And he felt sure there wasn't a place for them in Loden either. Tarish ought to realize how precarious their position was.

Tarish stalked over to him, leaning on the table. "Read, Merith. Finish the missive."

Merith stared at the paper, struggling to find his voice.

"Read!" shouted Tarish, slamming his fist onto the table.

Merith jumped, then hunched his shoulders. "Understand, Nazar, that my polite language should not be mistaken for a request. I order you to present yourself in Zelan, not as the Stravad Leader of Temeron, although that I am, and not as a kinsman, but as the living heir of Eldon himself. I order you to present yourself in Zelan at the prescribed time because I am the Nazarien order."

Merith lowered the letter and stared at the signature. Zeran Eldralin. *Zeran Eldralin.* The living heir of Eldon. He was not to be disobeyed.

Chancing a look up at Tarish, Merith wasn't sure what to expect. His silence was almost worse than the bombastic shouting of before.

Tarish's mouth twisted as if he'd eaten something rank. "We'll see," he said cryptically, then he nodded his head as if he'd come to some sort of conclusion. "We'll just see about that."

Without another word, he whirled on his boot heel and headed for the door. Merith scrambled to his feet, the letter still held in his grip.

"Nazar!" he shouted, but Tarish merely lifted a hand as he disappeared through the door, waving at him.

*   *   *

Alana swam up from a deep sleep and her eyes fluttered open. Sunlight streamed in the room and made her wince in pain. She shifted on the hard bed and more searing pain travelled up her right leg and through her body. She whimpered and lay still, not daring to move again. But the bed moved beneath her and a male cough came from her left side.

She blinked the dry, gritty feeling out of her eyes and shifted her head slowly. Trey lay beside her, his knees curled up and pressed to her left thigh on the too short bed. One arm lay over Alana's waist, curved protectively. It was one reason she felt so heavy. A dark lock of brown hair had fallen over his forehead and his lips were parted slightly. Black lashes rested on his sharp cheekbones and the lines she knew so well around his mouth and eyes were invisible in his relaxed pose.

She smiled despite the nagging pain travelling up her wounded leg. They were lying here, side by side, all night as if they really were married. She hadn't stopped to wonder why he'd told these people such a lie before, but she wasn't about to disclaim it now and risk his safety and her reputation.

The pain in her leg drew her attention. It was insistent and throbbing, much worse than she remembered in her fever delirium of the previous day. Added to the fullness of her bladder, she was uncomfortable.

Rising just a little on the bed, she clamped her teeth over the cry that nearly escaped her and looked down at the heavily swathed appendage. Fever made her head swim and the pain made her stomach roil, but she reached out a trembling hand and lifted the dense binding on her thigh. She held her breath and forced herself to look.

It wasn't as bad as they'd led her to believe the previous night. The puncture marks were still an angry red, but it wasn't swollen nearly as much as they'd said, not twice its normal size – swollen, yes, but mostly around the immediate area of the bite.

She collapsed on the bed, her eyes falling shut, her chest rising as she tried to still the rush of nausea and the agony that speared through her leg. Trey's arm tightened around her waist and then the bed shifted beneath them as he lifted himself.

"Allie?" he asked sleepily.

She opened eyes brimming with tears and looked into his confused, worried face. The single lock of hair hanging over his forehead made him look boyish and innocent. She forced a weak smile.

"Hi."

"What's wrong, honey?"

She shook her head, not trusting herself to speak. The pain wasn't easing as it should be. There was no denying it. It hurt a hell of a lot worse than the previous night, but she didn't want Trey to see what a coward she was. And she was afraid. If she complained too much, that doctor might come back and want to amputate.

His eyes moved from her face to her wounded leg. He eased into a sitting position and reached for the binding.

"Trey," she moaned, the fear overriding the blinding pain.

He glanced at her. "I just want to see how your leg is this morning, honey."

Before she could stop him, he lifted the binding and took a long look. Alana felt every muscle in her body tense and she shivered at the effort of denying how badly she hurt. He released his breath audibly and shifted on the bed until he was kneeling beside her and facing her. He removed the heavy binding completely, giving Alana a little relief, and his long fingers stroked gently over her thigh around the wound.

Alana shivered again, but this time it wasn't wholly from pain. Her eyes fluttered open and she fixed them on Trey. He lifted his head, dark hair falling away from his face, and he blinked rapidly a few times.

"It's better," he whispered. He seemed fascinated by her disfigured thigh, as if he didn't see anything wrong there at all.

"What do you mean?" she breathed, hardly daring to believe it was true when she hurt so badly.

He looked up and smiled. He was so handsome when he smiled. "Your thigh, honey. The swelling's gone down a lot. It was nearly twice this size, so distorted." He shook his head. "And it was so angry looking. But now, it looks almost normal again."

"Thanks," she said wryly, clenching her teeth.

To her surprise he lay down beside her once more and braced himself on an elbow, looking into her face. "Does it hurt?"

Tears rushed to her eyes again and she nodded. He reached out and brushed the tangled mass of hair from her forehead. "You still have a fever," he said with a hint of worry in his voice. "Not everything's healing yet, but I promise we'll get you well again." His fingers trailed down to her lips and he followed the line of each one. "I'm going to see where that doctor is." He said the words with contempt. "He's got to have something for pain, and I'll have another poultice made up." A smile crossed his hard features again, filling out the thin lines of his mouth. "That Eldralin blood's amazing stuff, Allie. Sure came through when we needed it."

Alana's brow furrowed. "What do you mean?"

Trey gave a chuckle. "The natural born healer in you came surging to the surface the moment you heard what that doctor wanted to do." His face grew serious again and he stared at her pointedly.

If Alana hadn't been so sick and hurt, she would have found more curiosity in that look. It was possessive and proud, and intimate. She felt a spiral of heat travel through her. Her eyes lowered to Trey's mouth and despite her discomfort, she wished for a moment that he'd kiss her again.

"In fact," he said, "you are a constant wonder to me, little girl. You're like no other woman that I've ever met. So damn special."

Alana exhaled and turned her face into his caress. It ended too soon as he rose and left the room, but when she closed her eyes, she could almost pretend he was still there.

* * *

Trey finally sat down to the meal Glynis, Moya and Zoel had prepared for the entire family in Miss Leev's crowded kitchen. It was late morning and he was starving, but he'd spent the last few hours hovering over that idiot doctor, making sure he didn't hurt Allie anymore than necessary.

Alana was sleeping quietly now. Although she hadn't complained even once, he'd known she was in a lot of pain. The doctor had confirmed it when he'd examined her leg. As the swelling went down, the feeling came back and with the feeling came the hurt. All in all, it was a good sign, but Trey didn't like seeing the tightening of Alana's mouth or the glistening of unshed tears in her eyes.

He speared half an egg and lifted it to his lips. He was starving. He and Alana hadn't eaten a proper meal in the last week. He intended to see that Alana was well fed and taken care of from now on, no matter what he had to do.

He smiled as he chewed his food. The doctor had been so damn surprised when he'd examined Allie. He'd expected her leg to be worse, even putrefying. It sickened Trey to think how ready he'd been to mutilate the most beautiful woman the bastard had surely ever seen. But Allie hadn't been worse. She'd been much better – not near to healed, but so much better he'd wanted to sing.

Bane dropped down heavily into the chair across from Trey and folded his hands together on the table. Trey lifted his teacup to his lips and took a drink, meeting the smaller man's eyes over the rim. Glynis set a plate down in front of her husband and stood behind him as if she were waiting to serve his every whim. Trey glanced between the two of them and returned to his meal.

Bane didn't touch his.

He cleared his throat and drummed his fingers on the checkered table cloth. Trey glanced up at him, but continued eating. He caught the nod Miss Leev gave her son from the corner of his eyes. They obviously wanted to talk to him, which was fine, but Trey wasn't going to open the conversation first.

"Well," said Bane, nodding his head a few times and continuing to drum his short, thick fingers.

Trey hid his smile behind his teacup. He'd gathered last night that Bane's father had died some five years ago, so as the oldest, Bane felt himself the head of their family. He didn't mind Bane approaching him at all. He sensed the love the people around him shared and a small part of him longed for the very thing he'd never known. It was similar to what Alana had with her family.

Thinking in that direction made Trey feel ill. He'd begun to forget who Alana really was and that was dangerous. She was an Eldralin – the single, most powerful family on all of Samar. No one, least of all an Eldralin, would deign to lower themselves with the likes of Trey Almsden.

"Well," said Bane again, drawing Trey's attention from his thoughts. "You want to explain how you got you and your wife into this mess."

"Bane!" snapped Miss Leev, but Trey could only smile. He liked honesty. He'd always hated wading through bull shit.

"You told me to find out, Mama. I'm doing what you said."

"Not so rudely," she said and then gave Trey an apologetic look.

Trey almost laughed at the ridiculousness of her chide. She'd been anything but coy with him when they'd had their little talk. She'd asked him more personal things than even his own mother had.

He shifted an amused look between mother and son. "I don't mind your forthrightness, Mister Greyson. What do you want to know?"

Bane shot his mother a glance and Glynis beamed with pride for her husband. The two other brothers and their wives moved closer to the table. They all looked so damn much alike that Trey could hardly tell them apart, and Trey possessed an uncanny memory. He shuddered to think of what anyone else would do in this situation. Zoel was obviously pregnant, so that narrowed the field just a little, but to make up for it, they had a passel of children of various ages that ran like wild beasts through the house, shrieking like banshees.

The banshees had been banished to the yard at the moment, so it was unnaturally quiet in the Greyson kitchen. Trey was the center of attention and it was a position he'd never much liked.

"You and your wife are both Stravad, at least partly."

Trey nodded.

"From Temeron?"

Trey nodded again. As a man of few words, neither of these questions needed elaboration.

Coming from a family who tended to talk over one another, Bane was uncomfortable with his unwanted guest's reticence. "Well?"

He extended his hands and popped his knuckles. The other Greysons didn't notice, but Trey flinched. He hated that sound.

Bane drummed his fingers on the table and then leaned forward, pushing his plate aside. Trey braced himself for the important part of the interrogation and hoped his sharp memory would assist him.

"So exactly what is a young couple doing so far from home with absolutely nothing to call their own?"

Trey thought of their half-empty pack. It was a damn good question and he hoped his lie would sound truthful. "Allie and I are recently married."

"I told you," said Miss Leev with a nod of her grey head.

Trey shot her a smile and looked back at her son. "We don't have much yet, but we hope to build a life for ourselves somewhere new."

"Don't you have family in Temeron?"

Trey nodded. "Allie does."

"And they didn't want to help you?"

"Not exactly."

"What exactly?" said the middle brother, Imre. He was the tallest at six inches below Trey.

Trey shifted in his chair, folding his long fingers around his warm cup. This part had to be good, convincing. Not for himself, but for Allie.

"Allie's family wasn't exactly thrilled with the prospect of our marriage."

"Why? You get her in trouble?" snarled Imre.

Trey's eyes lifted to the man's face and he hid his smile. If possible, he sensed Imre was the outspoken one in this clan. "No, Allie and I were in love. We wanted to marry, but I didn't have as much money behind me as her family wanted."

The three Greyson brothers nodded. He'd found some common ground with them.

"They were rich?" said Imre, his eyes fixed on a pregnant Zoel.

"Very wealthy, and I was still trying to make enough to meet the next month's rent."

"So when you asked for her hand, they refused and you did the only thing you could, you ran off to be wed," finished Imre with a sigh.

Sounding familiar, Imre old boy thought Trey. He was a better liar than he'd thought. Why hadn't it ever helped when Zeran Eldralin caught him stealing as a child?

"That's the gist of it."

Bane's fingers drummed on the table. "Where did you think you'd go?"

"What did you think you'd do?" added Morvan.

Before he could respond, the women piped up. "It's romantic."

"Very. Like a fairy tale."

Trey's eyes flashed between all of them and stopped on Miss Leev.

"You love her, don't you?"

Trey blinked in surprise and swallowed hard. Damn the old woman. She'd cut right to the heart of an irrelevant issue. Trey could only nod because a sudden, dreadful pain caught him square in the chest.

"She's going to need a lot of time to heal. Where were you planning to go?"

Trey shrugged. "No particular place. Wherever we felt comfortable enough to settle and start a business. I intend to make sure nothing bad ever happens to Allie again, Miss Leev."

She nodded, but her dark eyes watched him.

Bane's drumming fingers were getting irritating. "Here's the thing," Bane said. "We've all discussed it. The Lazy G's a large ranch and requires lots of hands to run. We hire as many as we can and work like dogs ourselves, but we can always use more help. We've all agreed that if you're interested, you can work here with us, doing odd jobs until your wife's better. We'll give you room and board, and pay your wife's medical expenses, plus we'll pay you based on the amount you do on a weekly schedule."

Trey swallowed again and sat straighter in the chair. It sounded like a damn good offer and one he couldn't refuse. He had so little money. He wouldn't make it to Taral without food and some other supplies. Even if he left Allie with these people, waiting for the eventual arrival of her father, Trey didn't stand much of a chance on his own. He needed this job and it would allow him time to watch over Allie a little longer. Should the Temerian guards track them here, Trey still believed in his heart this was the best way. He owed it to both the Greysons and Allie. She needed their help, food, bed and medical attention, and Trey was responsible for reimbursing them. It was a good solution.

"I can't thank you enough for your generosity."

"You'll earn every bit of it. We'll work you till you drop if you let us," said Imre frankly.

Trey nodded. "And I'll do whatever you ask of me. Even if it's just for room, board, and Allie's medical care."

He held his breath, waiting for their response. He needed the money, but honesty prompted him to acknowledge their benevolence. Likely Allie's medical costs would be more than Trey could work off in a year.

Bane shook his head. "You look strong and determined. We'll pay you for your work as we see fit. It'll help give you and your wife a start on your future." He held his hand out across the table and Trey accepted it.

"Welcome aboard," said the man.

"Thank you," answered Trey and he truly meant it.

*　*　*

Alana opened her eyes as Trey eased the door open. He was carrying a tray of food in his arms and had to shut the door with a foot. He crossed the floor and placed the tray over her lap, then sat down facing her.

"Hi, sprite."

Alana managed a smile for him. The doctor had given her a painkiller that made her feel a little light headed and relaxed. It worked and at the time that had seemed like the only prerequisite.

"If I'm a sprite, you must be the fairy king," she said, holding out a hand.

He took it between both of his own and graced her with one of his beautiful smiles. A shiver of pleasure raced up Alana's arm as his callused fingers stroked over the back of her hand.

"I brought you a little breakfast."

She wrinkled her nose and entwined her fingers with his. "I'm not very hungry."

"I don't care. You're going to eat. You're too damn thin, Allie."

She closed her eyes sleepily and shook her head. "Just like a monarch, giving ridiculous orders."

She opened her eyes in time to see Trey leaning close to her. "Believe me, honey, this is not a ridiculous order."

Before she could think of a comeback, he slid an arm beneath her head and lifted her, pushing pillows behind her back to keep her elevated. A stab of pain throbbed through her leg, but it quickly dissipated.

He pushed a bowl of gruel at her and motioned to the spoon. "Feed yourself, sprite, or I'll do it for you." Alana stared at him in astonishment. He pinned her with his gaze, then reached for the spoon and dished up a heaping amount. "Open, love."

She started to protest, but he plopped the gruel into her mouth. Alana was forced to chew or choke. Before Trey could dish up another spoonful, she took the utensil from his hand and started working at it herself. He never removed his stern gaze from her the entire time, but when she'd finished a fourth of the bowl, she found she couldn't eat anymore. She dropped the spoon on the tray and lay back, giving him a defiant stare.

He looked into the bowl. "That isn't even half."

"If you want half, you eat the rest," she said.

He gave a laugh and lifted the tray off the bed, placing it on the floor. "You did good, sprite."

"Thanks," she murmured, closing her eyes. She couldn't believe how tired she was or how pleasantly relaxed she felt. There was no fever or pain to keep her on edge.

She felt Trey's fingers against her cheek and she opened her eyes to find him staring at her, his face close to her. "You did real good, honey," he whispered and bent, placing his lips against hers.

Alana tried to follow him as he drew away, but the softness of the pillows were just too alluring. She lay back and placed her hand over his. As she'd done before, he entwined their fingers and smiled at her.

She frowned. "Trey, shouldn't we be leaving now?"

He shook his head. Usually she didn't mind his quietness, but now she wished she didn't have to drag all information from him like it was precious and should be hoarded.

"What if my father tracks us here?"

"Then he does."

Alana's frown deepened. "No, they'll take you back to Temeron." Her fingers tightened reflexively. "We need to go."

"You're still too sick, Allie. Besides we have no money, no provisions, and exactly how do you think you could walk?" He nodded at her bound leg.

He tried to make his words light, but she caught the hint of desperation beneath them.

"We could hitch a ride."

He shook his head.

She stared at him, a strange worry crawling through her. "Trey, if my father finds us..."

"Listen, honey. I think we have a little time. It'll be difficult to follow that weaving trail we made, especially yesterday's. Give us a few days – for you to heal and me to make some money." He took her other hand and held them both. "The Greysons have offered me a job here. Room, board, your medical expenses, and a little cash. We need all of that right now, so please don't argue with me."

"But what if my father shows up?"

"Then I'll try to slip away, and if I can't, well, I'll give up without a fight and maybe they'll take me back to Temeron alive. And there we can try to prove my innocence. Your father believed me once, maybe if he sees I never meant you to get hurt, he'll listen again."

She tightened her grip. "I'm scared, Trey."

He eased closer to her and sat at her side, folding one arm over her shoulders. She shifted just enough to place her head on his shoulder, curling one arm around his waist.

"Don't be scared, sprite. I promise you'll be well and on your way home before you know it."

"I'm not thinking about myself. I'm afraid for you."

"I'll be fine as soon as I see you eating more and see that leg back to its normal size."

She eased her hand up to the buttons on his shirt and fingered one. "The Greysons offered you a job. They've been very generous. Aren't they suspicious about where we came from?"

"They were suspicious, but I did some pretty good lying. I will say I was worried when you woke up last night and heard them calling you my wife."

She gave a laugh. "Did you think I'd deny it?"

"Of course I did."

Alana closed her eyes and allowed her body to sink into his warmth. He felt so good, so strong and alive. "What else would you tell them, my *husband*?" she said. "It's probably the best course of action until we reach Denortosal."

He made a noise in his throat and Alana didn't question it. No matter what he might be thinking, she knew she'd be with him when he went on to Denortosal. She'd made him that promise and suddenly it seemed very important that she carry it out.

"Trey?"

"Hmmm."

"Do you have to go to work today?"

"No, they gave me the day to rest and spend time with you. What would you like to do? Have a foot race?"

"No," said Alana, snuggling deeper against him. "I was thinking more along the lines of sword fighting."

"Or there's always dancing."

"'fraid not. I never learned how." She yawned.

"Well, Madame Eldralin, we'll have to work on that won't we."

"Just like your reading, Mister Almsden."

"Yep, just like my reading." He lifted a hand and ran it down her hair. "There's a lot we could do together, Allie. If only…"

She opened her eyes, a feeling of apprehension assailing her. "A lot we will do together, Trey. It's a long road to Denortosal, especially with a lame partner."

She felt the slight pressure of his lips on the top of her head. "A perfect, beautiful, amazing partner," he whispered and Alana fell asleep with his voice in her ears.

* * *

Zeran knelt, staring at the dried blood stains in the sand beside the hastily covered remains of a fire. A few feet away lay the decapitated body of a snake, but he'd taken one look at it and turned away. Somehow he knew the snake and his daughter were connected – just as he knew the blood in this spot was hers. He'd been sitting here so long, staring at her blood, that he'd nearly forgotten anyone else was with him. Until Tyrane's hand came down firm on his shoulder.

He glanced up at his foster brother and back to the blood. He reached out and touched the area around it. "It's hers, Ty."

Tyrane exhaled and tightened his hold on Zeran's shoulder. "Come away, Zeran. I need to talk with you."

Zeran nodded, but he didn't move. Lifting a hand, he ran his fingers through his hair and closed his eyes. Where was she? Was she calling for him? Could she? Anguish tightened his throat, making it difficult to breathe.

"Zeran, come away."

Opening his eyes once more, Zeran engraved the sight of her blood on his memory. Trey Almsden was a dead man. When he was found, Zeran wanted to be the one to end him.

He pushed himself wearily to his feet and faced his foster-brother. He saw concern and sympathy in Tyrane's eyes. Tyrane had always been close to Zeran's children, treating them like his own. Especially Allie. He'd tolerated all her questions and curiosities and her less than feminine ways.

He curled a hand around Zeran's arm and led him from the sight of the blood. Zeran looked once over his shoulder, but Ty's pull was insistent. Temerian warriors were swarming over the area, looking for any clues they could find. Zeran gave them an absent nod as he followed Tyrane to the hasty camp they'd set an hour ago.

Roe Manes was waiting for them with the tracker, Folen Tesseran. Tesseran had a hand curled around the necklace hanging in the middle of his chest. Zeran's heart sank. Roe and Tesseran had led a few other warriors on ahead, looking for tracks to indicate where Almsden had taken Alana. Their quick return didn't bode well.

Zeran drew himself to his full, formidable height and controlled his expression. "You've returned quickly. Are you sure your men have covered all the necessary ground?"

Roe glanced at Tesseran and then fixed his eyes on his leader. "We scoured the ground in every direction for at least a mile or more, Stravad Leader." He rested a hand on the hilt of his sword. "If there were any tracks, the winds have blown them away."

"Do you mean to tell me there's no trace? I found my daughter's blood just over there." He glared at the tracker. "Captain Petric assured me you were the best tracker in Temeron."

"And I am. I haven't given up. I'll find something."

Zeran took a step closer to the two men. "My daughter's bleeding."

Roe's gaze shifted to Tyrane. Tyrane placed both hands on Zeran's shoulders, pushing him back. "You found someone's blood, Zeran, in a sheltered location. He chose it for a campsite for that very reason. He wouldn't travel, though, where he might leave any traces."

"I won't believe they just disappeared. There aren't that many places he could have gone!"

As soon as the words left his mouth, Zeran knew they were foolish. He didn't have to look around to know there were mountains just behind him, not to mention the entire Protectorate of Denortosal a few days walk in each of the three remaining directions. Almsden could hide in the landscape until he made it to one of the larger cities in this area. Then he could disappear in truth.

Frustration and fear made him shrug off Tyrane's hold. "Go back out and search all night if you have to. Take every man we have and…"

"Zeran."

He ignored his brother and continued to shout orders at Roe. "…spread them out over the area. Cover it in mincing steps if you have to, but find something, damn it!" He pointed at the tracker. "Do your job!"

"Zeran!" Tyrane's voice rose above his own.

Zeran's eyes shifted to him, daring him to intervene. "Go!" he shouted at Roe without looking at him, his glare fixed on his brother.

"Stay!" commanded Tyrane in the same manner.

Zeran's eyes widened in astonishment. "Are you contradicting me?"

"Right now, I am."

"I'm Stravad Leader."

"No, Zeran," said Tyrane, placing his hands on Zeran's shoulders again. "Right now, you're just a father who's afraid."

The fight went out of Zeran and his shoulders slumped. He ran a shaken hand through his hair. "That's her blood, Ty. I feel it." The pain in his chest made his voice tremble.

Tyrane's hands flexed on Zeran's shoulders and he drew a deep breath. "It might be her blood, Zeran, but that doesn't change the fact that beyond this point there are no more tracks for us to follow."

"What do we do? Give up. What if she's hurt out there?"

"She might be and we're trying to get to her, but chasing after shadows won't help her." He looked over his shoulder at the men. "Roe has a decent idea, Zeran, the only one we've got. You need to listen to what he says and try to keep your fear for Allie out of it."

Zeran studied the young man standing behind his brother. "Speak freely."

Roe shifted from one foot to the other, then cleared his throat. "I believe the blood's Alana's, but I think it's related to the snake we found." At Zeran's frown, he paused to gather his thoughts. "I think she must have been bitten. Most people know how poisonous sand snakes are and he would have tried to extract the poison, which would explain the blood."

"Why does Allie have to be the one bitten?"

"Because if it were Almsden, she would have escaped him while he was in the throes of the sickness," offered Tyrane logically.

Roe nodded. "Since we can't find any trace of them, it seems logical that he carried Alana from this location in search of help."

"Go on."

Roe rubbed at his temples. He obviously didn't want to relate the rest of his assumption, but Zeran was too impatient to wait.

"Go on!"

"A bite from a sand snake to someone Alana's size would make her very ill, Stravad Leader. She'd need attention quickly. No matter what sort of a man he is, Almsden isn't stupid. He would recognize that. Therefore, he'd make for the closest location."

"Anatem," said Zeran.

Roe nodded. "Anatem's closest and large enough to have a physician."

"If he's headed in that direction, I'll find tracks," said Tesseran.

"What if Allie wasn't bitten?"

"There aren't any tracks to follow, Zeran. What choice do we have?" said Tyrane.

Zeran studied his brother, but he wasn't seeing him. His mind was tripping over all the possibilities. Each one led him to the same thing. Anatem.

"Round up the men and tell them to break camp. We've a few hours more light. When we make camp, we'll meet again. We'll have to approach this situation carefully. I don't want to take the chance of Almsden getting away because we blundered into the midst of a Human town. Let's make sure we have a sound plan."

Zeran felt Tyrane's eyes on him. He turned his attention back to his brother. "What?"

Tyrane drew a deep breath and exhaled. "You worry me, Zeran. Do you realize what might happen if Roe's right about this?"

"Right about Allie being bitten?"

Tyrane nodded.

"Get to the point, Ty."

"Allie isn't a large woman, Zeran. You and I have both seen men three times her size brought down by a sand snake."

"What's your point? That he might not get her to help in time?"

"Or that he might not care."

The color drained from Zeran's face. He couldn't answer his brother's question. He couldn't let himself believe that anything would happen to his child. He turned his back on his brother and started walking toward his horse. "We better plan this thing carefully," he muttered grimly, "because I want Almsden dead."

CHAPTER 10

Jonik Myar, the aging butler, stepped into the kitchen, his hands clasped behind his back. Mai looked up from kneading the dough for rolls, blowing loose strands of hair from her face. Jonik mainly left the kitchen as Mai's domain, but with her father gone and her mother sequestered in her room painting, Mai was the only one left to run the household.

Selia had been spending as much time with their mother as she could, trying to coax her out of her room, or to coax her into putting down the paintbrush, but as the days slipped by with no word about Alana, Alix pulled more and more into herself.

"Jonik," Mai said, brushing at the stray hair with her forearm.

"Master Aronsen is here to see you."

"I can announce myself," said the old man, caning his way into the kitchen. "I don't need you doing it for me."

Mai grabbed a towel and wiped the flour from her hands, then she draped another towel over the dough on the counter, going to her grandfather and kissing his cheek. "That's all, Jonik," she told the butler.

He executed a short bow and walked out of the room. Elyon caned over and sank down at the table, his joints creaking. Mai poured them both a cup of tea from the teapot warming on the stove and carried it over to him, then retrieved the honey from the pantry and set that down in front of him. He took the honey and poured a generous amount into his cup.

Mai watched him in amusement, curling her fingers over her own cup. "How are you, Grandfather?"

"Any word from your father?"

"A messenger came last night. They believe Almsden's headed for Anatem to disappear in a larger population, but they have a tracker, Folen Tesseran, who is supposedly the best tracker in Temeron on their trail."

Elyon lifted a spoon and stirred his tea. "I'd hoped they'd stop them before they got to a large city."

"We all did," said Mai, fighting the rush of worry that spread through her.

"How is your mother?"

Mai shook her head. "Painting. She hardly eats, she hardly sleeps. All she does is paint all day."

"I'll talk with her."

"Selia and I would appreciate it. We're getting worried about her, especially with my father not here."

"How is everything else running?"

Mai shrugged. She wasn't sure what he meant. "All right."

"Are you sure?"

"What do you mean?"

Elyon gave her a piercing stare from his blue eyes. "I hear things. The Nazarien are in turmoil and the Lord of Loden has demanded the new Nazar present himself in Zelan. Your father should be handling this."

"All he can think about is Allie, Granddad. You can't blame him for that."

"And I don't, but you, Mairin, are his oldest offspring. Perhaps you should address the council, demand to know what is being done to compel the Nazar to appear here and pledge his fealty to the Eldralin line."

Mai choked on her tea, blinking her watering eyes at him. "Excuse me."

Elyon gave her a patient smile. "You are made for more than kneading dough, child. You have a good head on your shoulders and Eldralin blood in your veins. You should take more notice of what happens in our world."

She waved that off. "I'm not Alana, Granddad. That was her roll. Alana has always been groomed to take over for our father when the time comes." She shrugged. "That is if she's elected by the people."

"An Eldralin will always rule Temeron as long as there is an Eldralin ready to serve, but as much as I want Alana home again, we have to be realistic. Should she return, she may no longer want to rule in your father's stead. She may have different ideas about her life."

Mai frowned. "Why would you say that? Alana has always wanted leadership of Temeron. Nothing will ever change that."

"Are you sure?"

Mai set down her teacup. "What are you getting at, Granddad?"

He folded his hands together. "I have prophetic dreams. Has your father ever told you that?"

"No, he's never mentioned it."

"Well, I've always had them."

"And?"

"And, Mairin, the Eldralin I see at the head of Temeron's council is not Alana."

Mai felt a shiver race down her spine. She didn't want to hear this. What if the reason for that was because Alana died? She couldn't accept losing her sister. She would never accept it. "Granddad," she began.

He leaned forward and clasped her hand. "Mairin, hear me, child. The Eldralin I saw leading Temeron in the future was you."

Mai sat back, her hands falling into her lap. Nothing had prepared her for this. She didn't want to lead Temeron, she didn't want any part of her father's job. She'd been more than happy to think that Alana would one day rule. And more than all of that, she couldn't accept a world where Alana wasn't in it. She would never accept that.

*　　*　　*

It took Alana four days before the fever was gone and she regained even a measure of her strength. She spent those four days sleeping and eating only what Trey forced upon her. The doctor came to visit and remarked at the rapid rate her leg was healing, but it wasn't quick enough for Alana.

She hated being confined to the tiny room off the kitchen, and she especially hated being confined to her bed. At first her body demanded so much sleep, she didn't have time to get bored, but as she healed, she found herself staring at the ceiling more and more.

When the boredom was too much, she turned to Trey's book. She did lose herself in the adventures of the faery folk, but even that lost some of its appeal when she had no one to discuss it with. At night, Trey came to their room and literally fell onto the bed asleep. He didn't seem to care that his hair was still damp from his bath or that he still wore his trousers. When the light peeked through the window, Alana would crack one eye and watch him roll out of bed and grab his boots before padding silently out of the room.

The only time she saw him when they could exchange a few words was during the noon meal. He'd stand in the doorway, leaning against the jam, his arms crossed over his chest. He wouldn't even come near her, telling her he was too dirty and smelled too bad, but his filthy condition didn't keep him from demanding she eat every bite of her meal with him looking on. She was usually so furious with him that their conversation was stilted, and then at night he was too tired to discuss anything interesting.

At the dawning of the fifth day, Alana woke moments before Trey and stretched her limbs. For the first time she could move her right leg a little without the throbbing pain she'd grown to expect.

Rising up on an elbow, she eased the covers off the leg and lifted the poultice. The swelling was nearly gone, the puncture marks healing nicely. A thin line of scabbing marked the areas that Trey had cut to draw out the poison.

She touched it gently with her fingertips and sucked in a quick breath of pain. Still too tender to touch, but there was no denying it was healing. She lay back on the pillows and stared up at the ceiling beams. She picked out the various shapes she'd found in the wood – the cow, the flower, the girl's twisted profile. With a sigh, she rolled to her side and studied Trey.

He was lying on his side facing her. As he had for the last four nights, he was dressed in a clean pair of trousers that were too short for his long legs and too loose around his middle, borrowed from one of the Greyson brothers. His chest was bare, a bronze expanse of hard muscle padding accentuated in ridges and smooth planes.

One arm lay over Alana's waist. The other was folded beneath him, the hand cradling his cheek. His hair was unbound and tousled, an errant lock falling over his forehead. His lips were slightly parted and he breathed in a steady rhythm. He looked young and vulnerable in his sleep, and Alana's heart did an unexpected somersault.

She could spend hours looking at him just like this.

When he was awake, he was demanding, but she had to admit she liked watching him even then. When he stood in the doorway nagging her to eat, she devoured the very sight of him, dirty and rumpled and weary from a long day doing back-breaking work. She wanted to ease the lines between his brows and relax the muscles in his shoulders, but he seemed to avoid all physical contact with her except in his sleep.

Reaching out a hand, she moved the lock of hair from his forehead, letting her fingers trail over his dark brows. His eyes flashed open and then, as always, he was moving, rolling to his other side and swinging his legs off the bed. Alana knew too well what came next. He'd grab his boots and hurry to the door. It would be the last she'd see of him until noon.

She placed a hand against his bare back to stop him. Every muscle in his body tensed and he looked over his shoulder at her.

"Aren't you going to ask how I'm feeling?"

Dark brows lifted in question.

"Don't you care?"

He shifted on the bed and stared at her. "Of course I care."

"Well, how would I know since you bolt out of here every morning and don't return until late at night?"

"I'm sorry, sprite. The Greysons have had no problem keeping me busy."

"I know," she said, stroking his back with her fingertips. "You're working too hard."

His eyes were soft in the half-light and beneath her caressing fingers she could swear he trembled. He turned suddenly and bent over her, pinning her with an arm on either side of her body. She dropped back on the pillows in surprise and stared up at him. He lowered his mouth until it was a breath from her own.

"So, exactly how are you feeling this morning, sprite?"

Boldly wrapping her arms around his neck, she lifted and claimed his lips with her own. While she'd only experienced a few of his kisses, he was an excellent instructor and she a quick learner. Alana tangled her fingers in his hair and reluctantly let his mouth trail away when he began nuzzling her throat. She dropped her head back.

Without warning, he tore his mouth from her throat and reared to his feet, backing away from the bed, his chest heaving. He stared down at her with blazing emerald eyes.

"Damn it, Allie, you tempt a man beyond reason."

Alana was having a difficult time calming her rampant emotions. "Trey, how can it be wrong?"

He shoved a hand through his tousled dark hair. "How can it be wrong?"

"If we both feel the same way then…"

"Now wait a moment, Alana Eldralin. You know this is wrong."

She was crestfallen. "How is it wrong?"

His eyes widened as he stared at her. "How could it be right? I'm a hunted man. You were my captive just a few days ago. I damn near got you killed. Everything about us is wrong."

Alana could only gape at him. He grabbed his boots and a shirt off a nearby chair before heading for the door. Only when his hand closed on the knob did Alana recover herself. With a cry of rage, she grabbed his pillow and cast it at him, striking him in the back.

He stopped and stood stock still facing the door. Alana sank down in the covers and wrinkled her nose. It hadn't exactly been an adult thing to do, she realized.

He turned slowly and regarded her a moment without expression. Then his eyes went from the pillow to her and back again. "My point exactly," he said and turned again.

Fury colored her words. "I hate you, Trey Almsden!" she shouted and slapped her hands on the bed, but the action jarred her leg and made her grimace in pain. She lay back on her remaining pillows and glared at the door, but she knew she'd been lying. She didn't hate him and that was the entire problem.

* * *

Trey halted on the other side of the door at Alana's shout of fury. All Greyson eyes lifted to him in surprise, then the men's look softened with sympathy. He felt like a fool as he eased away from the door and approached the table, slipping his arms into the shirt.

The three younger women watched him with interest as he covered his bare flesh, but the men had returned to eating. He took his usual seat, shoved his feet into his boots and gave Miss Leev a half-hearted smile. He'd wring Alana's neck later.

"Don't take it to heart," said the older woman. "Every young couple has a few arguments now and again. She's probably getting tired a being locked up in that little room." She lifted the tray she'd prepared for Alana and headed toward the hallway.

"It only gets worse when they're breeding," said Morvan, spooning fried potatoes into his mouth.

Trey stopped in the midst of dishing up his plate. He noted the unhappy looks from the younger women and judiciously redirected his attention.

Bane grunted in agreement. "Maybe that's your wife's problem. Maybe she's breeding."

Trey choked on the mouthful of potatoes he'd taken and the three women were helpful with water, napkins, and pats on the back.

"It ain't so bad after you get use to the idea," muttered Imre around a mouthful of food.

"No, it ain't. You just got to spend more hours away from the house working," added Bane.

Trey cleared his throat. "Allie isn't pregnant."

"Humph!" said Bane.

"Like you'd know," said Morvan.

Imre just shook his head and continued eating. Trey looked to the women for help. They all exchanged glances, blushed, and looked away. Trey was trapped. If only Zeran Eldralin could hear this conversation, he thought grimly. He'd gut him at the breakfast table.

Miss Leev returned to the kitchen and laid her hand on Trey's shoulder. "Bane, I need Trey to help me this afternoon so you better let him off early."

"What you need, Mama? Maybe one of us can help instead."

She shook her head. "Don't think so. If your wives didn't protest, Trey would likely gut you if you were here."

When Trey looked up curiously, she gave him a smile. "Your poor little wife wants a bath and I'm gonna need your assistance."

Trey could only blink at her in horror, but he didn't miss the renewed sounds of eating that echoed around the Greyson table.

*   *   *

Trey stood in the doorway of Miss Leev's kitchen, rubbing an anxious hand over the stubble on his chin. Miss Leev and Moya were sewing before the stove, talking cheerfully and laughing. They both looked up at Trey's appearance.

Miss Leev rose to her feet, balling her sewing up and setting it on the kitchen table. Then she came forward and took firm hold of Trey's arm, pulling him into the kitchen as if she was afraid he'd bolt. Truth to tell, Trey was quite likely to do just that.

He'd worked feverishly since early morning, alone, trying to blend in so no one would remember Miss Leev had commanded his assistance that afternoon. None of the Greyson men had proved his ally this day, however. They'd all remembered his appointment and reminded him of it so emphatically, he'd had little choice but to obey.

He slumped his shoulders miserably and cast his eyes on the older woman, hoping she'd comprehend his pleading look. She left him with Moya and hurried into the small hallway off the kitchen. Moya gave him a smile and rose to her feet, angling toward the stove. It was then Trey noticed the large pot of water heating on the stove, obviously for a bath.

Trey couldn't suppress the groan that escaped him. He figured he deserved this torture after what he'd done to Allie, but even this was straining what a healthy young man could bear. Miss Leev appeared then and motioned him to her. He walked like a man about to face his own execution. She pointed to the door at the end of the hall that led to an enclosed porch.

"We do our bathing back there. There's a tub hanging from the wall. Take it down and position it beside the drain. Imre's invention. He's a clever one, he is."

Trey nodded and swallowed hard. He had a little time left. Maybe if he set up the bath, he could escape back into the field and not have to witness anything. In fact, the more he thought on it, the more logical that notion seemed. There was absolutely no reason why he had to assist Allie in her bath.

He quickened his step and opened the back porch. He moved to the tin tub hanging on the wall and brought it down, placing it where Miss Leev had told him. Standing upright, he gave the small room a critical look. It was enclosed with screen which meant anyone coming around the side of the house would be able to view Allie bathing. The thought gave him a surge of protectiveness.

"Are you going to stand back here all day?" said Miss Leev. She was standing in the doorway, hands on hips.

Trey wheeled to face her. She followed the line of his look and nodded. "I know it seems exposed, but the men are all out working and won't be back till sundown. She'll be perfectly safe."

Not bloody likely thought Trey, but he didn't venture his opinion out loud.

"Come on. You'll need to carry the water. That's why you're here."

He went back to the kitchen, lifted the pot and carried it to the back porch where he poured it into the tub. It filled halfway. Miss Leev and Moya appeared with smaller buckets and handed them to Trey.

"Cold water to moderate the temperature."

Trey nodded and placed one hand in the tub to feel the water as he added the buckets. When the water felt perfect to him, he rose to his feet and faced the two women, his expression hopeful.

"Take the pot and fill it again. She'll need it to rinse her hair," said Miss Leev to her daughter-in-law. Moya did as the older woman commanded. Trey noted that no one balked at Miss Leev's commands, even himself. He wondered at the woman's strange power, but she pointed at him and then pointed to the hall.

Trey gave her a relieved nod and hurried down the passageway back to the kitchen. He heard Miss Leev's rapid footfalls behind him, but didn't consider it until she grasped his coarse work sleeve and pulled him to a halt. Trey looked down at her. She pointed an imperious finger at Alana's door and gave him a dark scowl. Trey blinked stupidly at her, but she only shook her head.

"You're going to have to help her get into the bath. I'll bring you soap, towels, and a clean sleeping gown, but I've got to start the evening meal." A mischievous look entered her dark eyes. "Besides, after this morning you should try to make up with the pretty little thing, cater to her a little."

She moved beyond him and gave him an unfeminine shove in the center of his back. Trey stumbled and caught himself on Allie's door. He looked back at Miss Leev, all hope deserting him now. He was caught. A little more punishment heaped on his crime.

He forced his hand to close around the knob and thrust open the door, peering around it at Allie. She was sitting up in bed, his book open on her lap. Trey felt a moment of guilt. She was much better and had to be getting tired of being locked in the small, dingy room.

"Hi, Allie," he said brightly, only now remembering their argument. It didn't help his predicament. "How are you feeling, honey?"

She gave him an appraising look. "Don't tell me you're really going through with this, Trey Almsden. I didn't think helping me with my bath gave you enough distance."

He stepped into the room and swallowed. If she only knew how tempted he was. "Don't bait me, Allie."

She looked surprised. "Bait you? But Trey, isn't this too intimate? Of course, I guess when you only see me as a child, it doesn't really count."

"I don't see you as a child, Allie, and that's the problem. Do you want a bath or not?" he ground out between his teeth.

"Yes," she said, closing the book.

Trey took it and put it on the nightstand beside them. Then he grasped the covers and pulled them back. He bent, eased an arm beneath her wounded thigh, and lifted her off the bed, yet when her foot touched the floor, she gasped, lost her balance and clutched at him.

Trey caught her, pressing his lips to the top of her head. "Sorry, sprite," he whispered.

"It's all right," she answered, her voice trembling.

He swept her up as gently as he could. "Think we'll forego the walking today, eh?"

She nodded, her face paler than he liked. He kissed her forehead impulsively and carried her from the room, dodging the door jamb. He maneuvered through the tight hall and into the back porch. Someone had placed a chair beside the tub and a steaming bucket of water. He lowered Allie to the chair and fixed an arm on her elbow as he helped her to sit. She eased her leg straight and shifted on the chair with a grimace of discomfort.

"Will you help me with the bindings?" she asked, looking up at him.

Trey ground his teeth, but knelt before her and eased the loose sleeping gown up until her bandaged thigh was bared. Untying her bindings, he unwrapped the leg, studying the wound. The leg was swollen only at the sight of the bite, so much better than it had been just a few days ago.

He lifted his head and looked into her eyes. "It looks good, honey." He rose to his feet and clenched his hands at his sides. "I'll wait outside until you're finished."

He walked to the door and stepped out as Moya came down the hallway with a fresh pot of water. "Can you help her into the tub?" he asked the other woman, relieved to see her.

"Of course," said Moya.

He leaned against the wall and closed his eyes, trying not to think of Allie, trying not to wish things might be different between them. In the last few days, she'd become the most important thing in his life. How could that happen so fast? How could the young woman he'd abducted suddenly become everything he lived for, worked for, wanted?

And the cruel hand of fate, making her believe he was worth her time. An Eldralin? Eldon's bloody star, he was really insane to think he had a right to touch the back of her hand, let alone have thoughts of building a future with her. Him – a man who couldn't read, who didn't know who his father was, who was on the run for murder.

He lost himself in his predicament until the door opened and Moya stuck her head out.

"You'll need to carry her back to bed. She's exhausted now."

He gave Moya a pained look. Being with Allie was torture and it was only becoming more so as the days went by. Still, he walked into the room and found her sitting on the chair in a clean night dress. Moya had even brushed her damp hair, keeping a towel around her shoulders so it didn't soak through.

Allie was breathing hard as she looked up at him and he could see the pain in her eyes. He bent and gathered her in his arms, carrying her back to the room without saying a word. When he got back to the room, he found Miss Leev waiting for them. She'd changed the sheets on the bed and fluffed the pillows at Allie's back as Trey settled her onto the mattress again.

Handing Allie a glass, she urged her to drink. "For the pain, honey," she said.

Allie downed the liquid, then accepted the glass of water Miss Leev passed to her next.

"How did the bath feel?" she asked.

Allie laid her head on the pillow and closed her eyes. "It felt good. I'm just tired."

Miss Leev fussed with the pillows some more, then she picked up the glasses. "You rest while I get supper ready. We'll get you something with a little more substance tonight. What do you say to that?"

Allie opened her eyes and clasped the older woman's hand. "Thank you for everything you've done for me," she said. "I can never repay you."

"Tush," said the woman, patting her hand. "You owe us nothing." She gave Trey a pointed look and left the room.

Trey shifted weight, wanting to bolt, but Allie's face was pale and her lips were drawn back against her teeth in pain. He grabbed the chair in the room and pulled it up beside the bed, sitting down and reaching out to take her hand. She opened her eyes and rolled her head on the pillow, staring at his fingers.

"Don't let me keep you," she grumbled.

He lifted her hand and kissed the back of it. "Come on, Allie. Cut me some slack. I'm trying to be a gentleman here."

She stared at him. "Did I ask you to do that?"

He sighed. "No, but let's be honest, honey. We don't exactly come from the same background, and..." He gave a weary laugh. "What the hell future can you possibly see for us? Your father is eventually going to find us and then, I'm dead."

She studied him and he could see the painkiller was beginning to take effect. "You didn't kill Trista."

"I know, but he's not going to care. I did abduct you. There's no denying that. Then I almost got you killed."

"Stop saying that! I got bit. It wasn't anyone's fault. You saved my life."

"And could that be what you're feeling? Could this attraction you have for me be because I got you to safety?"

She gave him a disappointed look, but he was afraid that was exactly what had happened. She was confused about her feelings because she thought she owed him something. "Tell me something, Trey, and be honest."

He nodded to indicate he'd try.

"Did you love Trista?"

He looked down at her hand, running his thumb across the back of it. "No, Allie, I didn't love her."

"But you slept with her."

"I did."

"You must have felt something."

He thought about that. He and Trista had done some talking about their lives. Trista felt trapped by her father's position, by the demands of being a councilman's daughter. She wanted to pursue her own path, she wanted to travel. He'd encouraged her to do that very thing, but she'd died before she'd gotten the chance. There was something sad about that.

"I made her a medallion out of wood."

"A medallion?" asked Allie, her eyes growing heavy.

Trey smiled, remembering the day he'd given it to her. He'd thought it was a poor gift. She was used to better things, but she'd been delighted with it. He'd strung it on a silver chain he'd bought in the market and she'd worn it whenever he'd been with her.

"It was a flower. I carved it in Master Elefson's shop and I bought a cheap chain. I don't know why I gave it to her, but I just wanted to."

"You cared about her." She eased deeper into the pillows. "Did you like working with Master Elefson?"

"I did. He treated me as an equal. He didn't care who my mother was. I was happy working there."

"I guess Trista didn't care who your mother was either."

"No, she didn't. I didn't want her to tell people about us, but she didn't care." His voice trailed away and he looked into Allie's eyes.

"I don't care either, Trey."

He shook his head miserably. "You're an Eldralin."

"Which means nothing. Why do you think that has any more meaning than anything else?"

"Because it does."

"My mother was an orphan. She doesn't even remember her parents. My father crossed an entire land to find her. Do you think it matters to him? He adores her. He worships her. Why do you think my lineage is more important than yours?"

He lifted her hand to his lips and kissed the back of it. "Because there's no future for me, Allie. I can't see anyway out of this. I can't see anything beyond the moment when your father finally tracks us down and he will. He'll find us." He stared deeply into her heavy eyes. "Can you tell me that you don't want to go home? Can you tell me that you don't want your parents or your sisters?"

She cupped his cheek in her hand, rubbing her thumb over his cheekbone. "I want my parents to stop worrying. I want to see my mother and father, I want to talk to my sisters, but not at the expense of you." Her eyes drifted closed and she didn't respond for a moment.

Trey thought she was asleep, especially when her hand fell away from his face. He placed it under the covers and smoothed them out, then he rose and kissed her forehead.

"I don't want to go home," she whispered, her eyes staying shut, "if it means I'll lose you."

He leaned back and looked at her, but her breathing had evened out and she was clearly asleep. He gave a wry chuckle. Damn it, why did this have to happen to him now? Why did he have to be shown everything he wanted just to have it taken away from him again?

The universe was a cruel child plucking the wings off a fly and he was that fly, damn it all, he was that fly.

.

CHAPTER 11

Alix stared at the sketch in her lap, seeing only the bright cobalt eyes and the impish grin on the little girl's face. She clutched it against her breast and closed her eyes, tears squeezing between her lashes to fall down her cheeks.

"Mama."

She opened her eyes again, letting the sketchpad fall into her lap and wiping at her tears. "Selia, come in, darling," she said, forcing a smile.

Selia crossed the room and knelt before her mother, taking her hands in her own. "Mama, are you all right?"

Alix nodded, keeping the false smile on her face. The need to stay strong for her daughters kept her going everyday without word from Zeran or Alana. Selia looked down at the pad in her mother's lap and then reached for it, holding it in front of her.

"Allie?" she asked, fighting tears of her own.

Alix nodded and blinked, blinded by her own anguish.

"Oh Mama," sobbed Selia, throwing herself in her mother's arms.

Alix stroked her daughter's chestnut brown hair and closed her eyes, enjoying the comfort of holding one of her children if only for a moment. "Shh, now, Sellie. Daddy's going to bring Allie home to us." She held her daughter off and wiped the tears from her face. "He promised me."

Selia nodded, but Alix knew it was only for her mother's benefit. "Mama, Talmar wants to see you. Do you want me to ask him to come back later?"

Alix drew a deep breath and shook her head. "No, send him in. I'll see him now."

Selia rose to her feet, letting her mother's hands go as she turned for the door. Forcing herself to climb out of the armchair, Alix settled the sketch pad on the table beside the chair and smoothed the gown of her skirt with her hands, then patted the loose strands of dark hair back from her temples. She turned when she heard Talmar's steps on the tiles.

He stood in the doorway, looking at her.

"Talmar, how are you?"

He took her hands in both of his and bent to give her a quick kiss on her cheek. "I'm fine. How are you holding up?"

She smiled and nodded, unable to answer him. There was no point in saying how she was feeling. "Won't you sit down? I'll just get us some tea or something to eat. Selia, can you tell Jonik to bring something up."

Selia nodded and left the room.

"I don't want anything to eat, Alix. I need to talk to you."

She frowned at him, uncertain what he had to talk with her about. He spent most of his time with Zeran now as a trusted advisor. He led her to the couch and pulled her down beside him. "You look exhausted," he remarked. "Are you getting any rest?"

"I'm fine," she said and looked away. She knew she looked bad, but she didn't care. Nothing seemed to matter right now. She suddenly wanted her husband so badly she could hardly breathe. Since the birth of Mairin twenty-five years earlier, they'd never been apart. She couldn't sleep without Zeran's warmth, his heart beating close to her ear. Having him and Allie gone were like two enormous holes inside of her.

"What did you need to talk to me about?"

"With Zeran gone, there are some issues that need to be handled." He clasped his hands before him. "I've taken care of as much as I can, but there are just some things that need more attention."

"I don't know what you want me to do. Usually, Tyrane would handle everything in Zeran's absence, but as you know, he's with Zeran."

"That's the problem. This has to be handled by an Eldralin."

Alix frowned. She felt a little fuzzy headed and she wasn't sure she was understanding him completely. "What has to be handled by an Eldralin?"

"The Nazarien have a new Nazar. Falco Leonhart is anxious about the way the new Nazar came by the position and he's demanded he present himself in Zelan. Zeran also sent a demand, but then he left with the tracker before we got an answer."

"Then it'll wait until Zeran gets back."

"I don't think that's a good idea. We got another message from the Lord of Loden. He's concerned this Tarish Enro is ignoring his summons."

"Tarish Enro's the new Nazar?" She didn't know why she was having trouble following this conversation.

"Right."

"And he came by the position how?"

"He killed Karnack Pretorian. Murdered him before the Nazarien Council."

"Eldon's star!" She blinked at Talmar. "What does Falco think Zeran can do?"

"Command the Nazarien," said Talmar. "The Nazarien must answer to an Eldralin."

"But Zeran isn't here."

"I know, which is why I'm bringing the issue to you."

"I'm not an Eldralin, not by blood."

Talmar sighed. "I know." He gave her a piercing look. "Elyon was here yesterday and I spoke with him."

Zeran's foster father? What did he have to do with any of this?

"He suggested that Mairin address the Temerian Council on her father's behalf."

Alix shook her head. A buzzing was in her ears and she really didn't understand what he was saying. "Mairin? Why Mairin?"

"She's the eldest Eldralin daughter."

"Right, but Alana…" She caught herself, a stab of pain lancing through her. Alana had been groomed to take over for her father, not Mairin. The loss was crippling.

Closing her eyes, Alix clutched a hand against her breast. She felt as if she couldn't breathe, as if her heart were being squeezed from her body. She gasped and swayed.

Talmar's frantic voice sounded in her ears, but she couldn't make out the words. Then there was running feet and her daughters' worried voices. She tried to soothe them, but she couldn't speak over the tremendous pounding of her heart or the burning of her lungs as she tried to draw in air. Then everything went black.

* * *

Alana sewed in the kitchen with Miss Leev. It was a bright, warm summer day and Alana was spending more time looking out the windows than working. Another few days had passed and her leg was healing. She'd been up every day, bathing and taking short walks around the yard within immediate view of Miss Leev's kitchen. It felt good to be alive and on the mend again.

Trey had been working himself half dead once more, getting up before daybreak and falling into bed well after dark. She hardly saw him, but got glowing reports of how strong and clever he was. Somehow it just wasn't enough.

As the time passed, a restless anxiety grew within her. She and Trey needed to leave. She didn't doubt her father was looking for them and would soon find them. They had to move location and leave a message for her father that she was travelling willingly with Trey, so that her father would call off the pursuit.

She was also worried about her family. She'd been gone more than a few weeks and they must be frantic. She worried most for her mother. While her father would be out actively hunting them, her mother would feel it necessary to stay home and hold everything together. Her mother had always been the backbone of the family, supporting all of them. Who would support her now?

Alana closed her eyes. She wanted her family so badly sometimes it hurt, but the thought of leaving Trey and never seeing him again hurt just as badly. It was a terrible dilemma and she didn't yet know how to solve it. Every way she looked at the situation someone was bound to get hurt.

Still, she needed to set her family's mind at ease and buy herself more time to explore her feelings for Trey. Trey was now an integral part of her life and she had to make certain he was safe, just as she had to know her family was safe. Somehow there had to be a way for both things to work to everyone's satisfaction. There had to be.

"You okay, love?" said Miss Leev at her side.

Alana opened her eyes and smiled at the older woman. "I'm fine, just thinking."

"About your home?"

"How did you know?"

"The look on your face. It's not easy following your heart, is it, honey?"

"No," said Alana, "not at all." *Especially when you didn't know what was in your heart.* She smiled at the older woman. "I owe you so much that I can never repay."

"Psht," said Miss Leev, waving Alana off. "You ain't owing me nothing. My Bane works your man to death out there."

"Trey's done a lot, but the debt was mine."

Miss Leev shook her head. "Once you marry, child, the debt belongs to both of you. That's for sure."

"I suppose," said Alana and looked out the window again.

"Where you thinking to settle, you and your man?"

Alana looked down and smoothed the skirt of the blue dress Trey had gotten for her. It was a modest, pretty dress, but Alana still couldn't get used to wearing it. "We haven't talked about it much since I got hurt."

Miss Leev nodded. "You know what you aiming to do for a living?"

Alana shook her head. She didn't know what would happen two days from now, but she allowed herself the fantasy of imagining a life, a future with Trey in it. She wanted it more than she could say.

"You ought to have a plan, child. I know when you're young it seems like being together is the most important, but what happens when it isn't just you and your man, what happens when there's another little life depending on you?"

Alana stared into the woman's eyes. How could she tell her there was no chance of a child between her and Trey because Trey didn't touch her, wouldn't touch her. She looked down at her sewing and tried to concentrate. It was too frightening thinking about the future, especially when the present was so volatile.

She concentrated on the pattern for a few moments, then her eyes lifted and she stared out the window again at the warm summer day. Trey and Bane had left that morning to go into Anatem. Alana had been filled with anxiety the entire time. What if Trey was discovered in Anatem; what if her father was there?

She'd given him a letter for her family to post. What if he decided not to post it for some reason? She dismissed that idea. Trey would do as she asked, but what if he decided it was best for him to head out on his own after posting her letter? What if he decided not to return to her?

Alana's heart beat frantically and she rose to her feet, dropping the sewing on the table. She crossed to the window and stared out, fighting the growing panic within her. He wouldn't leave without saying goodbye, would he? Could he leave her and never look back? After what they'd been through together?

"They'll be back before nightfall," said Miss Leev as if she read Alana's thoughts.

Alana couldn't tear her eyes from the yard. "Does it usually take this long?"

"Usually, sometimes longer, if we got a crop to bring to market, but I'll bet they're gathering supplies and heading back right now."

Alana's hands curled into fists. *Please let them be heading back.* She didn't know how she'd continue her life without Trey in it. He'd become so important to her. She realized in that moment that no matter what happened, no matter how much she missed her family, she wanted Trey in her life.

The front door banged shut and Alana whirled, ignoring the stab of pain that radiated up her thigh.

"Mama!" came Bane's voice.

Alana took a step forward, her heart beating. There was something wrong. She could hear it in his voice.

"In here, Bane," said Miss Leev, rising to her feet. She gave Alana an inquisitive look and turned to face her son as he barreled through the door.

He halted on the threshold, his eyes raking over Alana. Alana couldn't breathe, couldn't swallow. Trey wasn't with him and the look on his face told her that something was wrong.

"Get your hat, Mama, we got to go to Anatem now. I'm on my way to gather the others."

"What the devil you talking about, Bane?"

His eyes bore into Alana. "We got a criminal living here on our land, Mama."

Alana's knees nearly gave way, but so much blood pounded through her body, it held her upright.

"What the devil..."

"The Stravad, Mama," said Bane, turning to his mother. "He's a wanted man in Temeron. He killed a girl there and kidnapped the Stravad Leader's daughter." He pointed an accusing finger at

Alana. "She ain't his wife, Mama, and her daddy's in town looking for her."

Alana took a few steps forward, gripping the back of the nearest chair. "Where's Trey?"

"Are you sure, Bane?" asked Miss Leev, glancing at Alana.

"Sure as I can be. I talked to one of the Stravad myself. There's a whole passel of them in town, asking around, passing pictures of her and a drawing of him. It's them, Mama."

"Please," begged Alana, gripping the chair, "where's Trey?"

Miss Leev turned to her. "Is this true, child?"

Alana's eyes were pleading. "Part of it. Trey was accused of murder, but he didn't do it. He never had a chance to prove his innocence. They were going to execute him, so he escaped. He took me with him so he could get away, but he's never done anything to hurt me." She took a step forward, holding out her hand. "Please, you've got to believe me. You've seen how hard he's worked on your land, how good he's been to me and you. You can't believe what you heard."

"Come on, Mama," urged Bane, "we need to get off this land now."

Miss Leev tore her eyes from Alana's anguished face. "Where you want us to go, Bane?"

"Into town until he's caught."

Alana sucked in a ragged breath. Then he hadn't been caught yet. "Where is he?"

"We'll take her with us and return her to her daddy."

"No!" said Alana, drawing their attention. "You can't do this. Please. I need to know where he is, if he's all right."

"Once I heard about him, I left and came home fast as I could. Last I saw, he'd gone down to the post office to take care of some business. But it don't matter anyway, your daddy's been worried sick about you, girl. You got to go back."

"I can't. Not until I know Trey is safe."

"That's ridiculous!" said Bane, dragging a hand through his hair.

Alana limped to Miss Leev and clutched her hands. "Please, help me. I love my family with all my heart. I sent Trey to Anatem today to send a letter to them. It's my fault if he's been caught. I can't go back home until I know he's safe. I can't. Please understand." She swallowed as tears ran down her face. "I love him," she whispered.

Miss Leev patted her hands, then pulled her into her embrace. "It'll be all right, child. It'll be all right."

Alana sank into the older woman's arms and closed her eyes.

"Mama, we got to do what's right."

"Yes, we do. I ain't heard the boy's side of it and I don't intend to leave my land until I do."

"Mama, he could be dangerous. It makes me sick thinking of how often you and the other women have been around him. Who knows what he could have done?"

"He did nothing but work his fingers to the bone for my family. I ain't judging no one until they have a chance to defend themselves. Go on, Bane. Hitch up that rangy stallion only Trey seems able to ride. Figure he's bout worked off the price of it by now and that horse ain't much use to us, since none of you boys can ride him."

"Mama, I won't do it. I'm taking her to town."

"Do as I say. Alana and me will get together some food and some clothing. Also, count out what wages you owe the boy and bring it up to the house. They'll need some travelling cash. Get one of the little ones to help you. We don't have much time."

"No, Mama, this is one time I ain't gonna do it. It's wrong, I tell you."

"You will do it and do it at once, boy. I'm still head of this family."

All conversation ceased. Alana felt the tension ripple through Miss Leev's body and she lifted her head. Trey stood in the doorway, his eyes glued on her. Alana wanted to run to him and throw her arms around his neck, but her legs were suddenly too weak. Instead she stared at him while tears ran down her cheeks.

His green eyes were vulnerable. She knew what thoughts must be raging through his head. He held out a hand. "Allie?"

Alana glanced at Miss Leev and the older woman nodded at her. She stepped away and then she was across the room and in his arms. He folded her against him. She felt the pounding of his heart beneath her cheek and closed her eyes. He was all right and he'd come back for her.

"Go on, Bane," said Miss Leev at their back. "Get that stallion hitched."

Alana didn't know if Bane protested anymore. She only knew she was safe in Trey's arms again.

*   *   *

"What the hell do you mean she's gone?" shouted the handsome Stravad. Bane shrank before his angry glare and Miss Leev couldn't blame her son. The Stravad Leader was a big man, imposing, and about the most handsome man she'd ever seen in her life.

She'd thought Trey too handsome for his own good, but this man was something to behold, even in a rage. She understood his predicament. She saw the pain and worry in his cobalt eyes, eyes exactly like his daughter's.

"Easy, Zeran," said the smaller man beside him, placing a restraining hand on his shoulder.

Miss Leev raised appreciative brows. Lord, but these Stravad were fine specimens of masculine beauty. *Every one of them*, and there were a number of them standing like imposing statues in her front yard. Her own sons looked small and helpless against them.

"I tried to tell her she had to go back, sir, but she wouldn't hear of it," said Bane.

The tall leader raked his long fingers through his black hair and shook his head. "This is ridiculous. I want my daughter!"

Bane flinched again. Miss Leev came down the steps. Enough was enough. She stopped up in front of him and stared into his handsome face.

"Mama, no," said Bane behind her.

"Now listen here, fancy pants. You scared my boys enough for one day. I suggest you come inside and calm yourself. I can tell you all about your daughter and explain things to you, but I won't have my head bitten off. You hear!"

He stared at her with a grim expression. It didn't bother Miss Leev in the least. She wasn't afraid of his darkest look. She knew he'd never lift a hand to harm her or her kin, somehow she just knew.

She placed her hand on his arm and felt the tightly strung muscles in his forearm. "I understand you're a worried father, but I think I can ease your mind a little if you'll come inside."

Some of the steel left his expression and the muscles beneath her hand relaxed. He gave her a short nod and she released him, turning toward the house.

"Bane, see their horses watered and fed. Moya, get the other girls and help me put on a proper meal. They all look about ready to drop from exhaustion." She didn't stop to see if her orders were carried out as she entered the house.

The Stravad Leader turned and spoke in his own language to a number of his men. They turned and moved out, calling orders to the other men on horseback. Miss Leev ignored them. She didn't care what the rest did as long as they didn't harass her family.

She motioned the two men who'd followed her into chairs at the table and went to the stove. She poured out three mugs of strong tea and brought it back to the table, pushing it toward them. "Now," she said as she took a seat, "folks round here call me Miss Leev, but I guess you found that out in town."

The Stravad Leader looked at her with his piercing cobalt eyes, but the other man gave her a brief smile. "Yes, ma'am," he said, glancing at his companion. "My name's Tyrane, ma'am. I'm Zeran's brother and Alana's uncle. We'd appreciate any information you might have on her."

She nodded and looked the two men over, sipping at the hot tea. "Go on, handsome, drink something. You look about done in."

The one called Zeran blinked and looked down at the tea with a heavy sigh. He lifted a hand and pushed it through his mane of black hair before lifting the cup to his lips.

"Now, your little girl was just fine when she rode out of here earlier. She's a fine girl, a pleasure to have around."

Zeran's eyes lifted and fixed on the older woman with a pleading look. "She was really all right? We thought she'd been hurt."

Miss Leev nodded. "She was hurt, badly too. Sand snake bite."

Those beautiful cobalt eyes widened with misery.

"But she recovered. She's a smart little bit, that one. Told the doctor just what to do to save her leg. Good thing too, 'cause he was all for taking it off."

Anguish blazed across Zeran's handsome face. He rose to his feet and paced the length of the kitchen, raking his fingers through his hair again. His brother watched him with worried eyes.

"Eldon's star, what she's been through," muttered Zeran.

"Yes, it's been rough, but she's strong, your little girl. And she's got a good head on her shoulders. Knows just what she wants."

Zeran came back to the table and braced his fisted hands on it, staring down at her. "Why did she leave? Did he force her? Did he threaten you?"

"Don't loom over me, young man!" she said sharply and motioned to his chair. "Sit down now."

A look of surprise crossed his face, but he sank into the chair, clasping his hands in front of him as if to control himself.

Miss Leev leaned forward. "Now here's the funny thing. When he brought her here, none of us gave much hope for her survival. She was unconscious and burning with fever, but we did what we could. The doctor was all prepared to take off that leg when she suddenly comes around, calling for him. He'd told us she was his wife, so no one thought anything about it until now. She never once gave us any reason to think she wasn't with him willingly."

Zeran exchanged an anguished look with his brother.

Miss Leev patted his fists where they lay on the table. "He was good to her, strange as that may seem. He never left her side for a moment and he agonized over everything to do with her. The way they were together, I never would have suspected they weren't married."

"They weren't!" snapped Zeran. "He abducted her!"

"Easy, Zeran," said his brother.

"That's what I hear you say, and it might have been so at first, but it ain't so anymore. Those two are in love with each other and if they aren't married now, it won't be long before they find someone to do the deed for them. They belong together."

"He belongs dead!" snarled Zeran. "He took my daughter and Eldon knows what he's done to her."

Miss Leev gave him a critical stare. "I know it ain't easy for a man to think of his daughter as anything but an innocent child..."

"She is...was an innocent child."

"She's a grown woman in love, young man. I saw them together."

"And I know what that man is capable of doing."

"You know what you were told. That young man worked on this farm from sunup to sundown. He fought to save her life and he came back for her at risk to himself. No matter what you might have been told, he loves her and is willing to give his life for her. I saw that. I know that. And what's more, she loves him. She told me so herself."

"No!" He bolted to his feet and paced the kitchen like a wild thing.

Miss Leev looked to the brother.

Tyrane rose to his feet and moved around the table, halting his brother in mid-stride. "Maybe you should listen, Zeran. She's trying to tell you what she saw. She isn't the enemy."

"I won't believe it."

"If you won't believe it from me, why don't you listen to *her*?"

He stopped pacing and stared down at her. "What?"

"She left you a letter. Trey was posting it today in town when you arrived. I think she said it explained everything to you."

"She left me a letter?"

Miss Leev smiled sadly. "I know how hard this must be, but she told me how dearly she loved you and her family. She missed you terribly, but she said she couldn't leave him. She loved him."

The pain was stark in his face. Miss Leev wished she could offer him something else as comfort, but she had only the truth as she saw it. She rose to her feet and came to stand before him. "I know you're hurting, but you've got to believe me. He was a good boy. He worked hard and he never did anything to hurt her. I saw it."

He took a step back. "Somehow I just can't believe it. It's too crazy. My daughter couldn't fall in love with a man like that, she just couldn't."

He turned without another word and left the kitchen.

His brother drew a deep breath and forced a weary smile. "Thank you for your time, and thank you for everything you did for Allie. If there are any expenses still remaining…"

"None," she said. She held out her hand and he accepted it. "I wish you luck, but I hope he doesn't find what he's after."

Tyrane looked down. "He doesn't have a choice. She's his daughter."

Miss Leev drew a deep breath. "Hard as it is, every man's got to let go sometime. She's not a little girl anymore."

Tyrane nodded. "No, she's not."

*   *   *

Zeran crumpled the note in his fist. Here it was in her own writing, but he still couldn't allow himself to believe it. Alana said she was travelling with him willingly and she begged him to call off the search. Could it be true, could this be the little girl he'd cherished since the moment of her birth? How could she choose a criminal over her family? He put his head down and braced a fist against his forehead. Eldon's star, it couldn't be true. She must have been forced to write the letter. That was the only answer.

How could he call off the search and return home without her? What would he tell Alix? Ah, Alix. Was she all right? How was she holding up through this nightmare, and how did he tell her their daughter had chosen this man over them? It would kill her. He couldn't tell her. He just couldn't.

"Zeran."

He looked up into his brother's face. "How could she do this, Ty?"

Tyrane took a seat before him. "Love makes a person do funny things, Zeran."

Zeran shook his head. "No, I won't believe this is love. I can't. The man is a criminal, a murderer." He closed his eyes and fought the horrible images that came to mind.

"Zeran," said Tyrane, placing his hand on his brother's shoulder. "Remember before this happened, you weren't sure of his guilt. Remember, Zeran. Something inside told you that maybe things weren't what they seemed."

"Yes, before he kidnapped my daughter."

"Zeran, I know this is hard, but…" He paused and looked at the letter clutched in Zeran's fist. "Perhaps you should listen to her words with your head and not your heart. If he were keeping her by force, why would she write? Why would he have her write? And why would he risk capture to post the letter for her?" He sighed and leaned back. "Even more disturbing, why didn't she tell those people at sometime during her recovery that she was being held against her will? There were many times when she was alone with them, when he was working in the field. And if he is the man you think he is, why did he work so hard for them? Zeran, they gave him a horse and money, they helped them escape. It doesn't all add up."

Zeran bowed his head. "I know, but what can I do now?"

Tyrane drew a deep breath and clasped his hands together. "I think we should go home. I think you should let Alana make her own decision now. You belong in Temeron with your people and your wife."

Zeran opened his mouth to reply, but a knock sounded at their hotel room door. "Come."

Roe Manes and Folen Tesseran stepped inside. Roe folded his arms behind his back, giving Zeran an anxious look.

"Stravad Leader?"

Zeran nodded at him.

"Tesseran found their trail. It looks to be headed for Taral."

Zeran and Tyrane exchanged a look.

"I can't go home, Ty. Not until I see her, talk with her face to face."

"And if you succeed at capturing him?"

Zeran's eyes grew hard. "He returns to Temeron to await a second trial and sentencing."

Tyrane sighed and looked at the ground. After a moment, he lifted his eyes and pinned Zeran with a piercing look. "If you capture him and take him back, they'll execute him, Zeran."

"Maybe."

Tyrane shook his head. "If she's in love with him, you'll lose her forever. You understand that, don't you?"

Zeran forced the doubt down. "I have to do this. I just can't believe she's in love with him. This is too unlike my Allie."

Tyrane pushed himself to his feet. "Maybe," he said, a note of anger in his voice, "but you ought to remember what you did for love. It was even crazier."

With that, he pushed between Roe and the tracker and walked out the door.

Zeran stared down at the table and watched his hand close into a fist. He'd crossed two lands, one torn by war, to follow his dream of a chestnut-haired beauty. It had seemed perfectly sane at the time, at least to him. His life with Alix had started out rocky, but it had been the most important, most wonderful risk he'd ever taken. He sighed. He'd travel around the world again for his wife; he'd die for her. Could it really be the same for Allie? Could it?

He lifted his eyes to the young men waiting by the door. For some strange reason he found himself telling Roe to have the horses saddled and ready to depart at daybreak instead of immediately. He wasn't sure he understood his own motive, but he was too damn tired to question it anymore.

He waited until the door closed behind the men, then rose to his feet and went to the bed. He lay down on his back and folded one arm over his eyes, the other hand still clenched around Allie's letter. Before he could think anymore, he was asleep.

CHAPTER 12

Alana pushed back her blankets and sat up. By the light of the fire, she could see Trey's profile. A flutter of motion at his eyes told her he was still awake. Grabbing one of the blankets, she slung it over her shoulders and picked her way over to him.

He eased up on one elbow and stared at her in the darkness. "What, Allie?"

She sank down on her knees, grimacing at the pain in her thigh. It had been a more difficult day than she'd thought it would be. Her thigh hurt her, but worse was the rejection she felt from Trey. He'd spoken little to her and tonight, he'd deliberately set up their beds apart from each other. After sleeping beside him for so many weeks, Alana couldn't fall asleep alone.

She sensed he was angry at her, but she couldn't imagine what she'd done to anger him. She'd turned her back on her father and gone with him without hesitation. It hurt inside thinking about her father. How much she wanted to see him, talk to him, have him hold her for a moment, but she'd thrown that all away for a man who now turned away from her.

"Why are you angry with me, Trey?"

He blinked at her and his green eyes softened. "I'm not angry with you, Allie. I'm furious with myself."

"Why?"

He turned away, looking into the fire. "We need to sleep. We have to get up early tomorrow and spend the day riding."

She reached out and rested her hand against his cheek. "Don't shut me out, Trey. Talk to me."

He looked at her, holding her hand against him. "Just leave me alone tonight, Allie, please. Go to sleep."

Tears threatened in her eyes as she drew her hand away. "I can't."

"Why not?"

"I'm used to sleeping beside you."

He closed his eyes and groaned. "Not tonight, Allie."

The tears slipped down her cheeks. She wiped at them and moved to rise. His hand on her arm stopped her. Pulling aside his blankets, he motioned her in beside him. She curled into the warmth of his body and laid her head on his shoulder. He sank his fingers in her hair and stroked her scalp. She felt his breath against the top of her head as he placed a kiss there.

"Damn it all, Allie, I never should have come back to the farm for you. It was selfish of me. Damn selfish. I knew you'd come with me. I knew you'd keep your word."

She pressed her face against his throat and breathed deeply. "I'm glad you came back for me. I would have felt so betrayed if you hadn't."

"I've been using you since this whole thing started and you've gotten the raw end of the deal. I can't understand why you don't hate me."

"Because I can't," she whispered. Telling him she loved him was on the tip of her tongue, but she just couldn't. Not yet. Not while he was beating himself up this way.

"I would have understood if you refused. I wouldn't have held you to our deal."

She wrapped her arms around his waist. "It has nothing to do with that deal, Trey. I would have come with you even without the deal. I want to be with you."

He slid his hands down and wrapped them tightly around her. "We shouldn't be lying like this together. It's too hard. I want you too much."

She lifted her head and looked him in the eyes. "Trey, it doesn't have to be this difficult. I want you too."

He shook his head. "No, it's not right. I'm not right for you. I don't have a future, Allie."

She laid her head on his chest again and exhaled. She didn't know what she had to do to convince him she wanted him and him alone, but this obviously wasn't the time to make that known. He was already swamped in self-loathing and nothing she was going to say tonight was going to change that.

* * *

Since Alana had never seen Anatem, she was surprised by Taral. They arrived in late afternoon two days later. The days they'd spent on the trail had been difficult ones, fraught with tension.

Many people were stirring about Taral at this hour and a number eyed them with curiosity. This made Trey nervous. It wasn't difficult to miss two people riding on one horse, two Stravad no less, but Alana's interest was also hard to ignore.

She stared at the people and the businesses going by on either side of them. When they passed a noisy brothel, Alana's mouth actually dropped open. Trey would have laughed if he wasn't so anxious. They shouldn't have entered the town, but he didn't know what else to do. He wanted to get Alana a good, hot meal and a real bed to sleep in, not to mention a bath. He never wanted to make Alana suffer again, but he had already.

He turned the tired horse down less busy streets, winding through the heart of the town, his eyes marking and missing nothing as they passed. He saw no signs that Zeran had gotten ahead of them, but that didn't mean he wasn't moments behind.

Trey wanted to find an inconspicuous boarding house or hotel to rent a room. Tonight he intended to have an intent discussion with Alana about the future. Tomorrow, he would be on his way to Denortosal. In his mind, he told himself Alana would not be accompanying him, but his heart pounded frantically at the thought of being separated from her.

He deliberately edged to the outside of the town. Taral had grown over the years, sprawling out with little planning. Gaming houses and brothels stood next door to respectable businesses. If the people in Taral thought it strange or inappropriate, it didn't show on their faces. Young mothers guided their impressionable children past drunks on the street. Whores hung from the arms of well dressed business men. Trey missed none of it. By Alana's stunned expression, she wasn't missing anything either.

He caught sight of a small house set back from the street between a bar and a jewelry store. A sign on the front gate proclaimed it *Thesa's Boarding House*. The yard was clean, the porch neat, and the house itself well maintained. Trey brought the stallion to the gate and swung down, lifting his hands to Alana.

She slid to the ground, staring up at the little house, smoothing her skirt down around her legs. Trey smiled to himself.

He knew how much his Allie hated the dress, but he liked the way it looked on her, soft and feminine.

He tied the stallion to the wrought iron fencing and opened the gate, motioning Alana before him. She limped into the yard and headed toward the few stairs to the porch. As they reached them, the door opened and a heavy set woman stepped out. She was middle aged and grim faced, but her apron and dress were clean, as was her tightly pulled back hair.

"Yes?"

Trey placed a hand on Alana's waist. "We were wondering if you had two rooms available for tonight."

Alana glanced up at him, her brow furrowing.

The woman raked them with her dark eyes. "You're Stravad."

"Yes, ma'am. We just got into town and we need a place to stay for the night."

She folded her arms across her ample bosom. "You married?"

Before Trey could respond, Alana piped up. "Yes, we are, recently." She said and surprised Trey with a blush on her bronze cheeks.

Trey glared at her, then looked up at the woman, prepared to refute the claim. He and Alana didn't need to continue masquerading as husband and wife.

"Ma'am, we need two rooms," he stated emphatically. Alana shot him a glare, but he waggled his dark brows at her.

"Two? What *are* you talking about?" The woman was straight forward. "I knew Stravad were uppity, but I never guessed how much. Two rooms, lord be, they need a parlor and a bedroom for a night, do they? Well, I don't have two rooms available. I got one and it's small, so if that don't suit you, you just go on back out my gate and find some place more acceptable."

Alana smiled prettily. "Ma'am, whatever you have will be absolutely perfect."

Trey opened his mouth to protest, but she moved away from him and limped up the stairs toward the woman without looking back. At that moment Trey knew he was in deep trouble. Alana had won. Either she was more intelligent than he was or simply more devious. The latter was most likely, he decided, glaring at her as she disappeared inside the house. Definitely more devious – a hell of a lot more.

*   *   *

Trey was in a fine rage as he climbed the interminable stairs to the attic of the little house. It wasn't nearly as charming inside as it had seemed outside. The rooms and hallways were tight and narrow, the ceiling hanging threateningly over his head. And it was filled with people.

He'd had to press himself against the walls innumerable times to let one of the shorter, more portly patrons pass him. They'd all been friendly about it, but Trey was in anything but a friendly mood. In fact, he'd been making mental pictures of how he was going to turn Miss Alana Eldralin over his knee and paddle her enticing little bottom the moment he saw her again. That is, if he didn't get wedged in the hallway before he'd climbed enough stairs.

He'd left Alana here more than an hour before. The landlady had a stable in the back, which was convenient, but Trey had taken his time grooming the horse, trying to quiet his temper and find an appropriate way to tell Alana he was going to spend the night with the horse rather than her. It didn't make matters any better when the woman had told him Alana had ordered dinner for two in their room that night. The dour woman had seemed much more amiable upon his return, telling him how much she enjoyed having newlyweds in her boarding house. Trey had only growled his response. Yes, Alana was definitely ripe for a sound whipping.

He finally reached the door to her room. He knocked and stepped back, crossing his arms over his chest. He plastered the sternest look on his face that he could muster, but it was difficult to maintain a forbidding posture when one had to stoop over so as not to strike one's head on the ceiling.

Alana opened the door a moment later, her face bursting into a bright grin. She stepped back and motioned him inside. Trey had to duck further to escape knocking his head on the doorjamb. It only increased his temper.

He turned on her as she shut the door and glared. Her hair was loose and damp, and she'd tied a robe about her slight form. Trey drew a deep breath. She'd bathed while he fumed in the stable.

"You are in a lot of trouble, young woman!" he snapped, shaking a finger at her. "There is absolutely no reason for us to continue parading around as husband and wife. Furthermore, I have no intention of sharing this room with you. It's time you and I have a very serious talk."

He expected many things from Alana at any time, but silence wasn't one of them. She stood before him, barefoot and beautiful, staring up at him with her pixie face and her enormous cobalt eyes.

"I'm not kidding you, sprite. I'm furious."

"I know," she said calmly.

"Good, because we're going to talk whether you like it or not. We can't go on this way."

"Oh, I agree."

"Fine, then you should also agree that things have to change between us. We can't keep pretending to be married, sleeping together, without something happening between us."

"You're absolutely correct, Trey."

Trey closed his mouth and stared at her. This wasn't going the way he'd rehearsed it in the stable. Warnings sounded within him. She was being too agreeable, too amiable.

Before he could gather his wits about him, she moved forward to stand directly in front of him. She raised her hands and laid them on his chest. Trey's heart thumped in answer.

"Allie?"

"You're right about everything, Trey. I don't want to pretend any more." She slid her hands up his chest and curved her arms around his neck, pulling him down to her. For some reason, Trey lost all command of his muscles, allowing her to draw him close. "Let's end the game now."

"No, Allie. You know that's not what I meant."

She raised herself on tiptoes and breathed against his lips. "I belong to you, Trey," she whispered, "from the moment you kidnapped me from my father's house."

"Allie?" he groaned, but he knew it was a losing battle he fought. "You don't mean that."

Her lips curved in a beautiful smile. "I do mean it. And I suspect, you belong to me, Trey. A man doesn't do what you've done for me if he doesn't care for that person deeply." She brushed her lips against his. "I love you, Trey."

Trey pulled back, staring into her eyes. He couldn't believe what she'd just said. It was his most cherished dream, his impossible longing, but he saw only truth in her eyes.

"Allie?"

"I love you," she repeated.

He sank his hands in her damp hair and held her against him. "Don't play with me."

She smiled again. "I'm not."

"I mean it, Allie. Don't say that unless it's true."

"I love you, Trey Almsden. My future is irrevocably linked with yours."

"Allie," he whispered against her lips. "I didn't hope for this. I didn't expect it. I knew I was reaching way above me."

She gave him a tilt of her head. "And?"

He huffed out a laugh. "I love you, Alana Eldralin. More than the air I breathe." He was humbled by the longing and love he saw in her eyes. It didn't matter to her that he wasn't good enough. That he was a bastard with no future. She loved him.

Then she stepped away from him and held out her hand. Trey was lost. He moved toward her as if he couldn't resist the pull, wrapping his arms around her and lifting her off her feet. She laughed as they tumbled onto the bed together, but he silenced it with his mouth.

"I love you, Allie," he whispered, then he proceeded to show her just how much.

∗   ∗   ∗

Alana came awake to the knock at the door. She opened her eyes and stretched. The room was dark, but the high, small windows of the attic allowed the light from the lanterns on the street to spill through. She watched Trey move into a sitting position, running his fingers through his hair and rubbing at his eyes. He swung his legs to the floor and reached for his trousers, pulling them up.

He walked to the door, shirtless and barefoot. Alana smiled as he ducked the low ceiling to reach the knob. Love for him filled her. He was so strong and handsome. If she could only put a little more weight on his frame.

He opened the door and spoke quietly to the person on the other side. Alana pulled the covers higher about her as he opened the door wider. He muttered something more, shut the door with his foot and turned, a tray in hand.

Alana lifted to a sitting position and reached for the lodegem lighter beside the bed. She struck it and applied it to the wick on the lamp. Light flared and brightened the room, but she turned the lamp down and made room on the table for the tray.

Trey sat down beside her. "Hey."

"Hey," she said, tucking the sheets under her arms.

"Hungry?" he asked, reaching out to brush the hair from her shoulder.

She smiled at him and ran her fingers over the hard ridge of muscles in his chest. "A little," she said, lifting her eyes to his handsome face.

He bent forward and kissed her gently, then turned to the tray and lifted the lid from the plate. He fingered the bottle of wine and smiled at her. "This was a nice touch. Did you request it?"

She shook her head. "Miss Thesa said she liked newlyweds."

His expression sobered and his eyes narrowed. "We need to talk, Allie."

She placed her fingers against his lips, stopping him. A feeling of anxiety fluttered in her stomach. She didn't want to hear what he'd say. Not now. "Please, give me tonight. We'll talk tomorrow."

He drew a deep breath, but his expression was still troubled. He reached for the wine and poured a single glass, handing it to her. She sipped it and smiled.

"It's good." And it was. She'd never liked wine before, but the sensation of the warm, spicy liquid was pleasant as it ran down her throat and into her stomach.

His eyes darkened to glittering emeralds and he brought his lips to hers. "It is," he whispered. "I love you, sprite. I don't deserve you, but now that this has happened, I can't let you go."

She smiled. "Then don't. Why can't you accept I love you too?"

"I want us to marry tomorrow," he said softly.

She frowned. "What?" Stravad marriages were simple. They vowed to honor, love and protect each other in the privacy of their own homes and then they consummated that union. Once that was done, they were married in the eyes of Temerian law.

"I want us to make it official. I want us to be married by Human law."

"How? Why?"

"At first light, I'll find a preacher. Say you'll marry me, Allie."

"Of course, I'll marry you, but why does it have to be by Human law?"

His expression clouded. "I can't go back to Temeron. I can never go back to Temeron."

She brushed a strand of hair off his forehead. "You don't know that, Trey. We just have to prove you innocent."

He shook his head. "I know it, Allie. Your father will never let me return. Not now. Not after what's happened between us. The only way to keep you with me, the only way to make sure he can't tear us apart, is if you marry me in the eyes of the Humans."

Her frowned deepened. "That doesn't solve the problem of him taking you back to Temeron. We still have to prove you innocent."

"But it protects you, sprite."

"What are you talking about?"

"What do you think people in Temeron are going to say when you return?"

"I don't care."

"But I do. They're going to think you gave yourself to me to save your life. They're going to treat you like they treated my mother, but if we're married…"

It suddenly made sense to Alana. He was afraid everyone would gossip, would assume she had been used by Trey after all this time in his presence. They would never believe she loved him, chose to be with him, but if they were married, people wouldn't necessarily approve, but they wouldn't call her a whore. Trey couldn't stand the thought they'd lump her in with his mother.

Her fingers trailed down to his chin and she urged him to her. "I'll marry you whatever way you want me to."

Some of the worry eased from his expression.

"But I won't go back to Temeron without you. I will never go back unless you're beside me as my husband."

"You may not have a choice, Allie."

"That's not true. We just have to get away. I've been thinking about it and I think going to Denortosal is a mistake. My father will expect us to go there."

"Why do you think that?"

"It's a big city and doesn't always play by the same rules as the rest of the protectorates. He'll reason we think we can get lost in there."

He sighed and she felt the tension in his shoulders. "Where should we go then?"

"We need to think it through. We can't make a hasty decision."

"What about your parents and your sisters?"

She forced down the pang of longing when he mentioned them. "If they want me in their lives, they'll have to accept you. There's just no other way."

"They're never going to accept me, Allie. Never."

She stared into his green eyes – this man had stolen her from everything she loved, everything she knew, but he'd replaced her old life with something just as important. She'd never lacked for love growing up, but he had. She was all he had in the world. He gave her life a new meaning, a meaning it hadn't had before him. She loved him. She couldn't pretend any other way, and she couldn't pretend she could go back to the way things were. She'd never be happy, she'd never be satisfied with a life that didn't have him in it.

"Then you'll be the only family I need, Trey," she said, leaning forward to press her lips to his.

CHAPTER 13

"Just address their concerns. Don't offer any other information than what we have. Keep it simple," said Talmar, his hands on Mairin's shoulders.

She nodded, but she felt like she was going to be sick. This was supposed to be Alana's calling, not hers. She wasn't the one trained for diplomacy. She wasn't the one trained to lead in her father's stead, but with her mother sick, she had no choice. Selia gave her a nod of encouragement.

"Remember," said Talmar. "You're an Eldralin."

She was an Eldralin. Her eyes shifted to the statue of Talar Eldralin as a babe. It had occupied the central spot outside the Council Chambers for decades. Studying it, she forced herself to remember she was a member of one of the most important families in Loden, on Samar for that matter. She could do this. She sucked in a breath and held it, then slowly released it, rubbing her palms against her skirt.

"Are you ready?" asked Talmar.

"I'm ready," she said.

Talmar backed up a step and pushed open the double doors. The Council Chamber opened before Mairin, a massive hall with vaulted ceilings, marble tiled floors, and a semicircle of seats spread out before her. Council members occupied the seats with the exception of the largest chair in the center, the chair reserved for the Stravad Leader.

Selia moved up beside her as Mairin stepped toward the door. Once she got moving, it was easier to cross the echoing chamber, feeling the eyes of the Council lock on her. Talmar fell in behind her, matching pace with her sister as they came to a stop in the center of the room. Mairin's eyes swept over the assembly, pausing on Canto Lamer, Trista's father. He narrowed his gaze on her, his upper lip twitching. Seeing Trista's father made Mairin hesitate.

"You can do it, Mai," whispered Selia at her back.

Mairin straightened her shoulders and lifted her chin. She was Zeran Eldralin's oldest daughter. She could do this. "Council, I am

Mairin Eldralin, eldest daughter of the Stravad Leader Zeran Eldralin. I've come to address you in my father's stead."

A few council members exchanged glances, then a woman seated to the left of her father's chair leaned forward. She had long silver white hair and Stravad blue eyes ringed with thick dark lashes. It was always difficult to tell the ages of Stravad, but this woman moved with a grace that suggested she was in the prime of her life.

"I am Rania Adren, child. Welcome to the Council of Elders."

Mairin inclined her head, pressing her fist to her breast. The rest of the council did the same in return.

"Have you news of your father, Mairin Eldralin?" said Rania.

"We received a message two days ago. He tracked my sister and the fugitive, Trey Almsden, to Anatem, but he hadn't yet captured them."

Canto shifted in his chair, but he didn't speak.

"That is unfortunate, Mairin," said Rania. "There are matters before the council that need to be decided. Have you been chosen to assume the interim role of Stravad Leader?"

Mairin shot a panicked look at Talmar. He gave her a slight nod.

"I do not seek to assume my father's role. Rather, I've been informed you have concerns regarding the leadership of the Nazarien."

"We do have such concerns as does the Lord of Loden, Falco Leonhart. He has ordered the Nazar to present himself in Zelan, but the Nazar declines the invitation. This is an intolerable situation," said Rania, steepling her hands.

"And you want my father to summon the Nazarien through the Eldralin bond," she said, sweeping them all with her eyes.

"Exactly," said Rania. "The new Nazar must not be allowed to think he operates without oversight. He must pledge his fealty to the Eldralin line like all Nazars before him."

"What if the Council of Elders summons him in the name of the Eldralins?"

A smile touched Rania's lips. "You are a clever young woman, Mairin Eldralin, but this would not work. It must be an Eldralin who summons him. It must be an Eldralin who meets him in Zelan and forces him to swear fealty."

Mairin glanced at her two companions. Talmar chewed on his inner lip, but Selia drew a deep breath. "You have no choice. We don't know when Father will return. You're the oldest Eldralin after him. It has to be you."

Mairin didn't want this. She didn't want the leadership of Temeron. That had not been her role. She was more than happy to let Allie take it. Allie liked the intrigue, the machinations, the politics. Mairin hated it. The last female ruler of Temeron had been Tyla Eldralin and Mairin had no illusions about herself. Tyla had been a woman of uncommon power. Besides intuitively knowing what spices to use in her cooking, Mairin had believed all Stravad gifts had passed her by.

"You can do this," whispered Selia. "For Father, for Allie."

"I must make it clear to you, Mairin Eldralin," said Rania, "the dangers inherent in a rogue Nazarien. If Tarish Enro is not brought to heel, he could challenge the very foundation of our people. We have known peace with the Human protectorates in Loden for millennia. Tarish Enro cannot be allowed to thwart our will. He cannot be allowed to utilize the Nazarien in a fashion other than what Eldon himself envisioned."

Mairin wasn't sure she understood the entirety of this threat. The Nazarien operated in Nevaisser. They crossed into Loden only rarely. For the most part, they already operated outside her father's control.

"Please explain," she asked.

Rania shared a look with her fellow councilmembers as they shifted uncomfortably.

"Explain it to her," said Canto, his voice edged with contempt.

Rania focused her attention on Mairin again. Mairin felt a chill snake down her spine at the councilwoman's steady appraisal. In fact, she wondered if Rania was trying to probe her thoughts, gain some inside information about Mairin's true intentions.

"Nevaisser is a land of strife and warfare. Stravad are persecuted and hunted. The Human kingdoms round up unaffiliated Stravad and force them onto guarded tracts of land. Our people are not allowed to roam free. The Nazarien have been left untouched because they remain apart from the Human world in Chernow and

Tirsbor, but the resources of those lands are limited. The Nazarien are dying."

Mairin curled her arms around herself as another shiver raced over her.

"Karnack Pretorian was an isolationist. He did not challenge the rights of the Nazarien to expand beyond their limitations. In this, Tarish Enro is right. The Nazarien could no longer stay in isolation, but if he does not come to heel, if he believes his right as a Nazar subsumes his calling to protect the Eldralin line, he may decide to bring the Nazarien to Loden." Her voice trailed away and her eyes blazed. "He may decide to declare war to annex our land for his use."

Mairin felt the blood drain from her face. This is what Falco Leonhart feared as well.

"Now, Mairin Eldralin, daughter of Stravad Leader Zeran Eldralin, do you understand our concern?"

"I do."

Rania nodded. "And Mairin Eldralin, daughter of the Stravad Leader Zeran Eldralin, do you promise to act in your father's stead, to protect Temeron and her people?"

Mairin drew a deep breath and held it. She locked eyes with Rania Adren. "I do," she said.

*   *   *

Alana stood in her shift, her feet bare, her arms hugged tight around her body. Trey was bathing himself in the basin, combing back his sable hair, and tying it with a strip of leather. She shuddered, but not from cold, and leaned against the door to their room as if she could prevent him from leaving.

Dawn was a pale pink glow in the narrow window of the attic room. For some reason, they'd both come awake at the same time, their limbs tangled together. Immediately Trey had left the intimacy of their bed and began dressing. Alana had tried to lay still, but a terrible urgency had come on her, forcing her to rise and pace the room as he dressed.

He looked up into the mirror and met her anxious look. "I'll only be gone a little while. See if Miss Thesa has something pretty for you to wear for our wedding; although, I don't suppose anything she has will fit you." His eyes glittered like emeralds as his gaze raked her body.

"Don't go." She hated the way her voice sounded so small and frightened.

His brows lowered. "I have to, Allie. You promised me we'd marry this morning."

"It doesn't have to be this morning. It can wait."

His look turned fierce and he spun around abruptly. Alana backed against the door as he stalked her. His hands closed around her shoulders. "It can't wait."

"Why not?" she demanded. She didn't know why she was so afraid for him to leave her this morning, but the sensation was almost paralyzing in its intensity.

"Did it occur to you, sprite, that we might have started a baby last night?"

She made the mistake of shrugging. "We might have."

The expression on his face was so fierce that Alana experienced a moment of worry. "I won't have my child branded a *bastard*."

He spat the word out with such hatred and pain. Alana flinched and tears welled in her eyes. Eldon's star, would she ever get past the layers and layers of rejection he'd lived with all his life? She reached up and cupped his face in her hands.

"Trey, our child would never be a bastard. We are married where it counts most."

His eyes still glittered dangerously.

"It won't be the same for our child as it was for you, love," she said softly. "Our child will have two parents who adore him and adore each other. He'll never be alone, he'll never be ridiculed, and he'll never feel like he isn't worthy. I swear this to you. I swear it."

His eyes softened, but he still shook his head. "It isn't enough. It just isn't enough for me. I need a stupid piece of paper that tells me you are mine. I need that, sprite. Please. Please."

She smoothed back the hair at his temples, loving him. The fear was still there, stronger now, but she knew she had to let him go, she had to let him do what was so important to him. He would never feel married to her if he couldn't hold a piece of paper in his hands proclaiming it for the rest of the world. Loving him meant letting him walk away from her this morning, even though every instinct was screaming it was a mistake.

"I'll be back before you know I'm gone." There was such pleading in his eyes, such need for her acceptance. She nodded and fought the frantic panic that threatened to engulf her. Then she made the hardest move of her life and released him, stepping back.

He nodded at her and gave her a brilliant smile. Alana's heart slammed against her ribs. He turned away from her and hurried to the bed, slipping his arms into his shirt and shrugging it over his shoulders. He came back to the door and bent, capturing her mouth with his.

Alana clutched him, kissing him with such urgency they were both gasping when he broke away.

He ran his thumb over her lips and smiled. "Save that for later, sprite."

Alana wrapped her arms around herself and trembled.

He gave her another smile and moved around her, opening the door. "Get a little more sleep," he said.

She forced a tremulous smile and nodded. He frowned for a moment, then came back into the room and gave her another hard, passionate kiss. The tears filled her eyes as he pulled away. He frowned again and narrowed his eyes.

"I'll be back, Allie," he said firmly. "I swear it."

She nodded, but didn't trust herself to speak. He went to the door, but paused on the other side and glanced back at her a final time before pulling it closed.

Alana flinched at the soft sound of the latch catching. Closing her eyes, she forced herself to breathe deeply. Finally regaining control, she hurried and dressed in the dress he'd brought for her, then sat on the bed, preparing herself to wait. She knew he would need her in a little while, she just knew it.

*   *   *

Trey's steps were light as he went down the boardwalks of Taral. He forced the sight of Alana trembling in the middle of their room from his mind. She was just acting superstitious. He concentrated instead on the thought that soon she would be his in the eyes of the law. Then no one or nothing could come between them. She would be his.

Even though he was lost in thoughts of their future, he noted the flurry of motion across the street, the flash of forest green. His steps faltered and he turned toward the motion. A swath of green bolted around a building corner and disappeared from sight.

Trey drew a deep breath and felt every muscle in his body draw taut. He swallowed and glanced around the street, noting the position of each building, the number of people around him. His eyes passed and returned to a familiar pinto mare tied to a hitching post in front of the constable's office. Zeran's horse.

His mind whirled. He knew he should go back to Alana, but he couldn't. He just couldn't. She might be carrying his child even now and he would not, could not have it be born a bastard no matter what she said. If he were careful, he'd be able to get around them before they found him. If he were very, very careful.

He began walking again, trying not to draw attention. His eyes scanned the street, searching for Stravad faces. He couldn't get caught. Not now. He just couldn't get caught now. Turning the corner of the next street, he angled away from the constable's office. If he could get through the back streets, he might be able to keep out of the Stravads' way.

The thought hit him with force. Alana had somehow known her father was in Taral this morning. It was why she'd been so afraid to let him go. The knowledge of her insight stunned him. Had she also known more, sensed more? Did she know he was going to get caught today? Fear pounded in his throat. He couldn't get caught. Not now. Not when there was so much to live for. Not when he had a chance to redeem himself, make something of himself. Eldon please, not now.

Turning another corner, he came up short, his hands clenching into fists at his side. His vision narrowed on the three green clad men coming to a surprised halt before him on the busy street. Roe Manes was in the center and their eyes locked on one another.

Trey swallowed and took a step back.

Three bows came to bear against him. Trey halted and stared into Roe's eyes. Would he order them to shoot on so busy a street?

Would he order them to shoot no matter what? Trey's jaw hardened. It was a chance he had to take – for Allie.

He took another step back.

"Don't, Almsden!" said Roe fiercely.

Trey shook his head and took another step back.

"Don't make me shoot you, Trey!" He sounded worried about it.

"I'm sorry, Roe," he said and bolted.

A blaze of red hot pain seared his shoulder from behind. Trey stumbled and almost lost his footing, but the vision of Alana fueled him. He clutched a hand to his shirt front and ran on. Another bolt of pain caught him low on the back and this time he couldn't keep his feet. He watched as the ground came up to meet him, jarring his body.

He lay gasping, fighting for breath. He felt the presence of the three guardsmen as they knelt around him, then a gentle hand touched his back.

"Damn it, Trey, why did you make us shoot you?"

Trey laughed and felt a trickle of blood run from his mouth. "Sorry again, Roe," he said in a weak voice.

The hand was still there against his back, strangely comforting. "I didn't want it to be like this, Almsden. I mean it."

"I forgive you," said Trey, then he lost consciousness.

*   *   *

Zeran paced like a wild animal in the little office. Tyrane watched him, sitting on the edge of the constable's desk. The constable watched him, sitting in the chair behind the desk. He felt their eyes on him, but he didn't care if he acted like a lunatic. Alana was here somewhere and he had to find her. He had to see her and know she was all right. He just couldn't turn away and accept that she'd made such a stupid choice – that she'd chosen an outlaw over her family. He couldn't believe it…he wouldn't.

And then he saw him, carried between Roe Manes and Folen Tesseran. Blood spread across the front of Trey's shirt, but Zeran saw only the man who'd stolen his daughter's innocence. He yanked the door open and started outside, blind to anything but the burning fury raging inside of him. Tyrane and the constable scrambled to their feet, trying to catch him, but he was already out the door and into the street before they could stop him.

Valmir Petric stepped in front of his men and blocked Zeran with his own body. "He needs a healer!"

Zeran shoved against the captain. "Get out of my way!"

The constable moved to the captain's side, making the barrier solid against Zeran. "He's in my jurisdiction now."

Zeran gaped at the man. What the hell was he talking about? He hadn't said a word about claiming jurisdiction before this. "Get out of my way!"

Tyrane wrapped his arms around Zeran from behind. "Get control over yourself!" he shouted in Zeran's ear. Zeran threw him off and turned, glaring at him.

"He has my daughter!"

Tyrane caught Zeran behind the neck, dragging him forward. "Calm yourself before you bring this entire town down around our heads. Your damn eyes are glowing, Zeran!"

Zeran tried to take a deep breath. Power zigged in his fingertips and he knew he was close to losing control. Losing control here would be bad. Too many innocent people could get hurt.

"Look at him!" shouted Tyrane, spinning Zeran around to look at the fugitive. "He's bleeding to death. If you don't get a healer in here and quickly, you'll never find Alana."

"Bring him into the cell," said the constable, taking over.

Roe shot Zeran a look as he and Tesseran carried Trey's limp body into the building. Zeran watched after them noting the splatters of blood that dogged their steps. They'd shot him twice in the back. Glancing around the street, Zeran saw the many townspeople looking on with horrified expressions.

A moment later, the constable sent his own men out to disperse them, while one of his guards went to fetch a healer. Zeran curled his hands into fists and started for the jail cell. He saw Roe standing in the hallway outside the cell, talking to Tyrane. Rage spiraled to the front again and Zeran closed on them, shoving Roe back against the wall with his forearm across his throat.

"Why did you shoot him! I told you to take him alive!" he shouted in the younger man's face.

Roe's eyes grew wide and he tried to pry Zeran's arm away. Both Tyrane and Petric tugged on Zeran's shoulders, trying to pull him away, but he was too strong for them. Roe's eyes rolled up in his head and his fingers scrabbled against Zeran's arm before the two men were able to yank Zeran back.

Bending over and choking, Roe fought to regain his breath. Zeran paced away from him, raking his hands through his hair. He had to calm himself or he was going to bring the jail down around their ears.

"Are you okay?" asked Tyrane, bracing the younger man's shoulder.

Roe nodded, still rubbing his throat.

"Did you have to shoot him to get him to stop?"

Roe shook his head, unable to speak.

The tracker stepped out of the cell. "I shot him. I thought we were told to bring him in dead or alive."

Zeran whirled on the man, but Tyrane threw himself in front of Zeran to stop him. "Don't!"

"You shot him?" Zeran's voice thrummed with power.

"He was trying to run. He wasn't stopping." Tesseran shrugged. "You told me to track him, you told me to find him. You told me to stop him. I did that." He reached up and curled his hand around the wooden medallion hanging from his neck. "I did what you ordered me to do.

Zeran surged forward, but Tyrane and Petric shoved him back. "You took away any chance I have of finding my daughter! Now I don't know where he's keeping her!"

"She gave you a letter telling you she was traveling with him willingly!" said Tesseran.

Zeran shoved between Tyrane and Petric, slamming his fist into the tracker's mouth. He went down, his head smacking against the cot. Tyrane threw himself at Zeran, straddling the tracker to save him further harm.

"How do you know he didn't force her to write it!" Zeran raged at him.

"Zeran!" Tyrane shoved him backward. "Damn it, man, get a hold of yourself!"

Zeran paced out of the cell, walking to the end of the hallway and back again. The beams groaned overhead and Zeran caught all eyes watching them warily. He pointed at his brother, his hand trembling.

"Don't let him die, Ty! Promise me you won't let him die!"

Tyrane held up his empty hands. "I promise. Go outside." He shot a look upward as plaster rained down on him. "Please go outside and calm down."

Zeran fixed his gaze on the still form in the cell, then he drew a breath and exhaled, turning to storm out of the jail. The constable scuttled back as he shoved past him for the door. Zeran made it to the street, coming up short as the healer followed the constable's guard into the building. The man gave Zeran a wary look as he sidled around him.

Zeran clenched his fists and released them, looking up at the sun shining overhead. Where was his daughter? Where was his Allie? If Almsden died, Zeran might never find her. What if he hadn't even brought her into Taral? What if he'd left her bound and gagged somewhere that Zeran couldn't find until it was too late?

The energy leached out of him and he sank down on the boardwalk, clutching the rail. He couldn't stand the thought of Allie alone and afraid, calling for him. The child he'd held in his arms, the babe he'd sang songs to as she drifted to sleep. He couldn't lose her.

An insidious thought plagued him, a niggling doubt at the back of his mind. She'd left him a letter telling him she was traveling with this man willingly. She'd begged him to understand. How could he understand? How could he accept his daughter might actually be telling him the truth, that she might actually have feelings for a man who'd stolen her from her family? Who'd ripped her away from her home? He couldn't believe it.

He wouldn't believe it.

CHAPTER 14

Elyon opened the door to the tower built into the Temerian wall. He motioned Mairin and Talmar into it. Mairin approached with trepidation. She'd seen this tower her entire life. It stood to the right of the main gates, looming over the city like a watchful eye. She'd believed the Temerian warriors kept a watch on the roads into and out of the city from here. Apparently that was only one of its purposes.

She hooked her hand under Elyon's arm, helping him up the long, winding staircase. He gripped the railing with his other hand. Smiling at her, he paused for a moment. "Don't look so worried, child. You have every right to take this action."

She gave him a tense smile. "I hope you're right. I just wish my father or Uncle Ty were here to look it over."

He patted the back of her hand and began climbing again. "Talmar has seen it. So have I. Even Councilwoman Adren has approved."

"But this is summoning the Nazarien, Grandfather. This is something even my father hasn't done until now."

"True, but the Nazarien answer to the Eldralins, child. Do not forget that."

She hadn't. As she and Selia had poured over the letter last night, Selia had reminded her of this fact time and time again. Not for the first time did Mairin wonder if Selia wouldn't have been a better choice. Still, when she'd visited her mother in her bed this morning, she'd clasped Mairin's hands and told her how proud she was of her. It had banished a little of the doubt.

Talmar hurried up ahead of them, taking the stairs two at a time. Mairin could hear voices and a strange cooing noise the closer they came to the top. The tower had been made of stones, stacked on top of each other, the staircase spiraling around it forged from iron. At regular intervals in the walls, open embrasures allowed natural light to spill into the tower, and above these were iron sconces glowing with pale yellow lodestones.

By the time they reached the top, Elyon was breathing heavily. He leaned on the railing and motioned for her to go on without him. Mairin hesitated, but her attention was torn. The entire upper level of the tower was open, great windows without glass that overlooked both the countryside and Temeron in a vast circle. The roof of the tower was made of thatch and Mairin glanced up, wondering how anyone climbed to such heights to replace it.

A few Temerian guards stood at the embrasures, holding glasses to their eyes that enhanced their vision, but in the center of the room was a massive cage filled with small brown birds, the source of the cooing she'd heard earlier.

Mairin had heard of the trill cote, but she'd never seen it for herself. She knew her father received messages from the outlying lands by an avian delivery system, but the full implication of it had been lost on her. She immediately saw how ingenious the method was. A bird could cover a great deal more ground through air than a person on horseback, and far quicker.

Talmar approached, leading a stooped old man with white hair and rheumy blue eyes. "This is Dalgo Tereagan, Mairin. He's the keeper of the cote."

The old man held out his hand and Mairin placed her hand in his. His fingers were soft as butter and trembled in her grasp. "Pleasure to meet you, lady."

"Pleasure to meet you, sir," she said, smiling.

She caught sight of a young boy with a blond mop of hair peeking around the back of the cage. "And who is that?"

The old man peered over his shoulder, then gave a laugh. "My grandson, lady. He's learning the trade. Come here, Pip, you silly boy."

The young boy skidded over to them, clasping his hands behind his back. His blue eyes twinkled with mischief. "Howdy do, ma'am," he said.

Mairin laughed. "Howdy do, Pip," she answered.

The boy blushed and ducked his head, kicking at the rough stones of the tower floor.

"We need to send a missive to Chernow, Dalgo," said Elyon, moving up beside Mairin.

"I've just the bird." He held out a hand. "Do you have the missive, lady?"

Mairin shared a look with Talmar, feeling her stomach knot. What if her father was displeased by the missive? What if he felt she'd gone too far?

"Give it to him, child," said Elyon. "This is your right as an Eldralin."

Mairin removed the small roll of paper with the tiny falcon seal on it from her belt. She held it out to Dalgo. The old man took it and turned, placing a hand on the boy's head.

"Get the Westerlin," he ordered.

The boy ran over to the cage and slipped inside. As he entered, the birds fluttered from branch to branch, their coos changing to a high pitched trilling. Elyon grimaced and Talmar covered his ears. Dalgo turned to her, a wry look on his face.

"This is how they get their names!" he shouted above the cacophony.

Mairin nodded, wishing they would stop announcing themselves so. She glanced at the guards and noticed their hunched shoulders. They were used to this racket, but it was still unpleasant. A moment later, Pip emerged, holding a small grey bird in both hands, his thumbs stroking across the back of it.

"Is that the Westerlin?" Mairin asked.

Pip transferred the bird into Dalgo's hands and the old man began affixing the message to a special clasp on the bird's left leg. "This is the Westerlin," said Dalgo. "One of three. Born and bred in Chernow. They have a strong homing instinct. Once we release him, nothing short of death will keep him from returning home."

Mairin nodded, although she couldn't understand how an animal with such a small brain would be able to remember how to fly hundreds of miles home, but she wasn't going to be skeptical with these men standing around. She'd talk to Selia about it tonight in the privacy of their own rooms.

Once Dalgo handed the bird back to Pip, they all walked to the edge of the tower. Mairin rose on her tiptoes to look over. A touch of vertigo swept through her and she drew a deep breath. Pip climbed up on a step-stool and held the bird over the drop in both hands.

"Remember to throw him out and away from the tower," Dalgo said.

Pip nodded his shaggy blond head, then he surprised Mairin by drawing the bird back to his chest and pressing his lips to the top of its head. He murmured something softly to it, then he held his arms out again, waited a moment, and tossed.

Mairin caught her breath as the bird dropped, but the moment it opened its wings, it caught an updraft and shot away from the tower, becoming but a speck in the sky. Mairin laughed with delight, looking over at the boy.

Pip gave a proud nod of his head.

"What did you tell him?" she asked.

"Safe journey," he said, hopping off the stool.

Dalgo beamed with pride as he ruffled the boy's head. "He'll be a good keeper of the cote, won't he, lady?"

She smiled at the boy. "Yes, he will," she said, glancing over her shoulder to check the progress of the Westerlin, but the bird was gone. And so was her message.

*   *   *

Alana waited until mid-morning, pacing the attic room in the boarding house. Trey should have returned by now and a feeling of dread was twisting in her belly. She kept the door to the room open, hoping to hear the moment he entered the building. A few people came and went, clomping up and down the stairs, but not Trey. Each time she heard footfalls, she ran to the door and peered down, only to be disappointed.

She knew something was wrong. She'd known something was going to happen even before he left today. She should have tried harder to stop him. She should never have let him go. Her heart started hammering and a tingle of energy in her fingertips had her curling her hands into fists.

A loud male voice sounded from the bottom of the stairs, talking excitedly. She recognized Miss Thesa's voice answering him. She crept to the door again and peered out. She could see a man in a knit cap, talking to the landlady, his expression intense.

"I saw it myself. He was all bloody, Thesa. I tell you, you don't know what you brought in here."

Alana felt bile rise in her throat, but she choked it down. Throwing open the door, she rushed down the stairs.

"…not that I could tell. All I saw was them carrying him off…" His voice trailed away when Alana stopped in front of him.

He was human, tall, with dark eyes and a hooked nose. His eyes rounded as they raked over Alana's features. Miss Thesa turned, her expression falling.

"Oh, sweet girl," she said.

Alana shoved between her and the man, staring up at him. "What happened?"

The man opened his mouth, his eyes shifting between the two women.

Miss Thesa clasped her hands before her and lowered her head. "Tell her," she said.

"I saw them catch your man in town."

"Who? Who caught him?"

"Stravad. They were wearing uniforms. Temerian guard."

Alana felt the blood drain from her face. "Where did they take him?"

The man held out his empty hands. "I don't know. They shot him and he was bleeding."

Alana swayed and Miss Thesa caught her arm, bracing her. "Easy, child."

Alana turned and clasped the woman's hands. "Where would they take him? Do you have any idea?"

"The constable?" suggested Miss Thesa, her eyes lifting to the man.

"Yeah, even Stravad would have to check in with him before they could claim a prisoner."

"Will you show me?" Alana begged him.

He took a step back. "I don't think I should get involved."

"Cassidy Jonas! If you want to stay with me another night, you'll show this poor girl where they took her man. You hear me!"

Cassidy ducked his head. "Yes'm," he said, stepping back and opening the door.

Alana squeezed Miss Thesa's hands, even though her heart was pounding so hard she was afraid they could both hear it. Then she raced out the door. If anything happened to Trey, she didn't know what she was going to do.

* * *

The healer came through the door leading to the cells, wiping his hands on a towel. The constable looked up from his desk as Zeran turned to face him. The healer gave Zeran a cold look, then glanced over at the constable.

"He'll live. I removed the arrows. One was blocked by his shoulder blade, so it didn't penetrate as far as it might have and the other was stopped by his pelvic bone." He motioned to a spot just below his left hip. "I cleaned him up, gave him a sedative, and sewed the wounds closed." He stepped forward and placed a vial on the desk. "Give him a few drops of this every two hours in a glass of water for pain. I'll come by tomorrow to clean the wounds again."

The constable picked up the vial and closed it in his hand. "Thanks, Hunt, 'preciate it." He stroked a hand over his white moustache. "You'll be around if he takes a turn for the worse, right?"

"I'll be around, but he needs rest now. And a meal. The boy's thin as a reed." He shot a venomous look at Zeran.

Zeran didn't know what he expected him to do about it. He hadn't suggested Trey abduct his daughter. "When will he wake?"

"When he does," said the healer.

Zeran's lip twitched. He wanted to know where his daughter was. That's all that mattered. With another glare, the healer clutched his bag and lowered his head, moving toward the door. Before he got there, the door slammed open on its own, striking the wall, the glass shattering.

The constable surged to his feet. "What the hell!"

Zeran whirled around and both Tyrane and Petric bounded up, their hands on their weapons. Alana stalked into the room, stealing the breath from Zeran. Her dark hair was loose around her shoulders, her features were thinner but unmistakable from her turned up nose to her full lips. But her eyes...

Zeran could feel the power radiating off her. Her eyes glowed with it. He'd never felt such power from any of his daughters.

"Alana!" He started toward her, but she waved her hand and a wooden box holding papers on the constable's desk sailed in front of him, smashing into the wall on the opposite side. Tyrane and Petric danced back, while both the constable and the healer ducked.

Zeran didn't move. He couldn't believe he was seeing what he was seeing.

"Where is Trey!" she said in a low voice.

"Alana." He moved forward a step, a rush of emotion sweeping through him. She was here, she was alive. That's all that matter.

Tyrane put a hand out and stopped him. "Easy, Zeran!"

Alana's eyes never left her father's face. "Tell me where he is!"

"Alana, he's a crim…"

Her eyes rose to the doorway behind him and narrowed. The door slammed open, crashing into the wall. Zeran could hear scrambling feet as Roe Manes and Folen Tesseran ran out. A pitcher on the corner of the constable's desk sailed past Zeran's head and smashed into the wall, sending Roe and Tesseran scrambling for cover.

"Alana!" Zeran shouted, but the windows fronting the street suddenly exploded outward, showering the boardwalk. People on the street screamed. The constable cowered under his desk and both Tyrane and the captain hit the deck.

Alana's chest heaved and her hands were in fists. The glow in her eyes told Zeran she'd lost control and she couldn't figure out how to regain it. He had to get her to calm down. He took another step toward her, but a chair sailed across the room and slammed into his legs, forcing him to buckle.

Overhead the beams groaned and plaster rained down.

"She's going to bring the ceiling down on us!" shouted Tyrane.

Zeran knew he could blast her with his own power, but he couldn't chance hurting her. Not his daughter. He had to get her to calm down on his own. He shoved the chair away, prepared to rush her, but a voice cut through the mayhem.

"Alana!"

She blinked and took a step back. Zeran could feel the violent pulsation of her power ebb the tiniest amount. Glancing over his shoulder, he saw Trey clinging to the doorframe, his eyes fixed on Alana. She made a mewling noise and he staggered toward her. The healer had dressed him in a clean homespun shirt that hung past his waist. He put a hand on his lower back and took another step closer to her.

Zeran could still feel the energy emanating from his daughter and he knew it was a killing force. "She'll snap your neck. She doesn't know you. The power has taken her over."

"She knows me," Trey said, his jaw clenched in pain, sweat beading on his forehead. "Allie, look at me, sprite!"

She vibrated with energy and her eyes glowed eerily, even with the sunlight streaming through the broken windows. Zeran wasn't sure she recognized anyone at this moment. He knew what she was feeling, how easy it was to lose control when every cell hummed with power. He'd been here himself many times and he'd been trained extensively. How had he missed this much raw power in his own daughter?

"Allie, I'm here," said Trey, using the constable's desk to ease closer to her. He shook with pain and weakness. Zeran wasn't sure he could survive a blast from Alana at this close range. "Honey, you've got to get control."

Zeran felt himself bristle at the familiar endearment, but he never took his eyes off his daughter as the other man approached her. Overhead the beams groaned again. Trey shot a look up, then eased closer still.

"Honey, this place can't take much more. Pull back, Allie. Ramp down, honey."

She shivered violently and her hands curled into fists.

"That's it. Ease off."

Zeran felt the energy drop and her eyes dimmed.

"Come on, sprite. I know you can do it."

She bit her upper lip, her teeth chattering. Zeran could see her pupils finally. Trey stopped in front of her, holding out his empty hand. She started to reach for him, but hesitated. He nodded at her.

"It's okay, sprite. I'm here. I'm here with you."

She stepped forward and pressed her face to the hollow of his throat, her hands curling into fists in his shirt. He wrapped his arm around her, the other braced on the desk. Zeran felt the energy dissipate and everyone climbed to their feet.

As he watched the two of them, Allie sobbed into Trey's neck and he whispered in her ear, the intimacy of their greeting tearing him apart. He wanted to yank Trey away. He wanted to pummel him, but he could only watch as Roe Manes brought Trey a chair and helped him ease down into it.

* * *

Alana stepped away from Trey, cupping his cheek in her hand. "I begged you not to leave."

He gave her a weary smile. His skin was grey and perspiration dotted his forehead and upper lip. "You were right. I'll listen from now on." Sitting in the chair, he leaned on the constable's desk, his back hunched. He wasn't able to put weight on his left side.

Her gaze shot up to her father, watching her from a few steps away, then she looked around the room at the destruction she'd caused. She hadn't meant to do that, but everything had gotten away from her. Her uncle sported a cut on his cheek and Captain Petric was pulling a shard of glass from his arm. A man with a healer's bag eyed her warily from behind the constable's desk.

Roe moved up behind Trey. "He needs to lay down, Alana," he said.

She glared at him, but Trey took her hand.

"It's okay, sprite. He's right. I feel like I got hit by lightning."

"I'll stand guard," Roe said. "You have my word."

Alana nodded, watching as Roe put a hand under Trey's arm and helped him to his feet again. She moved to follow as Roe guided him toward the cells in back, but her father stepped in front of her, holding up his hand.

"Allie, wait."

Trey hesitated, looking over his shoulder.

Alana stopped, stiffening, her gaze rising to her father's face. She was so conflicted. She wanted to launch herself into his arms, she'd missed him so much, but he'd ordered Trey shot and she couldn't forgive that.

"Take him to rest, Roe. I'll be there in a moment," she called to the guard, then her eyes shifted back to her father, but she didn't move.

"Allie, I thought you were dead," Zeran said, his voice anguished. "I thought I'd never see you again." He moved closer, but she backed away, holding up her hand to stop him. "Allie, please."

"I gave you a letter."

"I couldn't believe it. I couldn't believe what you said in it."

"Why?" she hissed. Glass danced on the floor at the sudden burst of power that escaped her.

The constable ducked, his moustache quivering. "Just calm down, child. There isn't much of my building left as it is."

She didn't spare him a moment of her attention. She could see Roe and Trey disappear into a cell and she wanted to go after them.

"Allie, listen to me."

"No!" she said, slashing her hand. The rafters groaned and Zeran glanced up warily. "You never listen! You never hear me!"

Zeran held up his hands. "I'm listening now, Allie. I'm hearing you." He took a step closer to her. "I know you're confused and scared."

"I'm not either of those things."

Zeran looked around at the destruction. "Allie, this is all new. It has to be. You've never shown this ability before."

She glanced around herself and she had to admit he was right. She'd had no control over what happened here, not until Trey had gotten through to her.

"I can help you. I can teach you to control it. The way I was taught, the way Elyon trained me."

She met his gaze, anguish rising inside of her. She wanted to relent. She wanted to sink into his arms, but he'd ordered Trey shot. He'd nearly killed the man she loved.

"I promise you, Allie. I can help."

"You ordered them to shoot him."

Zeran briefly closed his eyes. "He was trying to run, Allie. I had to know where you were."

"You had him shot."

"I did. I would have done anything to find you. You can't blame me for that, Allie. You're my daughter. I did what any father would have done."

She gave him a disbelieving look.

He acknowledged her point. "I did what I felt I had to do as your father and as Stravad Leader, but he's alive. He will heal. Then we'll take him back to Temeron to stand trial..."

She shook her head as the constable cleared his throat.

"There's a bit of a problem with that, Stravad Leader."

Zeran frowned at the man. Alana gave him a confused look as well.

"The prisoner was apprehended in my jurisdiction."

"And?" asked Zeran.

"Technically, he's my prisoner."

"He's Stravad."

"Well," said the constable, bending over to right his chair. "He definitely has some Human in him, but it doesn't matter. He was apprehended here."

"You're going to try him for the murder of a Temerian citizen here?" asked Zeran, his voice edged.

"Well, actually, murder trials are tried in the capital, so we'd transport him to Denortosal and the King would preside."

"You're taking him to Denortosal?" said Zeran.

"Nope."

Zeran shared a look with his brother and Alana frowned.

"Since he's a Temerian citizen, but he was apprehended in Taral, jurisdiction is under dispute. And when jurisdiction is under dispute, we take the prisoner to..."

"Zelan," finished Zeran, slapping his hands against his thighs.

"What? Why?" said Alana.

"To keep the protectorates from going to war over a dispute," said Tyrane. "That was established when the Seven Protectorates were created."

Zeran moved toward the constable. "You can't be serious? You're going to take a Temerian issue to the Lord of Loden just because he was apprehended in your town?"

"Apprehended and shot down in the street," said the constable. "That's exactly what we're going to do."

Zeran gave his brother a disbelieving look. Tyrane shrugged.

"We'll give him a few days to get better, then we'll be on our way. We can catch the barge and that will make things easier on us."

Alana glared at her father. This was his fault. He had to pursue them even when she told him she was traveling with Trey willingly.

"And while we're at it," said the constable, crossing his arms over his chest, "let's talk about who's going to repair my office."

* * *

Alana sat outside Trey's cell on the ground. He was lying on his belly on the cot, the fingers of his left hand snaked through the bars, clasped in Alana's. He was resting easy, his breathing a steady rise and fall, his features relaxed. He couldn't be in any pain.

She tensed as the door creaked open and someone stepped inside the tight corridor. She wasn't ready to talk to anyone right now, especially not her father.

A Stravad she didn't recognize appeared around the corner of the first cell. He had golden hair that hung to the middle of his back and deep cocoa brown skin tones. He wore a Temerian guard uniform that had splatters of blood on the leg. Alana scrambled to her feet, pressing her back to the cinderblock of the outer wall.

"Who are you?" she demanded.

Trey's brow furrowed, but he didn't wake. Whatever Roe had given him had really knocked him out this time.

The man's gaze swept over Alana's body from her head to her toes and he smiled, but the smile didn't reach his eyes. There was something hard about his mouth. He reached up and curled his fingers around a medallion dangling over his uniform shirt, caressing it with his fingers. Alana couldn't see what it was.

"Alana Eldralin," he said, stalking toward her, his gaze penetrating. "You are fascinating."

Alana pressed back into the wall as he stopped in front of her, close enough to touch, but he didn't. "Who are you?" she demanded.

"Everyone talks about your sisters. Why is that? They pale in comparison to you." He rested a hand on the wall above Alana's head and leaned closer to her.

She shoved him in the chest and braced her legs. Power licked at her fingertips. "I won't ask you again. Identify yourself."

He smiled, slowly, and his eyes swept over her. "I'm Folen Tesseran. I'm the man who found you."

Alana felt her confidence slip. He was the man who'd tracked the two of them to Taral? He was the reason Trey was hurt?

He moved close again.

"Why do you think so many people find your sisters more interesting?" His upper lip twitched and he leaned his head down as if he were going to rub his face against her hair. Alana backed into the wall again. "*You* are the prize."

"Tesseran!" snapped a voice, making them both jump.

The tracker whirled around and blocked Alana with his back. She tried to peer around him and saw Roe Manes standing in the aisle, his hands clenched.

"The Stravad Leader wants you to guard the front of the building," he said in a voice that thrummed with authority.

Tesseran cast a look over his shoulder at Alana, then he smirked, lowered his head, and moved down the corridor, brushing past Roe as he went. Roe waited until he heard the door close at the end of the hallway before he strode toward Alana.

"Did he touch you?" he said, looming over her.

She put her hand on his arm. "No, he didn't touch me."

Roe looked back down the hallway, but he didn't say anything.

Alana glanced at Trey. His brow smoothed out and he'd fallen back into a deeper sleep.

"He's going to be okay, Alana," Roe said.

She glanced up at him and nodded, but she couldn't shake the guilt that he'd been hurt because of her. Roe took her elbow, directing her to a bench that was lined up along the wall fronting the cells. This room was depressing. Low light, no homey furniture, and only the barest of creature comforts.

Alana clasped her hands between her knees and stared at Trey's dark head. This was supposed to have been her wedding day. It was supposed to have been so very different than this. "What's going on?" she asked, nodding toward the constable's office.

Roe crossed one booted foot over his other leg, playing with the ragged fringe on his pants. "Your father's arguing with the constable about Lodenian law and how it doesn't really apply to Stravad."

"Poor constable."

Roe chuckled, then his face darkened. "I'm sorry about what happened, Allie. I really am."

"He didn't kill anyone, Roe."

"He abducted you. That pretty much sealed his fate."

"I left my father a letter..." She stopped herself and slapped her hands against her thighs. "What difference does it make now?

Everything's ruined. Trey lost his freedom, and I…I've lost my family."

"You haven't lost your family," said Roe, irritation evident in his voice. "They're waiting for you just as they've always been."

Alana rubbed her chin against her shoulder. She was getting tired. She'd used up a lot of energy today. "I love Trey, Roe. I love him."

"Well, that *is* a problem."

"I know it is. My father will never accept him and I…I'm not sure I can ever forgive my father."

Roe shifted to face her. "What did you expect him to do, Allie? He's a father. He had to find you."

"He could have believed me when I wrote him that letter."

The look Roe leveled on her said he thought her daft. "And what sort of leader would that make him, Allie? A girl is dead. She was murdered. Do you think he can just take your word for it and tell the Lamers he's sorry, but his daughter doesn't think the last man who was with her had anything to do with her death?"

Alana stared at him, frowning. She hadn't thought about it that way. She knew Trey hadn't killed Trista, but someone had. Someone had killed a Temerian citizen and it was her father's duty to figure out who.

She rested her head on Roe's shoulder. "I don't see anyway out of this mess."

He rested his head on hers. He'd always been like a brother to her. She trusted Roe, even when he was calling her out. "The first step is talking to your father, Allie. He's hurting. I've never seen him like this. He thought you were dead."

Alana nodded. "Okay. I guess you're right."

He nudged her with his shoulder. "Besides, you kinda scare the piss out of everyone now. You do realize you need some help controlling that Eldralin energy, right?"

"Right." She made a face. "I'm probably going to have to scrub floors for years to pay back the damage I've done to the constable's office."

"Years? I'm thinking decades. After you came in here, half the plaster fell off the roof out there. Everything's covered in white dust."

Alana laughed.

"Go talk to your daddy, Alana," said Roe, nudging her again. "I'll stay and guard Trey while you're gone."

Alana kissed Roe's cheek. "You're a good guy, Roe Manes," she said. "I hope Mairin finally realizes it someday."

Roe smiled up at her as she rose to her feet. "Maybe you can put in a good word for me?"

Alana smiled and touched his shoulder. "You know I will," she said and turned toward the empty corridor. Her father awaited her. Eldon protect her.

*   *   *

When Alana stepped out into the constable's office she found the constable and a few of his deputies trying to put everything to right again. She glanced up and saw a huge chunk of the plaster had fallen from the ceiling, exposing more beams. Workers were boarding up the windows and her uncle, Tyrane, was sweeping glass. Her father was nowhere to be seen.

She gave the constable a sheepish duck of her head and walked over to her uncle. Tyrane stopped sweeping and leaned on the broom as she encircled his waist with her arms and laid her head on his chest. After a moment, he wrapped his free arm around her.

"I'm sorry, Uncle Ty."

He kissed the top of her head. "For what, peanut? For getting caught up in all the excitement? Shesh, we've all done that."

She laughed and hugged him tighter. It felt so good to be held by him. She'd suspected for a long time that she was her uncle's favorite. He always said she had a spark of mischief in her. "Where's Daddy?"

"He's outside, love," said Ty, his voice rumbling under her ear. "You need to make right with him."

"I know."

"He's only doing his job."

"That's what Roe said."

"That Roe Manes is a sharp cookie. I've always liked him."

Alana leaned back and smiled up at her uncle. He touched her nose with his fingertip. "He's crazy about Mairin," she said.

"Ah, and he has good taste."

Alana laughed. "How come someone hasn't locked you down yet, Uncle Ty?"

He cupped her cheek. "Because I'm too much man for any one woman, peanut, that's why."

She kissed his cheek and pulled away. "I'd better get this over with."

"Go easy on the old man. He's been through hell," he said, holding onto her hand as she headed toward the door. "We all have, Allie," he answered.

She felt a rush of guilt, but she squeezed his fingers and released him, opening the door and stepping outside. A small crowd stood in the street, whispering and pointing to the broken windows, but the majority of them had dispersed. Alana looked around and found her father sitting on a bench a few doors down from the jail. She could feel the force of his cobalt eyes searing into her. She smoothed her hands down her sides, taking a deep breath.

She was not going to apologize for loving Trey. If he wanted to scold her for that, well, then, he was in for a fight. And she wasn't going to excuse his order to have Trey shot. That hadn't been necessary and she wasn't going to pretend it was. Trey had never shown any violence...well, except when he abducted her.

Damn, this wasn't going to be an easy talk.

She sat down on the bench next to him.

Zeran had his arms braced on his thighs, his hands clasped before him, his dark hair lying over his shoulders. "Hey," he said.

"Hey," she said, wanting to wrap her arms around him. "How is he?"

He? Couldn't he say Trey's name?

"Resting."

"Good."

"What happened with the constable?"

Zeran looked out to the street, sighing. "We're going to Zelan in a few days. I knew I wouldn't win that argument. I signed an update of the treaty last Valhall myself."

"Did you send a message home?"

He looked back at her, his blue eyes wary. "I did. You don't know how afraid we all were..."

"Please don't. Not right now," she said, holding up a hand. "Everything's still too raw."

He nodded. "I didn't have a choice, Allie."

"I know!" she snapped. Then she closed her eyes and drew a deep breath. "I know you didn't have a choice. I know what I put you through. I know how afraid you were. I missed you every day of my life, but I love him, Daddy."

Zeran flinched and looked away. "Don't..."

"Don't tell you that? Don't explain why I made the choice I made?"

"Don't say you love him!" spat Zeran.

Alana studied her father's handsome profile. She reached out and fingered a lock of his hair, brushing it off his shoulder. "Don't tell you the truth, Daddy."

He abruptly rose to his feet and paced to the edge of the boardwalk, gripping the handrail in his hands. She could feel the hum of his power. She realized she'd always been aware of it, but never so much so as now. He must always fight to control it.

"Is it always there?" she asked him. "Nipping at the edge of your conscious, wanting to be unleashed."

His back hunched. "Always," he said in a tortured voice.

She nodded. "I feel it too. Like something's crawling under my skin."

He turned and faced her, pressing his back to the railing. "Did it just happen?"

She considered that. "No, I guess I've always felt it. It's always been just there at the edge of my awareness, but I'd never been in a situation where I needed it before."

He nodded.

"The first time I brought a cave down. I didn't even realize what I was doing. Trey saved me from myself. I would have been buried alive." She stopped speaking when Zeran's hands curled, biting into the wood.

This wasn't going to be easy if he didn't want to hear anything about what she'd experienced.

"I thought you died, Allie. I saw the snake and I thought..." His voice was so tortured, Alana came to her feet.

"Trey saved my life, Daddy. Trey saved me."

He looked away, shaking his head.

She moved closer to him, lifting her hand to touch his cheek. He released a shuddered breath and closed his eyes. "I love you. I always will. No matter what, but I'm not a child anymore."

He looked back at her, his eyes roving over her face.

"You and Mama protected me, you taught me, you gave me everything, but you can't give me everything anymore, Daddy. Can't you understand that?"

He gave a moaning laugh. "I'm trying, Allie. I'm trying to understand." He sank his fingers in her hair and brushed it back from her face. "I'm trying to figure it out, but you've got to give me some time."

She nodded and moved closer, wrapping her arms around him. "I need you both, Daddy. I need you and Trey. I don't know how that's going to work out, but I need you both."

He folded her in his arms and his chest rose on a sigh. "I'm trying, little girl. I'm trying. But more than that, I'm here."

Alana pressed her face to his shirt and breathed in his familiar scent, tears blinding her. No matter how old she got, no matter where life took her, she loved this man, and she would until her dying breath. He was her center, her rock, her support. And she was home.

CHAPTER 15

Tarish whirled, a blur of motion, and struck the edge of his sword against the hilt of the trainee's blade. The trainee's sword dropped into the sand and he danced back, shaking his hand. Merith stood behind the line of trainees and mentors, trying to keep the disgust off his face. Tarish liked to show off. He liked to best the trainees. It wasn't much of a contest. He was one of the most skilled fighters Merith had seen. Perhaps that was his Stravad gift.

Tarish shoved the young man in the shoulder, knocking him off balance. "You'd be dead!" he roared in his face. His gaze swept the assembly, his jaw tense. "You'd all be dead. Worthless, lazy idiots! You've gone soft! I'm ashamed to be associated with you." He pointed his sword at the trainee. "Pick it up!"

The trainee's frightened eyes rose to Tarish's face.

"Are you stupid?" Tarish shouted.

A few of the elders looked away, including Merith. It was painful to watch a trainee be publicly humiliated this way.

"I said pick it up! We go again! I will not lead a band of weak willed, spineless animals! We've hidden in caves long enough!" He feinted at the trainee, tagging him on the upper arm. Bright red blood welled in the wound and the young man staggered back, staring at Tarish with enormous eyes.

Merith rubbed his hand over his temples. He hated seeing Tarish's cruelty, but he also agreed with him, to a point. They had become weak, they had become docile. They'd allowed the Humans to drive them into their caves and hold them there like captives. It was shameful.

"Do you see!" shouted Tarish, walking around the circle of the training grounds. "Do you see how he refuses to obey? How he refuses to protect himself?" He turned and stared at the trainee. "I should kill him for that!"

A grumble of protest rose from the mentors, and the trainees tried to meld back into the crowd so as not to be noticed. Merith cursed under his breath. He was going to have to intervene, but it was the last thing he wanted to do. Tarish was becoming increasingly unpredictable the more the current state of the Nazarien was revealed to him. Karnack Pretorian had done them no favors.

Pushing through the people, he positioned himself so Tarish would have to see him. The Nazar lowered his head and advanced on the trainee, his sword raised to deliver a killing strike. At the last possible second, the young man lunged forward and grabbed his own blade, dropping into a crouch to face his leader.

A cruel smile tilted the corners of Tarish's mouth and he straightened, then his eyes lifted from the trainee and fixed on Merith. Merith ducked his head and held up the missive in his hand, turning the seal outward so he could see it.

Tarish's expression shifted and he lowered his blade, striding past the trainee who shuffled around to keep the Nazar in sight, but Tarish was finished with him. He came to the fence and his gaze roved over Merith and the missive.

"Is that from Temeron?"

Merith nodded.

A waiting attendant handed Tarish a towel. He exchanged it for his blade, wiping his face on the towel as he ducked between the rails, rising in front of Merith. He snatched the missive from Merith's hand, rubbing his thumb over the seal.

Draping the towel over his shoulders, he made an amused noise. "Zeran Eldralin is getting desperate," he said, moving back toward the caves.

Merith fell into step beside him. "How long do you think you can ignore him, my lord Nazar?"

"For the rest of my days, Merith. For the rest of my days." He broke the seal and unrolled the tiny missive, stopping to squint at the elegant script it revealed.

Merith frowned. He'd seen Zeran's handwriting before and this was not it.

Tarish sucked in a breath and turned the paper over, looking for more, but there wasn't anything. He turned it back around and read it again, lifting a hand to rub his chin.

"Another summons?" asked Merith, trying to get a look at the paper.

Tarish's eyes lifted and they were filled with a strange light. "What do you know of Mairin Eldralin?"

"Mairin Eldralin?"

"Eldest daughter of Zeran Eldralin."

"Very little. We have been isolated…"

"Is she beautiful?"

"She's an Eldralin," said Merith and fortunately, it was enough to quell Tarish's interest.

"She is and all the bastards are comely, are they not?"

Merith nodded.

"But even if she had the face of a horse, she would intrigue me."

"I'm sorry, Lord Nazar, why are we discussing Zeran Eldralin's daughter?"

Tarish waved the missive in Merith's face. "She's the one summoning me to Zelan now!"

"Mairin Eldralin? A woman?"

Tarish nodded, his lips curling into an unsettling smile. "A woman? She dares to command me."

"Well, we are certainly not going to answer," said Merith.

Tarish went still, tilting his head in concentration. "Oh, we're going."

"But you said the Nazarien will no longer dance attendance on the Eldralins."

"That was before Mairin Eldralin summoned me." He draped an arm over Merith's shoulder, turning him toward the caves. "Of course, I have to think of the order, Merith, and thinking of the order means I'll have to sire progeny." He patted the older man's shoulder. "I can't imagine a better dame for my offspring. Can you?" He released Merith so suddenly, the older man stumbled. "It's as if fate took a hand in affairs, now, isn't it?"

*　　*　　*

Alana stared skeptically at the melon resting on a table in the courtyard behind Miss Thesa's boarding house. Zeran had set up the training grounds, as he called it, clearing a spot in the middle of the courtyard, ordering Roe and Tyrane to stack the furniture around the perimeter.

Miss Thesa watched them from the kitchen windows, frowning as they rearranged her patio. Alana shook her head in amusement. The woman had told Trey she had only the attic room available, but when confronted with Zeran and his handsome face, she'd suddenly managed to scare up three more rooms.

Alana had insisted on staying in the attic, rather than rooming with her father. Her most intimate memories of her time with Trey had happened in that room and she wasn't prepared to forget them now. Her thoughts turned to Trey and she wanted to check on him in the jail, but her father had been adamant that they would start her training today.

Their truce was tenuous, so she didn't argue. She wanted a relationship with her father, but she was having trouble forgiving him for locking Trey up and wounding him. She also couldn't accept that Zeran refused to acknowledge their relationship.

After Roe and Tyrane cleared the rest of the furniture, Zeran turned Alana to face the melon at the back of the yard, her own back to the brick boarding house wall. He put his hands on her shoulders and motioned Tyrane and Roe to step behind them.

"Okay, Allie, we already know you can move things when you're provoked." He pointed over her shoulder at the melon. "But can you move them when you're not provoked?"

Alana scrubbed her hands on the work pants and shook back her long hair. She didn't know. When she was provoked, the power roared out of her, but she'd never tried to summons it on her own. She glanced anxiously over her shoulder at her uncle and Roe. Tyrane gave her an encouraging nod, but Roe seemed unsettled.

"How do you call it up when you're not angry?" she asked.

"Close your eyes," came Zeran's voice in her ear. "Can you feel the power at the edge of your consciousness?"

She did as her father instructed, searching for the electrical energy of it. It hummed right at the back of her mind, snaking down into her fingertips, creating a tingle as it passed. She realized she always felt it, always heard a slight buzz in the back of her mind, but she'd learned to block it. She drew on that energy, feeling it filling her up like a glass.

"Good," said Zeran. She knew he could feel it too, the same way she'd always been aware of his power, heard the hum of it in her consciousness. "Now, establish a connection with the melon and will it to you."

Alana opened her eyes and stared at the yellow, round ball, imagining her power snaking out like lightning to wrap around it. The melon wobbled on the table and Tyrane sucked in a wild breath. His reaction snapped Alana's concentration and the melon wobbled to a stop.

"You've got to block everything else out of your mind, Allie," said Zeran. "Focus on the melon to the exclusion of all else."

Alana sucked in a breath and held it, trying to clear her mind, but worry for Trey kept pressing in on her.

"That's good. Deep breath in, then fully exhale."

"How do you clear your mind though?" she grumbled in frustration, plucking at her pants legs.

"I think of the ocean, the rhythmic motion of the waves against the shore."

"I've never seen the ocean," she reminded her father, realizing her childhood had been happy, but sheltered. Very sheltered.

"Okay, think of something else then. The sound of wind through the trees, the rustle of grass in a meadow."

Alana thought of combing her sisters' hair. She'd always styled it for them, dragging the brush through their long locks over and over again until it was smooth as silk. There had always been something soothing about the chore.

She focused on that memory and her mind cleared. The power responded to her summons, sparking in her fingertips, and she sent it out, wrapping it around the melon. The fruit rocked on the table, bouncing right to the edge, hovering, about to go over.

"Now, bring it to you," said Zeran in a soft voice.

Alana gave a mental tug.

The melon sprang violently off the table and careened toward them. She just had time to throw herself to the side before it blazed past their heads, slammed into the brick wall of Miss Thesa's boarding house, and burst open, spraying all of them with melon guts.

Alana flipped to her backside, staring at the mess on the wall as the men began climbing to their feet, dusting themselves off. Zeran walked over to her and held out a hand, a touch of amusement curving the lines of his mouth. She took his hand and let him yank her to her feet.

Tyrane gave her a skeptical look. "I'll go get more melon."

Roe exhaled heavily. "I'll get a mop."

Alana's gaze shifted to Miss Thesa where she was frowning, her arms crossed over her bosom. She looked ready to explode. That is until Zeran flashed her a dazzling smile. The older woman blushed and ducked her head, waving him off.

Alana made a noise of disgust. "Just what every daughter wants to see – her father flirting with another woman."

Still smiling for Miss Thesa's benefit, Zeran said, "A means to an end, baby girl. It's either this or we sleep in the bunkhouse with Roe and the other soldiers."

Alana patted his shoulder. "Then keep flirting, Daddy," she said.

*   *   *

Jonik Myar tapped his pen against the clipboard. "The bath off the study is leaking. The water containment tank has rusted. It needs to be replaced."

Selia poked her head out of the pantry where she was trying to take an inventory of their supplies. Her mother had always done this in the past, but her mother refused to leave her room, lying in bed or painting. She wasn't sure if it was Allie or Selia's father she mourned the absence of, but Alix hadn't been herself in weeks.

"Who usually does such repairs?"

"Your mother has a contractor on retainer. Would you like me to call her?"

"Her?"

"Yes, she's a woman. Your mother thought it was amusing to hire a female contractor."

Selia stepped out of the pantry. "I don't think she thought it amusing, Jonik. I think she felt she was the best one for the job."

Jonik made an airy wave of the hand. "That may be. Should I call her? There are few other things that she could repair, like the loose board on the back deck and the broken spindle in the banister."

"Fine."

"We'll have to go to the market. Our usual stores are running low."

Selia glanced over her shoulder, nodding. "Let me just tell Mairin where I'll be." She started toward the main part of the house, just as the bell over the front door rang. Jonik brushed by her in a hurry to answer the door himself. Selia exhaled a frustrated sigh. The old butler was efficient, but he'd always been so uptight.

As she passed the entrance hall, she glanced over to see who it was. She caught a glimpse of a forest green uniform before Jonik closed the door again and turned to face her. He held a letter in his hands.

"From your father," he said. "Should I bring it to Mairin?"

Selia's eyes widened. "No, give it here!" She held out her hand.

Jonik's expression was disapproving as he held the letter against his chest, but eventually he relinquished it to her hands. She tore the envelope open, snatching the paper from inside. Her eyes scanned the script, feeling a momentary pang of regret when she realized it was written to her mother.

Alix, love,

I've found our daughter. She is well. After all this time, you cannot know the joy it gives me to send this message to you. Please be comforted now, love. Tell Mairin and Selia I will bring their sister home to them as soon as the matter is settled. Based on our treaty with the Lord of Loden, I am honor bound to take the fugitive to Zelan for sentencing. However, as soon as that unpleasantness is finished, Alana and I will return home.

As always, I remain yours.

Zeran

"Mairin!" shouted Selia, hurrying for the stairs. "Mairin!"

Jonik put a hand over his heart. "Good heavens!" he complained, but Selia didn't care. She raced up the stairs two at a time, throwing open her mother's room. Alix sat before the windows, painting, but she looked over when Selia entered. For a moment, Selia was struck with how much weight her mother had lost in the time since Alana's abduction.

"Mama, I have a letter from Daddy!" she said, carrying it to her.

Mairin appeared in the doorway a moment later, breathing hard. "What is it, Selia, for heaven's sake!"

"A letter from Daddy," Selia said, placing it in her mother's hands.

Alix's hands trembled as she read the letter, then she covered her mouth with one hand and the tears fell. Mairin rushed to her mother's side in alarm as Selia gathered her into her arms, holding her close.

"She's coming home," whispered Alix. "My baby's coming home."

Mairin gave Selia a bewildered look.

"Daddy found Alana," Selia said. "She's all right."

Mairin burst into tears and wrapped her arms around Selia's where they held their mother and together the three of them wept.

*   *   *

Alana leaned on the railing of the bunkhouse porch, watching Roe assist Trey in walking the short distance between the jail and the bunkhouse, Roe supporting him with his shoulder. Trey still carried himself hunched over, but he seemed better each day. The constable had decided they would head toward Zelan by the end of the week. Constable Quell stood now, leaning against a support beam holding up the roof over the back porch of the jail, eating an apple and overseeing the prisoner. Alana bristled. Trey shouldn't be locked up like an animal. As if called by her thoughts, her father and uncle stepped out of the jail, greeting Quell with a lift of their chins.

"They're going to execute him," said a voice in Alana's ear.

She jumped and turned around, glaring at the tracker, Folen Tesseran, who stood in the doorway of the bunkhouse. "Don't sneak up on me," she hissed at him.

He held up his hands. "I'm sorry. I thought you heard me."

Of course she hadn't heard him. As a tracker, he'd trained to not be heard. Many Stravad were skilled at moving silently. "Why would you say something horrible like that to me? What have I ever done to you?"

He reached out and touched a strand of her black hair. "Nothing. I wasn't trying to hurt you. I want you to prepare yourself."

She tossed her head, yanking the strand free. "Well, I don't need you to prepare me for anything."

He smiled, slowly. "So much fire. I like it."

"Don't," she warned, narrowing her eyes.

"Look, Alana, let's be honest. We all know what happened between you and..." He gave Trey a disparaging look. Alana glanced over her shoulder at the two men. Trey was watching the exchange with wary eyes. She smiled reassuringly at him, then turned back to Tesseran.

"What are you talking about?"

"There aren't many men who would accept a woman like you knowing what happened with that murdering pig."

"Be careful what you say."

"I'm not blaming you. I'm sure it was the only way you could save yourself. I don't want you to be worried about it. I'm not like most men."

"What exactly are you implying?"

Tesseran shot a glance at Trey. "You had to sleep with him. We all know it, but back in Temeron, they're not going to be that forgiving." He reached out for her hair again, but she blocked him with her arm. "Listen to me, Alana. I'm not going to judge you. Your lineage and your fire are worth a hell of a lot more than whatever you had to do to survive that monster."

Alana's back snapped straight and she took a step closer to him. "Do not speak of this to me again. Do not say my name. Forget you even know I exist or I promise you, you will pay."

She started down the stairs and moved across the yard toward the jail. Tesseran caught her arm.

"Please stop," he said.

Alana saw her father straighten from his lean and her uncle got that look in his eyes that said Tesseran was about to get a beating. Even Roe turned, but it was Trey who worried her most of all. He pushed away from Roe and started toward them, his hands clenching into fists.

Alana's gaze focused on the half eaten apple in the constable's hand and she willed it to her. It sprang from his grasp and sailed across the yard beaming straight for Alana's head. At the last second, she ducked to the side and the projectile struck Tesseran in the forehead, knocking him backward.

He let out a whoosh and shook his head, dazed, as the apple burst into a rain of pulp, seeds, and juice. Amusement danced across all of the men's faces, except the constable, who was still staring at his empty hand.

Alana focused on her father. "Now that I've mastered moving fruit, I want you to teach me how to throw a body next," she said, glaring at Tesseran where he was wiping pulp off his forehead. "Don't ever lay your hands on me again!" she told him.

Then she went to Trey and looked up at him. He shook his head, chuckling. "You are something else, sprite, you know that?"

She wrapped her arm around his waist and directed him toward the jail. "Let's get you inside. You're looking a little grey."

He draped his arm over her shoulder and leaned on her a bit as they walked toward the jail. Alana didn't hesitate as she passed her father and the constable, helping Trey make it inside again. She was done listening to male silliness in her life.

* * *

Mairin rubbed at her forehead with the heel of her hand. The numbers Talmar was showing her had begun to blur. She'd never realized all that her father had overseen as Stravad Leader. It was daunting. Talmar was trying to make her understand the taxes they paid to Zelan every year to keep the peace among the Seven Protectorates.

Elyon lounged on the couch across from her, waiting to instruct her in the diplomatic part of her duties. He was forcing her to memorize all of the council member's names, their mate's names, and even the names of their children. If he asked her to memorize their pet's names, she was running away.

Alix entered the study, followed by Jonik who carried a tray with tea and biscuits. Mairin's mother had steadily improved after receiving her father's letter, but she was still too thin. Mairin smiled up at her, grateful for the distraction.

Elyon leaned forward, eying the tray. "What's say we have a splash of Trendarian brandy in the tea, Alix love?"

"What's say I tell your healer about the splashes?" she countered.

Elyon collapsed back on the couch. "I think I'm old enough to make my own decisions about what I eat and drink."

Alix sat down next to him, patting his knee. "Why don't I pour?"

He gave her a jaundiced eye. "Besides, you're the one who's far too thin."

Alix ignored it, beginning to pour. "Mairin, leave that for a bit, child. You're looking tired."

Mairin wouldn't mind a break, but there was still so much to do. She accepted the teacup Jonik held out to her, watching her mother dish up the pastries. She couldn't help but wonder who'd made them. That had always been her job before.

"Who baked?"

"Selia," said Alix in amazement. "They're actually quite good."

Mairin's brow lifted. Funny how all of their roles had changed so rapidly. She wondered about Allie. How much had she changed throughout this ordeal? The bell at the front door rang. Jonik handed Talmar a teacup and went to answer it. Alix patted the seat on the couch next to her.

"Come sit, Talmar. You must be tired too."

Talmar sank onto the couch next to Alix, sipping at his tea. Alix offered a cup to Elyon. He gave her a stern look, but he accepted it. Mairin smiled behind her own cup, delighted to have her mother more like herself again.

Jonik appeared in the doorway once more. "My lady," he said, addressing Mairin, "there's an urchin here to see you. He says it's urgent."

Mairin set down her cup, frowning. Pip Tereagan, the trill cote's apprentice, poked his head around Jonik's side.

"I have a missive, lady. Grandfather asked me to bring it to you lickety quickely."

Mairin beamed at the boy. "Come in, Pip. Come in. Would you like some tea and biscuits?"

"I would, ma'am, very much."

Alix began pouring him a cup and Talmar dished him up a plate of the pastries. Pip pulled a red cap off his blond mop and held it in one hand, extending the other to give Mairin the missive. She wasn't sure she recognized the seal, but both Elyon and Talmar went still. Elyon set down his cup and rose to his feet. Talmar did the same, motioning the boy to take his place on the couch.

Pip perched on the cushion next to Alix, while the two men stalked toward the desk.

"That's the seal of Chernow," said Talmar.

Mairin studied it carefully. She should have recognized the star and moon symbol instantly. Nazarien sported that very emblem in their ears. She broke the seal and rolled it open on the desk, glancing up at Elyon.

"It's in Nazarien. I can't read it."

Alix rose to her feet. "I can," she said, dusting her hands on her skirt.

Mairin knew her mother had a talent for spoken languages, but she hadn't realized she could read them as well. When she gave her mother a skeptical look, Alix shook her head in annoyance. "I was educated at the mission house in Adishian, then I worked for the magistrate translating for Nazarien in Marsino." She gave Mairin a frank look. "You don't know everything about me, child."

Mairin guessed she didn't. She handed the missive over to her mother. Alix scanned it, then her expression grew grim.

"What does it say?" demanded Elyon.

Alix's gaze met Mairin's. "Greetings, Mairin Eldralin, from Tarish Enro, the Nazar, leader of the Nazarien and keeper of Stravad history."

"Humble fellow," said Talmar.

Mairin smiled at him.

"My will is yours to command, dear Mairin. As you've summoned me to Zelan, I will respond. Upon the arrival of this missive, my men and I will have already departed Chernow. I look forward to meeting with you, discussing your plans for the future of the Nazarien. As always, I am ever at your service. Yours, Tarish Enro."

Nobody spoke for a moment, absorbing the letter. Finally, the squeak of the coils in the couch drew their attention. Pip was stuffing his face and kicking his legs back and forth under the couch, oblivious to the rest of them.

"Well, um, I guess I'm going to Zelan," said Mairin.

Alix exchanged a look with the two men. "What?"

"She has no choice, Alix," said Elyon. "Tarish Enro has refused your husband and the Lord of Loden himself. We have to know what his plans are. Mairin is the only one he's responded to."

"I don't care if she's the last woman on the planet. One of my daughters is already out there. I'm not sending another."

Talmar faced Alix. If anyone could talk sense to her, it was Talmar, sometimes even more so than Mairin's father. "We're concerned about the new Nazar, Alix. He's not responding the way past Nazars have responded. We can't afford to have him creating problems for us. A war between your people and the Nazarien would be devastating."

"War?" said Alix.

"It's what we fear," answered Elyon.

"Then I'm going with her," Alix said stubbornly.

"You can't," said the old man. "You'll have to stay here and run Temeron in her absence."

"She's not going to Zelan alone."

"I'll go with her and I propose Selia go as well," said Elyon. "Once we reach Zelan, her father will be there and he can help guide her."

Alix studied Mairin's face. Mairin waited to see what she would do. She'd prefer her mother come around on her own, but no matter what, Mairin was meeting Tarish Enro in Zelan.

"Selia can go with me, Mother," said Mairin. "That way Talmar can stay here with you and help you run things."

"I don't like this, Mairin. I've almost lost one child already."

Mairin rose to her feet, clasping her mother's hands. "You aren't going to lose me, Mama. I promise you, but you know I can't ignore this. You know I have to go."

Alix closed her eyes and rubbed her forehead. "Damn Eldralin blood," she swore, then she looked at her daughter again. "I know you have to go, but I don't have to like it."

Mairin smiled. "I know you don't," she said softly.

CHAPTER 16

Riding on the barge from Denortosal to Zelan might have been easier on Trey as he was healing, but Alana found it too restrictive. Trey had been chained under an overhang in the stern of the barge with at least one guard watching him at all times. Since this was also where the only shade was located, Zeran and company had set up camp here, but on the opposite side from Trey. Alana was never left alone long enough to talk to him, but she could watch him and he could watch her, a secret smile playing at the corners of his mouth.

Folen Tesseran also watched her. She felt his eyes following her no matter where she went, either on the barge or on the shore when they camped at night. He hadn't tried to talk to her again and he hadn't touched her, but she was tired of the way he looked at her. Still, she wasn't going to complain to her father about it. She didn't need him interfering in her business anymore than he already did.

Zeran placed a dagger on the ground in front of her, the speckled sunlight glinting off the blade. He glanced around for the barge operators. Almost everyone already knew what Alana could do, they'd been present at the jail, but Zeran had admonished them all that he didn't want anyone else knowing until it was time. What time he was waiting for, Alana wasn't sure, but the tenuousness of their relationship kept her from asking for answers.

"I want you to slowly lift the dagger into the air and keep it in control. We're not going to send it plunging into anything."

"Or anyone," Tyrane said, lounging on a deck chair beside her, his hands clasped on his belly.

Alana shot him a smile and he winked at her.

Zeran's expression wasn't amused. Alana rubbed her hands on her trousers and focused on the blade. "I only know how to blast something away from me or toward me."

"I know, which means you're going to have to ramp down on the power. Focus, Alana. Imagine controlling it. It might help to make a mental image for yourself. A box with a lid, build a wall around it."

"A music box with a lovely tune," said Tyrane.

Alana giggled.

"This is serious!" snapped Zeran.

"Everything's serious with you, brother. You've been on this girl from the moment she slammed a chair into your legs."

Alana lowered her head to hide her smile, but Zeran crossed his arms over his chest.

"Perhaps you'd like the next apple aimed at your head, brother," he said.

Tyrane's expression sobered and he sat up. "Concentrate, Alana," he said, nudging her. "I will not be part of your apple target practice."

Zeran's lips quirked upward in amusement, but behind her father, Alana caught sight of Folen Tesseran glaring in her direction. The heat in his stare made the hair on the back of Alana's neck stand on end.

"A box with a lid," she said. She wasn't sure how that mental image was going to work for her. She focused her attention on the blade, feeling the hum of power respond to her summons. It tingled in her fingertips, it zipped along her spine. She thought of it like static, like the times she'd shocked herself on something when the air was charged. She imagined it was a filament of power stretching from her body outward, wrapping it around the blade, and lifting it.

Zeran stepped out of the way as the knife rose into the air, hovering before her. She never broke contact with it, focusing all of her energy on keeping the power contained. She could hear muttering from the captain and Roe and from the few men the constable had brought with them. They were remarking how they'd never seen anything like it, but she drove the distraction out of her mind and brought the blade up to waist height, imaging grappling with the power as she might grapple with a heavy object, keeping it from getting away from her.

"Now, Alana, send it into the wall of the cabin. Send it with all of your might."

She narrowed her eyes and released the power, focusing it on the hilt of the blade. It slammed into the cabin, sending a couple of the men scrambling out of the way, and quivered there from the impact.

Zeran gave her a grim smile and Tyrane whooped. When she glanced over at Trey, he inclined his head with pride at what she'd done. When she looked back up at her father, she could see Folen Tesseran watching, a hooded expression in his eyes. The look made her shiver.

* * *

"Karnack Pretorian was a weak man. He kept the Nazarien in exile. He never confronted the governments in Nevaisser over their treatment of Stravad," said Elyon, riding on Mairin's right.

"Why not?" she asked, trying to absorb everything she could about the Nazarien in the few days they had before they reached Zelan.

"Who can say? He should have petitioned for help from Zelan or Terra Antiguo, he was within his right, but he never did."

"So that's why Tarish Enro challenged him?" asked Selia, riding on Mairin's left.

"He'll claim that was the reason, but you and I both know the seduction power represents."

Mairin chewed on her inner lip. There was too much to be remembered. She rubbed her back. She hadn't ridden for so many hours at a time in years. Her father had taken her and her sisters to Zelan for the Celebration of Valhall a few times, but not as they'd gotten older and life had become more complicated. In truth, Mairin hadn't left Temeron in months.

"Why did my father agree to take Trey to Zelan for sentencing?"

"Under the treaty of the Seven Protectorates, any dispute that happens between kingdoms will be settled in Zelan. It was put in place when the region was trying to ally itself together. A dispute between kingdoms threatens the Seven Protectorates. Your father would never jeopardize it."

"Well, Canto's not happy about it. He wants his daughter's murderer brought back to Temeron to be judged by the Temerian council," said Mairin. In fact, Canto had demanded that very thing and Mairin found it hard to deny the man his rights as Trista's father.

"I understand Canto's feelings, but he's forgetting our responsibility to the region," said Elyon.

"I don't think he's forgetting it, Granddad," said Mairin. "I think he wants justice for his daughter."

Selia shifted in her saddle, drawing Mairin's attention. Her sister was frowning.

"What?"

Selia blinked at her in surprise. "Nothing," she said, but Mairin knew she wasn't telling her the truth. She knew Selia too well and she knew when something was bothering her. Still, she let it go, focusing on the gait of the horse beneath her.

However, as she and Selia got ready for bed in their tent that night, Mairin set down her hairbrush and walked over, climbing on the end of Selia's cot. Selia closed the book she'd been reading and set it on the floor, giving Mairin a curious look.

"What's bothering you?" Mairin asked her. When Selia started to protest, Mairin held up her hand. "I know something's bothering you, so don't try to deny it. What is it?"

Selia folded her hands on the book's cover. "I was just thinking about what you said earlier. About Canto wanting justice for Trista. I get that completely. I feel for him."

"But?"

"But, are we sure Trey's responsible for Trista's death?"

"He abducted our sister to get away from prosecution. I think it's a fair assumption that he's guilty, Selia."

Selia's expression was troubled. "I know that, but…"

"But? Spit it out. I hate dragging things out of you."

Selia pursed her lips, then shrugged. "Okay. Here it is. Alana's still alive."

"Thank Eldon himself she is. Daddy got there in time."

"Did he though? Allie was with Trey for a long time before Daddy found them. Daddy said in his letter that Allie was fine." Selia held up a hand. "If Trey's a cold blooded murderer, why keep Allie alive?"

"He was using her as a hostage. To make sure Daddy didn't attack him."

"I guess," said Selia skeptically.

"Well, if Trey didn't kill Trista, then who did? He was with her the night she died. He abducted Allie. All things point to him, Selia."

"And that's what bothers me. It just seems a little convenient. Think about this, Mai. On the off-chance that Trey's innocent, that means there's still a murderer running around Temeron and no one is looking for him. We've all been concentrating on Trey Almsden to the exclusion of everything else."

Mairin chewed her inner lip. Selia had a point, but she couldn't worry about it right now. She wasn't in Temeron and she had the situation with the Nazar to contend with. There were too many things demanding her attention right now.

She leaned forward, hugging her sister. "We'll talk about this more later. Right now, we both need some sleep. My backside's killing me."

Selia laughed. "I know. I don't know how I'm going to sit in that saddle tomorrow, myself."

Mairin rose to her feet, smiling down at her sister. A part of her longed for the life she'd had before, when she and Selia only had to worry about what dresses to wear or if they could get Alana to do their hair in the latest styles. How fast everything had changed for both of them.

*   *   *

Zeran watched the prisoner playing chess with Roe Manes. They sat on camp chairs before a tent beside the river, Trey's wrist shackles clinking as he made his move. Roe threw back his head, grimacing as he lost another piece to his opponent.

The light from the lodegem lantern lit hollows in Trey's face. He held himself carefully still, the wounds closed, but sore. And although he'd never be a heavy man, some of the gaunt look was beginning to leave him now that he was no longer running.

Zeran wanted to hate him. He wanted to keep the level of rage against him that he'd felt when he'd discovered he'd abducted Allie, but that rage was cooling despite Zeran's attempts to keep it alive. He did things like this, play chess with one of the men, something so natural, so normal. And Zeran wasn't a fool. He saw the frequent looks he sent Allie's way, looks shared between a young couple who had memories together, who had a bond. He hated it, but he couldn't deny it.

Allie hadn't defied him, she hadn't insisted on spending time with Trey, but he thought it was a calculated move on his daughter's part. Allie hadn't given up her claim that she loved this man. She hadn't once denounced him. She was trying to win her way back into her father's heart and so she was biding her time, but once she got to Zelan, Zeran wasn't a fool, he knew she was plotting something.

"Are you sure about him?" asked the constable, coming up beside Zeran.

Zeran sighed. "I don't know. I know he abducted my daughter and he has to pay for that."

"Does he? According to what he told me, he was desperate. He had to get away. He knew he'd never get fair treatment from your council. And he never had any intention of hurting her. He planned to let her go as soon as they got out of Temeron, then…"

"Then he didn't. He kept her with him until Taral. She'd still be under his control now if we hadn't intervened."

The constable laid a hand on Zeran's shoulder. "I'm a father too, Stravad Leader. I know how vulnerable that makes you. I know what it's like to be afraid, a fear like nothing else. But I've seen that little girl of yours and trust me, man, no one controls her." He patted Zeran. "You might think about that for a moment, if I were you. She might be docile right now, but she's cooking up something in that pretty head of hers, you can be sure."

Zeran blew out air. He knew it. And he knew now that if Allie had wanted to get away from Trey at any point in their journey, he wouldn't have been able to stop her. Which meant only one thing. Allie hadn't wanted to get away.

Quell walked off, leaving Zeran standing in the shadows. Deciding this wasn't getting him the answers he needed, he stepped away from the trees and crossed the campsite, stopping before the camp table. Roe shot to his feet, coming to attention. Zeran couldn't help but wonder why Allie couldn't have fallen for someone like Roe. Roe was infinitely preferable to Trey.

He was steady, had a career, understood obedience, had a stable family.

Zeran pushed that thought aside. No use wishing for things that would never be.

"Let me talk to the prisoner," he told the young man.

"Yes, Stravad Leader," said Roe, ducking his head. "Do you want me to remove the game board?"

"No, leave it. You can continue when I'm done."

Roe walked off and Zeran took a seat, stretching out his long legs. The campground was settling and the last he'd seen, Allie was talking with her uncle around the campfire. He felt Trey's green eyes searching him, but he didn't exactly know what he wanted to say yet.

"I will never forgive you for the terror you put my family through," he said, surprised by how bitter he sounded.

Trey didn't respond, leaning back in the chair, his shackled hands clasped in his lap.

"You stole my daughter from her home. Her mother and I, we didn't know if she was alive or dead." Zeran looked at him, feeling rage spark, and he knew his eyes glowed with it. "We didn't know if she called for us."

Trey met his look without blinking. "I know."

"You know?" Zeran shifted in the chair, curling his hands into fists. He could kill him right now. He could send a bolt of power into him and stop his heart. "You know?"

"What do you want me to say, Stravad Leader? I'm sorry?"

Zeran clenched his jaw, his nails biting into his palms.

"I am sorry. I'm sorry I scared you. I'm sorry I gave you a moment of worry or fear or agony. If I had it to do over again, I want to tell you that I wouldn't do it, I wouldn't take her, but if you want me to say I'm sorry it happened, I'd be lying."

Zeran grappled to regain control. He wanted answers. He wanted to know what had made Trey do something like this. Raging at him would only make him close off again.

"You want to tell me you wouldn't take her?"

Trey's gaze never wavered. "I want to tell you that, but I'd probably do it again. I thought you were going to kill me. I thought you were going to have me executed for something I didn't do."

"For something you didn't do? Why would I ever believe you?"

"That's the point. You never will. No matter what. You'll never believe I didn't kill Trista. Nothing's changed. And yet, everything has."

Zeran frowned. "What do you mean? If the Lord of Loden orders you executed, I will make sure it's done."

"I know. I know you will."

Zeran looked away. This young man unsettled him. If Falco Leonhart ordered Trey executed, Allie would never forgive him. It suddenly became clear. She would never accept it. "She'll hate me."

Trey didn't answer. He didn't have to. Zeran was in a trap of his own making and he couldn't see a way out. His eyes rose to Trey's again.

"She says she loves you. Do you love her?"

"With everything I am."

Zeran shifted in the chair, facing him. "Alana is an Eldralin. Do you realize what that means?"

"Not entirely."

"You saw what she can do. She needs her people. She needs help controlling her gifts. Once others find out what she is, they'll be after her. They'll want her for their own use. The only hope Allie has is to stay with her family, to stay in Temeron, where we can protect her."

"Lock her up, you mean?"

Zeran shook his head. "Eldralins with her power are hunted, used and discarded. You can't want that for her."

"I don't, but I don't want you deciding what she does with her life either. She's worth so much more than that."

Zeran brushed that aside. He had a way to make all of this right again. A way to save this man's miserable life and still have his daughter's love. "Listen. Once we reach Zelan, you will stand trial in front of Falco Leonhart. He will have your fate in his hands and I can't interfere."

"I know."

"But before we reach Zelan, I can help you."

Trey's chin lifted.

"I can set you free. You can get away right here and now. I'll even give you supplies. If you go, if you head out now, I won't pursue you, I won't track you. You'll be free. You can go wherever you want."

The green eyes narrowed.

"I'll even give you money. I have money with me and it'll all be yours. You'll never want for anything else. It's more money than you've ever seen, Trey. You can start over in one of the protectorates. A new life." He held out his hands. "We can do it tonight. Just say the word. Just swear to me that you'll leave and never return. You leave and promise never to contact Alana again."

"That's all I have to do to get everything you're offering me? I just have to promise never to see Alana again?"

"Yes," said Zeran breathlessly. "That's all."

"And if I do? If I contact her?"

Zeran's voice came out like a growl. "I will hunt you down. You know I will. You know I will never stop, and I will kill you."

Trey didn't answer right away. He just sat and stared at Zeran, unblinking.

Zeran fidgeted, then he leaned forward, hissing. "What do you say? Do we have an agreement?"

"I didn't kill Trista. I never laid a hand on her."

Zeran waved that off. "It doesn't matter now. Answer me."

"It doesn't matter? You have a murderer in Temeron, Zeran Eldralin. How can that not matter?"

Zeran jerked back, surprised by the vehemence in his words. The doubt he'd harbored about Trey's guilt took new root, but he pushed the thought aside. He'd deal with that later. He had to make this accord. He had to get Trey away from his daughter. He wasn't Stravad Leader right now, he was a father who had to protect his child.

"I'll handle Temeron. Answer me. Do we have an agreement? Will you take the offer and leave?"

Trey's gaze never wavered, never shifted, never faltered. "No," he said. That and nothing more.

Zeran rose to his feet. "What?"

"No, we don't have a deal."

Zeran pointed to the barge. "Tomorrow we'll arrive in Zelan!" he shouted. "You will be tried and if you're found guilty, you will be executed!"

Trey didn't respond.

"They will kill you and I won't be able to do anything to stop it!"

Still he didn't respond.

Fury overwhelmed Zeran and he glared at the game board. It blasted upward, spraying chess pieces everywhere. Trey flinched as they struck him, but he didn't look away. Zeran walked a crazed circle, then jabbed a finger at him.

"You are not worthy of her!" he shouted. "You will never be worthy of her!"

Trey leaned back in the camp chair, adjusting the shackles on his wrist.

Zeran realized he was close to losing control and others were watching them. He whirled away, but before he could take a step, Trey called to him.

"Zeran."

Zeran looked over his shoulder at the younger man, hating him with everything he had.

"I will never tell her what you offered me. She'll never know. That will remain between the two of us forever."

Zeran felt a chill shiver over him as he realized what he'd done. If Trey had taken the offer, he'd have lost Allie forever. He closed his eyes and fought to contain himself, then he bowed his head and walked away, never feeling so defeated in his life.

*   *   *

The barge edged up to the landing. Standing at the end of the wooden structure were white horses with dark manes, their sides draped in white silk embroidered with gold thread. Sitting astride the largest horse was a man with long brown hair swept back from his brow with a gold crown, his hands loosely holding the reins. A large ring with a green lodegem inside winked from his left hand. His features were handsome, high cheekbones, slanted grey eyes, broad forehead, and regal bearing.

Alana had met Falco Leonhart many times. Her father and mother had brought all of them here for Valhall when they were younger and she'd come the previous year with her father as his heir to attend the meeting of the Seven Protectorates.

She liked Falco, but she couldn't control the flutter of nerves that set up in her belly as she watched the bargemen extend the ramp to the shore. If he denied her, she didn't know what else to do. Falco was her last hope.

Zeran moved up beside her. He'd been distant since the previous night when he'd gotten into a shouting match with Trey. She wasn't sure what it was about, but it didn't matter now. Either her relationship with her father would be irreparably harmed in the next few moments, or he'd learn to accept her decisions as an adult woman.

As Zeran stepped up on the ramp, Alana glanced over her shoulder, meeting Trey's gaze. He stood between Roe and the constable, his hands shackled before him. He gave her a confused look, but she smiled through her anxiety and followed her father.

Falco swung down off his horse, motioning for his entourage to do the same. The smile he gave Zeran was welcoming. "It is good to see you, old friend," he said, extending his hand.

Zeran clasped it in his own, shaking it. Alana stopped behind her father, waiting with Tyrane to be acknowledged. "We're very glad to see you, Lord of Loden," said Zeran.

Falco's grey eyes swept over Alana and Tyrane, then focused on Zeran again. "Your lovely wife isn't with you?"

"No, we have pressing matters and came ourselves."

Falco's brow lowered in a frown. "But I had word that your daughters and Elyon would be joining me?"

Zeran exchanged a glance with Tyrane, then gave Falco a confused look. "My daughters and Elyon? They're coming here."

"Yes, to meet with the new Nazar."

When Zeran's expression still showed confusion, Falco held out his hands. "You and I had both demanded Tarish Enro present himself in Zelan. Do you not remember?"

"I remember, Falco," said Zeran with an uncomfortable laugh. "But last I'd heard, he refused."

"True, but a week ago, we received word he'd left Chernow and was coming here to meet with both of us and your daughter, Mairin. I'll admit I was confused. I'd believed Alana was being groomed to take over as Stravad Leader, but Enro clearly stated he looked forward to meeting Mairin."

Zeran exhaled. "We've had a bit of a miscommunication, it seems. I haven't been in Temeron for weeks." He motioned Alana up beside him. "We've had a personal situation and frankly, we're here for your assistance. It's a delicate matter and I would ask that we speak in private if we may."

"Certainly," said Falco, smiling down at Alana. He wasn't as tall as her father, but she had to look up at him. His regal bearing had never intimidated her before, but she'd never been in a position where she needed his help. "Welcome, Alana," he said.

Alana swallowed hard, then she dropped to her knees before him, bowing her head. "Lord Falco, I beg you for asylum."

"Alana!" snapped Zeran, reaching down to draw her to her feet.

Falco also bent, drawing her up. He placed a hand under her chin and forced her to meet his eyes. "What in the world are you talking about, child?" he said.

Alana realized she was trembling, but she met Falco's eyes and forced herself to speak. "I'm begging for asylum for me and my husband, Lord Falco. We are entirely at your mercy."

Falco's eyes rose to Zeran. Alana could feel the spike of her father's power, but she held her ground, refusing to back down. She didn't want to betray her father, but she couldn't think of any other way to save Trey's life.

CHAPTER 17

"Her husband?" spat Zeran, pacing the room. "Did you hear her claim him as her husband?"

Tyrane lifted the stopper from the decanter and poured them both a drink. He carried one over to Zeran where he'd stopped pacing to look out over the gardens of Zelan. Sitting at the confluence of two rivers, Zelan had always sported magnificent grounds – fountains, and winding paths, and plants from all seven protectorates, grown in ornamental gardens representing their lands.

"Drink something."

Zeran glared into the glass, but he didn't take it.

"Drink, Zeran. You're not doing anyone any good acting like an angry bear."

"She claimed him as her husband." He took the glass and tossed back the entire amount, coughing.

Tyrane rolled his eyes. Sometimes it was difficult dealing with his brother. "Have you considered they might be married?"

Zeran went still, the back of his hand over his mouth to hold in a cough. He thrust the glass at Tyrane. "Get me another."

Tyrane took the glass and walked back to the table, pouring again. "You're going to have to accept that Allie isn't a child anymore. She's a grown woman and she's made a grown woman's decision."

"She asked Falco for asylum!"

"What choice did she have, Zeran?" He handed him the second drink, taking a seat in a plush burgundy armchair. Throwing one leg over the arm, he sipped at his own drink. "You tell her you're going to have him executed at every turn. I'm proud of her. She found the one solution to her problem and she exploited it."

Zeran took the seat next to him. "Do you think they're married?"

Tyrane met Zeran's tortured gaze. "I think there's a strong possibility, Zeran, yes. They may not have been in Temeron, but they're both Temerian citizens. They would be within their right."

Zeran scrubbed his hand across his face. "What am I going to do, Ty?"

"Accept it. Stop wanting revenge."

"What if he killed Trista?"

"Do you really believe that? Do you really think he'd continue to say he didn't do it facing what he's going to face now?"

"Someone killed her, Ty. If he wasn't the one, there's a murderer in Temeron right now."

"I know. I've been thinking about it and it makes my skin crawl. We need to get things finished up here and get back home."

"Without Allie?"

"You may have to accept that, Zeran. Especially if you can't let this need for revenge go."

Zeran finished off his drink and set the glass on the table between them. "I offered to free him."

Tyrane sat forward. "What?"

"I offered to give him all the money I have, some supplies, and let him go."

"Zeran…"

"He wouldn't take it. He refused."

Tyrane slumped back in his seat. "If Allie finds out, if he tells her…"

"He promised me he wouldn't." Zeran looked over at him. "He swore to me he'd never let her know."

Tyrane drained his own drink. "You'd better hope he doesn't or that will be it, Zeran. You'll lose her for good."

Zeran closed his eyes, exhaling.

* * *

Trey was allowed to bathe and eat, then he was given clean clothes and a room. The shackles were removed, but a guard manned the balcony outside his room and he felt certain another held guard duty outside the double doors. Trey wandered around the room, running his hand over the silk fabrics, the rich woods, the silver tray that held a meal like none he'd ever had before.

He wasn't sure what the hell was going on, but he didn't remember ever being treated like this. If this was being a prisoner of Falco Leonhart, then Trey wasn't going to complain. Except he wanted to see Allie. He knew something had happened on the dock this morning, but he'd been too far away to hear what she said. When she'd fallen to her knees, Trey had tried to go to her, but Roe and the constable had prevented him.

A knock sounded at the door, then Roe poked his head inside. "Are you decent?"

Trey turned to face him. "Of course."

Roe stepped into the room, wearing a dress uniform, his hair combed, his jaw shaved. He gave Trey a once-over. "I don't think you've ever looked this good."

Trey laughed, feeling the pull of the healing wound in his back. "I haven't felt this good since you shot me in the ass."

"I didn't shoot you and definitely not in the ass."

They both laughed. Under any other circumstances, he and Roe might actually have been friends. Roe was one of the few people who didn't look at Trey with either disgust or pity. Allie was the other.

"Have you seen Alana?"

"She's in a private meeting with Falco Leonhart still."

Trey rubbed a hand over the back of his neck. "I wish I knew what that was about. Her father didn't look happy."

"Oh, I know what it was about. She asked the Lord of Loden for asylum."

"Asylum? What?"

"For her and her husband," said Roe, meaningfully.

Trey went still. "She what?" He took a step closer to Roe. "Don't mess with me."

"That's what Tesseran heard. He has eagle ears, that one. Truthfully, it makes sense. She had no other option."

Trey thought about what she'd done. Her father would consider that a betrayal. He'd never accept that Allie was his wife. A slow smile spread across Trey's face and he took a seat in the chair at the table, his knees suddenly weak.

"Is it true?"

Trey glanced up at Roe, confused. "What?"

"Are you married?"

Trey shrugged. "In a way. I was going to find someone to marry us in a Human ceremony when you shot me in the ass. I mean, by Temerian law, you could say we're married."

Roe smiled. "Congratulations."

Trey shook his head. "Gods, that woman. She's clever. Too clever for me." He looked up at Roe. "Her father's going to lock her in a tower."

Roe came over and took the seat across from him. "After what I've seen Allie do, I don't think anyone's going to lock Allie anywhere."

Trey couldn't stop smiling. "I would do anything for her."

Before Roe could answer, the door opened and the captain poked his head inside. "The Lord of Loden wants to talk to Trey," he said.

Trey shared a worried look with Roe. His fate lay in the Lord of Loden's hands. He wished he knew more about Human nobility. He wasn't sure how to act around Falco Leonhart. He pushed himself to his feet and tried to smooth down the trousers they'd given him. The fabric wasn't as supple as the worn clothes he'd used for so long and the collar pinched his neck.

Captain Petric was waiting for him outside the doors and he held up the shackles. Trey gave him a wounded look, but he offered his arms. "We can't take any chances with the Lord of Loden's safety."

Trey didn't bother arguing with him.

Roe stepped out and shut the door at his back.

"You'll accompany us," Petric told Roe.

Roe nodded in agreement and fell a step behind them as they made their way down the lushly decorated hallway. The floor was polished, the walls meticulously painted. Accent tables in rich woods sported fresh bouquets of flowers. Trey had thought the Stravad Leader's home was opulent. He'd never seen anything to compare to this.

He was led down a broad staircase to the lower floor. Workers polished lamps and the banisters, scrubbed floors, and dusted the cobwebs from the corners. Petric led him into another hallway and to a set of double doors. He knocked on the right one and waited, his hands clasped behind his back.

A moment later the door opened and a man in a burgundy uniform bowed his head. "Please come in. The Lord of Loden awaits you."

Trey followed Petric into a circular room with a star pattern created by different pieces of wood inlaid into the floor. A massive desk sat in the center of the room with a burgundy leather chair behind it. On the left side of the room was a stone fireplace, large enough for a man to step inside. Above the fireplace was a portrait of a lion, golden mane, golden eyes keeping watch over the room. Behind the desk were floor to ceiling glass doors, framed by heavy brocade burgundy curtains, edged in gold.

Falco Leonhart turned at their entrance and gave them a smile. He wasn't as tall as Zeran, but there was something in his bearing that made Trey fight to make eye contact. The man in the burgundy uniform returned, carrying a tray with refreshments on it and placed it in the middle of the table.

"May I serve, Your Majesty?" he asked Falco.

"Thank you, Ganryn. I'd appreciate it." He motioned to a leather sofa with nailhead edging along the arms and back. "Please sit."

Trey waited for Petric to guide him. The captain nudged him toward the seat, then took up a position at Trey's back. Trey's spine tingled. The last time Petric had been behind him, he'd shot him in the shoulder. Trey sat on the edge of the seat, his shackles jangling, feeling completely out of place. Roe moved to Petric's side.

"Captain, surely one guard will be enough," said Falco, catching Trey's discomfort. "Wouldn't you like to check on your men?"

Petric looked like he might argue, but he sent Roe a severe look, then ducked his head. "As you wish, Your Majesty," he said, turning crisply on his heel and heading for the door. Falco waited until he was gone before he motioned to the spot on the sofa next to Trey.

"Sit, please, and tell me your name."

"Roe Manes, Your Majesty," said Roe, taking his seat.

Falco moved to a massive leather armchair across from the sofa and sank into it, curling his long fingers around the arms and rubbing his index finger across a nailhead. "And you are Trey Almsden?"

"Yes, Your Majesty," said Trey, distracted by the amount of food Ganryn was piling on a plate. He'd eaten not two hours ago and he wasn't hungry.

"You've gotten yourself in a bit of trouble, have you not?" said Falco.

Trey's eyes snapped back to his face. "Not all of it my fault, Your Majesty."

Falco's fingers drummed on the arms. A portrait on the wall opposite the fireplace showed the Lord of Loden with a woman and two children. Trey assumed those were the king's wife and offspring. He felt his heart sink when he saw the youngest was a girl. Falco Leonhart would have to be sympathetic to Zeran. Not that Trey figured it would go any other way. Zeran and Falco were of the same breed, the same sort of men, and Trey was not.

"I'm a direct man, Mr. Almsden," said Falco. "I'm not one to couch things in unnecessary frippery."

Trey wasn't sure what that meant, but he nodded, distracted as Ganryn handed his king the first heaping plate. Falco thanked him and settled it on the side table, touching nothing. The next plate was offered to Roe and the guard's blue eyes danced with delight. Finally, Ganryn gave Trey a dish, but Trey wasn't sure how he was supposed to eat anything with his hands bound. He leaned forward and carefully set his plate on the table, watching Roe tuck into his food from the corner of his eyes.

"Did you kill the young woman in Temeron?" said Falco, snapping Trey's attention back to him.

"No, Your Majesty," Trey said. He felt like he'd been saying the same thing for a lifetime now.

"Were you with her the night she died?"

"Yes."

"Did you abduct Alana Eldralin?"

Trey drew a deep breath and released it. "Yes."

"To escape Temeron?"

"Yes."

"Did you intend to let her go at any point?"

Trey stared at his shackles. "I want to believe I did, but then things got complicated."

"You developed feelings for her?"

Trey nodded, meeting Falco's eyes. "I fell in love with her."

"Are you married to her?"

Trey shrugged. "Technically, yes. According to Temerian law, we are. I wanted us to be married by Human customs and law, but I was caught before it could happen."

"Is it still your wish to marry her?"

"It is," said Trey without hesitation. And it was. He wanted nothing more than to be able to build a life with Allie, but he was beginning to realize that was a dream that got farther and farther away each day.

Falco's fingers tapped. "You know Zeran and I are kinsmen, yes?"

Trey hadn't given it much thought, but he guessed they were. Falco was descended of Taverand, the first Lord of Loden, and Zeran came directly from Talar's line, which had transected with Taverand through his niece Shara. Trey didn't think this required an answer. Drawing attention to their link only made Trey's future that uncertain.

"I'm being asked to intervene in an issue that's really a Temerian affair. Yes, you were caught in Taral, but I'm reluctant to interfere with Zeran's authority."

Trey felt his heart sink. That would mean Zeran would drag him back to Temeron to face the council and Canto Lamer, Trista's father. He was as good as dead if that happened. "I didn't kill anyone, Your Majesty. I took Alana because I didn't see anyway out, but I never intended to hurt her or anyone for that matter."

"You are not a father, Mr. Almsden."

"No, I'm not, but I know what I put the Stravad Leader and his wife through. I don't know how to make that up to them, but keeping Allie and me apart isn't the answer."

"What is?"

Trey found himself distracted as Roe polished off his plate. Roe Manes had been raised far better than Trey had, but one would never know it seeing the way he could polish off food. Trey eased his own plate over to Roe.

Roe's blue eyes flashed to his face. "You need it more than I do," he said.

"Just eat it," muttered Trey under his breath. When he looked up again, Falco fought a smile.

Finally Roe gave in and took Trey's plate, picking up a pastry and popping the whole thing in his mouth. "To be fair, Your Majesty,

Allie can take care of herself. She could have gotten away any time she wanted," Roe said with his mouth full.

Trey glared at Roe. Zeran wanted Allie's power kept a secret. He didn't know if that extended to Falco, but he sure wasn't going to break that promise. Roe had the grace to blush and drop his eyes.

"What do you mean by that?" asked Falco, his interest piqued.

Roe shifted uncomfortably. "Have you met Alana Eldralin?"

Falco smiled. "I have. I find her to be delightful."

"That's one way to put it."

"And head strong."

"And that's another," finished Roe.

"I need to consider the situation," said the Lord of Loden. "I have other pressing issues that also need my attention, but I will give your case much thought." Falco pushed himself to his feet. "Will you escort Mr. Almsden back to his room, Roe?"

Roe quickly rose to his feet and set the half-empty plate on the table. "As you wish, Your Majesty."

Trey rose also and faced the other man. "I took Allie, but I did it because I thought I was going to die. I never meant to hurt anyone."

Falco folded his hands before him. "I will take that into consideration," he said.

Walking to the door beside Roe, they paused as Ganryn opened it for them. "Pleasant afternoon," said the butler.

"Same to you," answered Roe, stepping into the hallway as the door closed behind them. He rubbed a hand over his belly. "Lord, you missed out. That was some of the best food I've ever eaten."

Trey gave him an annoyed look. "What's gotten into you? You're usually a lot more professional."

"I don't know," said Roe, heading down the hallway. "I guess I'm nervous."

"About?"

"Mairin is coming to Zelan."

"So?"

Roe stopped at the bottom of the stairs. "Mairin is coming here."

Trey wasn't sure what that had to do with anything. He had bigger problems to think about.

Roe blew out air. "She gets me all in knots," he said.

Trey shook his head and started up the stairs. "That's how all Eldralin women get us, in knots is a good way to describe it."

* * *

Alana rushed down the front stairs of the castle as her sisters and their entourage cantered into the front courtyard. Their father already stood next to Falco, waiting for them to arrive. As soon as the horses came to a stop, Selia swung down out of the saddle and ran across the courtyard, ignoring their father and grabbing Alana in a hug.

Alana hugged her back, laughing as Selia rocked her in her arms. Holding her off, Selia placed her hands on Alana's cheeks and kissed her forehead, her eyes swimming in tears. "We were so worried about you."

"I'm fine," said Alana, smiling up at her. She glanced over Selia's shoulder to where Mairin had stopped before their father, hugging him and Falco in turn. Alana caught Roe's eyes as he stood at attention behind them, his gaze fixed on Mairin.

Moving forward with her arm around Selia's waist, Alana stopped beside her father. Mairin's gaze shifted to her, then she moved forward, gathering her in her arms.

"I'm so glad to see you safe and sound," she whispered in Alana's ear.

Alana hugged her in return, then moved beyond her to wrap her arms around Elyon's waist. The older man kissed the top of her head.

"You're different, child," he said. "What's happened?"

Alana smiled up at him. "I grew up, Granddad," she said.

He laughed and chucked her under the chin. "It happens to all of us."

"Please, come inside. We have refreshments prepared," said Falco, waving expansively. "I'm certain you're tired from the trip."

Wrapping her arm through Elyon's, Alana followed her father and Falco back into the castle. As she passed the stairs though, she felt eyes on her and glanced behind to see Folen Tesseran tracking her with his gaze. He gave her a slow smile, then his attention shifted to Selia and he winked at her. Alana shivered, but dismissed him. Nothing was going to ruin her reunion with her sisters.

After taking lunch in the dining room, Mairin went to debrief their father and Tyrane, but Selia dragged Alana off to her room to catch up. Alana kicked off her shoes and climbed onto the end of Selia's bed, tucking her legs under her.

"How's Mama?" she asked.

"Better. Once we got the letter from Daddy that you were all right, Mama came out of her room and even helped Mairin run the city."

"Mairin running Temeron? That's something, isn't it?"

"She addressed the council," said Selia. "You should have seen her. And she's the reason Tarish Enro's coming to Zelan. He ignored Daddy and Falco's summons, but he agreed to meet with Mairin."

Alana played with a loose thread on the bedspread. "I never knew she was interested in politics."

"I'm not sure she is. She didn't really have any choice with you and Daddy both gone." Selia leaned forward and patted Alana's leg. "But as soon as you get home…"

"I'm not coming home, Selia."

Selia frowned. "What? Of course you're coming home."

Alana shook her head. "Trey can't return to Temeron, so I won't be returning either."

"What the hell does Trey have to do with anything?"

For the first time in her life, Alana didn't feel like scolding her sister for her profanity. "We're married."

Selia's face went still and she sat up straighter. "You're what?"

"Trey and I are married. We married each other in Taral. He wanted a Human ceremony, but they shot him before he could find anyone to do it."

Selia waved Alana off. "Hold on a minute. What are you talking about? You married the man who murdered Trista and abducted you?"

"He didn't murder anyone."

"He abducted you?"

"He did. Technically."

"Technically? What madness is this, Alana? We didn't know if you were dead or alive."

"I know and I'm sorry about that."

"But you went ahead and married him anyway?"

Alana shrugged. "I love him."

Selia slumped back against the pillows, stunned. "I don't understand what you're saying. He took you from our home and kept you prisoner."

"He saved my life and somewhere along the way, I fell in love with him."

"He feels the same way?"

"He does."

"What does Daddy say?"

Alana blew out air. "You know Daddy. He exploded, then he forbid it, then he ignored it."

Selia shook her head. "How can you think you're in love with him, Allie? He took you against your will."

Alana shrugged. "Somewhere along the way, things changed between us." She smiled softly. "I love him."

"And if he's executed for Trista's murder?"

Alana's expression grew grim. "I won't let that happen. He didn't murder Trista."

"What makes you think you have a choice? And if he didn't murder Trista, who did?"

Alana kept her thoughts to herself. Their father didn't want anyone else knowing what she could do. She wasn't going to break that trust. He had his reasons, but she had hers. If Falco Leonhart decided Trey was guilty of killing Trista, Alana knew she had to intervene, no matter what she had to do.

CHAPTER 18

Roe affixed the shackles to Trey's wrists again, giving him an apologetic look. Trey turned away, staring out over of the gardens of Zelan. His fate would be decided today – his future with or without Alana, his very life. Falco had called them all to his council chambers to hear his decision. Trey knew he hadn't killed anyone, but would it matter to a man like Falco? He and Falco Leonhart were not of the same world, not even close. The Lord of Loden would have no choice but to side with his kinsman and a man much more suited to his station.

"Are you ready?" Roe asked.

Trey looked back at the other man. Roe Manes was a good soul. "You should tell Mairin what you feel for her."

Roe made an uncomfortable face. "And have her laugh at me? Men like me don't get women like Mairin, Trey."

Trey shrugged, his shackles jangling. "That's not always true."

Roe chuckled and patted his shoulder. "I guess not." He motioned to the door. "We'd better go."

Trey swallowed hard, feeling the breakfast he'd eaten settle heavily in his gut. He hated that other people had his life in their hands. He hated that he had so little control, but he did. He was at their mercy and so far, mercy hadn't been high on their priorities.

He followed Roe from the room and down the hallway again. This time, however, they climbed another set of stairs to the third floor. A round antechamber opened before them with marble floors and portraits of people Trey had never seen before. Two guards in burgundy uniforms manned the double doors and they thrust them open when Roe and Trey arrived.

Roe led Trey into a massive room with a throne in the middle of it. The columns and flooring were all marble, cold and austere, the throne overlaid with gold leaf, the cushions a deep burgundy. Behind the throne were floor to ceiling windows framed in the same heavy burgundy brocade of the study Trey had been brought to the day before.

Falco Leonhart sat on the throne, a gold crown on his brow, his body clothed in rich robes, lined in fur. His dark hair lay across his shoulders and he surveyed Trey with those piercing grey eyes.

Standing before him to the right of the throne was the Stravad Leader, his brother, his father, and his three daughters. Behind them were Captain Petric and Folen Tesseran. Roe led Trey to the left and placed a hand on his elbow as if that would be enough to restrain him if he suddenly lost his mind and attacked. The constable moved up on Trey's other side, inclining his head toward the throne.

"Thank you all for attending," said Falco, clasping his hands before him. "Trey Almsden, you have been brought before me for judgment by Constable Quell. You were captured in Taral, but the crimes you are accused of committing happened in Temeron. Because there was a dispute between two sovereign nations, our treaties demand I must preside over the outcome."

Trey glanced over at Alana. She was staring at him, her heart in her eyes. He gave her a reassuring smile, but he felt like his own heart was going to pound out of his chest. The thought of losing her forever made his stomach roil.

"You have been accused of murdering a Temerian citizen. You have admitted you were with the young woman before her death. You've also been accused of abducting the Stravad Leader's daughter. You have admitted that you committed this crime."

Trey shifted his attention back to Falco.

"To complicate matters further, the young woman you abducted has asked for asylum for both herself and you, and claims that you are married."

Zeran shifted uncomfortably.

"You do not deny this marriage."

Trey could see Zeran's jaw clench from the corner of his eyes.

"I have spoken with you and with the Stravad Leader. He desires to have you brought back to Temeron to face the council for your crimes. The crime of murder carries a high penalty. Are you aware of that penalty?"

"I am," said Trey.

"The penalty for murder is the same here as it is in Temeron. Murderers are executed."

Trey inclined his head.

"That being said, I have my doubts you are guilty of that crime."

He looked up at the Lord of Loden.

"I have spoken with all parties involved and no one can provide me with a shred of evidence that you committed such a deplorable act."

Trey dared to breathe. If he was to be absolved of the murder charge, maybe Falco wouldn't have him taken to Temeron to face the council.

"It is not our practice to lock a man up for being accused of something when there isn't a shred of evidence that he did it. I order you to be released from that accusation until such a time as true evidence can be brought to bear."

Trey heard Alana's gasp, but he didn't know how to react. He stared at the marble floor, willing the buzzing in his head to go away. He felt dizzy with relief, sick with it. Roe's hand on his elbow tightened, keeping him upright.

"Regarding the request for asylum, I cannot give you that, Trey Almsden. You have admitted to abducting Alana Eldralin to effect your escape. That is an undisputed fact. You must be returned to Temeron to face the council for that transgression; however, if they should absolve you of that charge, I will reconsider your request for asylum. Should you wish to return to Zelan…"

Trey dared to breathe again.

"I will do everything in my power to find you gainful employment," finished the Lord of Loden. "Until such a time as the Stravad Leader wishes to depart Zelan, you are free of constraint."

Before he could react, Alana had flown across the room and was reaching for his shackles. "Take them off, Roe," she ordered, tugging on them. "Take them off now!"

Trey laughed at her as Roe scrambled for the keys to unlock them.

The constable patted his back. "Well done, young man."

"Constable Quell, thank you for your intervention," said Trey.

Alana threw her arms around the older man, hugging him tight. He patted her back awkwardly. "Yes, thank you," she said.

"My pleasure, dear," he answered.

"I will pay you back for the damage I did to your jail," she said, easing away from him.

He laughed. "Your daddy already took care of that, little one. Don't you worry about it." He chucked her under the chin, then waited until the shackles were removed, holding out his hand for Trey to shake. "I'm glad you're free."

"So am I, sir. It wouldn't have happened without you."

Quell blushed and released Trey. "Stay out of trouble, you hear?"

"I hear."

A moment later, Trey staggered as Alana launched herself into his arms, pressing her face to his neck. He wrapped his own arms around her, holding her tight and laughing. Nothing had ever felt so right as this moment.

"Congratulations, Trey," said Roe, dangling the shackles from his hand.

Trey gave him a nod, then he spun Allie around. She laughed, throwing back her head, her dark hair streaming behind her. Trey didn't give a damn who saw. He could feel their eyes on him, but it didn't matter. All that mattered was he was finally free again.

* * *

Standing on the wide balcony outside the bedrooms in the castle, Trey brushed a dark lock of hair from Alana's face. The moonlight bathed her in its glow, illuminating her cobalt eyes, eyes the exact shade of her father's.

Trey leaned down and pressed his lips to hers, savoring the moment, the knowledge that he was free, if only for a little while. Alana responded, wrapping her arms around his neck and deepening the kiss. He dragged her against him, splaying one hand across her back, the other in her dense hair. When they drew away from each other, they were both breathing hard. He buried his face in her hair, drawing in the scent of flowers, curving his hand around the back of her neck to hold her close to him.

She held him tightly, then she eased away, sliding her hand down to his. "Come on. Let's go to our room."

He pulled back, frowning. He wanted nothing more than to follow her, but he knew her father watched them from the windows in the study behind them. If he went with her now, she would lose everything and he loved her enough not to want that to happen.

Her expression grew confused. "What's wrong?"

"Allie," he began, sighing.

Her jaw firmed and she snatched her hand out of his. "I see. Now that you're free…"

He closed the distance between them, cupping her face in his hands. "Don't dare finish that sentence. I love you. I love you more than anything and nothing's going to change that."

"Then why don't you want to come with me?"

He resisted the impulse to look at her father. "Because I'm not sure you know what you'll be giving up if I go with you tonight."

She looked bewildered. "I don't understand. I thought we wanted to be together. You said you wanted us to marry in a Human ceremony."

"I do, but your father doesn't want us together. He will never accept me, Allie."

"I don't care."

He dropped his hands to her shoulders and sighed. "But I do. I can't ask you to give up your family for me. I can't ask you to walk away from your sisters, your parents, Temeron."

She shook her head in confusion. "I love you."

"And you'd hate me when you couldn't see them anymore. I'm going back to Temeron for the judgment of the council, but once my punishment is over, Allie, I'm coming back here. I'm taking the Lord of Loden up on his offer. I can't stay in Temeron."

She pulled his hands off her shoulders and cradled them in her own. "I know that, Trey. You think I hadn't already figured it out."

"Do you realize that coming with me would mean not being with your family?"

She dropped his hands and took a step away from him. "Yes, I realize that. I understand exactly what I'm giving up and I'm willing to do it. I love you, Trey. I'm willing to give up everything to be with you, but I guess you don't feel the same way." She turned on her heel and started off.

"Allie!" he called, moving toward her, but she never hesitated.

He stopped, curling his hand into a fist. She didn't understand. She couldn't know the conflict inside of him. She thought she could make this sacrifice in the heat of the moment, but after awhile, after days and weeks and months went by, she'd come to resent him and he couldn't stand that. He couldn't lose Allie now that he'd finally found her. He had to figure out a way to make things right with her father.

*　*　*

Sitting in an armchair before the fireplace, Selia watched her father. He stood at the windows, looking out over the balcony, his attention riveted on something, while Falco, Elyon and Mairin discussed the impending arrival of the Nazar and what it meant.

"He refused both your father and me," Falco told Mairin. "It makes me anxious that he's suddenly agreed to meet with us after you sent your request, Mairin."

Selia studied Falco. She'd known him her whole life. He had a wife and children, who were currently visiting her family in Trendaria. He and Zeran had always sided together on things, not only bound by their shared heritage, but by the fact their family had been raised with each other. He viewed Selia and her sisters like nieces.

"I don't know what to tell you. It makes me anxious as well. I don't know what he thinks I afford him," said Mairin. "Up until a week ago, the most complicated thing I did was bake a pie."

"You underestimate yourself," said Falco.

"That she does," replied Elyon, his heavy eyes showing his weariness. "She has a head for government, but she lacks confidence. It's the same plight that plagued her uncle."

Glancing up at Tyrane, Selia gave him a smile. He was staring into the empty fireplace, a glass of Trendarian brandy in his hand. He seemed pensive, but he gave her a playful wink, looking over his shoulder at his brother's tense back.

Selia knew Tyrane worried about Zeran's volatile personality. The only one who'd ever been able to curb it had been their mother, but she was in Temeron. Not that Zeran was an unfair man. He just didn't always see there were two sides to an issue. Often there was Zeran's side and the wrong side.

Selia climbed to her feet, wondering what had her father so transfixed. She moved up behind him and spotted Alana and Trey standing at the edge of the balcony. They were wrapped in each other's arms, the moonlight bathing them. Selia wasn't sure how she felt about Alana's attachment to Trey, but she could see they both felt something strong for each other.

As she watched, Alana backed up and they seemed to be having words. Zeran's head came up in interest and he curled his hands into fists. When Alana turned and stormed away, Zeran released his held breath and his hands opened. Shifting away from the window, he came up short and his eyes widened when he saw the look on Selia's face.

"We're not children anymore, Daddy," she told him.

He made a face. "I know that, Selia."

"Do you? I love you, Daddy, but sometimes it feels like you want to control everything we do. As grown women, we're going to find our own partners, start our own families."

"You think I don't know that."

"I'm not sure. It feels like you're trying to control Allie right now, denying her her own choices."

"I'm not denying anyone any choices. I know you're going to find your own husbands. I'm just trying to protect her from making the wrong choice, picking the wrong man!" he said, his voice rising.

Selia drew a deep breath and released it. She knew everyone in the room was watching them now. She stepped up to him and kissed him on the cheek. "You don't get to decide that either, Daddy," she said, then she turned and headed for the door.

When she got outside, she found the hallway empty. She was glad for it. For weeks now, tension had radiated around her. Finding Alana hadn't lessened it. Now people buzzed with tension about the Nazar coming. She wasn't sure what they were anxious about. They wanted him to report to Zelan. He was reporting to Zelan. Situation managed.

She headed toward the room Falco had given her, admiring the paintings on the walls. She'd skipped down these hallways as a child with Falco's daughter, Audra, never once looking at the beautiful artwork. Audra had a mischievous side and was always trying to spy on their fathers, hear what they were talking about. Alana had been right there with her, tagging along, caught up in the intrigue even at that young age, but all Selia had wanted to do was go to the stable and ride the horses. Falco had the most beautiful horses in his stable, ones gentle enough for a child to ride.

She paused at the portrait of Shara Eldralin. She sat on a stool in the study before the fireplace, her red hair a mane around her shoulders, her green eyes holding secrets Selia wanted to know. She was dressed in an emerald green gown that flowed around her, her hands clasped in her lap. She'd been the love of Talar Eldralin's life, the woman he couldn't live without. When Selia was younger, she'd begged Elyon to tell her the story of Shara.

They'd taken a walk to the mausoleum where Shara and Talar had been interred. It had seemed so romantic to her, to think of a man with Talar Eldralin's power, brought down by his love for a woman. Eldralins loved fiercely. Her own father felt that way about her mother, crossing an entire region to find the one woman who was his match. Selia sighed, wondering if such a match was out there for her, if she'd ever find the one man who made her feel whole.

This train of thought brought her full circle to Alana. Had she found her one true match? Was Trey the man who she would sacrifice everything for? She was risking her family, risking being ostracized by her own people. She was risking never returning to Temeron.

Without warning, something gripped the back of her neck and shoved her forward. Her head struck the wall and pain radiated across her skull. Fingers tightened beneath her hair and she felt a body press into hers from behind.

A voice hissed in her ear. "So sad, wandering these lonely hallways by yourself."

She didn't recognize the voice, but she fought against the hold he had on her. "Let me go!" she shouted.

He spun her around and slammed her back into the wall. Lights exploded in her eyes and pain ran down her spine, then his hand was on her throat, his fingers digging into her flesh. Selia blinked, panic edging to the surface. She recognized the Temerian guard uniform, but she didn't remember ever seeing this man before. She braced her hands against his chest and shoved, but he moved into her, pressing the length of his body against hers. He rubbed his face against her hair.

"Such a shame. You are lovely. I would enjoy playing with you."

Selia dug her fingers into his shirt, trying to twist away, but he slammed her back into the wall and blackness nearly engulfed her.

His fingers tightened and Selia couldn't draw a breath, her heart pounding frantically beneath her breast.

"This isn't your fault. You can thank your sister for this. If she hadn't rejected me for a piece of pond scum, you wouldn't be here right now."

Selia clawed at him, but lights danced in her peripheral vision and she couldn't get any air into her lungs. She tried to kick him, but he had his legs pressed so tight against her that she could hardly move. She knew that if she lost consciousness she was dead. She tried to raise her hands to rake her nails across his face, but he slammed her head into the wall again, drawing an agonized whimper from her.

His breath was hot against her ear. "Remember, as you die, you die for Alana," he whispered.

Selia felt the edge of blackness beckoning her and her fingers went numb. Against her will, her eyes started to close. It would be over soon, she thought. It'll be over, no more pain, no more struggle. Just as her hands fell away, something slammed into her attacker, his hand wrenched from her throat.

Air flooded her lungs.

She doubled over, clutching her chest, gasping in great breaths, pain radiating out into every part of her body. Someone grabbed her shoulders, holding her up.

"Selia! Are you okay?"

She clung to the arms supporting her and opened her eyes. She realized the frantic sounds were coming from her. Trey's green eyes looked into her own, panic in their depths. She couldn't get enough air to speak, but he held her up. Behind him lay the crumpled body of the guard, blood pooling beneath his head, one of Falco's bronze statues lying on his chest.

Suddenly the study door burst open and people came running down the hallway. Her father arrived first, shoving Trey away from her and pulling her into his arms.

"What the hell's going on!" he roared.

Selia clung to her father. "He tried to kill me," she sobbed, pointing at the downed man. "Trey saved my life." Tears streamed down her face and her throat throbbed with every beat of her heart. "He said he was going to kill me because Alana rejected him."

Trey glanced down at the man, then something caught his attention. He stepped over his legs and bent, grabbing something at his throat, yanking it free. Alana came running up the hallway, taking it all in, her eyes swallowing her face. She hurried over to Selia and gathered her in her arms. Selia melted against her sister, holding her as close as she could get her.

"What is it?" demanded Zeran.

Trey let a necklace dangle from his hand, a wooden medallion swinging from the bottom of it. "It's the necklace I carved for Trista. I gave this to her. I made it myself."

Alana's gaze snapped to her father as Roe Manes came to a skidding halt in the middle of the group. Zeran stalked over to the body and glared down at him.

"Who is he?" sobbed Selia, shivering now. Mairin moved to her other side and wrapped her arms around both of them.

"Folen Tesseran," said Alana through clenched teeth. "He was the tracker who found Trey in Taral and shot him."

Zeran looked back at them, his expression stricken.

"He's also the man who killed Trista," Alana finished. She brushed Selia's hair away from her face. "Come on. Let's get you to your room."

"I'll send a healer up," offered Falco.

Zeran turned to Roe. "Lock this bastard in a cell."

"Should I have a healer look at him too?" Roe asked, moving toward the body.

"No, let him rot," snarled Zeran. He held out his hand for the necklace and Trey passed it over. "If he dies, it'll save us an execution," he growled.

CHAPTER 19

Zeran went looking for Trey the following evening. He'd spent the day processing everything that had happened the previous night. He'd almost lost another daughter. He couldn't get his head around that. Selia had almost died.

Everything that he'd thought, his prejudices, his belief system had been under fire since that moment, the moment he came out and saw the bruises on her throat, saw her shivering in shock, gasping for her next breath, saw the man holding her up, the one he'd made an enemy in his mind.

It took him hours to sort through the conflict, to break down his old paradigm, to accept the truth. Had it really taken a nearly fatal mistake to prove to him he was wrong? He couldn't allow himself to think how much worse this could have been, how irretrievable the outcome. He couldn't accept that he'd almost lost Selia.

He finally tracked Trey to the library, thanks to Roe Manes. He pushed open the door and found the younger man sitting in a chair at the table, a lodegem lamp casting shadows in his face. He looked up as Zeran entered, his green eyes shining.

"I've been looking for you," Zeran said, feeling awkward, feeling conflicted. His old beliefs still warred with his new reality.

Trey motioned to the chair across from him and Zeran pulled it out, sinking into the burgundy leather. These Leonharts and their burgundy. Zeran was sick to death of the color on every surface.

Looking around the room with its vast shelves filled with books, Zeran had to admit this was the last place he'd expected to find Trey. "You like books?" he said, conversationally.

Trey laughed, shutting the book he held. "Honestly, I can't read. Allie's been teaching me. I thought I'd try to practice a little."

Zeran frowned. "You can't read?"

Trey shook his head, flattening his hand on the cover. "Let's just say Perrine wasn't any too concerned about me getting an education."

"But I saw you in the schoolyard when I picked up the girls."

Trey shrugged. "I'd go there to get away from home, be around the other kids. Perrine was usually…" His voice caught and he drew a deep breath. "…entertaining during that time."

Zeran felt a stab of guilt. "I should have taken you from her home."

"You can't save everyone, Stravad Leader. And having a bastard half-blood around your daughters wouldn't have been to anyone's liking."

Zeran looked at the book under Trey's hand. *History of Loden.* Interesting choice. "I owe you an apology."

Trey leaned back in the chair, wincing.

"Does your injury still hurt? I can get a healer."

Trey chuckled. "You wouldn't think getting shot in the ass would hurt so much, but apparently you have a lot of muscles back there."

Zeran smiled.

Trey waved him off. "I'm fine."

Zeran looked around the room, then rose to his feet, going to the refreshment table in the corner. A crystal decanter and a number of glasses were positioned on a silver tray. He pulled the stopper and filled two glasses with a few fingers of liquor, then he carried them back to the table, passing one to Trey.

Swirling the amber colored liquor in the glass, he watched it coat the sides. "I'm sorry for arresting you for Trista's murder. I'm sorry for taking your life away from you. I owe you for both of my daughters' lives and I will do everything I can to clear your name in Temeron. You will not have to face the council for Alana's abduction. If you come back to Temeron, I'll make sure you have employment, either with your old master or in anything else you want."

Trey considered what he was saying, lifting the glass to his lips. He took a sip, then made a face and put it on the table again, pushing it away from himself.

Zeran gave him an amused look. "You don't like it?"

"It tastes like shit," Trey said.

Zeran laughed. "That's Trendarian brandy. The finest brandy in the land."

"It's nasty."

Zeran shook his head and lifted it to his lips, taking his own sip. A sour, acidic bite struck his tongue and he shivered in disgust. "Dear lord," he said, setting it down.

Trey laughed.

Zeran shivered again. "Oh damn, that is off. So off."

Trey continued laughing.

Zeran's expression sobered. "Can you accept my apology? Can you accept my gratitude?"

"You don't owe me an apology, Stravad Leader. Nothing changes what I put you through. I owe you an apology for that."

"You didn't have much choice…"

Trey held up a hand. "Can we just stop? I'm not comfortable with this. It was an unfortunate event all the way around and nothing's going to change that."

Zeran sighed. "Agreed."

Trey looked up at him, his green eyes piercing. "I love your daughter. I'm not going to apologize for that. She's the best thing that's ever happened to me."

"Things looked tense between the two of you last night," Zeran said conversationally. He didn't really want to talk about Alana, but he knew he couldn't avoid it anymore. "Did something happen?"

"I know you can never approve of me. I understand that. I don't expect you to, but Allie says she's willing to choose me over Temeron, over her family. I just can't let her make that decision. She'll grow to hate me later if she does."

Zeran leaned back, splaying his hand on the table. He hadn't expected this. "You told her that? You told her you didn't want to be with her?"

"No, I'd never lie to her. I told her I wanted her to make sure she knew what she was giving up. I can't compete with you and her sisters. I can't offer her that." He looked down. "And I can't go back to Temeron. There's nothing there for me."

"Allie's there. Your past work is there."

"Do you know what prejudice Allie would face everyday if she picked me? Do you think anyone in Temeron is going to believe I didn't kill Trista?"

"If I tell them…"

Trey gave him a speaking look.

Zeran knew he was right. It wouldn't matter. Trey's fate was sealed the moment he was born a bastard to a prostitute. Temeron was progressive, but even Stravad had their prejudices. Zeran sighed.

"I'm not going to lie to you, Trey. I envisioned someone very different for my daughter."

"Did you envision anyone for your daughter?"

Zeran laughed, nodding in agreement. "You have a point. Selia called me out on that last night. I don't know. I guess I hoped I wouldn't have to face this, but the truth is my girls are grown women now. And honestly, Allie is more capable than anyone else of taking care of herself." He held up a hand and let it fall. "The one thing I know about Allie, the one thing that has always been true is when she says something, she means it. She told me she loves you. I don't deny that it's true. If you love her as you say you do, then I can't believe you'd let any obstacles get in the way of the two of you." He rubbed the back of his neck. "Take it from someone who crossed an entire land for the woman I loved, if it's meant to be, it's meant to be fought for. I've seen you fight for her and I've definitely seen her fight for you. Maybe you should stop worrying about what everyone else thinks and actually start living your life. I almost lost two daughters in the last few weeks. Seems to me life's a bit short to be worried about what everyone else thinks all the time." He sighed. "Even me."

Trey smiled. "This is just about killing you, isn't it?"

"Yeah, I really could have used a drink, but I'm not drinking this swill," he said, pushing the glass away. He rose to his feet. "In fact, I think I'll track down our host and see if he's got anything that doesn't taste like feet. It might be a good night to get rip-roaring drunk." He tapped his fingers on the table, then turned to leave. "If you really want to learn to read, I'd pick something a little more exciting than the *History of Loden*, unless you need an anesthetic."

*   *   *

Alana opened the door to her room to find Trey standing on the other side. She gave him a surprised look, tying her robe around her waist. Her hair was still damp from her bath and she hadn't expected to see anyone else tonight.

"Hey," he said.

"Hey," she answered.

He put his hands on her hips and guided her back into the room, closing the door behind him. "Can we talk?"

Talk? She blew out air. It had been a long day, working with her granddad to control her power, sitting with Selia and talking about what had happened, then listening to Falco lecture Mairin on Nazarien protocol. She still felt stung by Trey's rejection the previous night and wasn't feeling like forgiving him just yet.

She crossed her arms and gave him her coldest glare. "About what?"

"About us?"

"Is there an us?"

He briefly closed his eyes. "I know you're angry with me, sprite."

"Oh, I'm not angry."

He exhaled in frustration. "Can you please hear me out?"

She waved a hand airily. "Speak.

A smile spread across his face, lighting his eyes. She didn't know what the hell he found amusing and it made her angry all over again.

"Do you think this is funny?"

"I think I love you," he answered, taking her breath away. "I think you are the single best thing that's ever happened to me."

She looked down, fighting tears. He confused her. She didn't know what he actually felt and he kept changing the game on her. He stepped forward and sank his fingers into her hair.

"Look at me, Allie."

She looked up, blinking back the wetness.

"I'm sorry about last night. I just didn't want you making a mistake."

"I told you I knew what I wanted."

"I know, but I just wanted you to be sure."

"Then why are you here now? What's suddenly changed?"

"I talked to your father."

Alana blinked. "What?"

"He came to see me and we talked."

"And?"

"And I don't know if he approves of us or not, but he understands you're a grown woman now and the choice is yours." He lifted his other hand and cupped her cheek. "I will never second guess you again, sprite. If you tell me you want to be with me, I'll believe you. I'm not sure how I got this lucky, but I'm not going to question it. If you'll have me, Allie, I want nothing more than to be with you for the rest of my life."

Alana sniffed, lifting a hand to brush a tear off her cheek. "I love you, Trey. That's all I know."

"Then that's all that matters," he said. He brought his mouth down to hers. "Now, how about we pick up where we left off?"

And Alana had nothing more to say as she lifted to meet him.

* * *

Mairin sat in a chair next to her father, lined up at the head of the audience room to the left to Falco's throne. She wore a pair of trousers and a silk blouse buttoned to the neck with a military style jacket that came to mid-thigh and polished black boots. Alana had picked it out for her, telling her it was a power look. As Mairin glanced over at her father and Falco, she realized they'd chosen similar outfits, with the exception of the gold crown that lay on Falco's brow.

She rubbed her hands over the arms of the chair and gripped the ends, searching the gathered crowd for Alana. She stood next to Trey and Selia, giving her a nod of encouragement. Behind her was Tyrane, Elyon, and Captain Petric and to Mairin's right, standing against the wall, his arms clasped behind his back in parade position stood Roe Manes.

She shifted and looked back at him. He gave her a small smile and that one gesture eased some of the panic welling in Mairin's chest. They hadn't had a chance to talk much since she arrived in Zelan, but something about the way he stood at her back, tall and dignified soothed her.

Zeran reached over and covered her hand with his where it had a death grip on the chair arms. "Ease up, Mai. This is just a meet and greet, nothing more."

She nodded jerkily and swallowed. It should be Alana up here, not her. Alana had been trained for this. Alana had wanted this her entire life. How had *she* gotten mixed up in it? She didn't want to be a leader, she didn't want to be a politician. She just wanted to make her pastries and be satisfied with that. Except she didn't. Not anymore.

Running Temeron in her father's absence had given her a purpose she'd never known. She'd gotten up each morning, wondering what new thing awaited her. And listening to Falco last night, hearing him explain the way the alliance of the seven protectorates worked, had fascinated her.

She gave a start when the guards threw open the doors. A handsome man strode into the room, his step confident and sure, his head thrown back. He wore a black uniform with the scythe of the Nazarien embroidered in gold on his chest, medallions dangling from his ears. He had brown hair and piercing Stravad blue eyes and Mairin could feel the force of his presence as he came to a halt before them.

Behind him was a much older Nazarien, wearing the same uniform. He had to be very old because his face was lined and his eyes cloudy. Threads of silver shown in his black hair and his shoulders were rounded.

No others entered behind these two and to Mairin's surprise, the younger one turned to face her, placing his closed fist against his chest and bowing. A gasp of outrage rose in the room and Mairin shot a look at Falco. By Falco's clenched jaw, he understood the slight.

Straightening, the younger man shifted to face Falco again. "Lord of Loden, I presume."

Falco tilted up his proud head. "You presume right. State your name."

The young man made a flourish. "I am Tarish Enro, Nazar."

The older Nazarien bowed his head, his demeanor submissive and disapproving. Falco's attention shifted to him.

"Who is your companion and where is your retinue? I would speak with all of your followers."

Tarish made a sweep of the hand toward the older man. "This is Merith Daeglor. He is my closest advisor. I do not travel with a retinue; however, the entire Nazarien order has accompanied me to Loden."

Another murmur went up from those assembled. Tarish ignored it.

"They await my command at the Nazarien outpost on the Loden side of the Groziks."

Zeran stiffened and Falco narrowed his eyes.

"The entire Nazarien order?"

"Well, with the exception of the women and children, and a few guards to protect Chernow and Tirsbor, but we can discuss that more later. Right now, I am most intrigued to meet…"

"Tarish Enro!" thundered Falco's voice, echoing in the room. "I summoned you to appear before me twice and you ignored my summons."

Tarish folded his hands in front of him. "I did," he said simply.

Merith flinched, lowering his head further.

"Why would you ignore my summons?"

"That is a complicated issue, Lord of Loden."

"Beside me sits the heir of Eldon, Zeran Eldralin, the current Stravad Leader. You ignored his summons as well."

"I did."

"You cannot ignore the summons of an Eldralin. The purpose of your order, the purpose of your existence, is to serve the Eldralins."

Tarish gave a slow smile. Mairin shuddered. She'd never seen a Nazarien smile before and this was not a happy expression. His blue eyes shifted to hers. "But I did answer the summons of an Eldralin. I answered to Mairin Eldralin." He took a step toward her and suddenly Roe was between them, glaring him down.

Tarish hesitated, his brow quirking. "I wish only to pay my respects, guard," he said, dismissively. He dropped to one knee, his fist pressed to his chest, his head bowed. "You are truly as beautiful as I had heard and I am awestruck in your presence."

Mairin didn't know what to do. Something about his behavior sent alarms through her. He lifted his head and met her gaze.

"I will answer only to you, Mairin Eldralin."

"Enough!" shouted Falco, rising to his feet. "Tarish Enro, I am appalled by your behavior. This is not the way the order Eldon founded was meant to work."

Tarish rose to his feet and turned to face Falco, tearing his gaze from Mairin. "Then it appears we have much to discuss, Lord of Loden."

"It appears that way," said Falco through clenched teeth.

"My advisor and I are exhausted. It's been a grueling ride. I would like the opportunity to refresh myself." He glanced at Mairin again as he said it. "I feel as if I should present my best self to you."

"Fine. You will be shown quarters, but we will meet again tomorrow and you will explain yourself," said Falco. "Do not think for a moment your behavior has gone unnoticed."

Tarish tilted his head. "Oh, I'm certain it hasn't."

"I expect you will conduct yourself with the gravitas of your position in the future."

Tarish folded his hands again. "Lord of Loden, do not mistake my appearance here as a sign that you've brought me to heel. My appearance here has everything to do with my deep abiding dedication to the Eldralin line." His gaze shifted back to Mairin. "And my desire to serve it in every way possible," he said suggestively. "*Every* way possible."

Zeran rose abruptly from his chair and Roe's hand fell to the hilt of his sword.

Then Tarish Enro did the most surprising thing of all. He tilted back his head and laughed.

CHAPTER 20

Trey stayed back in the shadows, leaning against the wall of the barracks, watching the Nazar practice his weaponry in the training arena outside the castle in Zelan. He spun and whirled, striking the practice dummy and skating away so fast, it was difficult to follow him with the eye. He had a skill that only a Stravad could possess, a quickness and litheness unlike few that Trey had ever seen.

Roe stepped up beside him. "He's been at it for hours. It's like he never tires."

"I know."

"Something's not right about this visit. Something doesn't feel right."

"Maybe it's the entire Nazarien army stationed a day's ride from us," Trey said.

Roe crossed his arms over his chest and shook his head. "It's also this obsession with Mairin. I don't like it."

Trey gave him an amused look.

Roe glanced at him. "It's not for the reason you think."

"No?"

"No." Roe made a face. "Not entirely for the reason you think."

Trey chuckled.

"Nazarien do not marry. They procreate."

Trey considered that. Roe had a point. That did make him uneasy. "Who better to procreate with than Mairin Eldralin? I see your point. Have you told Mairin or the Stravad Leader your concern?"

Roe shifted weight uneasily. "It's not that easy. How do I cast disparagement on the Nazar?"

Trey started to answer, but the man suddenly turned, peering into the shadows as if he'd heard their quiet conversation. Roe stiffened and Trey eased away from the wall. Walking to the edge of the arena, the Nazar grabbed a towel and wiped his forehead with it, leaning the blade against the railing.

"Would either of you care to join me?"

Roe's hands clenched into fists and he took a step forward, but Trey stopped him with his arm, shaking his head at the guard. Roe clenched his jaw and eased back.

"No? What a shame. I could use a skilled sparring partner, except I have to be honest, there are few with my skill." His eyes shifted to Trey. "And you? Would you give it a go?"

"I would be far less of a challenge for you," Trey said, fighting down the rise of irritation. He wasn't going to be baited by this man. He clapped Roe on the shoulder. "Besides, we have other engagements to attend." He turned Roe and they started walking back to the castle.

"I could have held my own with him," said Roe, glancing back over his shoulder.

"And if you wounded him, what then? He's the Nazar, Roe. You aren't exactly in the same league."

Roe stopped walking, his face falling. Trey stopped and turned to face him.

"What?" he asked.

"You're right. I'm not in the same league. I'm no where near the same as a man like that."

"That's not what I meant."

Roe shook his head, giving a grim laugh. "What a damn fool. I have no right to even think about Mairin the way I do. I'm no match for her." He stepped closer to Trey. "Do you know I kissed her once? In the Stravad Leader's kitchen after Alana went missing? I kissed her. Me!" He slapped a hand against his chest. "What was I thinking? She'd never consider a lowly soldier. Lord, I'm such a fool."

Trey sighed. "Stop this. You have more right to court Mairin Eldralin than anyone else. You have always been loyal and dedicated and annoyingly upbeat about everything." He gripped Roe's shoulder. "Take it from me. You can't predict what an Eldralin's going to do, but if anyone has the right to pursue Mairin, it's you."

Roe forced an uncertain smile. "You make me regret having you shot in the ass."

"Well, I clocked you with a crowbar, so we're probably even."

Roe rubbed the back of his head in memory. "That's right. I almost forgot about that. Damn, that was a cold blooded thing to do, Almsden."

Trey shrugged. "You were holding me for execution, so it seemed a fair trade."

They both laughed as they turned toward the castle again.

*   *   *

Merith stepped out from behind the shed that held the practice equipment. Tarish sensed him, looming there for the last ten minutes. He watched the two young men wander back to the castle, both so disparate in nature – one dressed in the uniform of a Temerian warrior, the other dressed as a vagabond, too thin and ragged – still he sensed a bond between them. He wondered if he could use it to his advantage.

"Did you find out who the thin one is?"

"His name's Trey Almsden. He was brought here as a prisoner from Taral for judgment by the Lord of Loden."

Tarish didn't bother to turn to face his advisor. "What charge?"

"They believed he murdered a council member's daughter in Temeron."

"And yet he's free?"

"It was discovered that a member of the Stravad Leader's guard was the real culprit. The one they're holding."

"Did you get in to the cell to talk with him?"

"I did," said Merith.

"And no one saw you?"

"I had a few minutes to myself. When I was discovered by a guard, I feigned being lost."

"Did the prisoner have anything to tell you about the Stravad Leader's retinue?"

"He talked mostly about Almsden. He said Almsden's a bastard, the child of a whore and an unknown father. His life has been difficult, even in Temeron."

"And yet he walks around a free man?" said Tarish, rubbing the towel over the back of his neck.

"But he can never return to Temeron. They will never accept him."

"So, he's an outcast."

"Just so, my Lord Nazar."

Tarish rubbed the towel over his head. "I wonder where his loyalties lay. With the people who accused him of murder, with the people who denied him the basic necessities of life, or does he hate them?"

"He's apparently in love with one of the Stravad Leader's daughters, but the Stravad Leader is violently opposed to it."

"Of course he is. Eldralins are not without their prejudices. While the soldier is fiercely loyal. I've seen that firsthand." Tarish draped the towel around his neck, reaching for his sword. "This Trey Almsden, however, is vastly useable, I think." Then he picked up the sword and went back to his position, prepared to continue his training at least until the sun dropped down into the horizon.

$*$ $*$ $*$

Trey slipped out of the dining hall, taking a seat on the lion fountain in the central courtyard. The sound of running water was soothing and he breathed deeply of the night air. A chill touched his skin, reminding him autumn was pressing around the corner.

He looked back at the glowing lights in the dining hall. Falco had hosted a dinner in honor of his guest, although it had been a tense affair. Conversation had been stilted and no one had drank much of the wine that was prepared. Many anxious glances had gone around the table and Roe had loomed behind Mairin's chair, leaning against the wall like a statue the entire night. He hadn't been invited to dine with them, but as he'd maintained his vigil, Trey couldn't help but catch the covert glances he and Mairin shared.

Of course, Falco had ordered course after course of food. Trey couldn't get used to eating to the point of bursting. Once his stomach was filled, he felt like he'd be sick if he tried another bite. He'd told Alana he was going out for some fresh air and she'd squeezed his hand, giving him a smile that said she knew he'd had enough. He loved her for that, for understanding how hard this all was for him.

The door opened, the sound of conversation momentarily growing louder, and a figure stepped out. Trey instantly recognized the Nazar's effortless glide as he shut the door behind him and made his way to the fountain.

Trey straightened, feeling all the hairs on the back of his neck rise. There was something about this man that made him tense.

The Nazar stopped in front of him, his gaze roving over Trey. He was a handsome man, but there was a cruelty around his eyes and mouth that hardened his features. "You find these things as tiresome as I do," he said, conversationally, bracing his legs shoulder width apart.

He didn't take a seat and Trey resisted the impulse to rise. He didn't like having this man looming over him, but he wasn't going to give him the satisfaction of knowing that.

"I'm just not used to it."

The Nazar crossed his arms over his chest and glanced back at the dining hall. "The Nazarien live austere lives. We don't engage in such frivolities. They make a man weak, don't you think?"

Trey hid his smile. "There's austerity for the sake of austerity and then there's austerity when you have nothing more. The two are not the same."

The Nazar's gaze narrowed on Trey. "I'm guessing you've known the latter."

Trey didn't answer. He didn't need to justify his life to this man.

Tarish shook his head. "These Eldralins are a tight bunch, are they not? Hard to find a way into their inner circle."

"Yet you've proclaimed your interest in Mairin."

"She is magnificent, but I don't think her father approves. As I said, they are a tight bunch."

"With reason. People seem to always want a piece of them."

Tarish took a seat on the fountain. "Well, the Eldralins have that indefinable something about them. Eldon was said to have it and his son, Talar, was able to bend an entire nation of people to his will."

"He led them to a sanctuary, where they could live their lives."

Tarish gave him an amused look. "You know your history."

"I'm not a complete imbecile." Trey couldn't keep the bite out of his voice.

"No, but I suspect your knowledge has been hard won. I suspect things haven't been as easy as you'd like."

"Nothing is easy."

"Ah, but to chafe against the Eldralin shackles is not easy, and they are shackles. For generations, my people, the Nazarien, have been but pawns played on a chess board for the edification of the Eldralins. We exist solely for their benefit, to promote their line. It burns. It scalds." He jerked his chin toward the dining hall. "It goads me."

Trey felt alarms ringing inside of him, but he held his tongue. "It should goad you too."

"What exactly are you saying?"

Tarish's gaze swung back and pinned him. "I think it's time for the Eldralins to serve the Nazarien, not the other way around."

"You mean Mairin?"

Tarish nodded. "She's the first payment."

Trey rose to his feet, facing the Nazar. "Zeran Eldralin will never let you get near his daughter."

"Zeran Eldralin does not command me."

"He does. He's the reason for the Nazarien."

Tarish's lips quirked up in an unholy smile. "Perhaps that's about to change. I think you are a man who knows the way the tide flows."

"What?"

"You've survived for as long as you have because you can see the way things shift. A shift is about to happen here and I'd like you to be on the right side of the outcome."

"Are you threatening the Stravad Leader?"

Tarish held out his empty hands. "Not at all. I don't threaten, I do. Unlike my weak predecessor, I am a man of action."

"And what action do you intend to take?"

"I need a woman to breed me sons. A strong woman with an unparalleled bloodline."

"And you think Mairin will let you court her?"

"Nazarien do not court. I think her father will gift her to me."

Trey wanted to laugh, but there was nothing amusing in Tarish's tone or body language. He believed what he said. "Why would he do that?"

Tarish leaned back and folded his hands in front of him, bracing them on his crossed knee. "To save his people, naturally. He'll come to see it's an advantageous arrangement. Certainly better than a moonstruck soldier, wouldn't you say?"

"The Nazarien do not marry."

"No, we do not. And I have no intention of breaking that tradition, but Mairin will be a prized possession in my collection. She will want for nothing. Other fathers have made less advantageous arrangements for their young."

Trey felt a wave of nausea flow through him, but he fought it back. He had to learn more. He forced himself to take a seat on the fountain again. "Why are you telling me this?"

"Because, as I said, I sense a man who knows how to survive. Align yourself with me and I will grant you a position in my order."

"You'll make me a Nazarien?"

"Ah, I can't do that."

"No, because I'm not full-blooded Stravad."

"Just so."

"What does that leave me then?"

"A position as Mairin's guard, keeping her under control so I don't have to worry about it. You would be well compensated, you'd never want for anything else the rest of your life."

"And how do you know I won't go right to Zeran Eldralin and tell him what you've told me?"

Tarish considered that, his boot jogging up and down. "It really doesn't matter. He'll know my plans soon enough. I'm not trying to keep it a secret. All I'm doing is offering you a chance to get on the right side of history before the choice is taken away."

"You have only one man with you, and an old man at that. What makes you think Zeran won't just have you thrown in the dungeon?"

Tarish smiled again. It was the most chilling smile Trey had ever seen. "Because the entire Nazarien army is camped at the summit. If I don't appear before them in four days time, hale and hearty, they will descend on Zelan. Now, certainly Falco Leonhart has the command of Seven Protectorates at his fingertips, but how long will it take to assemble them, and in the meantime, my men are but half a day away."

Trey felt a chill race over him. This was the plot that Zeran had feared. This was the very thing that made Falco summon them to Zelan.

Tarish tilted his head toward Trey and blinked a few times, innocently. "So, now, fugitive, what'll it be? Will you join with me and make sure no one dies, or will you force me to tear out your heart and show it to your lovely lady…while…it…still…beats?"

CHAPTER 21

"I will throw him in the dungeon myself," raged Falco, pacing before his fireplace, his hands curled into fists.

"And his men will descend on Zelan," said Trey calmly, leaning against the wall by the door, his arms folded.

Captain Petric stood outside the door with some of Falco's men, guarding it against intrusion. Zeran stood at the windows, overlooking the balcony, his profile grim. Mairin sat in the chair by the fire, her hands clasped in her lap. Roe stood behind her chair, his hand resting on the top of it. Selia had taken a seat on the floor, next to Mairin's chair, her back to the fireplace and Alana sat across from them, her attention divided between Trey and her father.

Next to her on the divan was Tyrane and on his other side, Elyon, both deep in thought. It was impossible not to see the similarities between the two men around the eyes and cheekbones. They hadn't said much since Trey had brought them the news of his conversation with Tarish Enro. They all seemed torn between a mixture of shock and resignation. Trey figured his news wasn't anything they hadn't already suspected.

Falco braced a hand on the fireplace and ran his other hand through his hair. "I will send to the protectorates tonight. We can use the trill cote."

"And they won't arrive in time, Falco," said Tyrane. "Just to muster their men would take the four days Tarish has given us to make a decision. Zelan would fall in that time."

"I have my own army!" said Falco, whirling to face him.

"And is it enough to counter the entire Nazarien force?" said Tyrane angrily.

Falco's shoulders slumped.

"He's outmaneuvered us. He set us up and we walked right into the trap," continued Tyrane.

"The Nazarien answer to the Eldralins!" shouted Falco.

Tyrane gave the king a weary look.

"The Nazarien answer to the Eldralins," Falco said with less conviction.

"And that's why we're in this fix. We ignored the Nazarien for too long. I've warned against this for decades," said Elyon, bracing his face in his hands.

"Maybe he's lying," said Falco. "Maybe he didn't bring the entire army."

"What about your experience with the Nazarien has led you to believe they ever lie, Falco?" said Tyrane. "He brought his army. He knew what he was doing. He plotted this during all the time you ordered him to Zelan and he didn't answer. This is what he was doing and he just happened to be ready for action when Mairin contacted him."

Trey could see that Roe was working up to something. "You can't turn Mairin over to that animal!" he said, stepping up beside her chair, his hand on the hilt of his sword. "I will challenge him!"

Mairin looked up at her champion and lifted a hand to curl it through his free one. He gave her an anguished look.

"You can't challenge him, Roe. You're no match for his skill. He'd kill you and then what? It wouldn't stop anything," said Trey.

Zeran tilted his head down as if he were listening.

"I can't stand by and let him trade for her like she was a commodity!"

"No one's trading her like a commodity, Roe," said Tyrane with an edge to his voice. "Can everyone calm the hell down and let me think? This can't just be about Mairin. This is about something more."

Elyon nodded. "The Nazarien have been shunted to a corner of Nevaisser due to the persecution of the Human kingdoms," he said. "When Karnack Pretorian was Nazar, he was an ineffective leader. He chose isolation over confrontation. I warned you, Zeran, it wasn't a good move for an order that's used to action." He lowered his hands and looked up at Falco. "But because they were so far away from us, we didn't worry about them. In fact, we've paid little attention to the atrocities in Nevaisser for far too long. Our inattention, our inaction was bound to draw trouble to us."

"So if it isn't about Mairin, what is it about?" asked Falco, holding out his empty hands.

"He said Mairin was the first prize," answered Trey.

"And what is the rest of his prizes?" demanded Falco.

Trey didn't back down from the Lord of Loden's stare. "Temeron."

That brought Zeran around. His cobalt eyes blazed at Trey, but Trey didn't flinch away from him either.

"Temeron?" said Falco in disbelief.

"It makes sense," said Tyrane, nodding. "If he crushes Zelan with his army, the protectorates will mobilize to restore it, leaving Temeron vulnerable. Our army is highly trained, but it isn't trained the way the Nazarien are. If Temeron falls in a coup, the Seven Protectorate will have an enemy on their doorstep the like they've never seen and Tarish will have broken the Stravad people."

Selia raised a hand to her throat. "Dear lord, what can we do?"

Zeran drew a deep breath. "I have to challenge him."

That drew all eyes in the room to him and voices erupted in conflict. Trey listened to it for a moment, then he shook his head. "That's the worst thing you could do," he said loudly.

Zeran's gaze shifted to him. "What other choice do I have?"

"I've seen him fight and you're no match for him either."

"Trey's right," said Roe. "I've seen him as well. He's a demon."

"Then I'll use my power," said Zeran and Trey could feel it tickle against his skin. "I've killed with it before and I'll kill again to protect my people."

"Which creates a vacuum in the Nazarien," Trey said.

"Are you opposing me to oppose me?" said Zeran angrily.

Tyrane rose to his feet. "Listen to him. He's right. If you challenge him and Tarish dies, the Nazarien are still amassed at the summit with instructions to attack in four days. Who's going to be Nazar?"

"I am the Eldralin! I will command them!"

"For how long, Zeran? For the rest of your life? They need a leader. They need someone to turn them from the path they're on. They need someone who can dedicate his life to changing the order."

"And what of Temeron?" said Elyon. "What of our people? Who will lead them?"

"Mairin is capable."

"Not yet," said Mairin, rising to her feet. "I know nothing yet. I need years to understand everything that goes on in our government. You can't ask me to lead them by myself now."

Zeran gave his daughter a gentle smile. "Elyon will guide you and Tyrane. Falco will give you any assistance you need."

"And if you lose?" said Trey, pushing away from the wall. "What if he kills you?"

Zeran's gaze swung back to him. "You underestimate my power."

"But that's exactly what he wants, Zeran!" said Trey. "He wants you to challenge him, martyr him. In order for the Nazarien to change, they need new leadership, different leadership. They need to be taken in an entirely different direction from anything they've known before."

"And you think I can't do that?"

"I think your heart will always be in Temeron. I think Jarrett Murata tried to do that, but his allegiance was torn. I think his heart was in Temeron and that's why the changes he wrought only lasted so long. The Nazarien have to be rebuilt from the inside out. They must be broken and reassembled or you will have this same problem years from now."

Zeran took a step toward him. "Then what are you suggesting! Who do you think can do this?"

Trey's eyes shifted and landed on Alana. "Alana has to challenge him."

That caused mayhem. Both sisters were on their feet now, shouting and waving their arms. Roe gave him a disbelieving look that said he'd lost his mind. Even Falco seemed stunned. But Alana slowly smiled at him, her cobalt eyes shining. He smiled back at her, loving her so much in that moment.

Oddly enough, neither Elyon nor Zeran participated in the screaming match. They both had pensive looks on their faces. Finally Zeran held up a hand.

"Finish what you were saying," ordered the Stravad Leader.

"Alana is the only way to change the Nazarien for good. She must defeat Tarish Enro, preferably not kill him, so that he can be brought before his men and made an example of. The Nazarien respect such displays. Then she must order them to follow her rule. She has experience leading, since she's tutored at your knee her whole life and with the alliances she has in Loden, they will have to bend to her. She is an Eldralin. It's time an Eldralin lead the Nazarien."

"You said yourself that Tarish is skilled with the blade," said Zeran.

Alana rose to her feet. "I know how to handle a blade, Daddy," she answered.

Zeran frowned at her. "How?"

Alana put her arm around her uncle's waist and hugged him. "Uncle Ty taught me. He taught us all."

Tyrane kissed the top of her head and shrugged at his brother. "I figured it was more practical than the agricultural laws of DiNolfol," he said, rolling his eyes.

"What are you thinking, Daddy?" said Selia. "You can't send Alana out to fight a trained warrior. He'll kill her. What is this madness?"

Zeran never took his eyes off his middle daughter. "Alana, shatter that decanter of piss water Falco keeps in the corner."

Alana shifted her attention to it and the decanter exploded, glass shards spraying out across the table and striking the wall. Mairin and Selia jumped. Falco made an exclamation of surprise and Trey smiled.

"I'm also working on bringing things to me," she said, holding out her hand.

A glass ball on the table sprang toward her and she caught it, holding it out to her sister.

Selia took it, her eyes swallowing her face.

Roe chuckled.

Mairin struck him on the shoulder. "Did you know this?"

Roe flinched and stopped smiling, rubbing his shoulder with his hand. "Well, it was hard to ignore when she nearly brought the ceiling in the jail down on our heads."

"And busted out all the windows on the front of the constable's office," added Tyrane.

"My favorite was when she beamed that asswipe Tesseran in the head with an apple. I could hear the twunk," said Roe and they both broke off into laughter.

Zeran smiled at his youngest daughter and she smiled back. Then he shook his head. "I don't know. I need to think about this."

"You don't have much time, Zeran. We have four days beyond this one," answered Falco.

"I know that, but I can't put my daughter at risk that easily."

"He won't see it coming, Zeran," said Elyon, "and after what I've seen, the risks are minimal. I sense no power in Tarish Enro to rival that of our Alana." He folded his arms around her and kissed her temple.

"But it's not just about asking her to challenge the Nazar," said Zeran grimly. "You're asking her to become the Nazar, and that's something that requires more thought than the traffic of an evening. Much more thought," he said.

*   *   *

Falco arranged a private training facility in the basement of the castle. The room was cleared, a guard was posted, and Alana was brought down in secret. Trey, Zeran, and Elyon blocked the door and Captain Petric guarded the hallway. Tyrane and Roe were taking turns, running Alana through her paces, forcing her to defend herself with a sword, working out any rusty edges.

Zeran had to admit she was more proficient than he'd given her credit. He wasn't sure when his brother had taught the three girls how to handle themselves, but he'd done a good job. While Alana didn't match the two men in size or strength, she was quick and agile. Still Zeran shifted anxiously. This didn't sit right with him. Having his daughter fight a battle that was his to fight rankled and made him uneasy.

Not that he didn't see the logic in having Alana challenge Tarish. The Nazarien needed a leader and he agreed it needed an Eldralin leader. He certainly didn't see himself leading them, but then he didn't see Alana doing it either. For one thing, it would take her far away from her family, and for another, she was his daughter. He was supposed to protect her, to shield her from danger, not thrust her into the middle of it.

And yet, he couldn't deny that the fastest way to change the order was to put a woman in charge of it. Elyon was right. Jarrett had tried, but ultimately he'd failed. He'd wanted to be in Temeron with the woman he loved more than he wanted to rule the Nazarien. Zeran was no different. He'd already been away from Alix longer than he wanted and a great part of him just wanted to finish this mess and return to her. If he became Nazar, he would always be torn.

When Roe struck her blade, knocking it onto the ground, Zeran felt the blood drain from his face. She clutched her wrist and Roe immediately stopped, reaching to see if she was hurt. She shook her head angrily and backed away from him.

"I'm fine!"

"No," said Zeran, more to himself than anyone else. "No, I can't do this."

"Zeran," warned Elyon.

"No, I have to challenge him myself. That's the only way. I can't risk it."

Tyrane stepped in front of him, blocking him from going to Alana. "Stop! Look at me."

Zeran glared into his brother's eyes. "You're asking too much of both of us. She's just a girl." He threw his hand out to Alana.

"She's not a girl and she can do this. Would you have told Tyla Eldralin she was just a girl? Would you have denied her the right to fight for her life, to run Temeron?"

Zeran hated logic, especially when it was used against him.

Tyrane nodded as if he knew he'd won. "Roe, step back ten paces or so."

Roe did as commanded.

Tyrane gripped Zeran's shoulder. "Trust me, okay?"

Zeran nodded, but he didn't trust anyone where his daughter was concerned.

"Trust me!" said Tyrane more firmly, then he turned his back and took up a position at an angle to Alana and Roe, creating a triangle. "Now, when I move, we're both going to rush Alana at the same time. Do not hesitate, Roe. Do you hear me? Do not falter. You go at her with everything you've got. I cannot stress how important this is." He turned his head and gave the young soldier a pointed look. "Do you hear me?"

"I hear you."

"Alana, you disarm us anyway you can. Hold nothing back. You disarm both of us. Got it?"

"Got it," she said, bracing her legs and flexing her fingers.

"Tyrane," Zeran warned.

"Trust me!" hissed Tyrane.

Zeran glanced back at Trey. The younger man's face was tense, but he didn't move to intervene. Zeran wished he had a fraction of the faith Trey had in Alana, but when he looked at her, all he saw was the child he'd held in his arms.

"Now!" shouted Tyrane.

He and Roe raced at the slip of a girl, standing across the room from them. Both men raised their swords as if they intended to spit her upon them. Zeran fought the pulse of his power. It pressed at his control, wanting to slip free, wanting to kill them both for going after her, but he grappled it under control again.

Alana lowered her chin and her eyes suddenly flamed with brilliant white light. As if they struck a barrier, Roe and Tyrane were thrown backwards, landing in a heap while their swords slammed into the ground, vibrating on impact, the points imbedded in the stone.

Zeran released his breath in a rush as his brother and the guard rolled to their sides, giving her wide-eyed looks. Alana rose to her full height and flexed her hands.

"I didn't hurt you, did I?" she said, rushing over to Roe and helping him up.

Trey chuckled and walked over to Tyrane, giving him a hand.

Elyon nudged Zeran with his shoulder. "Still have doubts."

Zeran's gaze was fixated on the swords, still quivering. "Nope, none at all," he said in awe.

*　*　*

Zeran knocked on the door to Alana's room after they finished in the training chamber. He needed to talk to her, he needed to see her. Trey opened the door and Zeran fought his immediate violent reaction. He would probably never get used to being confronted with the man who'd taken his daughter from him. He wondered if they'd ever reach a moment where he accepted Alana's choice of mate.

"Can I talk to my daughter?" he asked, forcing down the immediate pulsation of his power.

"Of course," said Trey, stepping back.

Zeran walked into the room and found Alana sitting in a chair before the glass doors that looked over the balcony. She rose to her feet, seeming small in a bathrobe, her hair damp from a bath, her feet bare. Even so, Zeran could feel the hum of the power inside of her. She was so new to it, she hadn't learned how to hide it as well as he could.

"I'll go take a walk," Trey told her, motioning to the door.

Zeran held up a hand. "Stay. This concerns you as well."

"What's wrong, Daddy?"

What was wrong? What a loaded question. How did he answer her? What was wrong for him was so very different from how she would view the situation, but he had to make her understand. He had to know she was fully aware of the choices she was making.

"Sit down, Allie," he told her, taking her hands and guiding her back to the chair. She sank onto it, her cobalt eyes searching his face.

He grabbed another chair and pulled it in front of her, taking a seat himself. He braced his forearms on his thighs, glancing up as Trey moved to stand behind her chair, resting a hand on her shoulder. Absently, she reached up and curled her fingers around his.

"I wanted to talk to you about this whole situation." He motioned around them.

Trey's back stiffened and he saw Alana's chin lift. He knew immediately they both thought he was going to make another plea for Alana to cast Trey out of her life. While he might have thought about it a time or two (or a million), he wasn't a stupid man and he saw the writing on the wall. They were irretrievably linked to each other.

"If you challenge Tarish Enro for leadership of the Nazarien, there's no guarantee of the outcome. There's no guarantee the order will accept your claim."

"I'm an Eldralin."

"You're a woman."

She nodded. "I know, but it's time for the order to change. Everyone's right. It can't be left with a vacuum in leadership, but it also can't be run the way it's been run all these generations. It needs new blood, new ideas."

"This isn't going to be easy, Allie. You were trained to run Temeron, not an order that has been rudderless for so long. And in a land hostile to everything we are. You'll be half a world away from home. Have you thought of that?"

Her features grew grim. "I have. I hate the idea of not seeing you and Mama, Selia and Mairin everyday, but I have to do this, Daddy. I have to make this choice. It's the right one." She curled her free hand into a fist, pressing it to the middle of her chest. "I know this is the right path for me and for Trey."

"Trey will be giving up everything if he follows you."

"I'll be giving up nothing of importance," Trey said, touching her cheek with the back of his fingers. "Everything of importance for me is right here."

Zeran fought the urge to scoff at the sentimental drivel. Funny how it seemed romantic when he said things like this to Alix, but coming from the man who'd claimed his daughter, it sounded ridiculous.

"I need you to be sure, Allie, because once the challenge is made, there's no going back. I can still challenge him myself."

She leaned forward and clasped his hands. "You told me my whole life that being an Eldralin placed a burden on those of our line. You stood up and faced your challenge, you accepted the calling when it was thrust upon you. Now it's my turn. Every way I look at this, I see only this solution. I'm ready for it. You've trained me well. I can do this, Daddy."

He smoothed back her damp hair, tucking it behind her ear. "I know you can. I know you can do anything you set your mind to, but damn it, child, I'm going to miss you so very much."

She rose to her feet and wrapped her arms around his neck, pressing her cheek to his. "I'm going to miss you too, but you and Mama did a good job raising us. It's time now for you to let us make our lives what we will." She kissed his cheek. "I love you, Daddy."

He wrapped his arms around her and closed his eyes, etching the memory of this moment in his mind. He'd thought facing his father-in-law Hames had been the hardest thing he'd done, but it was nothing compared to letting his daughter go.

CHAPTER 22

Falco Leonhart sat on his throne as before, his hands clasped on the arms. On his left side sat Zeran Eldralin and on his right, Mairin with her guard in his customary spot behind her chair. The rest of the rag-tag band that had been at dinner stood on either side of the room, huddled together as if that would protect them.

A smile tugged at Tarish's mouth as he and Merith walked down the central aisle, pausing before the Lord of Loden. In a calculated move, Tarish placed his fist to his breast and bowed to Mairin, keeping his eyes fixed on her the entire time. The guard bristled and moved away from the wall, but Tarish merely gave him a slow wink.

"Tarish Enro," said Falco with a thundering voice.

"I prefer Nazar, if you please, Lord of Loden," said Tarish, feigning boredom. Lord, he was so not bored. He was anything but bored. For the first time in years, his brain buzzed with excitement. The Nazarien were so close to becoming the order they should have been for years now, unyoked from the Eldralins.

"You have made a threat against my people, Tarish. This is not in keeping with Nazarien faith and I cannot condone it."

Tarish swiveled his gaze to the ragged fugitive on the other side of the room. "Ah, so the loyalty to the Eldralins is still as strong as ever, even for those they've abused."

"Have you brought your army here to cripple us, Tarish?"

"That won't be necessary." Tarish held up his index finger. "Let me be more specific. That won't be necessary if you comply with my demands."

"Then your army is here for that purpose?"

"It is. If I don't report in four days, they will advance on Zelan. Once it is neutralized, they will turn their attention to Temeron."

"This is an act of war!" Falco grounded out. "I could have you jailed for even suggesting such a thing!"

"Which is why my men have instructions to attack if I do not appear at the designated time."

"What is it you want?" said Falco through clenched teeth.

"Ultimately, I want the Nazarien untethered from the Eldralins."

"There's no reason for the Nazarien, except to serve the Eldralin line."

"Times change and so do the Nazarien."

"If we agree to your demands, what prevents your soldiers from attacking Zelan?" said Falco.

Tarish couldn't deny he felt a bit disappointed. He'd hoped that Falco or Zeran Eldralin would at least challenge him, not roll over like dogs. He sighed. Now he was getting bored again. "I want you to declare the Nazarien independent from both you and the Eldralins. I want you to make a formal declaration of our parting. Then I want you to stay in your merry little castle and ignore everything that happens in Nevaisser."

Falco's eyes narrowed. "What *is* going to happen in Nevaisser?"

"Stravad have been the victims of Humans for too long. It ends in Nevaisser."

"What do you mean?"

"It's not for you to worry about...yet."

"Tell me!" thundered Falco.

Merith moved anxiously behind him, but Tarish wasn't intimidated. He knew Falco would do anything to protect his precious alliance with the Seven Protectorates.

"The Humans in Nevaisser have enslaved our people. They've murdered them and stolen from them. They've raped our women, and locked us on tiny tracts of infertile land. It stops. Now."

"What do you mean it stops?"

"I mean the Nazarien will wage war on the Human settlements until they are wiped from the face of Samar. Your pets here will be fine as long as they don't cross into Nevaisser, but if they decide to intervene, I will annihilate them too."

"You're talking genocide!" said Falco. "I can't allow that."

"You don't need to know anything about it. Leave me alone and your people stay safe."

Tarish felt the weight of his words settle over the room and he relished it. This was a coup. He couldn't help the exhilarated smile that played at the corners of his mouth. "Oh, and of course, I want

Mairin." He let his gaze rake over her. "She will bear me many hearty sons, I am sure."

"Why would you think we'd ever let you lay a hand on Mairin?" said Falco, lowering his head in an aggressive manner.

The guard positioned himself between Mairin and Tarish, glaring him down. Tarish almost wished he would challenge him. He'd love to gut the imbecile in front of Mairin.

"Are you going to challenge me, boy?" he said, grinning. "Are you going to fight for your woman's honor?"

"No," came a voice behind him.

Tarish looked over his shoulder, seeing Mairin's smallest sister with the huge blue eyes and the mane of wild dark hair step forward, the fugitive's woman. He narrowed his eyes on her. "What is this madness?" he asked, looking between Zeran and Falco.

Falco was grinning now and a chill raced down Tarish's spine.

"Tarish Enro, you murdering, vile piece of excrement!" she said, stopping in front of him. She had to look up to meet his gaze, but something made the hairs on the back of Tarish's arms rise. "I challenge you."

Tarish sputtered on a laugh, but Merith bowed his head, averting his eyes.

"You what?" he gasped in amusement.

"I challenge you for the position of Nazar."

"That's ridiculous. You're a woman."

She smiled, slowly, cunningly and Tarish again felt anxiety ripple through him. "I didn't take you for a coward, Enro. So disappointing."

"I fight with a sword," said Tarish, leaning over her. "Do you know how to use a sword, little bird?"

"I know how."

"This is ridiculous. Don't waste my time," he spat, turning away from her.

"According to the Nazarien bylaws, anyone can challenge the Nazar to a physical challenge. The Nazar may not refuse," said Falco.

"He can be challenged by another *Nazarien*," said Tarish.

"That's not what it says," stated Falco, smiling.

Tarish's expression sobered. "This is ridiculous." He looked over at Alana, his gaze chilling. "Do you want to die, little bird?"

"Do you?" she asked.

Tarish dismissed her. "I'm not fighting a woman. She has no right to challenge me."

"If you refuse her challenge," said Merith, speaking for the first time, "you will bring disgrace on the order and you will be hunted by all Nazarien from this day forward."

"What?" shouted Tarish. "This is insane! I'm not fighting this creature for leadership of the Nazarien."

"Then you should run," said Merith matter-of-factly. "The gauntlet was thrown down in front of witnesses. If you deny this young woman the right to challenge you, then your days are numbered."

Tarish struggled with himself to keep from raging. He moved up to Alana until they were almost nose to nose. "I will fight you, little bird, and I will destroy you. Then when you are lying in a puddle of your own blood, I will drag your sister away and I will rain such wrath down on your people that they will curse your name forever."

To Tarish's surprise, Alana smiled. "Oh, such arrogance. Hollow words from a hollow man. I pity you."

Tarish's eyes widened and he took a step back, lifting his arm as if he'd backhand her. The fugitive moved to intervene, but Merith was the one who caught his arm. "Do not bring dishonor to the order!" he growled.

Tarish yanked his arm free and turned to face Falco. "As you will," he said, bowing before the Lord of Loden. "I will gut your vixen and cut her tongue from her mouth. Then I will claim my prize," He gave Mairin a piercing look. "When I've done all that, I will annihilate you and your people, Falco Leonhart, and I will raze Temeron to the ground. The Eldralin oppression will end forever."

He spun on his shoe and stormed toward the doors.

*   *   *

Mairin watched Tarish attacking the practice dummy in the training arena outside the castle. He was savage, hacking at it until sand rained down from a tear in the shoulder. Even when all of the sand leaked out, he continued to slash at it, making the fabric dance on the end of the rope, his shouts of rage echoing back off the mountains. Mairin was very aware an entire army waited a half-day away, ready to annihilate all of them. And the man in the arena would attack her sister with the same ferocity, the same lack of compassion.

She couldn't allow it.

She couldn't allow Allie to face this raging bull of a man on her own. What was her father and Elyon thinking? How could they put her up to such nonsense? Mairin had seen what Allie could do in the parlor, but smashing a glass bottle and floating a bauble in the air were no match for the deadly skill of the man training in the arena before her.

She scrubbed her hands on her pants and fought down the panic. She had no choice. She had to try to save her family, her people, her land. She'd seen the reality in Tarish's eyes. He believed what he was doing and he wasn't going to give up.

As she started across the open grounds towards him, she marked that his advisor, Merith, lurked in the shadows, watching the Nazar warily. Mairin didn't think he approved of the turn the Nazarien had taken, but he was powerless to stop it.

Well, she wasn't.

Tarish stopped whirling as she approached, his chest heaving, sweat glistening on the skin of his throat, staining his tunic, and sliding down his temples. He gave a slow smile. Mairin had never seen Nazarien smile and she knew why. It was chilling.

She fought the urge to run and stopped on the other side of the fence from him. He came over, taking the towel hanging on the top rung, and wiped his face.

"I'd like to say this is a pleasant surprise, but you Eldralin women are a bit more trouble than I'm used to," he said, his eyes raking over her body.

She fought the shiver of revulsion that raced through her. "I want to parlay," she said, clenching her hands into fists. Now that she was here, she wasn't sure she could go through with this.

He draped the towel around his neck. "Speak. I'm listening."

"I will go with you willingly, but you must leave now and you must take your army from Loden."

His dark brows rose. "Really? That easy. You'll go with me without question. No fighting, no sobbing." He shuddered at the last. "No whining. Eldon's bloody star, I hate women who whine."

Mairin glanced away. "No, none of that, but you must swear on the order, on all you hold dear, that you will leave my family and my people alone."

"Come inside," he said, stepping back.

She took a shivering breath and crawled between the rails. Before she'd gotten through, he grabbed her by the hair and hauled her up against him, his hand twisting in her long locks. She could smell the sweat on him and see the pulse pounding in the hollow of his throat. And she knew she'd made a very bad mistake. This man would devour her and cast aside her empty body for the vultures.

He leaned close, his breath hot against her face. "Promise me you'll submit. Promise me you'll obey every order, even when I order you to my bed."

Mairin closed her eyes and shuddered in revulsion, but she nodded stiffly.

He yanked on her hair. "Say it out loud."

She drew a calming breath. "I will…"

"No!" he said, tugging her hair so hard it brought tears to her eyes. "Look at me when you say it."

Mairin forced herself to open her eyes. She took another shuddering breath. "I will…"

"Mairin!"

Mairin felt her heart stutter. She'd wanted to conclude this as fast as she could and leave with Tarish before anyone knew what she was planning, especially Roe. She couldn't let anything happen to Roe and she knew he'd never stop until he saved her from this decision.

"Roe, go back!" she pleaded.

Tarish held her hair so tight, she couldn't even turn to face him. She couldn't do anything to stop him.

"Let her go!" Roe shouted in a voice that vibrated with fury. "Let her go or I will cut your hand from your body!" He stepped through the rails and drew his sword. "I challenge you, Tarish Enro. I challenge you for the position of Nazar."

Mairin shook so hard her teeth chattered. Tarish tossed her away and she struck her back on the fence railing, falling into the dirt. Pain exploded in her skull, but she fought it, struggling to get to her feet.

Roe advanced on Tarish and Tarish turned to face him, twirling the sword around in his hand.

"No, Roe! Don't do this! He'll kill you!" she pleaded.

The two men continued to advance on each other, but Tarish laughed. "She has such faith in you, little soldier. Such belief that you will save her. Does it make your manhood shrink?"

Roe didn't take the bait. Mairin pushed away from the rail, but as she moved to intervene, Tarish roared and charged Roe. The two men came together so violently, sparks were struck from their swords.

Searching around the arena, Mairin looked for a weapon. She couldn't allow Tarish to kill Roe, but they circled each other like animals, striking and dancing away, their grunts of exertion hammering in Mairin's head. Her eyes fell on Merith, skulking around the shed that held the practice weapons. She ran toward it, yanking the door open and dashing inside, grabbing the first sword she saw. It was heavier than the one her uncle had trained her on, but she was determined.

Roe would not die for her.

She ran back out to the arena, but the two men had locked swords again and Tarish was grinning. "You love her, little soldier, don't you?"

Roe roared and threw Tarish off, swinging his blade, but Tarish danced out of the way, chuckling.

"Ah, it's such a pity. You've fought hard for her. I suspect you're willing to lay down your life for her," he said, circling Roe.

Mairin raised her own sword, prepared to dash between them if Tarish would just take one more step back.

"When she's lying in my bed, we will think of you, little soldier. We will think of you and all you sacrificed…for nothing!"

Tarish slammed into Roe, sending him sprawling on his back, the sword knocked from his hand. The Nazar continued on, throwing himself onto Roe's stomach. Roe tried to reach the sword, but Tarish slashed his blade across Roe's wrist, severing the tendon. Roe moaned in anguish and blood gushed from the wound.

"NO!" screamed Mairin, rushing forward, but Tarish looked up at her, flecks of blood on his cheeks, his blue eyes blazing as he put the edge of the blade against Roe's throat.

She stumbled to a halt, her heart pounding in her breast. He was going to kill Roe. He was going to murder him right here in front of her and she knew she'd go mad if he did. She dropped her own sword.

"Please, don't kill him! Please, I beg you! I will go with you willingly. I will do anything you say, just don't hurt him."

"You will go with me either way, little bird."

Mairin's face grew grim. "But if you kill him, I will never forget it. When you sleep, when you eat, when you turn your back for a moment, I will be there and I will kill you myself. I swear this in Eldon's name, I swear it on all that I hold dear. You will die by my hands if you do this."

Tarish glanced between Roe and Mairin, then he leaned back, easing his hold on the sword, and laughed. "Oh, this is rich. You Eldralin women and your love for the wrong sort of men. A lowly soldier, little bird, really?"

Mairin couldn't take her eyes off Roe. He was looking at her as well and she realized Tarish was right. She had loved this *simple* soldier for years, loved him for his kindness and his gentle ways, for the way he always made her feel special, treasured. He'd always been there for her family, sacrificing himself, as he was doing now.

Tarish rolled his eyes in disgust. "On the one hand, I really hate looking over my shoulder all the time, but on the other hand," he told Roe, "as Nazar, I already have to do that. Sorry, man, but you've got to go!"

He lifted the sword to deliver the killing strike and Mairin felt a scream tear out of her.

But as the sword came down, it suddenly jerked backward, throwing Tarish's arm behind him. The sword landed in the dirt, creating a furrow as it slid across the arena. Mairin looked back and saw Allie, flanked by Trey, standing outside the fence.

Tarish scrambled off Roe and grabbed the blade, but it gave Mairin enough time to pick up her own sword and run to step between Roe and the Nazar. He gave her a chilling look, but his attention was divided as Allie walked to the railings and slipped through.

"This ends now," Allie said, striding toward him, unarmed.

"I have no problem killing a woman," Tarish warned, bringing his sword around to face her.

"Well, that speaks to your utter lack of qualifications to be Nazar," she said.

He circled around them, then bent over, picking up Roe's fallen blade. He tossed it across the distance where it landed at Allie's feet. "Very well. I'm tired of playing this game with you, woman. Pick up the weapon and let's finish this."

Alana ignored the sword, deliberately circling wide away from Roe and Mairin, forcing Tarish to follow her around. Trey had ducked between the railings and stood, leaning against them, his arms crossed. Mairin wanted to scream at him to grab a weapon. Between the three of them, they might be able to kill the Nazar. She knew it wasn't a sporting thought, but she didn't give a damn anymore. This had now become survival.

Roe rolled to his side and rose to his feet. He held his bleeding arm pressed against his belly, but he took the blade from Mairin in his left hand, pushing her behind him. Mairin pressed a hand to the middle of his back, needing to touch him, needing to feel the beat of his heart and know he was alive.

Tarish's gaze raked down Alana's body. "I'll admit that was a cute trick with the sword." His eyes narrowed. "Perhaps I've been too hasty in which Eldralin I want to bed."

"Hasty seems like a good summation for all of your actions, Tarish," she said, holding her hands out to the sides.

"Why won't you pick up the sword?" he asked, shoving it with his boot. "I'll let you take a few swipes at me before I slit your throat."

"I don't need it," she said calmly.

Mairin never remembered seeing Allie in such control before. She'd worked him so his back was to the training shed and she was now between Mairin and Roe. Mairin was momentarily distracted by the spots of blood that dropped into the dirt at Roe's feet, but her attention snapped up as Tarish darted toward Allie, swiping the blade before him.

Allie never moved.

Suddenly Tarish went flying through the air, slamming into the shed. He slid down to crumple at its base, but he kept hold of the sword. For a moment, he seemed dazed. Mairin stepped out from behind Roe, shocked.

Quick as lightning, Tarish leapt to his feet and rushed Allie again. This time he struck the shed with such force the wood splintered and his sword clattered to the ground. He pushed himself to his feet, shaking his head like a dog.

"Fight me!" he screamed at her, wrenching his blade out of the dirt. "You want the leadership of the Nazarien, you have to fight me hand to hand!"

"Times change and so do the Nazarien," said Allie. "Isn't that what you told the Lord of Loden? Honestly, it's about time. The old order was an unholy mess."

Another charge sent him tumbling end over end, the sword flying out of his grasp. Merith ducked behind the shed to avoid it. Before he'd hardly stopped, Tarish lunged forward again, attempting to attack her with his bare hands, but she lifted him off his feet and threw him back into the shed with such force that a board snapped and weapons fell off the walls inside.

He struggled to rise. "Fight me like a man!" he shouted.

Allie's attention snapped to the blade and it rose, careening through the air and plunging into the shed right between Tarish's legs. He threw himself back into the shed to avoid it impaling him, blood trickling out of the side of his mouth. He stared at the blade as if he had no idea how it wound up there.

Allie walked over and looked him in the face.

"That's the whole point, now, isn't it? I'm not a man." She narrowed her eyes and Tarish gasped, his back arching, the chords in his neck popping out. "I've had enough of your threats. Yield to me, Tarish, or I will kill you!"

His face turned an unnatural shade of red and his hands clawed at the shed, but he still wasn't able to draw breath. Mairin had thought about killing him herself, but watching the brutality with which Alana threatened him frightened her.

She'd witnessed her father grappling with his power all these years, but to see it in the sister she'd held in her arms, she'd sung songs to, she'd pushed on a swing, to see her stop a man from breathing chilled her.

"Yield to me, Tarish or the pain will never end! I can keep you here for days, just enough breath to keep you alive while parts of your body die from lack of air."

Mairin glanced over to see her father and Tyrane racing for the arena, followed closely behind by Falco and a number of his guards. A motion at the corner of the shed caught Mairin's attention.

She started forward, alarmed, as Merith walked out of the shadows, but rather than bringing a weapon to challenge Alana, he stopped at Tarish's side and dropped to his knees, pressing his closed fist to his breast.

"You have vanquished the Nazar," he said, his voice ringing across the arena. "You have defeated him and he will never be allowed to lead the order again. Alana Eldralin, daughter of Zeran Eldralin, you are now the Nazar!"

Alana took a step back, releasing Tarish. He fell forward, gasping, his hands clawing at his throat. He dragged in huge breaths, hunching his back as he tried to fill his lungs. Then, in a final, ill-advised move, he surged upward, hands extended to grab Allie by the throat.

Everyone darted forward, but Tarish never touched her. He slammed into the shed with such force the wall gave way and he landed inside among the swords and other weapons. Falco's guards hurried across the arena, racing to secure him before he could do any more harm.

Alana stared at Merith's bowed head, then she looked around.

Mairin ran across the space between her and her sister, throwing her arms around Alana. They staggered and nearly went down, but a moment later, Alana was hugging her back, her face pressed to Mairin's neck.

CHAPTER 23

Alana brought her horse under control, staring at the outpost. Nazarien trained in the open area before a circle of buildings, horses danced around the corral, and the air felt charged with male energy. Tarish had not lied to them. He'd brought the entire Nazarien army to this point and they were preparing for war.

She wiped her hands on her trousers and looked over at Trey. He smiled at her.

"You can do this."

"What if they refuse to be led by a woman?"

"They'll be led."

Merith eased his horse to her side. In the day since she'd vanquished Tarish, he'd been trying to give her an emergency training course on how to approach the Nazarien. They didn't have time for her to learn everything. Tarish's four-day reprieve would end tomorrow.

"Make eye contact and do not look away. They must be the first to break. One of them will challenge you. It's inevitable, but you must face him. You must either kill him or make him realize he has no other option but to submit."

Alana didn't want to kill anyone. It wasn't in her nature. She glanced over her shoulder at Falco and the soldiers he'd brought, not to mention her sisters, her father, Tyrane and Elyon. Roe insisted on coming as well, his hand wrapped in bandages. The healer didn't know if he'd ever be able to hold a sword again. His tendons had been severed in his wrist, but Zeran had promised that Roe would always have a position in his government.

She hadn't been sure it was a good idea to bring all of these people, people who meant so much to her, on this expedition. If it went badly, someone might be hurt or Eldon protect her, killed. She knew she'd kill Nazarien warriors before she allowed them to harm her family.

Her gaze met her father's. He gave her a nod, nothing more. It was enough encouragement. She could do this. Merith had made it very clear. Ride into the middle of the training grounds outside the circle of barracks and stake her claim.

She took a deep breath, curled her hands around the reins, and touched the horse's side with her heels. He cantered into the middle of the training grounds, drawing immediate attention. Falco's soldiers fanned out, blocking the exits, ready for battle. Another soldier drove a wagon up behind Alana while her father, Tyrane, and Trey flanked her.

As one, they swung to the ground. Per Merith's instructions, she went around the back of the wagon and reached inside, curling her hand in Tarish's shirt and dragging him with all her weight to the end, where she let gravity do the rest. He tumbled out of the back, his hands and feet bound, landing on his side in the dirt. Merith had made it very clear that she had to move him herself. No one else must do it.

Her eyes swept over the rest of her retinue, landing on her sisters. Both looked anxious, Mairin standing beside Roe, her chin lifted, a sword strapped to her side. She looked like a warrior princess, ready to defend her man to the death. Her expression gave Alana courage as the Nazarien warriors began striding over from the corral and the barracks, all armed, all looking large and lethal.

Alana stepped in front of Tarish, ignoring the hateful glare he leveled on her, facing the advancing sea of men. Her power tickled at the edge of her awareness, sending shooting energy to her fingertips.

"Steady," said her father behind her. He could feel it himself.

She drew a deep breath and tilted her chin up as Mairin did, staring down the man who stepped out from the others to face her. He was over six feet tall, towering over her. His head was cleanly shaven, so much so that he had no eyebrows. His lashes were a pale blond that hardly registered in the brilliant sunlight. Nazarien medallions dangled from his ears and he had the moon and scythe tattooed on his neck. His body was thick and muscular, his legs like tree trunks. He was terrifying.

"What is the meaning of this?" he ordered, raking his gaze down Alana's body, then sneering at Tarish.

"I am Alana Eldralin!" she announced so all could hear, but she never removed her eyes from this mountain of a man. "And I am now Nazar. I fought the past Nazar and I won. You will yield to me!"

The mountain tilted his head, giving her a curious look. "We will never yield to a woman."

Alana forced herself to take a step closer to him. "Then you will die."

He glanced back at his fellow warriors in disbelief. Alana could hear a ripple of denial float through them, but no one outright challenged her, except the mountain.

"Idle threats from a tiny female," he said, looking back at her. "Step aside!"

Alana could feel the tension ripple over the area. Falco's men drew their weapons, causing some of the Nazarien to do the same. "Stop!" she shouted, holding up her hands. "I am Nazar. I earned the position through combat. You will yield to me!"

More anxious discussion and some of the Nazarien shuffled their feet. The mountain shook his head, then he started forward.

"Get out of my way! I'll slit the bastard's throat and then I'll be Nazar!" He took a dagger out of a sheath on his side and advanced toward Tarish. Alana moved to block him and he reached out to shove her to the side.

The moment his fingers brushed her shoulder, he was thrown backward into his companions, knocking a few over, the dagger dropping into the dirt. He struggled to right himself, giving her a look of sheer disbelief. Then he charged.

He hadn't take three steps before he was off his feet again, careening backward. Nazarien jumped out of the way and he crashed into a pole holding up the corral fencing. Gasping for air, he shook his head, stunned.

Murmurs floated through the Nazarien.

He rolled to his side to push himself up, but the dagger suddenly lifted into the air and shot across the space between him and Alana, slamming into the wooden post above his head and quivering.

He slumped on his backside, staring up at it, the whites of his eyes showing clear around his irises. That's when Merith came forward and dropped to his knee beside Alana, pressing his fist to his breast, his head bowed.

Alana curled her hands into fists, not daring to hope it was over.

"Bow before the next Nazar!" said Merith as loudly as he could.

The Nazarien shuffled their feet, looking between Merith and the mountain of a man. The mountain rolled to his feet and came toward Alana. She tensed, prepared to send him sailing again. Eldon's star, was the man thick in the head? This was getting boring.

He stared down at her, refusing to look away. Alana held her ground, the power humming throughout her body. She could see from her peripheral vision that his hands tightened into fists, a muscle in his jaw bulging.

She didn't even draw breath, swallow, twitch a muscle.

Then he broke eye contact and before she could react, he dropped to his knee, bowing his head, his fist pressed to his breast.

"All hail the next Nazar!" he shouted.

As Alana watched, the rest of the warriors dropped to their knees in a wave all the way to the very back of the yard.

And Alana finally dared to draw a breath and release it.

*　*　*

Alana motioned one of Falco's soldiers away from the storage shed where they'd chained Tarish after the confrontation with the Nazarien. He stepped aside and she opened the door, lifting the lodegem lantern so she could see. Tarish blinked up at her, his expression defiant, despite the chains on his ankles and wrists.

A row of buckets lined the shelves above his head and she took one down, turning it over and sitting on it. She clasped her hands before her and regarded him, placing the lantern at her feet. He stared back at her, the hatred in his eyes chilling.

"Come to gloat?" he asked.

"That isn't my plan," she answered. "Look, you're not without your points, Tarish. The Nazarien have been stagnant for too long and the atrocities in Nevaisser can't be allowed to continue. I agree with that."

He tilted back his head, staring down his nose at her. "Why would you tell me this?"

"Because I think you deserve to know. I think you deserve to know you aren't completely wrong, but you are misguided. Very, very misguided."

"You think you know about the Nazarien now. You think you understand the order. You who have stolen the leadership from me." He rattled his chains. "I have lived this my entire life. I have breathed in the Nazarien. They have been the very soul of me. And you stole it. You took it under dishonorable means."

"How do you figure that?"

"You used your power. All Nazars before have fought without their gifts. They have fought with only their strength and skill."

She sighed. "Then they have been fools. A Nazar should be the one who can lead the Nazarien the best. The one that is the most powerful. You don't seem to understand, Tarish, that the reason the order has grown stagnant is because you wouldn't change. You wouldn't adapt. You wouldn't grow." She held out her empty hands. "Nothing can survive if it doesn't adapt to the environment around it."

"And you think you can change them? You think they'll follow you just because you're an Eldralin?"

"No, I think they'll follow me because they'll see this is the only way for the order to survive. They'll follow me because they'll see I can lead them through this dark time and bring them safely to the other side."

He made a sneering motion with his upper lip. "You can? What makes you think you have the ability to do any of this?"

She leaned closer and a cunning smile curled the lines of her mouth. "Because I'm an Eldralin."

He dropped his gaze, shaking his head as if he found her amusing. Alana made a motion and Trey stepped into the shed. Tarish's eyes rose to his face and a look of panic washed over his features.

"So this is it, is it?" he said, his eyes dropping to the dagger hanging from Trey's side.

Alana stood up, stepping back so Trey could take her place. "This is it, Tarish. You can't stay my prisoner. One of your own people is bound to slit your throat now and that would undermine my authority. I can't have that."

"So you're going to do it yourself, or have your slave here do it."

Alana laid her hand on Trey's shoulder. "No, I'm letting you go."

Tarish's brows drew down into a frown. "You're what?"

"I'm letting you go." She picked up the lantern. "You have a few hours more of darkness, so I suggest you get as far away from here as you can. I'm not giving you provisions, so you'll be able to travel lightly, but you'll have to hunt for your food and find water somehow." She stared down at him. "I suggest you get far, far away or Eldon help you, I can't stop what might happen."

Trey unlocked the shackles.

Tarish stared up at Alana, rubbing his wrists, then he carefully climbed to his feet. Trey stood as well, blocking Tarish from getting near Alana. She touched him in the center of his back, but he didn't move.

Tarish circled around Trey and faced Alana. "This is a mistake, female. You will now have an enemy lurking in shadows that you cannot see."

Alana's gaze narrowed and she used her power to squeeze his heart. He dropped to one knee, clutching his chest. She leaned over him, lowering her voice. "You really need to work on your relationships with people. Get out of my sight, Tarish Enro, because the next time I see you, you die."

She released him and Tarish scrambled to his feet, darting out the door and disappearing into the night. Alana drew a deep breath, held it, then slowly released it. She hated threatening people and she'd had to do it more than she'd ever thought over the last few days.

Trey put his arm around her shoulders and led her from the shed, the lantern swinging from her hand. "You sure about this?" he asked.

"What? Being Nazar or letting Tarish go?"

"Both, but especially Tarish."

"I'm very much sure. I couldn't cart him around as a prisoner. That wasn't a good solution and he'll spend the rest of his life looking over his shoulder. This is the only solution I could come up with, other than executing him and I don't want that on my conscience."

"What about being Nazar?"

She snuggled closer to him. "If you're with me, I can do anything."

"Remind me never to cross you," he said, kissing the top of her head.

She turned and stepped into him. "Cross me anytime, Mr. Almsden, I'm all yours."

He smiled and drew her closer still. "I like the sound of that," he whispered, then he lowered his head and kissed her.

EPILOGUE

Alana and Mairin followed their father and Falco toward the edge of the outpost lands, where the mountains overlooked the whole of Loden. Alana drew a deep breath, staring out over the valley, feeling a pull in the center of her. She never wanted to leave. Loden was home. Temeron was home. How was she going to make it so far from everything she knew?

She glanced over her shoulder at the corral. Falco's son, Fadren, had arrived that morning, bringing news from Zelan. He was grooming his horse with Selia right now and Alana could hear Selia's laughter floating across the open area. Selia and Fadren had always flirted with each other as teenagers, but after greeting his father and Zeran, Fadren had sought Selia out. He seemed a lot more serious and dignified than he had when they'd seen him just a few years ago. Alana smiled to herself, wondering if Fadren wouldn't be spending a lot more time in Temeron this fall. She hoped so.

"We asked you out here for a reason," said Zeran, drawing their attention back to him. Alana felt sure her father was going to tell her he was going home, even though the Nazarien weren't ready to move out yet. She'd hoped he'd stay with her until the time came for her to lead them back to Chernow, but she'd known he might not wait that long.

Tarish Enro had marched his entire army out to Loden with the barest provisions and in the days they'd been here, a combined contingent of Nazarien and soldiers from Zelan had gone to Yonartison to secure supplies. They weren't due back for another few days, but Alana knew her father was itching to get home. The thought made her sad.

To her surprise, Zeran placed his hands on Mairin's shoulders. "You stepped up and took over as Stravad Leader at a time when our people needed you. I think it's time we made the transition a permanent one."

"What are you saying?" asked Mairin, curling her hands around his wrists.

"I think you should petition the Stravad to be their leader. I know they will accept you."

"What about you?" Alana could hear the panic edging up in Mairin's voice.

Zeran's eyes went beyond her to Alana. "I'm going to Chernow with Allie for a while."

"What?" they both said in unison. Mairin looked crestfallen, but Alana felt elated.

"Allie's just started her training and she needs someone to complete it. Elyon's too old, so he'll be returning to Temeron with you, Mai. He knows more than I ever did about running the Stravad capital. Plus you'll have Tyrane and Talmer, and your mother." He gave Mairin a smile and chucked her under the chin. "And Roe. Roe will move into an advisor role if you ask him."

Mairin blushed and lowered her head, making Alana smile. She couldn't believe her older sister was still so shy about her feelings for the soldier that everyone in her family loved.

Zeran reached into his back pocket and pulled out an envelope, holding it out for Alana. "This is from your mother, Allie. Fadren brought it with him when he came."

Alana felt tears in her eyes as she stepped forward, taking the letter. Going to Chernow meant not getting to see her mother for months, maybe years. She broke the seal and pulled the letter out, unfolding it.

My dearest Alana,

I am sorry that I won't be able to see you start your new life, but I know your father will make sure you are well prepared for anything you undertake. I am so proud of you, my darling. You've fully embraced what it means to be an Eldralin, a life of service to others. It isn't going to be an easy life, but I'm certain you already know that. For some, the burden is greater than for others, but to those people most burdened, the greatest gifts are given. Now that your father has decided to step down as Stravad Leader, it's our time again and I intend we spend it exploring as we once did. Do not be surprised to find your mother on your doorstep one day when you least expect it. I love you, my darling.

May Eldon's light shine brightly in your life.

Mama

Alana brushed the tears away, shivering. She missed her mother so very much at that moment, that it felt like a weight on her soul. Zeran and Mairin both came to her and held her in their arms, and Falco offered her a gentle smile.

"I'm glad you're coming with me, Daddy," she told him, hugging him tight.

He kissed her forehead, then pressed a kiss to Mairin's, releasing them. He reached into the neck of his shirt and drew out a chain. The shard of emerald he always wore dangled off it. He pulled it over his head and held it in his hands, nodding at Falco. Falco approached, removing a flat box from his satchel. He pried open the lid and a second shard of emerald lay on a black velvet background.

Mairin and Alana looked up at their father. He jerked his chin between the two stones. "These are two-thirds of the famed Karhartadon emerald," he said. "The very stone Eldon himself unearthed."

Alana knew part of the emerald's story, but her father's expression was so intense, she decided not to interrupt him.

"This is the same stone Kiameron carried into battle against Gava and bequeathed to his son, Tasamer Haldane. Tash placed it back into Eldralin hands when he gave it to Talar. When Talar lay dying, he pleaded with Tash to take it once more. Tash held it until Tyla Eldralin came to Temeron. She protected it for many years, but when she got word that her brothers, Kalas and Amaroq, were coming to Temeron, she went to retrieve it from her hiding place. To her surprise, she found the gem had broken into three shards. The largest shard she kept for herself, the second largest, she gave to Amaroq, and the third she offered to Kalas, but Kalas refused it."

Alana and Mairin exchanged a look. This part of it they'd only heard in passing. Everyone knew the historic part, but this new part was personal.

"Tyla offered the third part to Thalandar, past Stravad Leader. Thalandar had been instrumental in training the Eldralins from Talar to Amaroq, so it only seemed fitting he accept the shard. He did so and it remained with his line until I became Stravad Leader. I then gave Thalandar's shard to Falco to seal our alliance with one another."

He held up the shard he carried. "This shard has helped me to control my power, Allie. It has enabled me to maintain control when everything screamed at me to release it. I want you to have it and I will show you how to use it." He slipped the chain over her head and the weight of it settled between Alana's breasts. As it touched her, it flared with emerald light and Alana felt a throb somewhere in her core. She laid her hand over it and found it warm to the touch.

"Thank you," she said, tears blinding her. She didn't know what else to say. Words didn't seem adequate for such a monumental occasion.

Zeran smiled and turned to Mairin. "Falco and I decided you should have the second shard. That way you'll have a tangible reminder of the bond you share with your sister and how it bridges the difference between our people." He lifted the necklace out of the box and draped it over Mairin's neck. The shard glowed for a moment and Mairin gasped, covering it with her hand.

"What happened to the third shard?" asked Alana.

"No one knows," said Falco. "Amaroq and a few followers, including Talar's brother Shandar, went over the Madronic Range and never returned. They essentially disappeared."

Zeran drew a deep breath and released it, his eyes surveying his two daughters. "I am so very proud of both of you." He shook his head in amazement. "This certainly isn't the outcome I'd imagined for either of you, but I believe you will both be exceptional at your various undertakings. It seems fitting that the heirs of Tyla Eldralin now rule in Temeron and in Chernow. She would have been so very proud of you herself."

Mairin wrapped her arms around her sister and kissed her temple. Alana rested her head against hers and the emerald warmed her skin. Glancing down, she noticed they both glowed.

Selia's laughter floated to them and they looked over their shoulders to watch her. She ducked her head as Fadren said something to her, bringing a blush to her cheeks.

Alana turned back around. "What about Selia?" she asked.

Mairin's gaze flickered to their father. "She's right. What does Selia get?"

Zeran sighed and smiled at his middle daughter. Selia threw back her head and laughed again, stroking her hands through the horse's mane.

"Selia gets the most precious gift of all," said Zeran wistfully.

Alana and Mairin glanced at each other in confusion, but Zeran continued.

"Selia gets to live her life, undisturbed," he said, his eyes going distant. "Selia gets to have peace."

The End

BIOGRAPHY

ML Hamilton has been teaching high school English and journalism in Central California for the last 25 years. Teaching students to appreciate literature is rewarding; however, she always dreamed of publishing her own novel.

That dream came true. Her first novel, *Emerald*, was published by Wild Wolf Publishing in 2010. Since that time, there have been 33 other novels, eleven in the World of Samar series alone.

In addition to teaching and writing, she has three sons, two dogs, and three cats. And sometimes a stray rabbit living under her deck.

Now that you've finished, visit ML Hamilton at her website: authormlhamilton.net and sign up for her newsletter. Receive free offers and discounts once you sign up!

The Complete *Peyton Brooks' Mysteries* Collection:
Murder in the Painted Lady, Volume 0
Murder on Potrero Hill Volume 1
Murder in the Tenderloin Volume 2
Murder on Russian Hill Volume 3
Murder on Alcatraz Volume 4
Murder in Chinatown Volume 5
Murder in the Presidio Volume 6
Murder on Treasure Island Volume 7

Peyton Brooks FBI Collection:
Zombies in the Delta Volume 1
Mermaids in the Pacific Volume 2
Werewolves in London Volume 3
Vampires in Hollywood Volume 4
Mayan Gods in the Yucatan Volume 5
Haunts in Bodie Volume 6

Zion Sawyer Cozy Mystery Collection:
Cappuccino Volume 1
Café Au Lait Volume 2

The Complete *Avery Nolan Adventure* Collection:
Swift as a Shadow Volume 1
Short as Any Dream Volume 2
Brief as Lightning Volume 3
Momentary as a Sound Volume 4

The *World of Samar* Collection:
The Talisman of Eldon Emerald Volume 1
The Heirs of Eldon Volume 2
The Star of Eldon Volume 3
The Spirit of Eldon Volume 4
The Sanctuary of Eldon Volume 5
The Scions of Eldon Volume 6
The Watchers of Eldon Volume 7
The Followers of Eldon Volume 8
The Apostles of Eldon Volume 9
The Renegade of Eldon Volume 10
The Fugitive of Eldon Volume 11

Stand Alone Novels:
Ravensong
Serenity
Jaguar

Made in the USA
San Bernardino, CA
08 February 2019